PARTYgirl

PARTYgirl

Rachel Hollis

LAKE UNION
PUBLISHING

Published by Lake Union Publishing, Seattle

www.apub.com

Amazon, the Amazon logo, and Lake Union Publishing are trademarks of Amazon.com, Inc., or its affiliates.

ISBN-13: 9781477820667
ISBN-10: 1477820663

Cover design by Elsie Lyons
Cover photo by Jacqueline Pilar

Library of Congress Control Number: 2014946876

Printed in the United States of America

For Mama, who gave me wings
and
For Daddy, who taught me how to use them

Chapter ONE

I'm singing . . . or, really, bellowing might be a better word.

My voice is miserable, and I'm a far cry from Miley, who's wailing from my iPod dock, but I'm too happy to care.

This is the very first day, of my very first real job, in my very first week in my very new city. This is the first day of the rest of my life, and I'm going to kick this day's butt! Watch out LA, Landon Brinkley is here and she's . . . belting out every word of this song like her life depends on it!

I wrap another piece of long blonde hair around the outside of the flat iron and stare at my reflection in the mirror while the curl heats to perfection. My big blue eyes shine back, outlined all around by the perfect shade of teak liner. The few clusters of individual lashes I added are definitely the right choice; they really stand out against the shimmery champagne coating on my lids. The eye shadow matches the MAC Lipglass in glittery pink I've bought just for this day. There's a little shimmer in my bronzer too, so my makeup ties in beautifully with the gold rhinestones lining the collar of my fitted pink cardigan. I smile at my own shining reflection; all the light-catching glimmer is gorgeous, and so *me*. If I had a power color, it would definitely be *sparkle*.

I work the last length of hair down through the flat iron, creating the ideal bouncy curl I perfected in seventh grade. The door to the bathroom bursts open behind me, and I try not to flinch when Max glares at me through mascara-smudged eyes. Her dark pixie cut is sticking up in every possible direction, and I gather from the deep creases running down one side of her face that however few hours she's been in bed she's slept all of them on that cheek.

"I'm sorry, is the music too loud?" I smile sheepishly and lower the volume.

"Miley isn't appropriate at any time of day, but before eight is ridiculous for anyone over the age of eleven," she says with a scowl.

She rubs one eye aggressively and pushes a hand through her hair. The movement jangles the pile of bracelets she never seems to remove from her left wrist. Her "pajamas" are an oversize T-shirt with a picture of a muscle car and the words "My Other Ride is Your Mom" stamped across the front.

Charming.

I hope she's got underwear on, but the shirt's hanging down too low to tell. She's clearly comfortable walking around the apartment wearing just a top, and I suppose if I were that thin and tall and had legs that long, I'd probably run around naked. I sigh. At five foot three I suppose it's my lot in life to forever envy anyone taller than I am. Oh well, a little tease and a back comb and my hair gets me at least two inches closer to heaven.

"Oh, come on, she's edgier now. She got that crazy haircut, I thought you'd—" I try.

"We can't even debate this topic . . . My brain cells are *literally* dying right now in an attempt to contemplate something so inane."

She doesn't even look at me as she speaks. She just walks across the space of the small bathroom, pulls down the underwear that were indeed hidden by her shirt, and sits down on the toilet.

I want to act cool, like finishing my makeup while she pees three feet from me is totally normal. But we've been roommates for exactly six days, and during that time we've spent a sum total of forty-something minutes together. I'm not a prude or anything, but *Lord*, let's ease into this, shall we?

"Why are you even awake this early?" Max grumbles, standing back up.

"It's my first day, remember?" I sound way too perky, even to my own ears.

"Oh yeah. Well, good luck, I've heard Selah's a total asshole."

I start to ask her what that means, but she's already yawning out the door, presumably to sleep until the afternoon. I take one last look in the mirror and then head into my room to grab my purse. My bed is already made and covered with throw pillows in various shades of purple. Max made fun of the fact that I was already unpacked, with pictures hung and clothes organized by style, by the end of my first day here, but I can't stand disorganization. I told her that when she interviewed me on the phone for the roommate position. She told me she was the polar opposite but that she was home so rarely it shouldn't be an issue. Then she said that if I could cover half of the $1,650 monthly rent and promise not to bring home any douche bags (her words, not mine), I could move in. And $825 later I had a place to live . . . in *Hollywood*. I still smile every time I think about my new zip code.

I step into the pumps patiently waiting next to my bed and reach for my purse. Even though it's a couple months old, I grin every time I look at this bag. It's a velour Juicy Daydreamer in bubble-gum pink with satin bows and gold charms; I saved my tips for months to get it. I don't usually buy anything so expensive but it was *so* worth it. I glance at the clock on my phone: it's 8:17 a.m.

Perfect: I have just enough time to head down to the garage, get on the road, and drive from my apartment to my new office in

Beverly Hills. I might even get there a little before nine and have a chance to grab some coffee.

Beverly Hills. Eek! I almost can't believe it. I've dreamed about moving to LA for most of my life, and now I'm here!

The ancient elevator doors open to reveal our apartment's underground garage, which apparently always smells like trash no matter what day it is. With every step the butterflies in my stomach seem to grow in size and strength. I start whispering the mantra I've said to myself a thousand times over the last year whenever I've gotten nervous.

I am strong. I am smart. I am courageous.

I am strong. I am smart. I am courageous.

The words are a litany as my heels clip-clop on the cement and I home in on my battered Ford Explorer. I had it washed once I got here to get rid of the millions of bugs that were murdered against the windshield on the drive through four states, but it still looks beat-up. Even if the license plate weren't from Texas, the SUV, with its custom Longhorns trailer hitch, would be out of place on LA streets. But it's not like I can afford to get anything else.

I pull out of the garage and am just turning right onto Fountain when my iPhone starts playing "I Hope You Dance" by Lee Ann Womack . . . It's Mama.

I hit the button for speakerphone. I'm still not used to this whole hands-free thing in Cali.

"Hi—wait, hold on, I thought this lane was clear. Now I'm stuck behind a parked car—ugh! Come on, let me back in!"

"Are you hollerin' at me, baby?" Mama asks cheerfully.

"No, Mama, I'm tryin' to—wait, OK, I'm back in. Sorry, I was tryin' to merge. How are you?"

"Oh, I'm fine. Just workin' on my biscuits."

In the background I can hear the rolling pin hit the edge of the counter as she works her dough down to the perfect density. My parents have owned The Pit since before I was born, and even though they have plenty of faithful employees, Mama refuses to let anyone else in on her legendary buttermilk-biscuit recipe. Even I don't know what she puts in those things, because a southern woman would sooner give up her firstborn than share the secrets of her best recipe.

The Pit is famous for Daddy's barbecue, but no table ever leaves without working their way through at least two helpings of Mama's biscuits. Which is why, every day they're open, you'll find Mama in the kitchen making her biscuits.

"Ooh, I wish I had one right now. I'm starving!"

"Bless your heart, why didn't you eat somethin'?" she asks, concerned.

"I was too nervous before. I'll grab something later."

"Baby, don't start skippin' meals now; you're already too skinny."

"Oh, I won't. I was just in a hurry. Hmm, I wonder what's taking so long—" I glance at the clock on my dash: 8:41.

"What's that honey?"

"Sorry, it's just, I haven't gotten all that far down the street. I don't understand where all this traffic is coming from. I'm supposed to be there in nineteen minutes and I'm not even to La Cienega yet." I crane my neck to try and see around the car in front of me . . . All I see are more cars.

"All right, girl, I'll let ya go. Just wanted to check in. I miss ya."

"I miss you too, Mama. I'll call you after, OK?"

I push the end button and scoot my car forward a scant two feet in line.

"Oh *please*, I can't be late!" I cry out to the cars in front of me. The clock on the dash reads 8:45.

Oh God, Lord Jesus, I cannot be late on my first day!

I don't know if what Max has heard about Selah is true, but I certainly don't want to make a bad impression. Everything I know about my new boss is based on a Google search. She started Selah

Smith Events five years ago just after turning twenty-eight, and in that short time has become the most publicized event planner ever. SSE has produced some of the biggest celebrity weddings, baby showers, and movie premieres in the last few years, giving each one the stamp of edgy luxury Selah is known for. She isn't just the planner either; Selah has become a celebrity in her own right, often walking the red carpet at the same events she produces. She's model gorgeous, tall and thin, and her dark-brown hair never changes from her signature severe A-line bob.

Selah is easily the coolest woman alive, and I can't believe she's going to be my boss! I had to beg, *beg*, the planner I'd assisted last summer to make a call to her old colleague in Houston. That colleague called someone else in LA, who called someone else, who finally had a contact at SSE. I'd e-mailed back and forth with someone named McKenna for nearly two months before finally getting a ten-minute phone interview with some girl who was in such a hurry that I never even got her name. After another e-mail from McKenna asking for a picture of myself that was apparently approved, I got a formal offer letter via e-mail. The deal was for a three-month unpaid internship with the promise that if I proved myself I'd be offered a permanent position at one of the most successful event agencies on either coast.

Unpaid or otherwise, I am beside-myself-excited by the opportunity; my parents, less so. I'm their only child, so the idea of me leaving our small town in West Texas to move to Los Angeles was more than a little upsetting. But there was really nothing for it. I'd grown up in a big, loud southern family, surrounded by aunts, uncles, and cousins, with parents who made a huge fat celebration out of *everything*. I could set a dinner table with Mama's wedding china by the time I was four, write out my own invitations by six, and when I was thirteen I saw Jennifer Lopez in *The Wedding Planner*. It was the first time I realized there were people whose job it was to throw beautiful events. It's all I've ever wanted to do since.

Daddy couldn't fathom a world in which someone would pay hundreds of thousands of dollars for a single party, but he wasn't allowed to complain about my choices since I'd done everything he asked of me first.

I'd gone to all four years at the state college in the next town over and earned the teaching degree he'd insisted I have as a fall-back. I knew he had secretly hoped I'd find some reason to stay home during those years, but my resolve only grew. I took on every shift I could at The Pit and stockpiled my cash reserves so that I could move to LA and start the glamorous life I'd always dreamed about. By my calculations, the $9,342 in my savings account can last exactly five months. It's a big gamble, but one I am willing to make in the hopes that I'll be promoted to the job of my dreams.

Every single dream I have revolves around me working for the best in events, and that's Selah Smith. I have to go in there and show her what an asset I am to her team. I have to—

Crap!

The clock on the dash reads 8:58 a.m., and I'm nowhere near Beverly Hills.

Chapter TWO

I'd been so excited to find out that the offices of SSE sit on the busiest part of Beverly Drive, with its cute boutiques and great-looking restaurants, but I barely even notice them as I sprint down the street in heels.

It's 9:22 a.m. by the time the elevator stops at the top floor of the building where SSE is located.

The doors open, and I walk into a small reception area. It's all clean lines and stark white. A pretty girl, probably my age, sits at a modern-looking desk in the center of the small space. Behind her, a faux wall with the SSE logo on it separates the reception desk from the large industrial-style office behind her. The whole place looks expensive and gorgeous, and I'd be in awe if I wasn't sick with the knowledge that I'm probably never going to work here since I was incapable of showing up on time.

I walk over to the desk, but before I can get any words out, the receptionist's phone beeps. She punches a button with her finger and speaks into the microphone of her earpiece.

"SSE? Yes, absolutely." She punches a few buttons, then looks up at me waiting.

"Hi, I'm—"

As the phone beeps again the receptionist's finger flies up, the universal signal for I'll-be-with-you-in-a-second.

"SSE? Yes, may I ask who's calling? One moment." She jabs the buttons again, and I wonder fleetingly if she takes out her frustration on that poor phone. She speaks into her headset. "Hi, I have Meryl for you . . . I don't know, you know she never remembers your direct line. OK, here she is." She abuses the phone again and then looks up at me.

"I'm—" The phone beeps and that single digit flies up again, telling me to hold on. I'm already so late; my chances of keeping this job are depleting with every call she takes. When she looks up at me again, I pounce.

"Hi there, I'm Landon Brinkley," I explain.

"And?" Her eyes narrow, and because her hair is pulled back into such a tight ponytail, I think it has to be painful to make that expression.

"I, um . . . I'm starting my internship today."

"Of course you are," she says sarcastically. "Who's your contact?"

"Oh, my contact is McKenna. Um, gosh, now that I think about it, I don't actually know her last name." I laugh nervously.

The receptionist is not amused.

She punches numbers into the phone.

"Hi, there's an intern here for you. Hmm . . . OK, uh-huh . . ." As she listens to whoever is on the phone, she looks at me with even further disdain.

Crap! Crappity-crap-crap!

"You were supposed to be here at nine," she says.

It's the nail in my coffin; I can tell by her tone. Normally I would grovel, or cry, or start apologizing profusely, but I know instinctually it won't make any difference. I'm gonna have to lie. I hate lying, and I'm terrible at it, but it's my only option if I want to keep this job.

"There must be some confusion." I try and sound as authoritative as she does. "I was told to be here at nine thirty. In fact I came a bit early in case I couldn't find parking." Jeez, my first day on the job in LA and already my moral compass is bent sideways.

"She says she was supposed to be here at nine thirty," she speaks into her headset. "I don't know . . . Yes . . ." She gives me a quick once-over. "Cute enough, I guess . . . OK."

She stabs the phone with her finger and looks back up at me. "Wait over there." She nods in the direction of the modern white lounge furniture set up in the corner. The phone beeps again and she looks down, dismissing me.

I sag in relief. I don't think I'm out of the woods yet, but at least they didn't throw me out. I walk over to the waiting area, trying not to let my heels make too much noise on the polished cement floor.

I'm too nervous to sit down, so I stand next to the fancy sofa and stare at the framed photos that hang on the wall. They're a montage of sorts, hung gallery-style with images of various sizes and shapes. Each picture shows elements of different events: modern centerpieces at a cocktail party, a long elegant dinner table set for at least thirty people, red-carpet arrivals of various movie premieres . . . Each image is more gorgeous than the last, evidence of a designer with exceptional taste and an unlimited budget.

"You're lucky I couldn't find the e-mail with your arrival time," a voice says from behind me.

I whirl around to face the handsome, perfectly dressed manchild standing next to the reception desk. He's not much taller than I am and dressed like a professor from the 1950s with his oversize glasses and his bow tie. His outfit fits his thin frame to perfection, and each piece—slacks, button-down, dress shoes—is black and stands out against the all-white decor in the office.

"I'm sorry, what?" I ask, confused.

He smirks. "I said you're lucky that I can't find the e-mail proof that your start time was nine. I know for a fact you're late, but you get some credit for having the balls to lie about it. Follow me." He turns on his heel and starts walking off. I have no choice but to hurry after him.

Balls?

Behind the faux wall SSE is a hive of activity. The office is one large industrial-style room, with desks that look like white glass cubes, and is cooler than any workspace I've ever seen. The desks are arranged in a perfect rectangle of three rows of five. Even with big desktops, most of the workstations are overcrowded with paper, magazines, linen samples, centerpiece mock-ups, and invitations in every style imaginable. The employees are going at a feverish pace on computers, on phone calls, on design samples and mood boards . . . It's cooler and prettier than I ever could have imagined!

As I hurry to follow the professor, I notice the white decor continues in this room too. Everything—the walls, the desks, the oversize Apple screens—are all stark white. In contrast, the staff of SSE, who are fifteen or so of the prettiest under-thirty set I've ever seen, are dressed just like the professor and the receptionist in all black. I look down at my polka-dot pencil skirt, my blue blouse, my pink cardigan, and the bubble-gum purse in my hand.

Crap.

At the far end of the office, walls of opaque glass create one large room and a smaller one next to it. I follow the professor into the latter. He closes the door behind me and takes a seat at one of the two desks in the room. He puts a headset on while waving at me to take the chair next to his desk.

"OK, we're off to a bit of a rocky start here, Brinkley. You and I both know you were late, but since I can't prove it I'm giving you until the end of the day to impress the hell out of me, or you can pack off to whatever quaint hamlet in West Virginia you hail from."

"I'm—"

"Nope," he cuts me off, "not interested in whatever it is you're about to say. I don't have the time or the inclination to hear your excuses. I've got work to do. Do you want to be a part of that or not?"

I'm so embarrassed and don't trust myself to speak without breaking into tears. Instead, I nod.

He nods once in response and types quickly on his laptop. His iPhone chirps and he grabs it and reads the screen while talking.

"There are three things you need to remember here at all times. First of all, nobody wants to hear what you think."

I must wince or something because he looks annoyed.

"That's not me being an asshole, that's just a fact. Interns are a dime a dozen and everyone whose opinion *does* matter has earned the right to that position. So keep your mouth shut. Secondly, whatever someone asks you for, they needed it *yesterday*. We're constantly handling millions of dollars' worth of events at one time, and the pace here is fast. If you can't keep up, you'll get run over like roadkill. Got it?"

"Sure, I—"

"Nope," he cuts me off again, "remember, I'm not interested. Just nod please."

I nod.

"You'll be working directly for me, and I work directly for Quade. Quade, of course, works directly for Selah. Just do whatever either of us asks you to do as fast as possible without fucking it up. Understand?"

I nod again.

"OK, come with me."

I stand, place my bag under the small chair next to his desk, and follow him just outside the door. He points to a low bookshelf that runs the length of the frosted glass of the office wall. It holds a mess of binders in every color, some half-hanging off the shelf and some lying on their sides. Colorful pages have been ripped out of magazines and haphazardly inserted here and there in the lineup.

"Organize these." He points at the mess.

"Is there a particular order y'all want them in or—" I ask before I remember that I'm not supposed to be speaking.

"Oh, she'll *hate* that accent. You better do something about it." He turns to walk away while I stare after him, dumbfounded.

What? How is that even something to hate? I can't help the way I talk!

I want to tell him to shove it and that I'm from Texas, *not* West Virginia. I want to mention how hard I've worked to get here today and that I won't have it destroyed by some snobby, overdressed jerk. But I don't say any of those things; I just stand there and stare at his back as he goes to turn the corner, and before I can think better of it, I call out.

"What's your name?"

He turns back. "I thought you realized." He walks towards me with his hand out, apparently finding, or faking, some manners. "I'm McKenna."

"*You're* McKenna?" I say, shaking his hand. "I've never met a man named McKenna. I didn't realize who you were."

"My name is Will, but as far as Selah's concerned, I'm McKenna, Samantha is Quade, and you'll be Brinkley. It's last names only here."

"But my name is Landon," I say, more confused than defiant.

McKenna cocks his head to one side and smirks. "Don't you get it? Nobody cares what your name is, Kansas. You'll either fade into oblivion or find some way to earn your keep; the means by which you make your impression are up to you, but in either case your name is irrelevant."

With that he turns and goes back into the little office.

I stand there a moment, perplexed.

I'd always known people in LA were going to be tougher than people from back home, but I hadn't expected them to be so openly rude. Oh well, not much I can do about it now. I look down at the offensive bookshelf. I might not be able to make McKenna like me, but this cluttered disaster I can handle. I start pulling binders off the shelves and get to work.

———

I don't know how long I've been down on the glazed cement floor, but it's got to be hours because my knees hurt like hell. Even still, I've managed to organize each of the binders into some semblance of order.

It took awhile, but eventually I discovered that these binders are inspiration books filled with tear sheets. Every binder housed a different party element, and I'd labeled each one appropriately with the little label maker I'd found buried on the shelf. Some were obvious: centerpieces, candles, tablecloths in solid colors, and tablecloths in patterns. Others took a little more thought to figure out, and in some cases required a bold-faced assumption. Those included things like "fish-based appetizers," "unique cocktail vessels," and "atmosphere/air." This last binder was filled with images of bubbles and smoke . . . I took a guess.

Now that each binder has a label, I set out to alphabetize and place them back on the shelf. I grab the first stack and begin to sort through them on the floor around me. I'm on my third stack when I hear the clip of heels coming my direction. I look up just as a willowy brunette with a perfect A-line bob and an angry-looking girl with pin-straight black hair both come to a stop next to my binder city.

I look up in awe. Selah is easily one of the prettiest people I've ever seen in real life. She's also the only person in the room wearing color (well, besides me). She's in tight gray slacks that hug her long legs and an ivory blouse that's only partially tucked in messy perfection. Her black ankle boots have a peep toe and gold buttons laced over black suede. I can see the red peeking out from their bottoms, and even I know how expensive that makes them.

I smile up at her. She's so cool—exactly like I knew she'd be! Every single thing about her is crisp, tailored perfection. She's my biggest idol come to life, and she's . . . glaring at me like I'm the blight on her otherwise perfect day.

McKenna comes out of his office to meet her, but before he can say anything, she speaks in an overly loud voice as if she needs everyone in the room to pay attention.

"Isn't there something else *this girl* could be doing with her time other than cluttering up my floor?"

I hold my breath, too terrified to respond. McKenna told me that no one cared what I had to say. It doesn't escape me that Selah spit the words "this girl" with the same venom one might use to say the words "crack addict" or "puppy rapist."

My stomach is churning. I'd imagined meeting Selah Smith for years. I had it all planned out. I was going to tell her how much I loved her design aesthetic and how the Pucci tablecloth she used for Margo Reeve's fiftieth birthday party set the stage for one of the prettiest tablescapes I'd ever seen. I never imagined she'd hate me before I'd even opened my mouth, or that she'd blow away just as quickly as she'd arrived with her two minions in tow, leaving me sitting on the floor with a binder labeled "Animal Entertainment (Mammals)" on my lap.

I am still staring down at the binder when a pair of scuffed black combat boots come into view on the floor next to me. I look up at a petite Asian girl with wild, choppy shoulder-length hair in an outfit of perfectly styled disarray. She's wearing all black, but her ensemble is a bit edgier than the sharp designer duds everyone else has on.

She looks down at the binder on my lap and then back into my eyes with a serious expression.

"The definition of a mammal?" she asks without preamble.

I'm a little nonplussed by the question so I hesitate for a moment. Unsure of what else to do, I answer.

"Animals that nurse their babies."

"And the secretary of state?" She's still staring intently at me.

"John Kerry."

"Before him?"

"Hillary Clinton."

"Capital of Uruguay?"

Is this girl crazy?

"Montevideo."

"Your opinion of Kesha?"

"She's kind of gross looking, but her music's good for cardio."

Her serious expression is replaced quickly by a genuine smile.

"May I ask why you're asking such odd questions?"

She looks surprised by my curiosity, as if the definition of mammal is a valid topic in the intern interview process.

"They call me Jin," she says, sticking out her hand. Each nail is perfectly manicured in neon yellow. "What's your name?"

"I'm . . . Brinkley, I guess?" I reach to shake her hand, and she uses the opportunity to pull me to my feet.

"And your actual name is . . ."

"Landon."

"Well, Landon Brinkley, most girls who roll through here, and believe me there are a few, are dumb as a box of rocks. If I'm going to take you under my wing, I have to make sure you're not a moron," she says decisively.

"You're going to take me under your wing?" I ask, confused.

She considers me for a second, then seems to come to a conclusion with a nod. "Yes, I am. And here's your first lesson: you'll do better with her if you don't show fear."

"I wasn't afraid."

"Like hell! Selah can strike fear into the heart of an intern from a mile away!" She giggles. "Have they given you a break or let you eat lunch or anything?"

I look nervously in the direction Selah has gone.

Is this some test? Like, if I admit I haven't eaten today or that I have a functioning bladder, she'll tear around the corner and call me *girl* again. My new friend must sense my hesitation.

"Don't worry, they're in an update meeting. They won't be out for at least an hour. Come on, I'll give you a tour."

When I still don't move, she giggles. "She'll hate you even more if you piss yourself, and there's far too much white uphol-stery around here to risk it. But if for some miraculous reason they pull their heads out of their asses long enough to check on you, I'll tell them I needed you for a project. Alec and Jane won't mess with me, I promise."

Even though I don't feel much like smiling, my mouth twitches at her comment. I consider not saying anything, but the book nerd in me can't ignore it.

"*Twilight* . . . really?" I ask with mock incredulity.

Her smile just grows bigger. "The fact that you got the nebu-lous Volturi reference only means you're at least as big a nerd as I am. Come on."

For someone so petite, she certainly seems sure of herself. With one more glance at the forbidding closed office door, I follow along after her.

———

Jin, whose first name is actually Miko, shows me to the bathroom first. Thank God!

Next it's the kitchen, where I gratefully grab some string cheese and carrot sticks from the fridge. I've never been so appreciative of free, communal snack food in my life, even if it is all suspiciously healthy. Miko shows me where to get coffee, where the printers are, how to find office supplies, and then how everything is laid out. Every single part of the office is sleek and gorgeous and some variation of glass, chrome, and white. I'm afraid to touch any of it.

Miko, as it turns out, is part of the design team—in fact the head of the design team. It's a little hard to believe because she can't be older than twenty-five, but I clearly don't know anything, so I choose not to question it.

There's also a production department and an in-house floral team that is in what Miko calls "full crisis mode" about some shipment of orchids that is stuck in customs. Apparently, "full crisis mode" happens a lot around here.

Next I meet a man named Revere whose highlights are better than mine and whose black ensemble is almost entirely silk. He's the head of the culinary arts team; I'm guessing that means catering?

At some point on the quick tour I ask about the whole last-name thing, and Miko sighs dramatically.

"Just another one of Selah's edicts. She tells anyone who asks that it's chic and catchy, but really she doesn't like anything she can't control. She says if our parents could be trusted to choose good names, we wouldn't be forced to forgo them in her presence. Evidently, she's never met a first name yet that meets her approval, and now it's just a thing everyone accepts. They're like pod-people. No one here even questions it anymore. If you meet them outside of work, they'll still only go by their last name."

"Gosh, I guess it's a good thing everyone has a nice last name then."

"Ha, hardly! Revere's last name is actually Warchenstein. No way he was ever gonna get away with that. He changed it before she could even ask, so now his alias is an alias. It's ridiculous!"

I can't help laughing along with her. It is sort of ridiculous, but clearly Selah knows something about what it means to be cool, chic, and elegant because everywhere I look the assembled groups are working on beautiful things. I so badly want the opportunity to work on those things too, and if the only way to beautiful flowers and silk linens is through a bunch of messy binders, then by God I am going to organize the heck out of them!

Hours later I am still on the floor putting the last of the binders onto the shelves when I hear a little *snap-snap-snap*. I look around me, unsure from where the noise is coming. Then I hear it again. I turn my head and see fingers snapping aggressively, reaching beyond the frame of the door of the small office. I jump up and hurry towards the angry hand.

Inside the small office both Quade and McKenna are barking orders into their headsets and simultaneously punching the keys on laptops in rapid succession. I stand awkwardly in the doorway; I have no idea what to do next.

McKenna glares at me and removes one manicured hand from his keys long enough to point at a Post-it on the edge of his desk. I walk over quickly and pick it up. Scribbled in near-illegible handwriting is a coffee order. It isn't entirely clear what the order is, but based on the penmanship, I'm guessing it's written by a serial killer.

"You want me to go pick this up?" I whisper.

He covers the mouthpiece of his headset with one hand. *"Obviously."*

I look at the list again.

Q – Lrg Blk
Mc – ~~Sm~~ Lrg Blk
SS – SFV/Ice Blended /Xtreme /Xtra Ice

Ice Blended? Like a blended iced coffee? Or is that a specific thing from a specific coffee place?

"I'm sorry to bug you, but is this from a specific—"

McKenna pushes the mute button on his phone and swings around to where I am nervously clutching the neon-colored Post-it.

"If you can't pick up a simple coffee order, what makes you think you can handle an actual job?" He sneers. "I suggest you figure it out quickly; Selah's leaving in twenty minutes for a meeting and better have a coffee in her hand when she goes."

Right.

I turn quickly and rush to grab my bag. Twenty minutes to drive and get special coffee from I-don't-know-where and be back here.

Crap.

How am I going to pull this off? I look around me in a small panic as if the answer will be painted on the wall or something. Miko and the design team are deep in discussion about some kind of room layout printed on a poster-sized piece of paper that takes up the space of a whole desk. I'd love to ask her for advice, but I'm hesitant to bug anyone more than I already have. I look down at the list once more and decide to Google it on my cell as I rush towards the door. On the way by Miko's desk, she holds out a magazine towards me.

"Brinkley, I need you to pick up this month's edition while you're out." She says this with a wink and then turns back to her group, most of which don't even acknowledge my presence.

I look down at the copy of *Elle Decor* in my hands; it's got thick black ink scribbled on the cover.

Coffee Bean.
She'll want it every day.
Down the street to your left.
#deathtothevolturi

I'm officially in love with this girl!

———

Thanks to Miko's help I find a place called Coffee Bean that does in fact have something called an Ice Blended. And when I tell them Selah's order, they seem to know exactly what I'm asking for. I have a small panic attack when the barista asks if she wants whipped cream or not. It will occur to me later—when I go over this day in my mind—that whipped topping shouldn't ever be the cause for anxiety. But at the time it seems like a life-or-death decision. Since I have no idea what the answer is, I decide that someone as skinny as Selah wouldn't be caught dead with whipped cream on her coffee. It's only when they ring me up that I realize no one gave me money. *Am I buying coffee for them now?* My budget is definitely not going to accommodate that. I hand over my debit card and decide to figure it out later; I have only eight minutes to get back.

I rush back up the street, balancing the coffee tray while inhaling a stale piece of coffee cake, which was the only pastry left in the display case this late in the afternoon. It's dry and cold, but I'm starving, and therefore it's the most delicious snack ever.

I'm back up the elevator and in the small office with three minutes to spare. I hold out the tray to McKenna and Quade, who turn around long enough to grab their own coffees. Neither says thank you.

When I stand there waiting for someone to take the last drink from the tray, McKenna nods in the direction of the larger office next door.

"You want me to take it to her?" I ask, unsure.

"Obviously," he replies and spins back around in his chair.

Someone should really explain the definition of the word "obvious" to McKenna. As in, whatever is obvious should possibly be obvious to people other than him, but whatever.

I sheepishly go to the frosted door to Selah's office and knock.

"Yes?" she calls from behind the door.

I turn the handle and open the door. Selah sits behind an all-glass table that's twice the size of any single desk I've ever seen. Her office feels very similar to everything in the common area: it's clean, sleek, and luxurious. A set of framed, oversize black-and-white prints dominates one wall, but beyond that there are no other photos. No paintings, no colorful throw pillows . . . Even the expensive-looking flowers on her desk are all white.

"Yes?" she asks again, clearly annoyed.

I haven't realized I've just been standing in the doorway like an idiot.

Way to impress, Landon!

"I have your coffee," I say, without moving to step foot in the room.

"Bring it."

I do as I'm told, removing the drink from the tray on the short trip across her office. I place a napkin down first, set the drink on top of it, and then lay a straw down next to the drink. I straighten up to leave the room.

"Why the napkin?" she asks without looking up from the screen of her computer.

I want to ask her to clarify the question, but I'm fearful of speaking unnecessarily.

"I—the drink is cold. I didn't want the condensation to drip onto your desk." I answer very carefully as if I'm competing in a spelling bee.

Intimidated, I-N-T-I-M-I-D-A-T-E-D, intimidated.

Her eyes flicker in my direction for a single heartbeat.

"What's your name?"

"Landon Brinkley."

She keeps typing. *Should I keep standing here? Should I go?* I have no idea.

"That'll be all, Brinkley," she says.

I smile weakly even though she's not looking up to see it and leave the office. Next door, Quade and McKenna are still hunched over their laptops. As soon as I walk in McKenna speaks.

"You survived day one, Mississippi, you can go. I hope I don't need to tell you that a similar ensemble will not be allowed inside this building tomorrow."

Quade snorts quietly.

I blush all the way down to my toes.

"So I'm done for the day?"

"You are, in fact. Just a reminder, we start at nine. I suggest you don't forget it."

"Of course. Thank you so much for the—"

"Selah Smith's office," McKenna chirps into his earpiece, and once again I am dismissed.

———

I slam the driver's side door of my car and melt into the familiar seat. I feel like I've been holding my breath the entire day, and now that I've let it out, I have an overwhelming urge to cry. God, this day hasn't turned out at all like I thought it would. I've made so many mistakes, and people were so mean. I just . . . I guess I thought I'd make some friends.

The first traitorous tear slides down my cheek, and I swipe at it angrily with my palm.

"No! You will *not* cry!" I tell myself furiously.

I am strong. I am smart. I am courageous.

I throw the car into reverse and make my way out of the congested garage and onto Beverly.

I am strong. I am smart. I am courageous.

It's just, I've been dreaming of this day for so long, and I thought . . . I thought maybe I'd get to learn about events, or help with something creative, or . . . Another tear falls. Nope, we're not going to do this. I drag my index finger below my lash line to clean away whatever mascara is trying to pull a Tammy Faye on me.

"This is what you came here for, Landon?" I chastise myself. "To cry your way home because the big kids are mean to you?"

I am stronger than this. I will not cry, I will not cry, I will . . . I need something to focus on, I need . . . the right song! I scroll quickly through the playlist on my phone and find what I'm looking for.

When the first few lines of the Taylor Swift song come on, I already feel better. I crank the volume until the windows shake with the twang of her guitar strings in my crappy stereo. By the time the chorus hits, I'm belting the words along with her and slamming my hand down on the steering wheel to punctuate our shared angst at being picked on by bullies. I'm sure the other cars around me are enjoying the view of the crazy girl crying and singing at the top of her lungs, but I don't care. I don't have time to wallow; I've got a dream job to land.

Over an hour later, when I pull into my own parking spot at home, I've cried off all my makeup and most of my eyelashes, but I'm resolved and ready to go back tomorrow and show them that I don't scare easily.

Chapter THREE

I walk into the Volturi's office the next morning at 8:57 a.m. McKenna is dressed in another set of perfectly tailored slacks, and his pin-striped suit jacket is draped over the back of his chair. I wonder if this professor thing is his signature look. He does a once-over of my all-black ensemble: a dress that can really be described only as "cocktail attire" and black pumps. It is one of my few options since I don't really own a lot of black. McKenna's eyes widen slightly as if I just walked into his office in a clown suit, but I just stand there and smile back at him like I'm competing for Miss America. I've decided that no matter what they say to me today, I'm going to keep this look on my face.

"Sit." He points to my chair from yesterday that's been rolled into the small space between the open door and the wall . . . I'm literally sitting in the corner.

I slide my bag under the chair and look up at him expectantly.

"OK, Brinkley, there's no shallow area here. You'll be thrown directly into the deep end. If you can't swim, you'll drown, got it?"

I nod.

"First you'll need to—" He shudders with a tremor of annoy-ance. "Are you going to take notes, or do you have something bet-ter to do?"

"Of course. I'm sorry." I scramble for my bag and remove a glittery pink notebook and a matching pen. He starts talking again before I've even cracked the page.

"First of all you'll need to speak with Chadwick. He's sup-posed to have centerpiece options for the Rhinestone after-party. Speaking of which, we'll need a collection of decor inspiration, something unique and original for that event. Come up with a list of jewel-themed ideas . . . You did bring your laptop, correct?"

"No, I—"

"Ugh! Go borrow one from Taylor. Don't show up here again without bringing your own."

"OK, I—"

"Now Brinkley. Get the laptop now." He sighs heavily as if dealing with me is the most tedious chore on earth, so I hop to my feet before I can annoy him further.

The central office area is at the same level of chaos as yesterday, only with new outfits. I look around, confused; I'm not really sure who Taylor is or where he sits. Rather than embarrass myself by wandering aimlessly, I sneak over to Miko to ask directions. She smiles up at me, but before I can open my mouth, I realize she's on a call; I don't want to bug her. I raise my hand in apology and start to back away, but she covers her phone receiver before I can sneak away.

"It's OK. What do you need?" she whispers.

"Sorry! Do you know who Taylor is?" I whisper back.

"He's the head of production, sits on the far side of the office, but you'll probably find him out in the production room."

"Thanks!"

Miko smiles and waves after me.

I hurry off in the direction that Miko has pointed out and find myself next to the kitchen and a doorway I hadn't really noticed yesterday. I open the heavy door and realize it's actually the entrance to a large workroom, nearly half the size of the entire office.

Nirvana is wafting out of a small wireless speaker on a far table, and several guys are unpacking what looks like the leftover accessories from an event. I pause for a moment, unsure of who to ask. Most of the men are on the other side of the room and one guy is unloading a crate nearby, so I head towards him. He's in black jeans, a black T-shirt, and black leather Converse. His arms are cut around perfect lean muscle, each with a full sleeve of tattoos, and even from back here he looks like the lead singer of your favorite band. He must hear me tapping over in my heels because he turns around, and I'm surprised at how young he is. He's got dark-brown hair and chocolaty eyes, and he's definitely rocking a sort of sexy bad-boy look. If I were into the whole Adam Levine thing, I'd probably be drooling right now.

"Can I help you with something?" He smiles down at me, and I hear a little southern twang that somehow softens his sharper edges. I wonder where he's from.

"I'm so sorry to bother you, but I'm looking for Taylor. Can you help me?"

He stares at my face more intently; I wonder if he hears my accent too. I fight the urge to fluff my hair.

"I'd love to help you," he drawls. "Why don't you tell me what you need him for?"

What is he, the door guard? I don't have time to waste with twenty questions, and I don't want to flirt. I just want to borrow a laptop.

"I just need to speak with your boss. Can you tell me where Taylor is?"

He sets down the glass vase he's holding on the table behind
him.

"I'm a little confused—" he starts.

"And I don't want to be rude, but this is already taking way
longer than it's supposed to. Can you please just point me towards
the head of production?" I look around the room trying to figure
out who that might be. "I just need to borrow a laptop for the day,
so if you could tell me who is in charge here . . ."

His smile has turned into a full-on grin now.

"I could have fun with this moment, I really could," he says
conversationally. "But alas, it'd take too long and you'd get into
trouble and you'd hate me and then we'd never be friends." He sighs
dramatically. "Come on, I'll get you set up with something." He
starts to walk to the door, and I scurry after him.

"Wait! Are you sure you're allowed to do this?"

"I'm sure," he says as I fall in step next to him.

"What if Taylor finds out. Will you be OK?"

He chuckles and comes to an abrupt halt just past the kitchen.
I do too.

"Like I said, I'd love to draw this out into some epic game of
tease-the-new-girl, but I think my manners are already dangerously lacking. I should have done this when you first walked into
the room." He sticks out his hand to me. "I'm Bennett Taylor, but
everyone's called me Taylor since peewee football, so you can too."
He gives me a cheeky smile, and I wonder how many girls have
fallen for that grin since peewee football.

I take his hand in my own and smile back. How is this guy
anyone's boss? He can't be older than thirty, but then, I guess, not
many people at this company are. Everyone here has one thing in
common, though. They may have different styles, different ethnic-
ities, and different backgrounds, but they're all the coolest people
you've ever met, and this guy is definitely one of them.

"I'm Landon Brinkley. Nice to meet you."

We turn and keep walking.

"How exactly were you going to pull off the epic game?" I ask after a second.

"Oh, ya know, misdirection, misadventure . . . Almost all my ideas centered on telling you that Big Pretty was the boss just to watch you embarrass yourself."

"And Big Pretty is?"

"One of our drivers. He can be a little intimidating." He smiles but doesn't look at me.

"Well that's not very nice." I can't help but smile a little too.

"I know, Brinkley, that's why I resisted temptation."

"I guess chivalry isn't dead."

"No ma'am." He touches the brim of an imaginary hat, and I roll my eyes dramatically, which only makes him chuckle.

———

Back in my corner I'm busy taking notes while McKenna runs through my to-do list.

"And Lee's team should have linen samples for the Kessler-Glen wedding—"

I don't mean to interrupt him, but I actually squeal at the mention of Hollywood's "it" couple. His eyes narrow into slits.

"I don't need to remind you that you signed a confidentiality agreement, do I?"

My face falls.

"Of course not. I won't mention it to anyone. I'm just such a huge fan of Kira Glen; I can't believe I'll be working on her wedding."

"I wouldn't say *you'll* be working on it so much as running around in the background schlepping. You won't even be doing that if Selah finds out you're a star-fucker."

What did he just say?

"I'm not a—" I can't even say the words. I've never heard the phrase before, but the way he just spat it at me means it's definitely not a good thing.

"Brinkley, I'm going to tell you the most important lesson you'll learn, and I expect you to commit it to memory since I don't have the time to hire a new intern. Are you ready?"

Even though he's being condescending, I nod . . . with the all-day smile plastered on my face.

"The celebrity clients are *everything*. Let me say it again—everything. They're the most important part of this whole deal." He swings his index finger in a wide lasso, gesturing to the whole office. "They're the bread and butter, they're who make it possible for SSE to charge what it does, they're where we get the press and the clout, and she'd stab her own mother before she'd risk her reputation with A-list clients. Nod if you understand."

I swallow nervously and nod.

"So like I said, the most important lesson is this: piss off a celebrity client and you can find another job. Serious as a heart attack. No joke."

I nod again. He looks at me through narrowed eyes as if assessing my understanding of the topic and then continues on as if the whole celebrity aside hadn't taken place.

"Next I need you to pull some entertainment options for the Lerner bar mitzvah; use the binders out front."

"You know, I was wondering yesterday if y'all have ever considered creating Pinterest boards for each event element, or even the event itself. It'd be so much more efficient than the binders, and I can—"

"How about you work here more than a week before you start trying to change business practices?" he bites out.

Damn it! I'll never learn to keep my mouth shut! I nod again. I'm getting really good at expressing chagrin with a single bob of my head.

"Now as for the mitzvah, I also need you to check with operations on the delivery of the kippot." He rubs the space where his glasses meet his nose like he's already exhausted. It's only 10:18 a.m. "They're supposed to have hand-stitched anchors on them, but Mrs. Lerner sent a panicked e-mail at, like, three this morning, freaking out because Ari went to another mitzvah last weekend and that kid had anchor kippot, and we can't possibly have the same thing this weekend. We'll need to reorder sailboat kippot instead."

I nod again, like I have any clue what he just said. I write a note to myself in the top corner of my page: *Google KeyPah (sp??)*.

McKenna pushes himself to his feet, and the sound makes me look up.

"Time for the all-hands meeting," he says, slipping back into his pin-striped jacket. He considers me for a moment like I'm a particularly interesting species of insect.

"Fine, you can come. Say nothing." He says this as if he's answering the question I hadn't asked.

I follow him quickly out the door with my notebook in my hands. We walk the length of the office before coming to the door of the conference room. One whole side of the room is lined with large windows that show off a postcard view of Beverly Hills. In the middle of the room is a long glass conference table, surrounded on all sides by Louis XIV acrylic ghost chairs. I run my fingers reverently along the back of one. I've never seen these chairs in person, and I can't believe they use them as conference chairs . . . Actually, *of course* they use them as conference chairs!

McKenna is typing feverishly on his smartphone, but he takes the chair to the right of the table's head and nods for me to sit next to him. All around us the room is quickly filling with staff members. Then it hits me: all-hands, as in all hands on deck. I try and stop my smile from forming but it's really tough. I'm so excited to be included!

The beautiful people are finding their seats and sipping on lattes and chatting about everything from a favorite pinot noir to a new band someone saw last night at Hotel Café. It's all so very LA, and I can't believe I'm here in the midst of it!

Miko walks in the room with a large sketchpad under one arm and gold oversize headphones on her ears. She's wearing leather leggings and wedge sneakers in black suede that I didn't even know existed before seeing them on her feet. Her oversize black T-shirt is falling off one shoulder and has a screen print of an angry cat on the front. On anyone else that shirt would look ridiculous, but somehow she manages to make it, like, the coolest cat T-shirt ever! I look down at my too-short dress and sigh.

I need to go shopping.

Miko sits down across the table and looks up just as Selah and Quade walk in the door. The whole room goes silent, except for Selah, who's on her phone. Quade takes the seat across from McKenna, and Selah sits down at the helm. And then we all . . . just sit there.

Selah chats on her phone as if she's got nothing better to do, as if the room full of people waiting for her doesn't have anything better to do either.

"No, of course I don't. You promised you were taking me out." She's smiling and happy, her voice oozing flirtatiousness. "That's not true. I loved your last selection." It's quiet as she waits for the person on the phone to argue the point. She laughs deep in her throat. "Well perhaps you should try a little harder to impress me?" she asks with an over-the-top pout.

Eew! Barf!

I look down the table to Miko, who rolls her eyes and leans back in her chair, getting comfortable. Clearly this is nothing new, and we might be here awhile. I wonder if the person on the other end of the phone realizes Selah's having this chat with a captive audience around her.

"I can't wait, Brody. See you then," she says, breathless and far too sexy for the workplace.

In quick succession the phone is off her ear and now in her hands. She's reading something on the screen. She starts to type. She doesn't look up, and the room stays quiet waiting for her.

"Quade, I assume I'm not the only one with a million other things to do," Selah says without looking up from the tiny screen. All hint of the flirty girl is gone.

Apparently, that is the gunshot we've all been waiting for, because Quade leaps from her seat with the eagerness of a thoroughbred on race day. She looks down at the iPad she's holding and then to the far end of the table.

"Lerner mitzvah. Taylor, can you tell us what's going on with production?"

I look down the table at Taylor. Despite the bad-boy looks and his age, he holds the attention of the room with confidence.

"We're good. Rentals are delivered on Friday; A/V loads in that afternoon. Client was annoyed about the need for on-site security to watch it all overnight, but it can't be helped. Timeline is finished. Walker sent it out this morning." Taylor points to a woman sitting next to him.

"Sunset?" Selah says without looking up.

Is that a question or a statement?

Man, I wish I understood this lingo!

"Seven thirteen," Taylor answers, so apparently it was a question.

"We're going to have to see what we can get away with there." Selah looks up. "Let me see the timeline."

She reaches out towards Quade, who's already handing her the iPad, but instead of grabbing the tablet she seizes one of Quade's hands.

"Is this the new metallic polish from OPI?" She looks closer at Quade's manicure.

"It is," Quade answers, a little unsure. "But just on the fringe; they call it an inverted French tip."

Selah takes another half second to inspect the nails while the room holds its breath.

"It's fabulous, Q!" she finally decrees, and Quade's gaunt frame literally ripples as she preens under the compliment.

"I saw it on someone's Latergram," she tells Selah and, evidently, the room at large, because she's raised her voice confidently.

"It looks a lot like what Prabal's models had on at the last show. You're so on trend, Q. Let's do something like this at the Riverton party . . . Maybe on the servers?" Selah's voice is sweet and playful, and she suddenly seems exactly like I thought she would be, like the coolest girl in school. If you can just impress her, she'll make you cool too.

"Definitely," Quade answers, and hands off the iPad.

It's about now that I remember I was told to take notes. I don't know which part of this conversation is important, so I just start writing down everything I hear. The room is quiet again as Selah contemplates the screen in front of her.

"It's really tight." She looks down the table at the production team, seeming annoyed, and her cool-girl moment is over.

"There's two bands, a party host, and the kid's performing a violin solo. The dinner is six courses, we have four food trucks for the teenagers, and there's a Venetian dessert table." Taylor throws an irked look at the culinary arts team. Revere responds with a dramatic shrug, as if to say, *Not my fault.* "And the klezmer band during cocktail hour. There was no other option with the timing."

"What time is strike?" Selah asks, looking back down at the screen.

"Midnight," Taylor says.

My head volleys back and forth between them like I'm at a tennis match. I have no idea what they're saying at all, but it's obviously a hot topic because Selah is radiating annoyance.

"It's tight," Selah says again.

"We'll get it all in," Taylor says, cool as a cucumber.

Selah looks back down at the screen, dismissing the conversation. I know now where McKenna learned that little trick.

"Floral?" Quade looks to an older woman three seats down from her. The woman has bright-red hair and a petite build. I'm a shorty, but she's so small I feel like she might fit inside my pocket. When she speaks she's got a thick British accent, and I immediately imagine her as some sort of spritely garden gnome.

"We lost the lady slippers. We're still unsure they'll make it out of customs, and even if they do, I don't trust the quality after so much time. We've reworked it with phalaenopsis."

"It'll feel too tropical. That's not the aesthetic at all," Selah snaps, glaring at the older woman. It seems like too harsh a response for a conversation about flowers.

Before the Gnome can defend herself, Miko chimes in.

"Not at all." She stands up from her chair and pulls her headphones back until they hang around her neck like a yoke. She walks over to Selah, opening the cover of her sketchpad. I'm already nervous for Miko because she's the only person in the room who hasn't waited to be spoken to before speaking herself. Selah doesn't seem to question it, though, and just looks at the sketch in front of her.

"See, we just added a bit in here for the color," Miko says, pointing to something on the page.

"And the cymbidiums?" Selah asks.

"Overkill I think," Miko says decisively.

Selah considers the page again. "Agreed," she says finally, then looks up at the Gnome again. "You've made her aware of the changes." It's not really a question.

"Yes, she's excited about this direction," the Gnome responds.

"She's *excited* about the dissolution of her design scheme three days before her event?" Selah raises her voice.

Miko interrupts again, waving a hand through the air in a staying motion. "She is. We showed her the new design, and I mentioned that I haven't incorporated this combination into a piece before. She's thrilled to set the trend."

The Gnome looks relieved at not having to answer. Selah looks irate, kind of like the angry cat on Miko's shirt.

"Well done, Jin," Selah finally says begrudgingly, and Miko walks back to her chair without acknowledging the praise. More than a few people throw pointed looks at the little designer as she takes her seat, but she either doesn't know or doesn't care. Miko's clearly a Selah-favorite whether she wants the title or not.

"The Riverton party is new, but since it's moving so quickly I suggest we discuss it next," Quade says.

"About the venue—" Selah begins, but McKenna interrupts, suddenly overeager.

"I was able to secure Milk Studios. I had to beg to get them to release the date, but JJ owes me a favor and—"

"And who approved that?" Selah's sharp tone ricochets off the windows behind me, and the already-quiet room grows ominously more so.

Holy crap.

"You asked me to get—" McKenna tries.

"Absolutely not! The brand asked for something exclusive and fresh, and Milk is so overdone it's nearly pedestrian." Selah attacks with far more venom than seems necessary. "In fact, last time I checked it was *my* name on the wall. So maybe you can explain why decisions are being made about *my* company without *my* input."

"It must have been a miscommunication," McKenna says quietly. "When you asked me to book it I—"

"Tell me you weren't idiot enough to confirm!" she hisses.

It takes everything I have not to cower down in the seat alongside McKenna, who looks like a beaten puppy.

"I did, but I'm sure I can—" McKenna tries.

"Oh, you will. It's not my job to correct your mistakes. I'm not even sure why I'm having this conversation with a *second assistant.*"

She says his title the same way she called me "this girl," and even though he's a jerk, I feel so badly for McKenna. The entire room is looking anywhere but his direction.

"The party will be at Twenty-Five." Selah announces it like a proclamation.

All around me murmurs rise up in a swirl, praising her decision.

"Gorgeous space," someone says.

"Go there all the time—"

"Love the vibe."

"Oh, it's sexy and masculine, a great departure from other Riverton parties." I'm surprised to hear McKenna agree loudest of all.

I can't believe he can even find his voice after she just ripped him a new one in front of everybody. But apparently he rebounds quickly, because as she starts to describe her vision for the party, he nods along emphatically like a church lady listening to a testimony. I half-expect him to throw out an "Amen!" when she starts talking about the celebrity DJ she has in mind. I don't know how she's gone from flirtatious to complimentary to ruthless in the span of one meeting, or how her staff has learned to keep up.

My gaze slides tentatively down the table to Miko, and at my wide-eyed stare she mouths the exact words I'm thinking.

Pod-people.

Chapter FOUR

After the uncomfortable meeting we make our way back to the office in silence. If it were me, I'd be railing to anyone who would listen about my nightmare boss or crying in a stairwell somewhere, but McKenna is doing his best to act like nothing happened.

I excuse myself for the restroom, and once I've locked myself in the stall my mind starts spinning.

What do you do when you realize the woman you've idolized for years is a horrible person? Successful, brilliant, beautiful? Sure. But also kind of crazy harsh. I mean, I guess she needs to be sort of hard-core to run her team and her company, but she's so vicious, and it seems almost like she enjoys being mean. And that whole deal with the phone call and making everyone wait for her, and the way she can intone the simplest words with the venom of a rattlesnake?

No, she's definitely not a nice person.

I can't help it; I laugh.

Not a nice person? God, I am such a country mouse!

She's a crazy B! Even I can see that! What am I gonna do, though? It's only my second day, and I've worked so long to get this position!

I rub my now-clammy palms down the front of the skirt of my dress and think about what it took to get here. Years and years of going home every day with my hair smelling like barbecue sauce and never spending the money I made on anything fun. Years of imagining what it would be like to help a bride choose the perfect flowers for her bouquet or how it would feel to see my favorite actresses walk the red carpet at an event I produced. It's all I've dreamed about for as long as I can remember.

Selah is the best, period. I wanted to work for her so I could learn from the best, not because I want to be some evil minion she crushes in the all-hands meeting. I'm not here because I want to *just work* for her; I'm here because I want to *be* her. I want to be a fabulous event planner in my own right, and the only way I'm going to be able to do that is stick it out and learn from the best. I've got to secure a real position here, even if it's hard. I've got to make myself stand out, to be the absolute best intern I can be, so I can learn everything I need to know. I've got to—

The door opens and closes as someone comes in, reminding me where I'm standing. I throw my shoulders back and turn the latch of the stall door. I will take this place by storm. But first I've got to leave this bathroom.

———

By the time afternoon rolls around I'm deep in my hidey-hole behind the office door, working on the borrowed laptop on jewel-themed decor ideas. My locale has proved treacherous: someone came barreling into the room and the door slammed into my elbow. I had to bite my tongue to keep from yelping out a blasphemous curse. That spot's going to bruise for sure.

I'll be honest. Being stuck in the corner is pretty degrading, but I suppose it's better than sitting outside the room on the floor. The partial obstruction of the door also means that I'm able to listen in on all of the phone calls and conversations and they mostly forget I'm here unless they need to bark an order at me.

From their conversations I've learned that we have an event this weekend . . . the aforementioned Lerner bar mitzvah with the rush-order, sailboat-themed kippot. Something, by the way, that Google informed me is another name for yarmulke, and apparently it's OK to have them custom designed to match your party so long as they cover your head. I looked up some pictures of them too, and I thought the little themed hats were adorable. I wish Presbyterians got to wear something so cool!

Snap-snap-snap.

My head flies up at the sound of McKenna's fingers. He points down to the Post-it on his desk.

Time for Coffee Bean.

———

This time, as I make my way back up Beverly munching the lonely bran muffin that was all that remained of the pastry section, I don't feel as terrified as I did yesterday. For one thing Miko has explained to me how to pull petty cash for these coffee runs, so at least I won't go broke keeping my bosses supplied with caffeine. As far as those bosses go, Quade hasn't ever spoken to me directly and McKenna is even ruder than normal after the morning meeting. But I haven't openly pissed off anyone today, and that's going a long way towards boosting my confidence.

On another positive note, I'm going to work my first SSE event this weekend! I should probably be a little more terrified after seeing Selah's temper firsthand, but I *know* I can impress her at this party. At least I think I can.

Back in the lobby of the SSE building I juggle the coffee tray and hit the button for the elevator. I step in and, as the doors slide together, shove the entirety of the remaining muffin into my mouth in an attempt to finish it before I reach the top floor. No one has expressly forbidden it, but I'm pretty sure carbs aren't allowed inside this building.

I have just started chewing the gorged mouthful when a hand flies between the closing elevator doors. The doors slide back open and standing there is . . . Jesus, in his human form.

OK, not Jesus. Not Jesus, but easily the hottest man I have ever seen in my life! Did I just call Jesus a hottie? I did. I think I did, and I'm for sure going to burn in hell. I guess I just meant that this guy is so beautiful, he's got to be some kind of deity. He's well over six feet tall and has perfectly tousled dark-blonde hair and the lightest blue eyes I've ever seen. His skin is sun-browned surfer perfection, he's rocking this sort of scruffy five o'clock shadow, and he's got lips that no one of the male species deserves to have. He's wearing a perfectly cut, light-gray suit, a crisp white button-down, and no tie. He doesn't necessarily look old, but he seems very grown-up. He fairly oozes confidence and money, and I'm sure his suit probably cost more than my car.

The guy takes a step inside the elevator and resumes typing into the phone in his hands. I see him open another e-mail on his screen and start reading, completely unaware of my presence. It's only after he starts typing a response that I realize I have a mouthful of muffin that I've stopped chewing, and I'm just staring at him like a deranged chipmunk.

Kill me!

I duck my head and do one massive swallow.

Big mistake.

Like all late-in-the-day pastries, this one is totally dried out, and it absolutely refuses to go down my throat! My eyes dart to him to make sure he's not looking at me.

Of course he's looking at me!

My eyes are bugging out, and I'm trying not to spill the coffees.

I start choking and coughing like a moron, but I swear I'm doing my best to asphyxiate as demurely as possible!

No go.

There's dreamy guy, looking all pulled together and gorgeous, and here's me, being all *cough-spastic, breath-wheeze-cough-cough death rattle.* This is it. I'm going to choke to death in an elevator dressed like I'm on my way to a hooker's funeral, and this blonde male model is going to watch me die!

All of a sudden he steps in front of me, looking concerned.

"Are you OK?"

Even as I'm coughing bits of bran muffin into my hand, I can't help but stare up at his mouth. His teeth are perfect. I wonder if he ever had braces.

He doesn't wait for my response, since clearly I'm in no position to give him one. He just takes the coffee tray from me with one hand and starts pounding me on the back way too hard. My coughing fades slightly, and he reaches to grab a drink at random.

"Here, drink this." He hands me the coffee.

I shake my head, my voice coming out squeaky. "Not mine."

He looks at me like I'm an idiot. "I'm sure whomever it belongs to won't mind."

I clear my throat about fourteen times and then try and speak again.

"She'd mind," I choke out. "I doubt she'd use the liquid in it to put me out if I was on fire." I reach out to take the tray back.

The model looks at me skeptically but relinquishes the tray. "If you say so."

I nod stupidly and take one giant sideways step to give myself some space. He watches me for a beat and then turns around to face the elevator doors again.

Through the speaker in the ceiling Lionel Richie reminds me
that he's easy like Sunday morning. It's the perfect awkward song
for this horrendously awkward moment. God, can't this thing
move any faster? I look up to see the progress of the elevator car
. . . Three more floors to go.

Right then is when I realize that he hasn't hit the button for a
different floor. Which means he's also going to the top floor, and
SSE is the only office up there. Which means he's headed there too.
Ugh!

Finally, blessedly, the doors open, and I don't even look at my
companion or the rude receptionist. I make a beeline past the partition and head for my chair. I've never been so desperate to sit in a
hidden corner in my life! Only, as I'm walking, I realize the model
is following me. I don't hear him speak with the receptionist or
anyone else, and no one acknowledges him as he trails behind me.
So, clearly, he being in this space isn't unusual.

Oh please Lord and Baby Jesus, do not let him be . . .

"Brody Ashton, you've kept me waiting," Selah purrs from the
doorframe of her office.

She's reapplied her lip gloss; I can see the shine all the way
from here. Also that flirty voice is back, and I know without question this is the "Brody" from her phone call earlier.

I continue walking, but for the smallest moment I squeeze my
eyes shut as if it might erase this car wreck that is my life.

Just keep moving forward. Keep smiling. Nothing to see here,
people.

I walk towards Selah since she's standing directly in front of
me and clearly sees that I've got her coffee in my hand. When I'm
a few feet away she nods towards her office.

"Put it on my desk, Brinkley," she says, looking past me.

I walk past her and set the drink down on the desk. All the
while I'm wondering if maybe I should have just let the bran muffin take me when it had the chance.

I turn from the desk, tray in hand, and keep my eyes trained on my shoes. When I get to the door Selah is in my way, and I have no choice but to look up at her and Brody. Light blue eyes consider me for a second before looking away.

"We seem to be in the way here," he says, pulling Selah to the side to let me pass.

"I didn't even think of getting you something, B. I can send her back if you want," Selah tells him.

She doesn't even look at me when she asks, just continues to stare at him, smiling her glossy, fake smile.

"No, I'm good. Thank you, though. Are you ready?"

I don't wait to hear what she says; I'm already back in the small office handing out the other coffees and thinking very seriously about how much alcohol I might need to drink to forget the last hour of my life.

———

That night McKenna doesn't let me leave until after seven. By the time I'm dismissed I have copied, filed, collated, stapled, schlepped, and researched until I can't see straight, and I've done everything so fast I haven't had time to sit down in between. At this point I'm so tired I can't imagine anything better than putting on my oldest sweatpants and eating a vat of mac'n'cheese on the couch. I head out to the elevator and spy Miko headed in the same direction. She takes one look at my face and declares that we're going to find a happy hour.

"I don't know if I'm up for going out," I say dejectedly.

"Oh no, you need a drink! You look exactly like Clari when she found out she couldn't make out with Jace anymore because he was actually her brother."

"I'm embarrassed that I recognize that reference." The elevator doors open, and we both get inside.

"Why is that embarrassing? Those books are epic." Miko hits the elevator button. "Though I do sometimes wish I didn't get so addicted to YA series. I mean, it's like book after book filled with heavy petting, and all I want the characters to do is get it on. It's so frustrating!" Miko says, rifling through the giant neon bag she has slung over her shoulder.

"I guess you could stop reading YA," I try helpfully.

"It's a love story about teenage half-angel warriors . . . I'm not made of stone." She says this through a giggle, like it's the most absurd thing I could ever suggest. She finally finds the lip balm she's looking for and dabs it on her lips.

"OK, where are we getting the drink?" I ask, watching as she drops the balm back into the black hole of clutter in her bag.

I will never understand how people can live with such chaos. The inside of my bag is a collection of smaller bags, each with its own special purpose in the organizational hierarchy.

"You get to choose; you're the one who got dream-crushed today." Miko opens the door to the lobby and lets us out onto the sidewalk. It's early October, and back home it's already chilly, but here it still feels tepid. We walk along the sidewalk in silence.

"What do you mean I got dream-crushed?" I ask.

Miko takes a deep breath.

"I mean that today you learned that this job isn't what you thought it was going to be. I mean that you can already tell how terrible Selah is, and it's only day two. That makes you wonder what that means she's like on day 22 or day 137. It means you realized that you're working for one of the worst people you'll likely ever meet and that you understand if you want whatever future you dreamed up for yourself, you're going to have to keep working for her for the foreseeable future. You had a vision for the way this was all going to go down, and today that got blown to hell and back."

She finishes succinctly: "*Dream-crushed.*"

I stare down at my heels eating up the pavement beneath me.

"That sounds about right," I finally concede.

"Yep. Let's find you some vodka!"

———

Since I haven't actually been out yet in LA, I pick the only place I even know the name of.

Gander, as it turns out, is a restaurant inside the Buchanan. The large wraparound bar that services both the restaurant and the hotel lobby at large is gigantic and sleek and surrounded by an eclectic mix of people who can afford the overpriced cocktails. It's a place to see and be seen and the ideal locale for anyone starting or ending a night in Hollywood. I'm thankful I haven't picked out something supremely cheesy, and I owe my knowledge of this cool location to the gorgeous but annoyed-looking bartender rocking a now perfectly styled pixie cut behind the bar.

Max looks up from the cocktail she is mixing just as Miko and I find seats at the bar. She calls down to me.

"You finally decided to come in?"

She is dressed the same as all the other bartenders here: skinny jeans, tight linen button-down shirt, thin suspenders. If I were wearing the uniform, I'd look like the ride operator on Big Thunder Mountain. On Max it looks flawless.

"Desperate times," I reply as she walks over.

"What can I get you guys?" Max asks.

Miuko pipes up. "Any kind of cocktail involving liquor, and then we'll also need a sidecar of more liquor. I'm Miko by the way," she says, tossing her neon bag onto the floor at her feet.

"Bad day?" Max is already pulling unknown ingredients from below the bar to mix us something.

"Decidedly not the best day I've ever had," I sigh.

"I told you she's an asshole," Max says.

"You did in fact."

"How'd you know she's an asshole?" Miko asks.

"I know some guys who've worked with her," Max answers while sliding us two tall, sleek shot glasses filled with an opaque pink liquid.

"What's this?" I ask, sniffing the shot dubiously.

"A new creation. I call it Cereal Milk. It tastes just like milk left at the bottom of the cereal bowl. You seem like a pink-shot kind of girl." Max's voice is sharp but her smile is teasing. I'm beginning to suspect her bark is worse than her bite.

I smile at my shot and the girl who made it, then down it in one swallow. She's right; it tastes exactly like cereal milk.

"This is delicious!" Miko sips on hers gingerly.

"It is delicious. How'd you come up with that?"

Max shrugs. "It's slow sometimes in the late afternoon, and I have to fill up the time."

"Well, I'll have another." Miko slams her now empty glass on the countertop.

"And I'd like another drink too, just not this exactly." I smile at her. "Can I have a Jack rocks?"

Max looks surprised, but then the shock fades into the first real grin she's ever given me.

"Well, well, well, Miss Landon, I'd never have pegged you for a Jack girl." She pulls the bottle off the glass shelf behind her.

"I was born and raised in a dry county . . . Had to get your alcohol content in hard and fast."

Max holds up an ice cube at the end of small tongs. I hold up two fingers in response. She drops the cubes in the finger of whiskey and sets it down in front of me.

"There may just be hope for you yet."

"There is. There definitely is hope . . . There is also some slight depression mixed with disillusionment and maybe the teensiest bit of dark thoughts," Miko agrees, studying me along with my roommate.

"And how do you know that?" I ask.

"Because I've competed as a tribute in the Games myself." Miko's gaze moves from me to her empty glass. She nudges it towards Max with her index finger. Max takes the hint and starts to make her another one.

"You're right . . . I'm definitely bummed out." I look down into my glass. "But my mama always said you can get mad and happy in the same pants."

I raise my glass to both of them in salute and down a hearty swallow. I don't even wince as it washes down my throat. Jack and I are old friends.

"What the hell does that mean?" Max sets the new shot down in front of Miko.

"It means that I refuse to let this get me down. I've worked too hard to get here; I won't be detoured. I'll find a way to get through this and come out the other side better for it. I *will* impress Selah. I *will* get promoted. I *will* start my own event-planning firm and have a feature in *InStyle*. I'll do it all!"

I'm not sure if I'm trying to convince them or myself.

"Oh man." Max shakes her head slowly.

"I know, right?" Miko agrees, even though Max didn't actually make a statement.

"Oh man, what?" I ask, confused.

"This town is going to chew you up and spit you out." Max is still shaking her head.

Miko is using one hand to prop up her head on the bar, but she's nodding along with Max now. "It's a definite possibility."

I consider their words for a moment, and then a smile slowly curves my lips. Both of them stare at me like I'm going insane, but then they don't know me yet. They don't know that my parents lost four babies before I was born two months too early. They don't know that because I was a preemie, I've always been the littlest kid in every class and have had to fight for acceptance for as long as

I've been alive. They don't know that I've been doubted since the moment I was born, and because of that nothing, *nothing*, motivates me more than someone telling me I *can't* do something.

My smile is a Cheshire-Cat grin now.

"Oh, girls, you have no idea how much I'm gonna enjoy proving you both wrong." I wink and knock back the rest of my drink.

Chapter FIVE

I walk into the office the next morning wearing an all-black version of a Catholic schoolgirl uniform, complete with Mary Janes. It's not a look I'd ever gravitate to but, like I said, my options are limited. It hadn't looked *that* bad when I stared at it in the full-length mirror on my closet door, but as I walk through the office I feel like a moron on parade.

I've got to go shopping!

"Walker needs you this morning," McKenna directs me before I'm even all the way into his office.

"OK." I drop my bag under the chair in the corner. "Walker is . . ."

"Production," he sighs. "You should know that by now."

"Sorry. I'll make flash cards or something," I grumble.

I swear McKenna's lip quivers in an almost-smile, but then he turns his head and gets a load of my ensemble.

"Holy Britney! Where'd you dig up this outfit?"

"Do you need anything before I go?" I ask, ignoring the jibe.

"I'd tell you if I did." He turns back to his computer.

I run to the kitchen quickly for a coffee fix and then hurry down to the end of the large room where I see Miko clustered around a desk with a few other people. Today Miko is wearing little black shorts over black tights, an oversize black blouse, a black tuxedo jacket, and faded black Converse. As I walk up I hear her talking to the group.

"I like this better; it feels more nautical."

"Totally. I'll handle it, thanks." I recognize the light-haired girl from the meeting the day before.

The small cluster breaks up, having come to a conclusion, and I step up.

"Hi, I'm looking for Walker." I smile at them.

"Walker, this is Brinkley," Miko says to the light-haired girl.

"Brinkley, I'm so grateful we have your help today. We're working on the programs for Saturday, and I need some help with production." Walker flashes me a small smile.

Programs? How exciting! I can't wait to see how we make something here!

"Of course. Anything you need," I tell her.

Walker holds out a program to me.

Back home we have programs at weddings. Usually the couple will print them out on card stock . . . Something designed on their computer at home with pictures of themselves and a list of the bridal party and the songs they're playing at the wedding. The program in my hands is like the daddy of those back-home programs.

No, that's not the right explanation. It's like the father of this program was an oil baron and he married a Rockefeller, and they had the richest, classiest baby program ever. That's what I'm holding in my hands.

The thick navy-blue paper shimmers a little with the light. It's been folded over itself to create a rectangle about the size of a business envelope. *Ari* is embossed in gold in the middle, and the whole thing is held together by a thin white rope tied with a really cool little knot. I can tell there's paper inside, but I wouldn't dare

open it. I'm hesitant to drop it, it's so fancy. It's nautical and masculine and so awesome-looking!

"This is the knot we decided on," Walker says, pointing to the
little white rope. "It's called the single carrick bend. You can see
how I did it here." She hands me a computer printout that shows
the steps necessary to create the intricate knot. "You want to try
one?" She hands me a new program and a length of white rope.

It's not really a question. She looks at me expectantly, and
Miko looks along with her.

OK.

I put the finished program and the directions down on Walker's
desk and follow them awkwardly. It takes me a few tries, and it's
kind of stressful with them watching, but eventually I create something similar to the perfect example Walker has made. I hold it out
to them for inspection. Walker reaches out and adjusts it a little.

"You see, if you pull here it'll look a bit neater," she says while
she works.

"OK, thanks." I study the way her fingers adjust the knot.

"Great. You can help us tie these then." She stands and starts
walking towards the production room, and Miko and I follow her.

Once we step inside I'm immediately overwhelmed by the
flurry of activity and the scent of flowers. One whole side of the
room is lined with high worktables at which four women are
working with what looks like thousands of white flowers. Tons of
buckets overflowing with roses cover the floor around them. They
work quickly, cutting stems and removing leaves, prepping them
for something great, I'm sure.

I'm so spellbound by the flower production line that I don't
even see where I'm following Walker. I turn around just in time
to avoid running into her. She's standing in front of worktables
covered with stacks upon stacks upon stacks of shimmery navy-
blue rectangles. Next to those rectangles are box after box of short
lengths of little white rope. It takes a minute for my brain to catch

up to my eyes and realize I'm looking at my very own production line of hundreds of unfinished programs. My mouth falls open.

"You can pull over one of those stools." Walker gestures towards the floral side of the room. "I'll be back in a while to check on you."

I nod absentmindedly.

I shouldn't ask, but I have to know.

"How . . . How many guests are you expecting?" I try and sound casual.

"Uh, I think we're at 417 last count, right, Jin?" Walker asks.

I look over at Miko, who's not even trying to hide her smile. I realize now that she's followed us here just to see the look on my face when I realize the amount of rope tying I'll be doing today.

"That's right, but you know Selah always wants extra just in case, so I'm guessing there's five hundred here. Better get at it, sailor." She actually salutes me.

Both of them turn to leave, and I look down at the now wrinkled computer printout of maritime knot-tying directions in my hands.

Excuse my language, but it's gonna be a long-ass day.

———

Later that afternoon, around I don't know what time, Miko shows up at my worktable with a brown bag in one hand and a to-go coffee cup in the other.

"I've brought provisions," she says, setting them both down in front of me.

"God bless you!" I grab the coffee and take a sip. The sugary nirvana of a pumpkin spice latte permeates me all the way down to my toes, and I feel a million times better. In the bag is a sandwich wrap. I don't even look to see what kind it is before I take a gigantic bite.

"You know, one of the perks about being on program duty is that no one is looking over your shoulder," Miko says, leaning one of her slim hips against the table. "You could leave to get yourself food and caffeine. No one would notice if you were gone for a few minutes."

"I've only finished 174. I don't have time to leave." I talk between bites. "Plus with my luck I'd leave at the exact moment they come to check on me."

"This is true; your luck is pretty bad. I mean, in only a few days here you've seen Selah go full-bitch at least twice that I know of. Then the Ken doll fries your synapses and now you're earning your knot-tying patch." She fiddles with a loose piece of rope in the box.

"Ken doll?" I shove the last of the wrap into my mouth.

"Brody Ashton. I saw you dealing with the two of them yesterday. Being trapped by that much combined gorgeousness isn't good for anyone's self-esteem."

"You saw that?" I wipe my hands on a napkin from the bag.

"Of course I saw that! Anyone with a functioning uterus eye-banged him all the way across the room."

"I guess," I mutter, picking up another piece of rope to tie.

Miko leans down to get a better look at my face.

"Well, now I know you're full of it! Only a blind woman wouldn't find him sexy as hell, and even then the guide dog would lead her to him!" She giggles.

"I guess he's just not my type." I continue to work on my knot with the tips of my now-raw fingers.

"He's *everyone's* type. Even I'd give him a go, and I hate blondes."

"Thanks," I say, mock offended.

"You're the exception to the rule, but that's neither here nor there. He's gorgeous and wildly successful. And if rumor is to be believed, he only dates Victoria's Secret models. Why do you think she wants him so badly?"

"His superhuman ability to attract both man and beast isn't reason enough?" I ask, bemused.

"One of the first things you will learn about your new boss is that she cares about appearance first and foremost. Brody is the toy that all the other kids want to own, so obviously Selah wants to be the one to lock him down. He's a fill-in-the-blank . . . It could be a purse, a car, a trip, a new pair of shoes. She's constantly in pursuit of shiny things, and well, he's very shiny."

Selah's pursuit or Brody's prowess or both aren't any of my business or concern. I shrug one shoulder, my own way of saying *I don't care either way*. I have ropes to tie.

"How many now?" Miko asks, throwing away my lunch trash for me.

"One hundred seventy-six." I sigh, continuing to work on the knot.

"I'll leave you to it. I've got to completely redesign the lounge layout for Saturday now. Don't ask me why." She turns to go.

"Miko, thank you for lunch." I smile at her. "I have no idea why you're so nice to me, but I really, really appreciate it."

Miko stops a few feet away and smiles back at me. "Landon, I'm nice because I like you and because I used to *be* you. And when I was you, I was always, *always*, starving and thirsty and afraid to leave to pee."

"Really?" I ask shyly.

"Really. Someday you'll buy a newbie intern a latte, and the circle of life will be complete."

She throws a nonchalant peace sign over her shoulder and saunters away and out the door. On the other side of the room, the floral ladies are still at it, only now someone is blasting the Bee Gees station on Pandora, and they're all humming along.

I turn back to my programs feeling infinitely better. If Miko used to be a lowly, losery intern like me and is now the coolest person I know, then surely there's hope for me too.

Only 322 more ropes to tie.

I finish the programs around nine thirty that night. Apparently, Selah doesn't like anything to be finished last minute. I have to admit that I agree with the idea . . . in the light of day. But this night I'm not feeling very generous during the last hour of work. When I finally do stumble my way out of the production-room door, I am shocked to find the office still alive with people. I'm somewhat mollified by the idea that everyone else is hustling to finish their own projects just like I am . . . everyone except Selah, of course. She clearly doesn't stay late when she has droves of minions to stay for her.

When I come in the next morning I'm down to the last conceivable all-black ensemble I can pull off. I've got on black skinny jeans, black ballet flats, and a plain black T-shirt. The shirt is sort of schlumpy and something I'd never normally be caught dead in outside of the house, but I compensated with a pretty red lip stain and a few more lashes than I'd normally wear . . . A girl's got to get her glam in where she can.

As I pass by the angry receptionist—whose name is Ambrose, by the way—I am surprised by the quiet in the office. I'd expected the pandemonium of pre-event chaos to greet me, but it looks like half the staff isn't even here.

I stop by Miko's desk on my way back to the small office.

"Where is everyone?" I ask, setting a latte down on her desk.

"At the load-in. What's this?" She taps the latte with her pen.

"Repayment beverage. Today we're going to try a red-velvet latte." I'm sipping on my own.

"Thanks! I've been here since six, and I'm hanging on by a thread. Also, I do love thousand-calorie coffees," she says, sniffing the drink through the hole in the lid.

"Well, since it's likely the only thing I'll eat today, and you can't weigh more than a hundred pounds soaking wet, I thought we'd be OK."

"A valid point." She sips her drink with relish. "This is amazing!"

"I know, right?" I turn to head to the office.

"I'm headed to the load-in to oversee setup." She starts throwing random things from her desk into her already-overstuffed bag. "But I'll catch you later."

I stop short and turn back around.

"*You're* overseeing the setup? Shouldn't she be doing that?" I whisper back at her.

"Oh, Landon," she says with dismay. "The second thing you'll learn about this new boss of yours is that she just shows up at the last minute, wreaks havoc for an hour, and then takes credit for it all."

"Really?" I walk back over to her. I can't imagine not being there for every minute of an event setup if my name is the one on the wall.

"Really." Miko is back to packing up. "Besides, it's not just me. All the team heads go."

What must that be like? To get to watch the whole party come together from the ground up?

"I'm so jealous. I can't imagine how cool it must be to put all the pieces together."

"Don't worry, you'll see more than enough. By tomorrow night just the sight of navy dupioni silk will make you want to gag."

"You realize I don't know what that is, right?"

"You will." Miko runs a hand through her perfectly disheveled hair, grabs her latte, and walks off towards the elevator.

———

That afternoon the little office is noisier than usual. From my corner I hear McKenna and Quade field call after call about the bar mitzvah. Mixed in with all those calls is the usual load regarding the event we have next week and the three others before month's end. For the first time it occurs to me how hard it must be to juggle so many high-profile parties at one time. You're not allowed to tell one client you're busy with another client's event, so you're forced to take calls and chat like you're not drowning in your to-do list.

Both Quade and McKenna look worn down, and around three o'clock that afternoon they send me to get them lunch. It's the first time I've seen either of them eat, and even though it's just sushi I'm sort of relieved that, in their own anorexic way, they're emotional eaters just like I am.

On my way home that night I'm stuck in traffic near Robertson. Katy Perry is crooning on the radio and my windows are down, letting in air that's only slightly chilly. Down the sidewalk and across the street I see a tall, extremely tan older man wearing a pair of boy shorts, old sneakers, and headphones. His lack of clothing on its own would have caught my eye, but it's the fact that he's dancing wildly that has me inching my car forward, trying to figure out what his deal is. As I draw closer I realize he's dancing along with his own reflection in a storefront window, and I can't help but giggle.

Mama would say he's drunker than a run-over yard dog, but I like him. He's clearly a little nuts, but you know what? He's working with it. There he is on this busy street, wearing his skivvies, and finding his own little moment of joy. My first thought is *I need to be more like that guy!* The second is to wonder what this says about the turn my life has taken—I'm idealizing the crazy, naked dancing man on Robertson.

Chapter SIX

McKenna tells me the dress code for the mitzvah is . . . *wait for it* . . . all black.

I have to recycle my black cocktail dress from earlier in the week, but this time I pair it with black tights and my black ballet flats. I didn't do many events back in Texas, but it only took one for me to understand that running around in heels for ten hours is a special kind of torture.

I curl my blonde hair like normal, but then I get nervous that maybe I should look a little more conservative since this is a religious event, so I pin it back. I add the pearl earrings Mama and Daddy gave me for graduation and toss a mint-green cardigan into my bag. Surely, if it gets really chilly, they'll let me wear it even though it's colorful.

The party is at the Lerner's home in Bel Air, and I have no earthly idea how anyone can host a party for four hundred people in their own home. I'm dying to see how it's done!

It's 3:47 p.m. when I pull up to a gate at the address I've been given. Thank God I left over an hour ago, or I never would have made it here on time! I'm not sure what I'm supposed to do now.

Do I call McKenna? Should I park? Is there a doorbell or something? I chew on my lower lip and lean forward in my seat, trying
to spot the way to gain access through this ominous-looking gate.
Just when I'm about to reverse and try and find street parking, the
gate starts to glide open. Before I can put my car into drive a big
guy in a dark suit comes out from behind the gate with a clipboard
in his hands and motions for me to roll down my window.

"Can I help you?"

"Oh gosh, thanks! I was startin' to worry I'd sit out here all
day!" I say brightly.

His eyebrows pull in towards his nose, and he gives me a skep-
tical once-over.

"I'm with SSE. I'm here to help with the party?" I don't know
why that comes out like a question.

"Name?" he asks, annoyed.

"Landon—or, um, maybe Brinkley? Landon Brinkley."

The guy runs through several pages on his clipboard before
finding whatever it is he's looking for.

"ID?"

"Is this in case I order a body shot or something? I promise I'm
over twenty-one," I say, trying to tease a smile out of him.

Security Guy is not amused.

"Sure, sorry. Let me just—" I reach into the backseat and grab
my bag, which is sort of hard to do without flashing Security Guy
the control top of my tights. I finally get to my purse, then my wallet, and produce the ID.

He looks at the photo, compares it to my face, and then checks
the name on the list. He hands it back and points down the long
driveway in front of me.

"Follow the drive all the way around and back. Staff is parking
on the second gravel lot at the bottom of the hill."

"Thanks, have a nice day!" I say with a smile. No response.

The driveway winds for a moment between well-manicured lawns before the house comes into view. No, not house, *mansion*. Surely something this big and this beautiful gets mansion status. It looks like what you might find in the Italian countryside. At least I'm assuming this is what homes look like in the Italian country-side. It's peaceful and statuesque, but as soon as I pass by it and continue down the drive I see the SSE staff scurrying about like a colony of ants.

I park my car alongside a bunch of other cars and jump out to look at the spectacle of the backyard. The first answer to the whole how-do-you-host-a-party-for-four-hundred-at-home question is that you need a backyard the size of Phoenix. There's got to be at least two acres of lawn and landscaping that match the Italian feel of the house. Farther on the lawn slopes downward, and at the bottom I can see a tennis court and a guesthouse that's bigger than the home I grew up in. But closer still is the second thing you need for hosting a party this large: a gigantic tent sitting in the center of the lawn.

I've never seen anything like it. It's completely clear on all sides; the only hint of color is the frame, which is all white. The clear roof shines in the sun like glass; for all I know it *is* glass. It's so pretty! Through the clear sidewalls of the tent, I can see a flurry of activity, with people setting up tables and chairs and those lounges that Miko worked so hard to rearrange yesterday. Every single area in the tent is buzzing. There's got to be at least fifty staff members setting, straightening, bringing crates in and out, and working on flowers. I'm in awe. I lock my car and head towards the tent. I can't wait to help!

Once I walk inside the tent, I'm too flabbergasted to move another step. It's literally too amazing, and my brain cannot pro-cess what I'm seeing.

I've never been inside a tent that had an actual floor built in. And this tent doesn't have just flooring: the floor is weathered plank hardwood that's been whitewashed and aged in a fantastic play on the nautical theme. The dinner tables are all draped with navy-blue silk linens, which must be the dupioni Miko was talking about. I've only ever seen round tables for big dinners like this one, but this layout is a mix of squares and rectangles. The tables surround the dance floor on all sides except for a small area where a white stage sits on a pedestal, which has white acrylic walls that come up to the waist of the DJ, who's inside setting up his equipment. In the center of the dance floor a few men are playing with a remote. Each time they mess with it, the lighting in the tent changes color. It's hard to tell what they're adjusting because it's still so bright in here through the clear walls, but they keep changing it . . . adding a bit more pink or a little purple. I watch as the linens on the tables change color subtly. I wonder what it will look like tonight when it's dark in here.

To my left the ladies from the floral team are placing flowers on the tables. The centerpieces are collections of three or four square glass vases in varying sizes, filled with the white floral arrangements I had seen them working on in the production room. A team of servers wearing black slacks, white button-down shirts, and navy-blue neck ties (of course they match the tablecloths exactly) is setting glassware and plates down on what must be at least fifty tables. Small lounge areas are set up throughout the room, creating cool little vignettes with small sofas and chairs. Everything is stunning and themed but with the underlying touch of SSE's clean, modern design. It's amazing.

I force my slack jaw to close and start walking again to find McKenna. As I move between the tables to the center of the room, I notice the dance floor is thick, clear glass that's covering the span of a lit pool below it.

Holy crap! Coolest. Party. Ever.

McKenna looks up just as I come upon him giving instructions to a handful of servers.

"The napkins should be a pocket fold." He looks up when he sees me. "Brinkley, find the menus and then tuck one inside each napkin. Oh, and let's get you a walkie." He doesn't sound snide or rude, just busy and efficient. This is a pleasant surprise.

He turns, and I follow him to the far side of the tent where several tables hide behind waist-high, white acrylic walls. A handful of men are sitting behind tables covered with computer monitors, wires, mics, and a thousand buttons and knobs.

"This is the A/V team. Mike, can we get another walkie?" he calls to one of the guys as he looks at the screen of his phone. While we wait, I can't help it. I have to say something.

"Everything looks—it's fantastic!" I come *very* close to squealing the words.

McKenna looks up from whatever he's typing into his phone with a nostalgic smile on his face.

"I remember being that excited once."

"And now?" I can't help but ask.

"Now—" He glances around the room along with me, then sighs. "You'll see."

"Here you go." A big guy dressed in a black T-shirt and black slacks hands me a heavy walkie-talkie. "This is your earpiece." He points to the different elements. "This is your mic. You can clip it on and press this button to speak. SSE is channel one, A/V is on two, catering is three. Got it?"

"Sure." I smile at him.

"Testing for Brinkley," McKenna says into the mouthpiece clipped to his lapel, and I hear it crisply on the earpiece I've just put on.

"Can you hear me?" I ask back to him into my own mouthpiece, and he nods at me.

I grin like an idiot; I've got an earpiece on just like J-Lo in the movie!

"All right. Head over to catering and find the menus; one goes into each napkin. We're room-ready at six fifteen for photography so make it snappy."

"Definitely." Holding my walkie, I scurry off in search of the menus. The walkie is pretty heavy, and I have nowhere to put it or clip it. Next time I have to remember to wear something with a waistband so I can attach this beast to something.

Music bursts through the speakers as the DJ starts to work with the A/V team on the sound. Britney, will.i.am, and a thumping bass fill the tent, and I bob along to the beat while tucking expensive-looking embossed menus inside each napkin. Working an event is way more fun than I thought!

While I'm on napkin duty I hear people speaking back and forth in my earpiece in some kind of special walkie-talkie language I've never heard before.

"McKenna for Taylor," I hear McKenna say.

"Go for Taylor," Taylor replies.

"Where are the throw pillows for the lounge setups?"

"Walker is bringing them in now," Taylor replies, and the conversation ends.

"Davies for McKenna," a sweet, British-accented voice says.

"Go for McKenna."

"Did Selah decide on whether we're doing votives in clusters or lines?"

"Lines."

"Cheers. Thanks," Davies answers sweetly.

"Taylor for Revere," Taylor says.

"He's on channel three," someone else responds.

"Do you need help with those?"

I've been so busy tucking menus and listening to walkie-talk, I haven't even noticed the three servers who are standing behind me. One of them points to the menus in my hand.

"Oh, y'all, that would be great. Thank you so much!" I hand each of them a large stack.

"The photo booth is here. Can someone show him to the Lido Deck?" McKenna asks into the walkie. When no one responds I jump on it, eager to help.

"This is Lan—. Er, Brinkley. I'll do it."

"Roger," McKenna says back.

I hurry out to the front of the tent and see a man waiting there expectantly.

"Photo booth?" I ask.

"Yes, I'm Greg. Are you Walker? I think we spoke on the phone."

"No, that wasn't me." I smile and shake his hand. "I'm Brinkley."

"Oh, sorry. Do you know where I'm supposed to set up?"

"The Lido Deck is where you're headed. Just give me two seconds, and I'll figure out what that means and where it's located." I look around me, confused.

"No problem. Let me just back the truck down here, and then you can tell me where we're headed, OK?"

"Sounds like a plan." I hurry off in search.

After ten minutes of searching the grounds I still can't figure out where the photo booth is supposed to go, and I'm getting anxious about making the delivery guy wait to unload it. I consider asking someone directions on the walkie, but then everyone will know that I'm clueless. Between admitting to the crew that I can't do a simple job and asking McKenna, the latter seems like the lesser of two evils, and since I can see him on the far side of the tent, I head towards him at a near jog.

McKenna looks up as I hurry over and slows me with a pointed look.

"Brinkley," he chides, "we *never* run at an event."

He reaches out and straightens the centerpiece on the table in front of him to a precise right angle.

"I get it. It's not ladylike or classy, but I couldn't figure out where the Lido Deck is, and I felt bad because he's out there waitin'—"

"Your being ladylike is the least of my concerns and, frankly, a project that's possibly beyond the scope of even my considerable talents. We don't run at events because when party guests see you run, they assume something bad has happened and"—he glares at me as if willing his words to imprint on my brain—"nothing bad happens at an SSE party."

This piece of information is incredible. I knew their team was talented, but it has never occurred to me they might be so well-oiled that they never had to troubleshoot. I have to learn what they do to ensure they don't have any issues day-of.

"Really? Back in Texas we always had at least one or two disasters at any of the events I interned." McKenna looks increasingly annoyed with every word that falls from my mouth, which makes me nervous, and only serves to make me talk faster and makes my accent more pronounced. "Miss Opal Teagarten, that's the planner I worked for over in Houston last summer, her motto was 'Prepare for the Flood.' But no matter how much we tried to do that, there was always something that—"

He finally snaps. "Why are you still speaking?"

I stare at him blankly.

"Of course things happen at our events. Don't be an idiot! The point is that our guests are never aware of them. So whatever happens, keep yourself in check until you're out of sight. Perception is reality. Got it?"

I nod at him at the same time he grabs a packet of paperwork out of the binder under his arm and hands it to me.

"You made the copies of this; you think you'd grab one for yourself." He turns to walk away. "The map is on the last page. I suggest you take a preemptive approach to that timeline going forward."

I look down at the twelve-page timeline in my hands and feel like the big idiot he said I was. I'd spent at least an hour printing, collating, and stapling the agenda for the SSE team. It should have occurred to me to look at it for directions on where setup should be. I flip quickly to the last page, heading back towards the delivery guy at a brisk walk instead of a run.

Turns out the Lido Deck is the name for a second tent that is set up in back. I'd never heard the name before, but when I mention it to Miko later, she assures me that rich people with boats find it clever.

The Lido Deck is about a quarter of the size of the main tent, but it doesn't have clear walls. This tent is white on the outside, and inside a thick, velvety drape covers every square inch from floor to ceiling. Because no sunlight can peek through the walls of the tent, the lighting in here is stellar. It's all blues and greens morphed into cool shapes or thrown around the room by lasers. In the center of the space a light shines onto the ground big bold letters that spell *Ari*, in case anyone forgets who the party is for.

Lights shift and move in time with the music coming from yet another DJ, and every inch of the space is filled with activity stations. There's the photo booth currently being set up, a vintage arcade with at least seven games, a place to screen-print your own T-shirt, tables full of glass vases filled with different kinds of candy (all of which are blue), and even a bar featuring "mocktails." I can't believe this space, which has to cost at least fifty grand, is for a bunch of thirteen-year-olds.

All I'd wanted for my thirteenth birthday was a purple velour Juicy jumpsuit, and, no joke, my daddy gave me a shotgun and a gift certificate for hunter's education classes down at the sporting goods store. Clearly Ari and I come from different worlds.

"The bars need their framed menus. Who's on it?" someone asks into the walkie.

"This is Brinkley. I'll grab them." I hurry out of the little tent and off in search of the menus.

"We need pens! The guest book has no pens," McKenna barks into the walkie.

"This is Brinkley again. I'll get pens when I grab the menus. Give me two minutes."

I hope I don't come across as a teacher's pet, but I can't seem to help myself.

"Roger."

"Did photo booth get set up?" someone asks as I head up to the production van.

"Yes, he's just finishing his setup now. I told them we're room-ready at six fifteen for photos."

I feel very official and important answering questions into my mouthpiece and fetching bar menus.

It can't take me more than a handful of minutes to grab the supplies, but by the time I walk back into the main tent the mood has changed. Selah has arrived and is fit to be tied. From what I can tell she hates the setup of the lounges, and now everyone is scrambling to change them around. At least twelve people are working with her trying to lay out the room differently, which is actually really tough since there is so much furniture in the tent; moving one thing means moving everything else around it too.

I try not to draw attention to myself as I walk the menus to each bar and then turn back to the chaos. I don't really want to enter Selah's orbit, but she's with Quade and McKenna. Since they're my bosses I don't really have a choice.

Selah is wearing a black sheath dress with black stiletto boots. She looks flawless but for the snarl on her face.

"I can't fathom why it's never ready when I arrive on site," she says hatefully. "This layout looks terrible. And now I have to stand here and wait while you put everything back the way it should have been to begin with."

I come up and stand off to the side of the group.

"Production sets up," McKenna sighs.

"Yes, and don't you have eyes? Surely you could see that the room looked like shit," she bites back. "This is what happens when a design is altered at the last minute."

Wait, wasn't she the one who had them change the whole design at the last minute?

"I know. It's so frustrating. Thank God you're here. It already looks so much better," McKenna says, coddling her.

I look around the space before me. It looks great this new way. But it also looked great the old way, and there really isn't enough of a change to warrant the scramble. All around me people are hurried and nervous-looking. It's odd because half an hour ago I thought we all seemed prepared and confident.

———

We're only a few minutes into the party when I hear Quade's voice screech through my earpiece.

"What the fuck is going on with these bar menus?" she demands to no one in particular.

I look at the bar across the tent from where I've been stationed, greeting guests. I'm expecting to see Quade's body language reflecting the angry tone in her voice, but at this distance she looks totally controlled and normal as she whispers viciously into her walkie.

"These menus are for the Lido Deck! We've got guests wondering why their signature drinks are named after Halo characters, and parents freaking out because the menus in the deck have alcohol listed in them!"

The bottom drops out of my stomach. I hadn't even thought to check and see which bar menu went where; I'd assumed they were all the same. I reach for my walkie so I can apologize.

"My bad. I'll swap those out right now." I haven't heard him on the walkie much today, but I recognize the little twang of Taylor's voice.

Why is he covering for me? I don't want anyone getting in trouble on my behalf. By the time I arrive at the bar Taylor is already there, swapping out the menus.

"I'm so sorry about that. I thought they were all the same." I can't get the apology out fast enough.

"Don't worry about it." He gives me a grin. "Nothing at SSE is ever done simply. There are always a dozen versions of every party element, and each is more expensive than the next. If whatever you're working on seems straightforward, you're probably doing something wrong." He gestures to the kids' bar menus that are stacked in his arms. "Want to help me switch these out?"

"Of course." I grab half the stack of frames from him, and we start to make our way out of the tent through the crowds of guests that are already deep into the party spirit. I'm so grateful for his kindness. McKenna has brought me to near tears for far lesser offenses.

"You didn't have to take the bullet, you know. Quade might have gotten upset with you, and she's already pretty scary under normal circumstances."

When I glance over he's looking at me like the notion is ridiculous.

"Don't worry. I haven't met a woman yet who could ever stay mad at me for long."

"I'll bet," I grumble under my breath at his bravado, and his smile stretches to reveal one perfect dimple.

I'm running our conversation over in my head when he starts talking again.

"You'll see. I—" I stop short. "You mentioned that nothing is ever the simplest choice . . . Does that include the guest book pens?" I'm so nervous.

He looks bemused.

"There should have been eight of them. They were Montblanc. Each had a different inscription—"

"Oh Lord!" I quickly hand him my stack of frames. "I just grabbed a handful of blue Bics from the production kit!" I screech and hurry to correct the problem, hopefully before anyone on staff notices. The sound of Taylor's laughter follows me all the way out of the tent.

———

The next day I don't open my eyes until well past eleven. I *never* sleep that late, but I didn't get home from the mitzvah until after two and I am exhausted. I sit up and let my legs dangle over the side of the bed and stretch them to ease some of the tension. You'd think that years of hauling gigantic trays of ribs through a restaurant would have prepared my body for one night spent working an event, but you'd be wrong. I hurt in places I didn't even know existed!

Once I stepped into that tent yesterday, I didn't sit down until I got into my car to drive home. Ten hours of hurrying back and forth through the party, pulling props and setting out the guest favors, moving 450 gift bags after Selah didn't like their first location, and then assisting with wrap-up at the end of the night . . . I'm pretty sure I've burned off the calorie equivalent of five Zumba classes.

The night had been exhausting, but it was also fast-paced and exciting. I learned so much about how the SSE team lays out a timeline and how they constantly troubleshoot to keep the event as on time as possible. Watching everyone move behind the scenes like a well-oiled machine made me realize for the first time how much work is actually required to make something look so flawless and simple.

I stand up and stretch out my whole body, then go out to the kitchen in search of a cup of coffee the size of my head.

Max is sitting on the kitchen countertop, eating a giant bowl of what looks like hamster food, so I'm guessing it's some sort of diet-y cereal. She's wearing an old flannel button-down, underwear, a pair of UGG boots, and nothing else . . . *What is with this girl and pants?*

"What is it with you and pants?" I ask quizzically.

"Said the cheerleader." Max scowls at my pink boy shorts and the baby tee I got at cheer camp in freshmen year of high school.

"Touché." I smile in spite of myself and head towards the coffee maker only to find that there's a fresh pot waiting for me. "I take back the pants comment. You can walk around here nude if you're willing to make me coffee!" I joyfully pour myself a cup and add two Splendas and a little of the milk that's sitting next to Max on the counter.

Max just grumbles into her cereal bowl in response; she's clearly not a morning person. Well, actually it's almost noon, so technically she's not a mid-morning person either . . . I wonder if there's any time of day when she's not grouchy. I smile down into my coffee as I take a sip. *Probably not.*

"Doing anything fun today?" I ask happily.

"You're looking at it." She points to the cabinet behind my head without moving from her perch. "Can you hand me a mug?"

"I'll get it. How do you take it?"

"Black."

Of course.

I pour her a cup and hand it over.

"I need to go shopping today for work clothes. Can you tell me where to find a Forever 21 or an H&M or something?" I grab a bowl from the cabinet behind me and pour myself some of her bran-filled cereal. She looks briefly affronted at my thievery but chooses to let it go.

"Hollywood & Highland is the closest, but it's filled with douche-y tourists and sweaty guys in Avengers costumes. You should go to The Grove."

"That's on Fairfax, right?" I ask before swallowing a spoonful. My taste buds openly revolt against the amount of flax packed into each flake; I fight the urge to spit it back out. Instead I put the bowl down on the counter behind me and hope she doesn't notice that I've stopped eating it.

"Fairfax and Third." She jumps down from the counter, flashing her Star Wars panties. "I can take you if you want."

"Really?" I can't keep the shock out of my voice. "You want to hang out with me? You're not too busy?"

"Calm down. I don't want to take a blood oath or anything. I need a break; I studied for six hours yesterday. If I have to look at another textbook, I'll scrape my eyes out with this spoon." She holds up the spoon from her cereal bowl and then turns to put them both in the dishwasher.

"What textbook—what are you studying?" I'm confused . . . This is news to me.

"I'm in the last year of my masters at UCLA," she responds, transferring a few dirty dishes from the sink to the dishwasher.

At first I'm dumbstruck, and then I'm unnaturally proud of her.

"You're getting your masters? That's so great! I had no idea. Why didn't you tell me?"

Max closes the dishwasher. "You never asked." She gives me a nonchalant shrug and turns to leave the kitchen. It's only then that I see the words stamped across the underwear on her bum.

These Are Not the Droids You Seek.

This girl is so weird.
I jump off the counter and follow her to get dressed.

Chapter SEVEN

The next morning I head into the office, and for the first time I don't stick out like a sore thumb. With Max's help I have acquired a new wardrobe in only one color. It's harder than you'd think for me to maintain my own personal style without color involved, but after hitting several stores, having the glass of wine Max insisted was necessary to deal with The Grove on a Sunday, and finding a clearance rack at Banana, I found a ton of stuff to mix and match.

Today I have on a gingham black-and-white button-down tucked into black skinny jeans, with black wedge booties and a black cardigan. My necklace is gold with red chevrons hanging just below the collar of my blouse . . . Yes, technically that's *color*, but nobody said anything about *accessories* being black. At least this is the case I plan to make if anyone says anything.

My hair is styled in bouncy waves, and my makeup is pretty and polished. I realize I'm still dressed a lot peppier than anyone else at SSE, but well, while you can take the girl out of Texas . . .

In the little office McKenna is already typing away at his laptop, and I sit down in my corner seat and fire up my old Mac.

"Have you worked a phone before?" McKenna asks out of nowhere.

A phone? Yes, I'm not a monkey. But that thing in front of him looks more like mission control than a telephone.

"Um, no, but I'm sure I can figure it out," I say, staring warily at the millions of buttons.

"Let me show you quickly." He gestures impatiently for me to come over, and I hop up.

"OK, this is the call log."

He opens up a program on his computer screen that looks like the inner workings of the Pentagon. There are names and numbers and notations and dates and times . . . How does he even keep all this straight?

"If someone calls, and Selah is unavailable, just put their info here," he says, using the cursor to show me a new line entry in the program.

"You hit this button to answer—" The phone buzzes as if on cue. He hits the answer button in question and speaks into his mouthpiece. "Selah Smith's office? Yes, hello Maya. How are you? Great—good . . . No, unfortunately she's out of the office. Can I have her return? On cell? Great, we'll buzz you later." He types the info into the call sheet. "And that button," he continues right along, "is to end a call. This is to transfer, just remember to dial one first. This button is to connect someone on a conference." I keep nodding like I have any idea what he's talking about. "Just hit conference, dial the number, and then hit conference again to connect. Got it?"

"Got it."

I *so* don't got it.

"Great, I'm going to get a coffee. Cover the phones." He pulls off the headset and holds it out to me.

I recoil like he's offering me crack.

"I'm not really sure I can—"

"Jesus, Alabama, you can either do this job or you can't! Which is it?" he demands.

I bite my lower lip nervously.

"Can." I grab the headset and put it on with more aggression than necessary, as if jamming it on my head with brute force proves to him that I'm more capable than I actually am. He's already out the office door before I even sit down in his chair. I stare at the open call log in front of me. I guess I can just write things down on Post-its until he gets back. Or maybe no one will even call; maybe I'll just sit here silently until he gets back. No harm, no foul.

The phone buzzes and instantly my stomach fills with acid. I hit "Answer."

"S-Selah Smith's office. This is Brinkley. How may I help you?" I stutter.

"Wow, who let you answer the phone?" Ambrose asks rudely.

"What can I do for you?" I try and sound as rude as she does.

"Where's McKenna?"

"Getting coffee. May I help you with something?"

"No, I'll ask him. In the meantime, answer the phone the way he does. If you recite that monologue each time the phone rings, you'll never get to all your calls."

"OK, thanks. I really app—" Before I even finish the sentence, the line goes dead. I hit "End" just to be sure it's hung up, and it immediately buzzes again.

"Selah Smith's office," I say brightly.

"It's Dawn. Is she available?" a woman asks.

"I'm so sorry she's unavailable. Can I—"

"Just tell her I called." She hangs up with a click before I can get her last name or number. Shoot!

The phone buzzes again.

"Selah Smith's office?"

The phone buzzes again and line two lights up.

"Hi, Quade. It's Billy from Superior. Is she available?"

"Hi, Billy. This is actually—" Line three buzzes. "You know what, Billy? Can I just put you on hold for one moment?" I am staring at two blinking, unanswered lines.

"Sure thing," he says.

"One second." I push the button to put Billy on hold and accidentally hang up on him.

Noooooooo!

I hit the button for line two.

"Selah Smith's office, can you please hold a moment?" I put them on hold before they even answer. This time I actually do it right. I hit line three.

"Selah Smith's office?"

"I have Michael Field calling."

"She's unavailable; can I take a message?" I ask hurriedly.

"Have her return here to the office," she says and hangs up.

Man, I hope we have these numbers saved in contacts somewhere! I push the button for line two, and line one buzzes again, and then line three does too.

"Sorry about that," I tell line two.

"No problem. Is she available?" a man asks.

"She's just—" The three other lines keep buzzing at me, angry. I panic. "I am so sorry; can I just put you on hold right quick?" Darn it, my accent always sneaks up when I'm nervous!

"Sure," he says. I hit "Hold."

"Selah Smith's office. Please hold." I say to line three, then put them on hold.

"Selah Smith's office. Please hold." I say to line four, then put them on hold.

"Selah Smith's office?" I say to one finally.

"It's—." The phone breaks up in a garble, and I can barely make out the woman's voice on the other end.

"I'm so sorry, your phone is breaking up." I raise my voice a little.

"It's La—." Her heavily accented voice barely breaks through to my end.

Line three hangs up. Lines two and four are still blinking.

Crap!

"I apologize, miss, but I cannot understand you; your phone is breaking up," I say louder.

"It's La—uise; is Sel—ere?" she says again.

"I'm sorry, who?" I'm almost yelling now.

"Lana Cruise! Can you hear me? I need to speak with Selah." Her voice suddenly comes in loud and clear, and instantly I realize I'm speaking with the gorgeous Spanish actress I've seen in a dozen movies . . . *And* I've just yelled at her on the phone.

Crap!

"Hi, Ms. Cruise, I'm so sorry she's out of the office. Can I have her return?" I try and sound professional, but my voice is shaking. I've never talked to an Oscar winner before.

"Yes, she has the number." She hangs up just as line four drops off. Line two still blinks. I hit the button for it.

"I am *so* sorry about that. How can I help you?"

"I'm guessing this is Brinkley," he says dryly.

Who in the world would know my name?

"And why would you guess that?" I ask nervously.

"Neither of the other two assistants would have let me sit on hold for five minutes."

He sounds annoyed, and I have the strongest urge to "accidentally" hang up on him. I eye the other lines, hoping one of them will buzz and save me.

"It is Brinkley, and I beg your pardon. It's my first time on the phones, and I'm not, well, gosh, you don't have time to listen to me—"

"No, I'm afraid I don't."

Cue: flop sweat.

"Right, of course. She's actually out of the office, though. Can I take a message, Mr.—?"

"Ashton. Just tell her I called, please."

It's *him*.

I wish, *wish*, that I'd stop making an idiot of myself in front of this person. Whatever their relationship he obviously has Selah's ear, and her hearing about what a moron I am doesn't really bode well for my career. It takes a real effort to get myself in check, but I do.

"I will, and I'm sorry again, Mr. Ashton. I'll tell her you called."

"Thanks."

The line goes dead.

Well . . . That was interesting.

———

The next month flies by so quickly I barely notice. By mid-November I'm working at least sixty hours a week, and I've helped SSE with six events, so I feel like I've officially been jumped into their gang. It's easier now to anticipate what McKenna and Quade expect from me and to steer clear of Selah's mood swings. I can handle the phones now too, though I still really hate to do it since I'm positive I'll destroy the whole infrastructure with one misplaced phone message.

And teacher's pet or not, after that first event I sort of become an assistant for the entire office. I'm not sure if this is because people like me now, or because they know I'll do anything they ask. But I don't care because it means I'm constantly doing several projects at once, and I love it because I'm learning so much about how each team functions. Most evenings I don't leave until after eight, but I've learned that in this office, and in this city, that's not so unusual.

The Kessler-Glen wedding is the second week of December, and I'm sort of desperate to see it all come together. First of all I've never worked a wedding with Selah, and I'm excited to see how she handles it. Also, the sketches Miko has shown me literally take my breath away they're so pretty. Next week is the Riverton party, but that's the last event we have before Thanksgiving. The SSE office is closed Wednesday through Sunday that week, and I can't believe I get to spend five whole days at home. I plan on wearing sweatpants and eating my weight in starches and carbs.

Snap-snap-snap.

My head pops up from where it's buried in my laptop, researching transvestite DJs for an upcoming party. (Apparently, they're all the rage.) McKenna as usual isn't looking up at me, but he's holding out a Post-it with an order for him and Quade. I glance at the time on my laptop; it's only 11:45. That's early even for them. This doesn't bode well for me; I can just feel it.

When I come back twenty minutes later McKenna and Quade are giggling, which is a fairly odd sound coming from such grouchy people. In another office, in another place, I'd ask what was so funny. I'd try and engage and befriend them both, but I've learned that these two don't see me as an equal and sure as heck don't want me as a friend. I hand them their drinks and sit down to get back to work.

"It's so true," McKenna says, still giggling. "She's got to have gained at least sixty pounds, and she's not even due until February or something."

"Did you see her on Kimmel talking about her pregnancy cravings?" Quade asks while typing something into her phone.

"Oh God, I know, so tragic!" McKenna agrees.

I realize now that they're talking about Paige Blakely. She's a new client of Selah's, and we're working on the shower for her first baby. Since she and her rock-star baby daddy are still unmarried, Selah is hopeful that she'll also be asked to plan the rumored post-baby nuptials. Paige is a popular country singer (so you know I love her), but she's made some headlines lately for the amount of weight she's gained with her pregnancy. Personally I think making fun of a pregnant woman's weight is downright evil, but being mean is nothing new for these two. Maybe they'll head out later and punch some babies for kicks.

"And you saw her e-mail, right? She wants a duck-themed shower. What is this, 1987? You hire the most expensive event planner on earth and then ask her for ducks?"

"Piglets would have been more appropriate"—McKenna chuckles again—"and the barnyard theme might be a better fit for a country girl, right, Brink—" He spins around in his chair, presumably to mock me too, but his eyes bug out of his head before they can focus on me. At McKenna's silence Quade rotates in her chair, and her face turns even paler than it is already. Both of them stare in silence, and even though I'm hidden by the door, I want to crawl under the chair and cower from whatever is in the doorway. Finally, I hear the slightest clearing of a throat and then Selah's voice.

"Paige and I were just headed down to lunch and she wanted to see the office." She speaks with the menace of a snake.

"Paige, I'm so sorry you had to—" McKenna tries to cover smoothly, and Quade looks like she's about to be run over by a train. I guess on some level she is. Selah cuts him off.

"No, you won't apologize. What you will do, both of you, is remove yourselves from my office. You don't work here anymore."

If it's possible, Quade becomes even more ashen. McKenna swallows audibly. It's like watching a car wreck, and I literally can't look away.

"Brinkley?" Selah calls out to me, and both Quade and McKenna slide their eyes to me in the corner. I didn't even know she knew I was back here.

"Yes ma'am?" I step out from behind the door nervously. Selah is boiling mad, but she's doing her best to mask it in front of the very pregnant blonde country singer standing next to her.

"Will you walk Paige back out to the lounge? I'll be there momentarily."

"Of course," I say, walking forward, "if you'll just follow me, Ms. Blakely."

Paige starts waddling through the office with a smile plastered on her face, but as she turns I can see that her eyes are watery. She's the cutest little thing I've ever seen, in her brightly colored maxi dress and her wedge sandals and her big, bouncy blonde hair. She's short like me, so the added weight is even more noticeable, but she's still gorgeous and glowing. Screw those A-holes for making fun of her! Before I can think better of it, I say what I'm thinking.

"Ms. Blakely, please excuse my language, but they're both total assholes. You look fantastic."

She sniffs and looks up at me. "It's OK. It's nothin' I haven't heard before." She sniffs again.

"No." I'm shaking my head. "It's not OK. They're idiots. They couldn't find their butt if they had both hands in their back pockets." I scowl.

"My mama always says that." Paige smiles her first real smile as we reach the lounge.

"Mine too." I smile back.

"Where are you from?" she asks as she lowers herself slowly onto a sofa.

"West Texas."

"Half my family's from Texas." She smiles sweetly. "Where 'bouts?"

And just like that both of our accents are going in full force.

"Odessa?"

"Of course I know Odessa! My granny's from Midland. When I was younger we used to head into Odessa for this great barbecue place I loved."

"The Pit?" I ask with a smile.

"The Pit! Lord, I haven't been there in ages but I loved that place!" She absently rubs her belly with one hand.

Mama's gonna die when I tell her Paige Blakely knows The Pit!!

"Actually, that's my mama and daddy's place."

She actually moans in response. "I'm so jealous! One of my pregnancy fantasies is having unlimited access to brisket!" She giggles.

Before I can agree I hear Selah behind me.

"Paige, just one more minute and we'll head down. Brinkley, a word?"

How long has she been standing there? I turn and follow her back behind the wall that separates reception from the rest of the office. At the far end of the room I can see Quade and McKenna packing up their desks. Oh no! She really has fired them! What does this mean for me?

"You're good with people." Selah says it like an accusation. I look up into her face, still strained in anger, and just nod.

She lowers her voice, presumably so Paige can't overhear. "Quade and McKenna were my entire support team, and they're gone. I don't allow anyone to insult my clientele, and they should know better."

I think of all the times I've listened to her insult her clientele . . . I guess it's only OK if none of them catch you doing it. I nod again.

She gives me a quick head-to-toe perusal, and then her eyes narrow.

"I don't have the time or the inclination to spend the height of the holiday-party season finding and training a new assistant. I need you to start immediately."

I think I stare at her for a full ten seconds before I find my voice to respond.

"I'm sorry, what?" I ask in shock.

"The job . . . as my assistant . . . It's what you're working towards, right?" If possible, she's even more annoyed. She looks down at the phone in her hand and starts to search through its contents.

"Yes ma'am. I mean, of course. I just—"

"You can either do this job or you can't, which is it?" she snaps.

It's exactly the same question McKenna asked when he taught me to use the phone. I wonder now if Selah asked him the same question once.

I can't believe any of this is happening. This morning I was excited about the prospect of watching *The Bachelorette* tonight on TV, and now Selah's offering me a job it should have taken years for me to acquire. She looks up from her phone, and I don't have time to debate it any longer. I decided when I came here that Selah was a means to an end, and she's offering me a chance to get to that end far faster than I could have anticipated. I muster every ounce of confidence I've acquired in my twenty-three years and look her dead in the eye.

I am strong. I am smart. I am courageous.

"I can."

"Good." She stares at me a beat longer, then looks back to her phone. "I've told McKenna to leave the handbook out and any pertinent notes available for you. They should be gone within the quarter hour. I'm off with Paige for lunch, but I'll be back by four. Tell Taylor I want the revised rental order on my desk by then, and make sure it's printed out. I don't like looking at those line items on a screen."

And then she's gone.

I turn slowly on my heel and see Miko staring, her eyes twice as big as they normally are. Before I can even get to her, Quade and McKenna come out of the small office with their stuff, looking annoyed but confident. Neither of them acknowledges anyone; it's as if their colleagues are somehow responsible for all of this. They start to pass me and, as usual, I'm not smart enough to keep my mouth shut.

"I'm sorry, guys, I—"

McKenna stops mid-step and glares at me, his angry face daring me to say another word. Then he resumes walking and they both carry on, refusing to look at me. How embarrassing for them! I wonder what they'll do now . . . What kind of reference would Selah give them? I don't even have time to contemplate it because I can hear Selah's phone buzzing, and I'm apparently the person who answers that now. I hurry past the room that's come to a standstill with all of this drama, past Miko's confused expression, and into the little office that's now all mine. I sit down at McKenna's desk and put in the earpiece as I punch the button for line one.

"Selah Smith's office?" I chirp, but the caller has already hung up. I look down at the white desk and see a thick black binder with the title "SSE Assistant Handbook," and right next to it is a bright Post-it. I realize it's the note Selah asked him to write, the one with any pertinent information I should have. McKenna's serial-killer handwriting is scribbled furiously across the top.

You won't last the week, Texas.

Well . . . At least this time he got the state right.

While Selah is at her lunch meeting I do my level best to memorize the assistant binder. It's something like fifty-two pages, single spaced, and mostly includes info about how to properly format an e-mail and answer the phone, but it's a lifeline and I'm clinging to it with both hands.

The phone is quiet through most of the afternoon, and while I'm thankful for the reprieve, there's something ominous about the silence. I'm guessing that the rumor of the Volturi's untimely demise has quickly made the rounds throughout the event industry and that none of the vendors want to risk speaking with Selah when there's already blood in the water.

"Brinkley, my office." Selah's clipped tone whips into my little room, and my head snaps up. She's already passed by, not bothering to confirm that I've heard her, just confident that her request will be met. I hurry to follow her with a notepad at the ready.

I walk just inside the door of her office and pause, waiting for her next command.

"Close the door and take a seat," she says without looking up from the screen of her cell phone.

I do as I'm told.

Selah angrily jabs a few buttons on the phone and then puts it down on the desk. Her eyes narrow on me like a hawk.

"I don't have time for this!" she barks.

"I'm sorry—should I come back later?" I'm confused.

"I've had Quade for almost two years and McKenna for half that; I don't know how I'm expected to continue at this level without proper support." Her tone is accusatory. As if *I'm* the one who has done something wrong. I just stare at her and try not to show how nervous I am.

When I don't reply she plows ahead.

"Whatever you don't know, you need to figure out."

I have *zero* idea what she's talking about but, as McKenna has taught me to do, I nod anyway. Selah pointedly glares down at the notebook in my hands. Since it's clear she wants me to make a note, I write:

1. Figure out whatever I don't know!???

"Next, the all-hands meeting is tomorrow morning. I shouldn't have to remind you of this, but that's your responsibility now."

I continue to write notes, but my stomach just drops out. I'm supposed to run a meeting? Like, a *real* one? The last meeting I led was back in Girl Scouts.

"Also, Margo e-mailed last week about some brunch or something she wants to do. We'll need to talk to Jin about the pulls she's done for that. Production should have three proposals going out today; confirm their delivery. I have drinks tonight with the team from Haiku, but I'm exhausted, this day is for shit, I need to reschedule. Make an appointment with the acupuncturist—my shoulders are too tense—and switch my Pilates back to Friday." She keeps listing things in rapid fire, and I scribble furiously without comment.

Thirty minutes later I'm dismissed, and it takes everything in me not to sag with relief. I hope that I've filled up five pages of notes because I'm new at this, and not because this is typical for a random Selah weekday.

I'm just barely at the door when Selah calls out again.

"And Brinkley?"

I turn around with the pageant-contestant smile on my face.

"This . . ." She points her index finger at my hair and then sweeps it around to encompass my face, "is ridiculous. The aesthetic here is chic, not cheap. You're a representation of my brand now, and as such I expect you to look presentable."

I will not cry. I will not cry.

I won't cry, but I don't trust myself to speak. I simply nod and turn to leave the room.

I walk back into the little office without looking at anyone else. Once inside I sit down with my back to the door and fight to see the computer screen through the tears in my eyes. When I hear Selah's door open I quickly dab at the tears with my sleeve and pray to God that none of my mascara is running.

"Brinkley, I'm headed out. I won't be back today, but I'm available on e-mail."

I swivel around to speak to her, but she's already walked off. I'm still staring at the empty doorway when Miko bursts through it and closes it quickly behind her.

"What. The. Hell."

"I'm her new assistant?" I meant that as a statement.

"And that's what you want?" she asks, serious.

"Yeah—Yes. That's what I've always wanted. I just thought it would come when I was actually prepared to do the job. I haven't really done any of this yet." Defeated, I wave my hands desperately around the small office and then let them plop into my lap. "And I have all these notes from her, but I don't know who half the people are or what she's talking about." I grab hold of my notepad and wave it at Miko spastically. The defeat I felt just minutes ago is slowly turning into panic. "I mean, I can figure out just about anything, and I can usually handle whatever anyone wants to throw my way, but I'm so far out of my league with her. I'll never catch up, and if I can't figure it out she's not going to let me stay, and I—"

"OK. Hold on!" Miko looks at me sternly, waits to make sure I am, in fact, holding on, and then abruptly leaves the office. She walks back through the door forty seconds later and puts something into my hands.

"First, eat this. It'll help," she says.

I blink down at my hands.

"Fig Newtons?" I look up at her, dismayed.

"It's the only sugar I have at my desk. I wasn't anticipating a crisis today, or I'd be better prepared. Just eat it. I'll be right back."

She leaves and I look back down at the little package of cookies. Well, it can't hurt.

I'm on the second cookie when Miko comes back with Holt in tow. I don't really know Holt well. She mostly works on PR and marketing for SSE, so I haven't interacted with her much. She's a really pretty blonde, but she seems perpetually annoyed . . . Right now is no exception. Miko pulls the angry Barbie through the office door and then closes it behind them.

"Brinkley, this is Holt. Holt's going to be super helpful and answer any questions you have about this new job of yours." Miko eyeballs her companion, silently daring her to disagree.

My eyes fly to my new savior.

"Oh my gosh! Really? What can you tell me?" I squeak.

"Everything." Holt sounds exasperated, but she takes Quade's old seat.

"How do you know so much?" I ask, curious.

"I'm the one who wrote that." Holt points to the manual on my desk and my eyes bug out.

"You were Selah's assistant?"

"The very first," she says, and I can't tell if the bitterness in her voice is from having to talk to me or the memory of what it meant to blaze that particular trail.

Oh man, this is so awesome! I had no idea any former assistants still worked here. Maybe I'm not going to get fired after all!

"And you don't mind helping me out?"

Holt eyes Miko speculatively and then finally says, "Actually, yes, I have about a thousand other things to do, and as I pointed out to Jin, no one taught *me* how to do this job. I just figured it out!"

"And as Jin pointed out to you," Miko says, sounding patronizing, "that was back when this company was much smaller and the job description not nearly so intense."

Holt opens her mouth to argue further, but Miko holds her hand up.

"I also pointed out to Holt that were she unable to assist you with this, it might be difficult for my design team to keep working on all the marketing materials that continue to make her look so good at her job. Isn't that right, Holt?" Miko asks with mock sweetness.

Holt allows herself a thirty-second death stare, but she must really need Miko's help because she turns to me with a bland expression.

"Let's start with personal assistant work. That's what's gonna make you want to slit your wrists the most, so you may as well know what you're in for."

I look at Miko and then back at Holt. Apparently, she's not joking. I grab the notepad off my desk and spin back around.

"Tell me everything." My voice sounds a lot more confident than I actually feel.

Chapter EIGHT

I worked until ten trying to cram as much information as I could into my brain while Selah wasn't in the office to harass me. This morning I spend forty-five minutes in front of my closet trying to pick out an outfit that she won't find "ridiculous." I settle for a black Zara jumper over black tights and black heeled booties. The little black blazer I've got on is a recent acquisition from a "shopping trip" into Miko's closet. Since she owns more clothes than any single human I've ever met, she's more than willing to let me swipe a few pieces. I've toned down my hair and makeup as requested, though I have to tell you, I feel totally naked without my lashes! My one act of defiance is a thin, neon-pink, patent-leather belt around my waist. I've decided that if Selah makes any comment about it, I'll use it to strangle her.

I'm the first one in the conference room for the all-hands meeting, and as the space slowly starts to fill up I review my notes for the fiftieth time. Everyone glances at me surreptitiously as they make their way to their seats, but no one says anything. I'm sure they're all just dying to see how many ways the intern can screw this one up. Someone takes the seat next to mine, and I look up to see Miko sliding a Starbucks cup to me with a smile.

"What kind of coffee is this?" I ask.

"The don't-piss-your-big-girl-pants kind," she says with a grin.

I take a sip of the caramel latte and smile back. Selah chooses that moment to breeze into the room, and my stomach seriously considers rejecting that sip of latte, but I keep it in check.

I am strong. I am smart. I am courageous.

I am strong. I am smart. I am courageous.

I plaster a smile on my face and we all wait while she finishes typing on her phone. After a few minutes of nervously staring at my boss, I look around the room at all the faces waiting anxiously along with me. It only then occurs to me: this is just another one of her intimidation techniques. She loves that a whole room of adults sits watching her like an audience. In fact, if this is anything like the other meetings I've been to, she'll look for any and every opportunity to embarrass me or put me in my place. I will not let her have the satisfaction of catching me unaware. I watch her facial features like a hawk, and the second I see her mouth open to say something, I spring to my feet.

"Should we get started then?" I ask quickly.

For a second she just stares at me, and everyone else does too. I didn't wait for her to call on me, but she was about to do just that and everyone knows it; it's not like she can chew me out for doing my job . . . *Can she?*

"By all means." She waves at me impatiently.

"The Riverton party is coming up next Tuesday. Taylor, would you give us a production status, please?" I say it with a smile that only slightly wobbles.

Taylor looks at me, bemused. "Guest list is confirmed at 287. Rentals come in Monday afternoon. Finalizing the DJ's rider and the special VIP section for the Riverton team."

"How many of that total are VIPs?" Selah asks Taylor.

Taylor looks to Walker, who consults her notes, but I have the information so I just jump in.

"Thirty-three are VIPs, fourteen of those are SSE clients. You mentioned you'd double-confirm arrival times with PR on Monday, correct, Walker?" I ask down the table.

Sixteen sets of eyes are staring at me in open shock, and believe me, no one is more surprised by the confidence in my tone than I am.

But here's the thing: last night while I lay under my purple comforter and vacillated between excitement about this opportunity and open panic that I'd be fired before lunchtime, I finally made a decision. I decided that if I was going to do this job, I was going to have the courage to do it to the best of my abilities. That way, if Selah decides to can me, at least I will know I've tried my best. *Just do your best*, I hear my mama say in the back of my mind. And so that's what I'm doing.

"That is correct, isn't it?" I ask again when no one answers.

"Yes, that's correct," Walker agrees quickly.

"Carpet arrivals start when?" Selah asks the production team.

"Eight," I answer again.

"Maybe I'd know that if I had the—"

"Timeline," I finish Selah's sentence, pointing to the iPad I had turned on and placed before her at the beginning of the meeting. The timeline for the Riverton event is open on the screen.

"Well aren't you just full of surprises," Selah says.

I choose to take that as a compliment regardless of whether she is offering one. I smile at her, waiting for instruction. Selah scans the timeline then looks up at Taylor.

"Did we get the cigar guy for Diego?"

"Of course. According to him he's born and raised in Havana, can't get any more authentic than that," Taylor says.

"And he's set up where?"

"Next to the Riverton sampling table in the VIP lounge," he replies.

"And that is *where* exactly? Honestly, Taylor, how am I supposed to know what that means?" she snaps at him.

I slide the party diagram from my stack of paperwork out where she can look it over. Look at me everyone; I'm Johnny-on-the-spot!

Selah studies it for a moment and then looks up again.

"I want to change the VIP seating around. Jin, you and I can discuss that later."

Miko nods at her, and Selah continues.

"I don't think I need to remind everyone how important this client is. The tequila line is Diego's baby, but Riverton Spirits has multiple liquor brands and incredibly deep pockets. Every element has to be beyond reproach." She glares up and down the table and everyone nods quickly to appease her.

At last, she asks, "All right, what's next Brinkley?"

———

I'm so thrilled at having made it out of my first all-hands meeting in one piece, I don't even mind when Selah barks for her coffee later that afternoon. I ask Ambrose to cover the phones and hurry out to grab the order.

When I bring it back to the office her door is closed and I knock quietly. She calls for me to enter, but as I open the door I can hear that she's on a call. I try and stay as quiet as possible as I walk across the room.

"I understand your interest, Meryl—" she says into the phone without looking up. "I mean, obviously I've only ever hired the best, but that no longer includes Will McKenna."

I almost trip over my shoes when I realize she's talking about McKenna and Quade. I need to get out of this room as quickly as possible. I set down the coffee cup and see her eyes flash as she listens to what the person on the other end of the line is saying.

"Of course. Well, ultimately it's your decision, but I have to tell you . . . I'd have real issues associating with any company who'd be willing to work with someone I've had to let go." Her tone is sharp and serious, and I hope she doesn't call out to me before I get to the door. "No, I do mean it. I'd hate to stop sending you business but, really, you'd be forcing my hand if you brought him on. My trust has been broken, and once that happens I'm afraid I just don't feel comfortable working with any company who employs—Oh, you do? I'm so glad to hear it. I'd hate to lose you as a partner, Mer." She's back to using her sweet "client" voice again, happy with the response the person on the phone has given.

I close the door quickly behind me and head back to my office. I'm trying to process what I've just heard. I'm pretty sure she was talking to Meryl Franklin, who owns the event-rental company we use most often, and that Meryl was considering hiring McKenna. Clearly, Selah has stopped it from happening. Plus Selah has just let Meryl, one of the biggest gossips in this industry, know that she won't do business with anyone who does hire either McKenna or Quade. Selah's connections and budgets are big and deep; I can't imagine any vendor in town is willing to cross her. So, she's effectively just signed the death certificates of her former assistants' event careers.

I can never, ever cross this woman.

———

"We need alcohol!" Miko yells down the bar to Max, who is clearly busy with another customer as we walk up to the bar.

"I'm pretty sure she blackballed them." I continue the conversation we'd started in the car.

"It wouldn't be the first time." Miko reaches for the happy-hour menu even though we surely have it memorized by now.

"You mean she's done this before?" I'm shocked.

A cute, hipster bartender walks up to us.

"What can I get you, ladies?" he asks in what I'm guessing is his most alluring voice.

Miko waves him away dismissively with the menu in her hand. "Nope. Not you." She doesn't react at all to his startled expression, but I give him an apologetic look as he scoots away. "Of course she's done it before. Selah's friendships and the power with which she wields them are a thing of beauty. If there's a bitchy well-connected publicist in a one-hundred-mile radius, you can bet Selah will be her maid of honor when she gets hitched to whatever junior development exec she convinces to marry her without a prenup."

"I don't understand. What do Selah's friends have to do with anything?"

Miko looks at me like she can't believe I'd ask such an idiotic question.

"Everything. Selah is besties with every A-hole publicist in town because they're the ones who bring her their biggest clients. Big clients mean big budgets and therefore a lot of power where vendors are concerned. Nobody is going to mess with her and she knows it." She yells again. "Max, come on, did you hear me? We need to drink! She survived the day!"

Max scowls at her but comes down to us all the same.

"Did you hear?" Miko asks, excited.

"That you need alcohol?" Max asks. "Yeah, I'm pretty sure everyone north of Sunset heard that."

"Yes, alcohol. We're celebrating; she survived!" In the nearly two months we've been hanging out, Miko, bless her heart, has blatantly refused to acknowledge Max's bad moods. She simply carries on as if my roommate isn't glaring at her.

"So you're still employed?" Max asks.

"Come on now." Miko does a little snap, whistle, and move-it-along rolling of her finger. "You can work while you chat, barkeep!"

Max glowers but dutifully starts to mix up something for us.

"I'm still employed, and get this, they're paying me now." I'm being sarcastic.

"Hourly rate or salary?" Max adds some odds and ends to her cocktail shaker.

"Salary," I answer proudly. "Did you just put mint and tomatoes in that?" I eyeball the shaker skeptically.

"Do *you* want to make the drinks?" Max stops using her pestle to grind the ingredients in the shaker.

Miko elbows me in the ribs. "Don't poke the bear, Landon."

I smile sheepishly at Max until she resumes making the drink.

"We're all salary, by the way," Miko adds, eagerly reaching for the lowball glass Max passes her way.

"Really? That seems so expensive." I sniff my cocktail and then take a sip. The heady sweet-and-sour combination swims all the way to my toes. "This is delicious! It's sort of like . . . a tomato mojito."

"That's what I was going for." Max shrugs.

"Expensive would be if she actually had to pay us for all of our overtime. Salary only seems exciting until you realize how many hours you're working. I'd suggest never actually doing the math on what your hourly rate ends up being at the end of an event week. It'll only depress you." Miko takes her first tentative sip of the drink. Her face lights up and she takes another huge swallow. "You're a wizard," she pronounces to Max.

"Glad you think so." Max gives her a little smile and then turns her head to take someone else's order.

"And now a toast." Miko turns to me with her glass already raised. "To surviving day one."

"To day one." I clink glasses with her.

"Now you just have to make it through 364 more of them," she says solemnly. I look at her, she looks at me, and then she turns her head to Max. Raising her glass, she announces, "We're gonna need more of these!"

Chapter NINE

I drive up and down Sunset three times before I realize that Twenty-Five, the location for the Riverton party, is the two-story brick building half covered with ivy on the corner. In my defense the only signage is the small silver XXV next to the door, and I don't realize they are Roman numerals until my third time past.

I park around back and make my way to the rear door, where several members of our production team are scurrying in and out. The Riverton party is supposed to be hip Hollywood luxury, and I tried to dress the part. I splurged on a pair of leather leggings with my first paycheck. They were sort of ridiculously expensive, but honestly, anything that makes my butt look this good might be worth twice as much. The leggings are tucked down inside ridiculously high-heeled boots that come up just above my knees. My top is a blousy black silk that ties into a big bow around my neck . . . sort of chic librarian. My hair is teased within an inch of its life and pulled back into a perfectly messy pony, and my one pop of color is the deep-berry lip stain. At the last minute I'd added a few lashes. Selah might think they are ridiculous, but the Texan in me can't imagine going to a party without them. I think my whole look is a good mash-up of LA cool meets conservative southern girl. Here's hoping I don't look like an idiot.

As I come through the back door of the club I see Taylor looking over some paperwork in his hands. He is as good a place to start as any.

"How's everything going?" I ask as I walk down the hallway towards him.

He looks up with a smile already on his face.

"It's going just fine. Want a quick walk-through?"

"That'd be great, thanks." I haul my big bag higher up on my shoulder and fight to keep the weight from sliding back down my arm as we head towards the front of the club. Taylor notices me fighting with it and gestures towards it with the paperwork rolled in his hand.

"Can I help you with that?"

"Thanks, but I'll manage." I smile at his manners, which only furthers my belief that he's from the south. "I'm dying to know whether or not that's an accent I detect."

Taylor's face spreads into a boyish grin at complete odds with his rough-looking exterior.

"Now here I thought it wasn't even noticeable anymore."

"Well, maybe not to everyone else, but I'd recognize a native at ten paces." I eye him speculatively. "I'm guessing . . . Oklahoma?"

"Born and bred."

"You a Cowboy?"

He smiles lazily. "I'm a Sooner."

My scowl makes him laugh.

"You?"

"Lone Star State."

"Makes sense." He nods thoughtfully.

"And what's that supposed to mean?"

He looks at me out of the corner of his eye. "You're far too polite to be anything but a good southern girl."

"Are you teasing me?"

"Of course not," he says in a serious tone. "I love southern girls!"

"Oh, I'm sure you do," I answer sarcastically.

We come to a fork in the road, and I'm unsure of which direction to turn. I look to him.

"You've never been to Twenty-Five?" He points to the left.

With every step we take, the deep bass of the club's sound system rumbles louder.

"I thought everyone on staff came here. It's got one of the toughest doors in LA, but the SSE connection makes it easy to get on the list."

He has to raise his voice a little louder as we pass through an industrial kitchen bustling with food prep.

"To be honest, all I've done since I moved to town is work and sleep. I haven't really had time to go out." I pick my way slowly over the huge rubber mats that line the floor to keep people from slipping. If I'm not careful my heel is going to get stuck in one of the little grooves and kamikaze me to the floor.

Taylor stops and spins around abruptly. I nearly run into the tight black T-shirt that covers his . . . upon closer inspection . . . really defined chest.

"Maybe you'll let me remedy that sometime." He smiles down at me with a sly grin.

"I'm sorry, what?" I'm flustered.

"Your never going out; I'd like to remedy that."

Oh.

"Oh, um, sure—maybe we can all do a happy hour after work or something?" I say dumbly.

I'm not really good at this sort of thing and definitely not with someone who looks like he does. Also, I'm pretty sure my daddy would have a heart attack if he saw all those tats, southern or not!

He must see the distress written on my face because he smiles, and it's not flirtatious, just friendly.

"I promise I'm not nearly as dangerous as I look. I just thought we could hang out. It doesn't have to be drinks; it can be something totally harmless."

"OK?" I answer, unsure.

We finally find ourselves in the main room of the club, and all other thoughts flit from my mind because I can't stop gaping at the club space around me. Twenty-Five is a perfect mix of masculine old-world furnishings and whimsical touches. The club is big, but not overwhelming. Everything from the bar to the second-floor lounges flows together, but each area is divided into sections throughout the space, and each feels slightly different yet somehow all part of a whole.

One section is a cluster of dark leather chaises and fur throws, and another looks like an old library in dark amber tones. The bar, an island in the middle of the room, is a mix of modern LED lights and old wood. In each space the severity of the furnishings is muted by odd touches . . . a vintage brass scuba mask on a coffee table, a mountain-goat bust mounted on exposed brick, huge oversize black-and-white pictures of cows covering the expanse of one wall. None of it makes any sense together, and yet it totally works. It's all mix-and-match luxury; the sort of space that makes you feel comfortable even though the sofa you're sitting on surely costs more than your life is worth. *I love it!*

Three guys from the production team come through the room carrying equipment to set up for the red carpet out front. They stop when they get close to us, and I see them give me a sleazy once-over. The look is bad enough, but then one of them decides to add soundtrack.

"Damn, look who's all grown up." His eyes run all the way down my body and back up again.

Back when I was a waitress, I had to deal with this sort of thing all the time, but I'm unsure of what I can say in this situation. Is this normal LA work behavior?

Before I can respond, Taylor does it for me.

"Well now, that's appropriate," he says with sarcasm. "You guys get back to work."

He's at least ten years younger than all of them, but they obey without hesitation and walk away.

"Sorry about that. Smith's actually not a bad guy; he's just trapped in the body of an eleven-year-old."

Awkward silence descends, and I want to change the subject.

"How much of this decor did we bring in?" I run a hand over the top of an ancient-looking pool table that's been reupholstered in a bright purple velvet.

"Decor?" Taylor looks confused. "Nothing. We only brought in some extra lounges for seating. You really haven't been out in LA, have you?"

"Why do you say that?" I look back at him.

"Because this is a Barker-Ash property."

"Barker-Ash, as in the hotel chain?"

"Barker-Ash, as in the *everything*. Hotels, restaurants, a handful of the best clubs in town." That bemused expression is back; it's like I'm some sort of Martian who needs him to explain the intricacies of earth life.

"OK, but what does that have to do with the decor?" I ask slowly.

"Each Barker-Ash property has a similar aesthetic; it's our signature design." A man speaks up from behind us.

I turn around to acknowledge him, and the look on my face—a smile? a mask of horror? I have no idea—freezes in place. Brody Ashton, gorgeous, uptight, and apparently the wealthy owner of this club, is standing in front of me looking like the cover of GQ. Next to Brody is a beautiful woman who's nearly as gorgeous-looking as he is. Her long dark hair is sleek, shiny perfection, and I'm pretty sure just her legs alone are taller than I am. She's dressed for something far fancier than our event tonight, which makes me wonder what they're doing here now, especially way before the party starts.

Brody is in dark wool slacks with a blue button-down under a dark gray vest. His sleeves are rolled and pushed up on his tan forearms, and his hair is way past the need for a cut but still looks all rumpled bedhead perfection. I'm not sure how someone can look simultaneously casual/sexy/stoic businessman, but he's somehow cornered the market. I have a small moment of panic that he and his girl Friday might have just seen the creepy, sleazy interaction with the production guy, but she looks too bored to care and his face is entirely unreadable.

He leans over and whispers something into her ear, and she nods and heads off towards the bar. I can't stop staring at them; they're both beautiful in a way I thought was achievable only through airbrushing.

"Do you like what you see?" he asks.

Oh Lord, he caught me staring! I'm pretty sure I just swallowed my tongue.

"Excuse me?" I squeak when I'm able to produce sound again.

He frowns slightly, like I'm an idiot or a waste of time or both.

"The club aesthetic; do you like what you see? Does everything look OK for the event?"

"It's, er—" I mumble eloquently. Taylor saves me.

"You heard about the issues with the alarm?"

"Yeah, Bennett, thanks for calling. I was on my way out and thought I'd stop by to check on it." Brody reaches out and shakes his hand. "There shouldn't be any other problems, but Marco is on site if you need anything. Since I am here, though, can I just confirm that guest count again?"

"I think we're at 215 or something like that," Taylor replies quickly.

Brody inspects us both, like he doesn't believe what Taylor's saying, and he's wise not to: our guest count was at 301 as of this morning.

"I've told Selah this, but I'll just remind you again, capacity is 250 and that includes staff. I won't do battle with the fire marshal again over her numbers." Brody's face is calm, but his tone leaves no room for discussion. He does not seem like someone you'd want to piss off.

Taylor must agree because he nods emphatically. "Absolutely, totally understand."

"Well, I'll leave you both to it."

Without another word Brody turns and heads back, presumably to find his date.

"We're room-ready in an hour, Brinks. You still want me to show you the layout?" Taylor says to me.

Brinks? I blink at him. What am I, an armored truck?

"Sure, yeah. Show me everything."

———

I'm checking things off the list on the clipboard when Selah pours into the club forty-five minutes later with a group of impeccably dressed men all around her. I attach the pen to the edge of my clipboard and walk over to meet them. She doesn't acknowledge me, but I'm not dumb enough to leave her presence without permission. At every event I've worked so far, Quade never left Selah's side for one minute. I've wondered what would happen if she had to use the restroom; I guess tonight I am going to find out. I stand off to the side as Selah walks the clients through the room.

"Diego," she practically purrs, "let me show you around." She slips her arm through the arm of an attractive older man and starts to tow him through the space.

"The guests enter through there?" Diego asks in a thick Latin accent.

"Yes, with the exception of some of the VIPs, who'll come through the back entrance," she says in what I've come to think of as her "client" voice. It is the overly sweet, kiss-up tone she uses when speaking to anyone with money or power, and it's as fake as my eyelashes. One second she's on the phone using the purr to tell a client how fabulous they are, and in the span of a heartbeat she's off the phone and hissing at me.

"But if the VIPs are coming through the back, how will they walk the red carpet?" Diego asks.

"Don't you trust me?" She wags a finger at him playfully. "I'll handle it, don't worry."

Diego eyes her speculatively, clearly not eating up her tone the way her clients usually do.

"Of course I trust you; had I not, I certainly wouldn't have approved the quarter million dollars we're spending on this event tonight. Not to mention the—Paul, what was it we spent on a talent wrangler?" Diego turns back to another member of his team, forcing Selah to release him from her clutches.

"Twenty-five thousand dollars," a studious-looking man answers him.

"Yes, not to mention the twenty-five thousand you insisted was necessary to get those VIPs here in the first place. So perhaps you'll indulge this old man and explain to me how that works."

Diego's tone and smile are easy and practiced, but his eyes are shrewd. He isn't easily impressed by Selah, and I think she knows it.

"Of course." Selah plows forward, refusing to drop her act. "VIPs come through the back. Part of our agreement with their teams is that they won't be harassed except by our in-house photographer who has access to them. But of course we have paparazzi arranged to catch them as they leave for the night. We're in constant communication with those paps. This event will get coverage in every weekly, don't worry. Let me show you the cigar roller; we had him brought in all the way from Havana!" she says brightly as she pulls Diego after her.

I walk quietly up the stairs behind the group, lost in my own thoughts. Miko has told me this is how it works. Event producers or club promoters get celebrities to their parties by promising them privacy, then turn right around and rat them out to the paparazzi. I'd told her I was surprised Selah's publicist friends put up with it, and she'd just laughed at me. Apparently, the publicists are often the "inside source" you read about in gossip magazines, tipping off the press about their clients' whereabouts. As much as an actress might hate being captured looking like hell on her way out of the gym, that's exactly the kind of shot that gets coverage, which boosts both her (and her publicist's) career.

At the top of the stairs I stand back from the group as Selah shows them the space. The brand is displayed throughout the party but in subtle ways. Each lounge area has bottle service, complete with a scantily clad Riverton girl. Each server wears a tight black baby tee with the Riverton logo stretched across her chest, teeny-tiny black shorts, and black heels. It's the sort of outfit I'd typically judge openly, but every single one of these women is so stupid-pretty, they somehow make the miniature uniform work.

Diego eyes the room with a bland expression, then walks over to inspect the small satellite bar in the middle of the space. He picks up the framed bar menu. "These are the featured drinks?" he asks, reading through it.

"Yes, guests can mix their Riverton tequila with any of our specialty freshly squeezed juices," Selah assures him quickly.

I wonder if anyone else catches the strain in her voice. Diego looks more closely at the menu in his hands, then back at Selah.

"No, that isn't what we discussed. We discussed specialty featured cocktails, not tequila with juice." With every word Diego becomes more agitated and his accent more pronounced. "The entire point of the event was to highlight tequila as a feature *in a cocktail*. We discussed this." He speaks emphatically.

"My apologies. We've recently changed up some of our team. Perhaps this detail was a miscommunication." Selah starts to look around, probably for someone to throw under the bus.

"No. This is a conversation *we* had," Diego says, "when you and Alex and I sat down last month at the . . . the . . ." He turns quickly to his team. "*¿Como se llama el hotel cerca de la playa?*"

"Shutters," someone tells him.

"Shutters, *sí*. When we had drinks there last month, you remember?" He looks pointedly at Selah.

"I'm so sorry, Diego, I don't recall." She touches her forehead nervously. "But not to worry, it'll take two seconds to come up with a menu of featured drinks."

Selah looks at the pretty bartender behind the bar.

"Can you suggest some tequila-based cocktails for our featured drinks?"

The bartender chews on her lower lip nervously and looks back and forth between Selah and Diego.

"I'm sorry, I'm not a regular bartender. I'm from the model service. I know how to make a margarita, but beyond that . . ."

Her voice trails off as Diego whirls around to his team. Even from back here it looks like his eyes are going to bug out of his head. He's barking a torrent of Spanish over the music, and I'm only catching bits and pieces, but between the curse words and the mention of the party budget, I'm pretty sure he's questioning why they've spent this much on our firm. Selah's composure is wearing down as she looks around for help, and the bartender, bless her heart, looks like she might throw up. Before I even realize what I'm doing I've pushed my way up through the group and am reaching my hand out to Diego.

"*Señor Riverton, soy Brinkley. Yo trabajo para Selah. Tal vez pueda ayudar,*" I say with the biggest smile I've got.

Diego hesitates a moment, then reaches his hand out to shake mine.

"*Encantado, señorita. Yo no sabia nadie a SSE habla español.*"

"No, with all the bad language you were throwing around, I'm sure you didn't realize anyone on our team could understand you," I challenge him playfully.

The Riverton team tenses, and I wonder if maybe I shouldn't have taunted him. Diego stares at me for a moment and then throws back his head and laughs out loud.

"You're absolutely right, *mi querida*. I beg your pardon." Diego takes me by the elbow and steers me towards the bar. "Tell me, how do you think you can help?"

"I happen to know a few different ways to dress up tequila." My tone is half-flirtatious and half-reprimand . . . A persona I used for years as a waitress to keep more than one customer in line.

"You drink tequila?" Diego asks.

"Only if it's Riverton," I answer with a cheeky grin.

Diego laughs again and this time the rest of his minions join in as well.

"By all means, *querida*; show us what you can do." Diego waves elegantly for me to head behind the bar. As I go I peek quickly at Selah. She's throwing me a screw-this-up-and-I'll-run-you-over-with-my-car look, and I almost trip over my boots.

You've gone too far to turn back now.

I walk over to the back of the bar and duck under the island to get inside. When I pop up I see Brody walking over to join the audience . . . As if I need more witnesses. Rather than look out into a sea of curious expressions, I start looking around for things to make my drink. Behind the bar is a small built-in fridge full of every possible garnish I might dream up, including some bright, perfect-looking cherry tomatoes. It gives me an idea.

"Diego, how is everything?" Brody asks.

Diego turns at the sound and reaches out to shake Brody's hand with a smile.

"Much better now. This charming creature was just about to make me a cocktail." He turns back to me. *"¿Tal vez algo dulce como tú?"* he says, and all of a sudden he's a sexy Latin lover instead of an angry client.

Come on, buddy, you're old enough to be my dad!

"¿O tal vez algo añejo como tú?" I challenge him back, not looking up from my work.

Diego laughs like my audacity is the funniest thing he's ever heard, and the rest of the group, including Selah, join in. I doubt she understands what I've just said, so maybe laughing is just something everyone does to fit in, like trying bangs or that one semester when I joined the FFA. When I look up, I notice that not everyone is laughing. Brody is looking at me with an unreadable expression. I look quickly down at the tools in my hands.

"¿Cuando usted aprende a hablar español?" Brody asks in perfectly accented Spanish.

"I grew up in Texas," I say with a shrug.

I drop a handful of the tomatoes down into the shaker along with the other necessary ingredients and use a spoon I find behind the bar to crush everything into oblivion. The group chats among themselves while I work nervously, and I can feel Selah staring me down, but I keep looking at the concoction in my hands. I add ice, some simple syrup, and the tequila and shake it all up exactly like Max does.

I pour the concoction into a lowball glass and drop a cocktail straw into it. I cover the straw with my finger and remove it quickly as a little makeshift syringe to pop into my mouth for a taste test. It's perfect. I hand the drink to Diego. He takes a hesitant sip, then another. His eyebrows raise in surprise.

"I love it!" he says, handing the cocktail to Brody's outstretched hand.

"Of course you do!" Selah chirps. "We knew you would. B has mad skills, and you know I hire only the best!" She says it like this whole scenario was the plan all along. It takes me a minute to realize she's talking about me. I get only about three seconds to savor the praise before she's ushering Diego away. "We're about to open the door; why don't you let me get you settled at your lounge so Brinkley and I can get back to work."

As I watch them walk away, Brody takes a sip of the cocktail. I start to clean up the mess I've made behind the bar, though I'd kind of like to see his reaction.

"It's like a tomato mojito," he says, sounding surprised.

I'm inordinately happy to have surprised him by doing something good instead of something idiotic like the first time we met. I channel Max in an attempt to sound cool. "That's what I was going for."

I hear the ice tinkle around in the glass as he takes another drink.

"Let me guess . . . It was the signature drink at all your sorority mixers."

My head snaps up at his tone, and his eyes narrow at my surprise.

"Excuse me?"

"The drink. I'm guessing all the other Tri Delts were big fans." He raises the drink in reference. "Is that where you learned to make it?"

He's not even trying to hide his patronizing tone, and the harsh little smirk on his face says he's got me all figured out now. It pisses me off.

"Actually, the school I went to wasn't big enough to be part of the Greek system." I grab a handful of dirty utensils and throw them into scullery with more force than necessary. "And even if it was, I wouldn't know a thing about it. I spent every waking hour I wasn't in class serving and busing tables so I could get to where I am right now." I look him right in the eye so he can see how angry I am. "Isn't this what every wannabe sorority girl dreams of?" I gesture wildly around the bar. "Impressing a group of spoiled millionaires by making drinks and flirting with them in Spanish?"

I see the muscle in his jaw jump twice as he looks back at me, his gaze inscrutable. He inclines his head by the slightest degree and sets the glass down on the counter. Maybe he didn't expect me to fight back, and maybe I shouldn't have, but I get enough bullying at work that I don't need it from this guy I barely know. He turns and walks away, and I look back down to finish my task. His voice pulls my head up again.

"Brinkley?"

He's walking back over, and the look on his face makes me think it's against his better judgment.

"Can I offer you some advice?" He sounds earnest.

I'm baffled by his tone. I have no idea how he went from antagonizing me to offering me advice. Where does he get off suddenly trying to be polite? I'm just ready to have this awkward confrontation over with.

"Sure," I answer, more than a little petulantly.

He shoves both hands into his pockets and looks down at his shoes for a moment, seeming to search for the words. When he speaks again his voice is quieter, maybe to avoid having the servers on the other side of the room overhear. He looks up at me again.

"If you were my little sister . . ." I have to physically restrain myself from rolling my eyes. He must see the annoyance flit across my face because a little smile starts playing at his lips. He starts again. "If you were my little sister, I'd tell you that people treat you with as much or as little respect as you allow them to."

I look back at him confused, unsure of what he's trying to say.

"I saw the interaction between you and your production team earlier," he says meaningfully.

I can actually feel the blush rise in my cheeks.

"He's harmless, but Diego *is* flirtatious and will continue to be so long as you allow it. I'm guessing this is your first professional job?" He looks at me for confirmation and I nod, too embarrassed to find my voice.

"Then start as you intend to finish. If you want respect, then demand it from the beginning. If you let them treat you like a silly little girl, that's all you'll ever be, no matter how hard you work."

I try so very hard to maintain my composure, but I buckle under the pressure of the stern look on his face and look down at my hands. Even though he's harsh, I actually think he's trying to be helpful, but I can't get his words out of my head. They pulse in time with my rapidly beating heart.

Silly. Little. Girl.

To have someone as successful as he is see me that way, when I consider myself so professional, is almost more than I can stand. I look up to defend myself, but I'm silenced by the apology in his light-blue eyes. I open my mouth to say something, but his date saunters up the stairs behind him and effectively cuts me off. She reaches for his hand, and I watch his face change the moment their skin makes contact. In her presence he's a cool, aloof businessman again . . . Apparently I don't rank high enough to impress with that persona.

I continue to watch as he shrugs out of her grip to put a hand on her back, and the move seems fitting. This does not seem like the kind of guy who does touchy-feely.

"Shall we?" he asks her.

She nods and murmurs something, and he guides her back down the stairs without acknowledging me again.

Once they're out of sight I force myself to take three deep breaths and decide not to think about what just happened for the rest of my natural life. This decision, while childish, helps me plaster on my best fake smile and get through the night in one piece.

Selah and the clients leave at ten, and at eleven the club opens up for the public so my work is done. I've spent the night nipping at Selah's heels yet somehow failing to do a single thing to her exacting standards. My mood is as low as my now-defunct ponytail.

Between Selah's attitude and Brody Ashton's, um, *whatever that was*, I am ready to go to sleep and forget this day ever happened. I grab my oversize shoulder bag and toss my purse into it. As I spin around to make a beeline to my car, I slam directly into Taylor. He reaches out to steady me quickly and then drops his hands.

"I'm glad I caught you before you left." He takes in my bedraggled appearance. "I heard what happened."

"Yeah, well—" I gesture ineffectually, because really, that's the best I can come up with right now.

"I have a plan," Taylor says with way more enthusiasm than this moment calls for, surely.

It's been a long night, and I'm emotionally exhausted, so as pretty as this boy is, I think it's best for all involved if I leave here as quickly as possible.

I start shuffling towards the door. "A plan for, like, life, or—"

He falls in step with me. "No. A plan for you. I'm taking you somewhere; it's going to make everything better."

"Thanks, but I'm tired and it's late. I think I'll just head home."

"Come on, where's the fun in that?" He nudges me playfully with his shoulder.

I keep walking, and when my voice finally does come out it's grouchy.

"*Very* few things about this night have been fun for me. Why would we start now?"

"Well now *that's* just a challenge," he says seriously. "You can't say something like that with big sad eyes and expect me to let you go home. No, you most definitely need to eat something. I'm taking you to the perfect place."

We are almost to the employee parking lot, and I look up at him in frustration. I'm annoyed because he won't let me politely decline. I'm annoyed with Selah for being unreasonable, and this night for being cold, and my life for sucking. Ugh! The list is too long to add up right now, and I just want to go home.

"Why do people always try and feed me when I'm upset? Maybe I don't need food. Maybe I just need to stew in my own indignation!"

He responds with an indulgent smile that only pisses me off more! I pluck my keys out of my bag and march towards my car with renewed purpose. Taylor snatches them out of my fingers before I can protest and tucks them into his pocket.

"Maybe everyone tries to feed you because good food makes people happy. Or maybe they feed you because you work way too many hours and you clearly don't eat enough. Either scenario works for my purposes this evening. But mostly I just want to hang out with you, and I'm hungry too. Now come on."

For the first time in hours I smile a little; he takes that as his green light and walks me towards a shiny black Escalade. Now that I've acquiesced I feel a little bit better already. It's sweet of him to try and cheer me up, and sweeter still to find me food, because I haven't eaten since breakfast and I *am* starving.

I hop up into the seat, and Taylor closes the door behind me. When he gets in the driver's side it's just us inside this dark little space. He drives out onto the street, and I suddenly feel nervous because I really don't know much about this guy at all. I grasp for something to say.

"So where are we headed?" I look out the window, trying to guess which direction we're going.

"Just a little place I know," he answers.

Well, that doesn't go far along the path of making me feel better. I'm about to demand a better explanation because, colleagues or not, I'm not in the habit of visiting unknown locations with random guys late at night. Then, something catches my eye in the dark. There's a photo propped up on the glass in between his speedometer and his mileage. It seems so out of place that I momentarily forget what I'm about to ask.

"Is that a cat?" I ask incredulously.

Taylor grins and glances at me. "Of course not. Only a total nerd would drive around with a picture of his cat in his truck."

I squint to get a closer look of the fat orange tabby looking out from the picture with utter disdain.

"But if it *were* a cat," Taylor continues, "his name would be Holden and he'd be the greatest cat ever."

I can't help my giggle.

"Your cat's name is Holden?"

"I went through a pretty intense Salinger period," he says, smiling.

"Wow." I'm bewildered. "You seem so cool, but you're secretly . . . not."

Taylor laughs. "I'm really, really not."

I laugh with him and then glance around, confused.

"Are you getting on the freeway? I thought we were getting something to eat," I say warily.

"We are. I know this seems suspect, but I really want to surprise you. I swear it's worth it. Are you up for a little road trip?"

I look at him, unsure. "This is a little unusual, Taylor."

"It is unusual, but I promise not even a little bit inappropriate. You'll understand when we get there."

It's tempting, but really, I don't even know him that well and this feels like the start of every Lifetime movie Tori Spelling ever died in. I see him glance at me quickly, then back at the road.

"Come on, Brinks, surely someone at work would have told you if I made a habit of chopping up coworkers and burying them in the desert."

"That's a very specific visual." I laugh.

He's right, though; Miko hates almost everyone but she loves Taylor. She would have told me to steer clear if he was a creeper. He's trying so hard to cheer me up. I decide to just sit back and let him.

We spend the rest of the drive talking about pets and books and our families back home. It's so easy to talk to him and, I realize, more than a little exciting to be on some mysterious road trip in the middle of the night with a cute guy. It's absolutely the kind of adventure I thought I'd have when I came to somewhere as magical as LA, and look at me now! *I'm totally doing it.*

When we get near Anaheim after forty-five minutes, I have a brief excited mental freak-out because I think maybe we're going to Disneyland. Then I realize it's late and that visiting a theme park for a midnight snack makes no earthly sense. We follow a series of random streets to head farther into the middle of nowhere, and just as I start to think that maybe he *is* going to bury me in the desert, I see a glowing red sign hovering over a familiar-looking drive-in. I literally yelp with joy.

"There's a Sonic here? You brought me to Sonic!"

I'm bouncing up and down in my seat and clapping my hands, which makes Taylor laugh.

"I guess that answers the question about whether or not you loved it as much as I did growing up." He smiles as he pulls into an empty slot between an older couple in a sedan and a truck full of teenage boys.

"I didn't even know they had these in Southern California." I look around me in wonder.

"Only two in LA County. Both of them take forever to get to, but sometimes a cherry limeade is worth the traffic." He rolls down the windows a little so we can pick up the fifties music wafting from the outdoor speakers. Carhops whip back and forth in front of us on their roller skates. "Do you know what you want?"

"I think I want *everything*!" I eyeball the glowing menu outside his window, trying to decide. Then I notice the dessert menu on my passenger side. "Ooh, milkshakes! I forgot about the milkshakes!" Then I clap again, because I can't even help it.

Taylor laughs. "I wish every girl were this easy to please."

And I am easy to please, actually, because I have an entire Brown Bag Special, a vanilla Coke, and a peanut-butter milkshake, and I am in a blissful food coma the whole way back to LA. We laugh and chat, and it really is an unbelievably nice end to an otherwise crap-tastic day.

Once we pull up to my car in the parking lot, he puts his truck in park and I unbuckle my seat belt.

"This was seriously the best. Thank you for talking me into it . . . and for not murdering me in the desert." I grin.

"Well, there's always next time." He smiles back.

I open the door and jump down into the cool night and head for my car. He waits until I'm buckled up and behind the wheel before he drives off. I wonder how many other guys in LA have those sorts of manners.

Chapter TEN

The phone buzzes once and abruptly stops, and I look up to see that Selah's calling from her office. I grab my notepad and go to see what she needs. This is her own unique paging system, a way to get me in front of her without deigning to use her vocal cords.

Being called into her lair isn't ever really a good thing, but I am in too good a mood to care. Even if she's annoyed with me, the Riverton event and its guest list have gotten coverage everywhere, and the clients are thrilled. A successful event, topped by the fact that I am leaving this evening to head home, means that my good mood is unflappable. Tomorrow I'll be stuffing myself comatose with Mama's best Thanksgiving dishes, surrounded by my big loud family, and I am practically vibrating with excitement. I can't wait to see everyone!

I don't wait by the door like I might have a week ago; I simply walk over and take a seat. After a moment she starts to speak.

"Have you confirmed the floral deliveries for tomorrow?" she asks without looking up.

"Of course, Davies has three of them already delivered because they were needed before the guests' arrival this evening. The rest are going out early tomorrow morning," I say, reviewing some of the details in my notes.

Apparently, many of Selah's clients use her for any sort of party at their homes, and that includes holidays. Even though these efforts are much smaller (designing a holiday table, hiring the caterer for dinner, and so on) she still takes them on and, from what I've seen from the invoices, charges quite a bit for the "consultation."

"The wine for the Andersons?" she continues.

"Arrived directly from the vineyard this morning; I just received confirmation."

"Excellent," she says, starting to gather and pack things into her black Birkin. "And you've confirmed that my flight is still on time?"

"Yes, it's on time. Leaving from terminal four at three forty-five direct to Denver, and your driver will be waiting to take you up to the house in Vail. I've already checked you in, and the car will pick you up for the airport at one-thirty."

"One-thirty?" she groans. "It won't take that long to get to LAX!"

"It's a holiday weekend; I thought it was better to be safe than sorry." I smile at her politely.

She considers me a moment and finally sighs and goes to shut down her laptop.

"Fine. I'm going to go ahead and take off then. I haven't even packed yet." She stands up and tucks her closed laptop under her arm. "You've given everyone your cell?"

"My cell?" I'm confused.

"The Andersons, the Meyers, Kira and Jake, Paige," she recites. She looks at me like I'm a little slow.

"Oh, I didn't know they needed my cell, but I can definitely—"

"Of course they need your cell. How will they get ahold of you this weekend if they don't have it?" She's stopped looking at her own phone. Now she is staring me down in a challenge.

"This weekend?" I ask stupidly.

Somewhere in the back of my mind, I already know what she is going to say. My stomach gurgles in anticipation of her words.

"Yes, *this weekend*. You're on call. I shouldn't have to tell you this!" she snaps.

I haven't been her assistant very long, but I can tell you with confidence that *I shouldn't have to tell you this* is one of her favorite lines.

"Of course. I'll give them all my cell number and keep it on me. They can contact me throughout the weekend, and I'll handle anything that pops up." I say all of this like I am trying to talk her off the ledge. Maybe if I sound like I have a plan, she'll go along with it.

"You'll handle anything that *pops* up," she says condescendingly, "and you'll be there *in person* for whatever the clients might need."

What?

I can't help it; my shoulders slump a little at this declaration.

"But I'm flying home . . . Tomorrow's Thanksgiving," I try weakly.

"I know it's *Thanksgiving*. Why do you think you're on call?" She says this like I am a total idiot, then she glances at her watch. "There are, what, six clients paying for consultation?"

"Eight," I say, defeated.

"Eight clients paying for consultation, and that means that someone is on call throughout the weekend to take care of them. This is a huge opportunity for you, to get to interact with clients of this caliber directly, but perhaps that's not something you care about. Or not something you think you can handle?" She looks down her nose at me, daring me to say something.

I square my shoulders and sit up straighter. What choice do I have?

"Of course. Thank you so much for the opportunity. I'll take care of them." I try for a small smile.

Selah nods at my acquiescence and heads for the door. Right before she gets there she turns back, looking thoughtful. Maybe she's reconsidered and will ask someone else to cover—maybe one of the staff who won't have to cancel a flight in order to do it.

"Brinkley, why don't you reach out to the rental property and have some Dom waiting on ice for us when we arrive? Three or four bottles, I think, and some cheese and charcuterie." She develops a sudden French accent for the pronunciation of the last word, and I want to gag . . . Just call it salami!

"It'll be nice for everyone to have a little nosh after traveling all day to get there, don't you think?" She sounds uncharacteristically lighthearted. I nod.

"Wonderful. Happy Thanksgiving." She heads out the door.

I'm pretty sure "happy Thanksgiving" is the nicest thing she's said to me to date. Too bad that having a happy Thanksgiving is virtually impossible now.

I've never been away from home on a holiday; I can't even imagine what Mama and Daddy are gonna say about this. What am I going to do tomorrow? Sit alone in the apartment while my family eats Mama's pumpkin pies without me?

The first tear falls onto the page of my notepad, and I wipe it off with the palm of my hand.

Stop acting like a baby. This is your job now.

I stand up and take a deep breath. I have a ton of work to do, and I need to get on with it. First I need to call Mama and tell her that I won't need a ride from the airport after all. Then I have to reach out to all our retainer clients and let them know my contact info for the weekend. Lastly I have to go order champagne and salami for a group of vapid socialites. Oh yes, *this* is my job now.

When I walk into the kitchen the next morning Max is bent over, digging around the fridge in her pajamas. I glance at the clock, confused; it's not like her to be up so early.

"Hey, look at you wearing pants before noon," I call as I walk in to make some coffee.

She stands up to glare at me. She is wearing sweatpants that are at least three sizes too big and an old shirt with a religious painting of Christ ascending to heaven and a tagline that reads "Jesus Hates the Yankees."

When all I do is smile back at her, the scowl only increases . . . She might be up before noon, but she isn't happy about it.

"What are you working on there?" I eye the things she is piling on the countertop while I pour us some coffee: butter, sugar, flour. I hand her the full cup as soon as her hands are empty. Grouchy she might be, but she's always made me coffee if she got up first and it's only right that she gets the first cup here.

"I'm making a pie," she says after a sip.

I swallow too quickly and burn my tongue.

"A pie?" I sputter.

"Yes, a pie. It's Thanksgiving," she says, taking another drink of her coffee.

"You know how to bake?" I come closer to inspect her pile of goods. It does, actually, look like the necessary ingredients for pie.

"Yes, I know how to bake!" she scoffs indignantly. "I'm not a mutant!"

"You're right, I'm sorry. I just never thought of you as the baking type." I hop up on the counter behind me and pick up my coffee again.

"What are you doing here, anyway? I thought your flight was last night." Max puts down her coffee and pulls a big bowl from the cabinet next to the oven.

"It was," I sigh. "Apparently I'm on call this weekend. I get to sit by my cell phone and wait for a possible holiday emergency. Which won't happen, by the way—everything has been delivered, everyone is fine. Selah's riding her broom down a mountain in Colorado, and I'm stuck here probably eating Taco Bell for dinner. Or not even! Taco Bell is probably closed because it gives its employees the holiday off! So they get, like, all-you-can-eat Doritos tacos *and* they get holidays off, which is *way* better perks than anything I get at SSE!"

Somewhere during that explanation I start raising my voice in panic, and when I finish Max's eyebrows are nearly in her hairline.

"Dramatic much?" she asks sardonically.

I sigh. "Sorry. What kind are you making?"

"Chocolate cream; it's my specialty."

"Yeah?" I ask, looking down into my almost empty coffee cup.

Max turns back around to her ingredients and starts to measure them out in the bowl.

"You can come home with me."

For a minute I just stare at her back. I don't know why it hasn't occurred to me she'd be going home to her family today.

"Home?" I ask stupidly.

She whirls around.

"Yes, *home*. I have a family, Landon. I didn't just spring into the world fully formed like Dionysus!"

"I didn't study enough Greek mythology to know who you're talking about," I say, grinning, "but I really appreciate your offer. I'd love to go home with you."

"Be ready at four." She spins back around and begins working the butter into the flour mixture with her fingers.

My phone chirps from our small dining room, and I jump down to grab it. On the way there I hear another chirp, and then another two on top of each other.

I grab the phone and see a series of text messages, one right after another. The area code is 310, but I don't recognize the number. Then I start to read the frantic message.

Need Help!! Was trying 2
make the thing but can't
forgive ou how 2 work my
oven. Also, don't know
what almond meal is.

Can I chopped up almonds
or is meal, like, a thing??
I have 2 B there soon and I'm
FREAKING out!! HELP!!!

Clearly someone's autocorrect is on. I type a quick reply.

I'm sorry, I think you have
the wrong number.

And just as quickly as it's sent, I get one back.

Isn't this Selah's assistant?

Oh man. I'm such an idiot! It hasn't occurred to me that almond meal might be considered a "holiday emergency" to one of Selah's clients.

Sorry, of course. This is Brinkley
how can I help you?

I drum my fingertips on the tabletop, waiting for the response, and then the reply pops up.

352 Camden Dr in BH. Pls come
straight away! Jake's mum is coming
to lunch. Can't screw this up!

My eyes bug out as I reread it for the second time. There's only one client on retainer today named Jake, and he's one half of the most famous celebrity couple in America.

Holy crap. I'm spending Thanksgiving with Kira Glen!

Chapter ELEVEN

It takes me only twenty minutes to get to Beverly Hills because LA is surprisingly dead on this holiday. I pull up to the little silver intercom box next to the front gate and press the button.

"Are you Brinkley?" a woman demands through the speaker.

"Yes ma'am—" But before I can even finish the sentence, a loud series of beeps blare from the box, and the gate starts to roll open. *OK.*

I follow the little drive and pull up in front of a modern white house that looks straight out of *Architectural Digest.* I jump out of the car and hustle up the driveway in the jeans and sweater I've pulled on quickly before rushing out of the apartment. Before I can even get to the gigantic front door, it swings open. Kira Glen is standing in the doorframe, inhaling the last miniscule centimeters of a cigarette. She's not wearing any makeup and has on the most basic black workout clothes Lululemon makes, but she's unbelievably gorgeous. Her shoulder-length brown hair looks like it's been blown out professionally, or maybe actresses just have naturally perfect hair. I have no idea. I bite my tongue to keep myself from telling her what a huge fan I am. *I can't believe I'm standing this close to her.*

"It's a fucking disaster is what it is!" She flicks the cigarette butt out her front door into the planter bed. Her British accent is so charming that even the cussword sounds adorable.

"Did something happen with your flowers or the caterer? I had them set delivery for a different address but I can—"

"No, no, they're fine!" She grabs my hand impatiently and pulls me into the house.

Ohmylordkiraglenisholdingmyhand!

I follow her mutely and stare around her house in wide-eyed wonder as she drags me through it. It's one big open space with wall-to-wall windows overlooking the backyard. The furniture is all sharp, industrial-looking pieces that don't look very comfortable, and the decor is modern art and weird sculptures that are no discernable form I can name. All of a sudden she stops us both, and we're standing in the gigantic kitchen. All around me are the remains of what was clearly a valiantly fought battle between a bag of flour and one of *People's* "Fifty Most Beautiful" women.

"It's a—" I gape.

"Supposed to be a cake. A bloody marmalade cake and I've destroyed it, haven't I?" She looks at me in desperation.

I don't even know how to tell her the *cake* isn't destroyed because I'm not even sure the lump of orange goo splattered across the counter got anywhere near "cake" status.

"Do you need *this particular* cake?" I eyeball the mess.

"Shit. I've ruined it. Just tell me, I've ruined it, haven't I?"

"I think—" I start delicately.

"Wait. Hold on!" She throws up a hand and starts looking around the kitchen. She moves around a bowl, a collection of measuring cups, and finally a dirty kitchen towel before finding a pack of cigarettes hidden underneath. She lights one quickly and takes a deep inhale.

"OK. Now tell me. Did I destroy the bloody cake?"

A dollop of batter drips from the edge of a mixing bowl and falls onto the cigarette lighter she's just put down. I look into her anxious face.

"You destroyed the bloody cake," I say gently.

"Fuck me," she groans, "what can I do?"

I push up the sleeves of my sweater and start dropping dirty baking dishes into the sink.

"Maybe you can tell me what exactly you need it for."

"Jake's hosting Thanksgiving at his house. It's like thirty-two people and most of them from the Midwest." She uses her current cigarette to light another one and starts pacing around the large center island. "I volunteered to do the dessert, and Meg, she told me not to, she said, *Don't offer to bake Kir, you don't know a bloody thing about the kitchen.* But did I listen to her?" She looks at me.

"No?"

"No! I didn't bloody listen! And his mum hates me already—"

"I'm sure she doesn't—" I try to soothe her while carefully removing eggshells from the countertop.

"She absolutely does! I tried cooking for them all once and I burnt everything! She's this good little housewife, and I'm just the ridiculous, whorey actress who's stolen her perfect golden boy!"

Is "whorey" even a word?

"I'm from Roehampton. I've never even been to a Thanksgiving! But I'm *trying*, I really am. Even though she's a nightmare, she's still his mum, and he loves her, and I just wanted to do this one thing right." She keeps circling the island like an angry terrier. "What am I going to do now?"

It's a little odd to have a person you've only just met tell you such private details about her life. When you factor in the idea that she's hugely famous, it really starts to boggle the mind. But I shake that thought aside because, either way, she needs help. And in the grand scheme of things, this is a fairly simple problem to fix.

"What time do you need to leave for your lunch?" I sweep the last bit of flour off the counter and into my hand.

"In about two hours," she says, glancing at the clock on the oven. "Why? Do you know how to make marmalade cake?"

"No, but I know how to make a Dr. Pepper cake," I tell her confidently.

"Is that a dessert?" she asks nervously.

"It is where I come from."

———

"So you baked her a cake?" Max asks as she pulls up her Prius to the stop sign.

"Actually, I baked her two cakes. Then I texted her just enough detail so when they ask about the process she can tell them how she made them."

"Unbelievable."

"Not really. If you think about it, she'll probably be pretty convincing. She is an actress after all." I hold on tight to the perfect chocolate cream pie in my lap and hope it's not getting anything sticky on my skirt.

Max takes another left off the main road, and I realize we're actually not that far from Kira's house. Palm trees flank the wide street on either side of us, and all the houses I can see look like the opening credits of *Real Housewives*.

"Did you grow up around here?" I'm in awe.

"Yeah," Max says, clearly unwilling to offer more detail. She stops the car in front of a big iron gate and presses a button on her console. The gate swings wide, and she pulls up the driveway before parking her car next to a long row of vehicles too expensive for me to even know what they are. I lean forward to take in the mansion in front of me.

"Your parents live here?" I squeak.

"Yep," she says, and cuts the engine.

"And you don't want to live here too? It's, like, seven minutes from your school!"

"And?"

"And our apartment smells like cabbage," I sputter.

I look around at the fountain in the courtyard, the perfectly manicured grounds, and the windows spilling warm light into the evening. It's a fairy tale.

Max gets out and slams her door before coming over to take the pie from my hands. The maroon blouse and black leggings she's got on are designer; they're the nicest things I've ever seen her wear.

"Of course I don't want to live here; don't be ridiculous." She turns and starts walking up the front steps.

I smooth my hands down the front of my long-sleeved blue babydoll dress, give my curls one last fluff, and walk up the steps after her.

"One more thing," she says, glaring at me over her shoulder. "If you mention anything that happens today as any sort of future ammunition, I will murder you in cold blood."

She's giving me her best scowl, but I can't help it; I laugh right in her face.

"All right, Dexter, open the door. This I've got to see."

———

"Mackenzie!" A gorgeous blonde woman comes shrieking towards us the second our boots hit the marble entryway. One of her hands is clutching a rather massive pour of white wine, and I'm amazed that she doesn't spill it in her hurry towards us. She's holding out both arms before she's even within striking distance and uses her one empty hand to pull Max into a ferocious hug. She forces them both into that little hug-sway-back-and-forth thing that always feels awkward, and Max, despite her general dislike for the human race, sways right along with her while holding the pie out to one side.

"Mom, this is Landon," she says, sounding more polite than I thought capable.

Mom?

I'd thought at first that this woman was closer to our age. Her clothes are perfect, her boobs are so perky they're nearly touching her chin, and her body is way better than mine. But on closer inspection I can see that she's just a very well-preserved older woman, maybe a little younger than my own mom but not by much.

"Mrs.—" I reach my hand out.

"Don't you dare! It's Vivian; calling me 'Mrs.' makes me feel old. Now get in here for the real thing!" She reaches for me and before I know it I'm caught up in her bosomy embrace. She holds me out at arm's length and gives me a head-to-toe perusal.

"Well, you're just gorgeous, aren't you?" she says sweetly, and I smile back at her.

"Thank you, ma'am—"

"Tsk, tsk." She chides me for the formality, but it goes against everything I know to use her first name.

"Now then." Vivian starts ushering us through the massive entryway and down a hallway beyond it. "You two come right in! You're the last ones here, and you're way behind on drinks." She says the last line to us in a singsong.

"Clearly," Max says, eyeing her mother's wine. Her usual sarcasm is there, but there's no heat in it.

"Oh, don't you start with me, Mackenzie." Vivian playfully swats Max's butt. "It's a holiday, and Daddy brought up the good wine from the cellar."

Max reaches out for the wine glass and takes a sip.

"And did he see you adding *ice* to the good wine?" she says, handing back the glass.

Vivian giggles and continues down the hallway "No! And you don't tell him either."

Usually when you meet someone's family you understand them a little better, but as I follow these two women down the hallway I feel the opposite. If you'd offered me a million dollars and a hundred guesses, I wouldn't ever have come up with this vivacious, bubbly woman as Max's mom.

We head first into a kitchen where a crew of caterers is busy making dinner. Max sets down her pie on a countertop with a bunch of other desserts and then grabs us both a glass of wine from a backup stash in the kitchen. She takes a big gulp of hers and looks at the swinging kitchen door speculatively. On the other side of the door the loud murmur of a big crowd can be heard.

"You ready for this?" Max asks me, serious.

"Your mom seems really sweet, actually. Why do you seem so nervous?" I ask.

"Because there are at least fifty people on the other side of that door, and once they spot us we won't stop talking again until we leave tonight." She takes another drink.

"Isn't that what you're supposed to do with your family—talk?"

"*Ugh!* I guess. Come on!" Max says, and I follow her through the swinging door.

The beautifully designed living room is full of clusters of people having loud, boisterous conversations. They're all variations of "LA pretty," but while their looks might be intimidating they seem, at least at first glance, nice enough.

Vivian spies us through the crowd and waves us over, and I follow Max to the corner where people are concentrated around a bar chatting and grabbing drinks. She walks me to her mother and the handsome older blonde man next to her. Max leans up and kisses his cheek sweetly.

"Daddy, this is Landon," she says to him in a sweet tone I didn't even know she possessed.

Now I know why she's promised murder if I made fun of her, because I totally would have. Under that grouchy, mean exterior, she's a total sweetie . . . At least with her family.

"So nice to meet you, Landon. I'm Charlie." He reaches out to shake my hand. "Mackenzie's told us so much about you."

I'm shocked to hear it, but I don't let it show. I reach out and grab his hand with a smile.

"It's nice to meet you both. Thank you so much for inviting me over."

"No, we're glad to meet you. We worry so much about Kenzie in that apartment, all alone. But God forbid she let us help her—"

"Who else is here?" Max cuts her mother off.

Vivian sighs, guessing, I'm sure, that Max is trying to distract her. She slips her hand into Charlie's lovingly and allows the subject change.

"Miran couldn't come home. Some excuse about schoolwork or something, but really, I think it's a new boyfriend." Vivian pauses long enough to sip her wine and Charlie picks up the conversation as if she's tossed him a slow underhand pitch.

"And Liam stayed with his mother's family, but your other brother is around here somewhere," Charlie says, looking off over my shoulder. "Oh, here he is."

Max looks up and smiles at someone behind me.

"Brody, this is Landon. My new roommate, remember?"

Brody? What are the odds that another Brody might be behind me? Given my luck, not great. I turn as slowly as I can without seeming like I'm having a stroke, but I know who I'll find before I even look up into his too-perfect face.

Oh man.

For a second he doesn't school his features and I see surprise. But then it's quickly replaced with that same bland expression that seems to be his go-to.

"Landon, is it?" He says it like an accusation.

"Yes, happy Thanksgiving," I answer, because I'm not sure what else to say but now I wish I'd just said nothing at all because even that comes out awkwardly. Inside my head is a tumble of incoherent screams that sound an awful lot like someone speaking in tongues. Apparently my inner voice is Pentecostal.

I turn back to Max's parents, purposefully cutting off further communication with Brody. The family around me goes back to friendly conversation, but I'm still in shock. I can't even wrap my head around this much exposure to him in less than forty-eight hours. And I fully intend to deal with him as little as possible. He's Max's brother? How is this even possible?

Against my will the words pop into my head. *Silly. Little. Girl.*

"Would you excuse us for just one moment?" I interrupt the conversation, reaching out to tug on Max's arm, and all eyes look at me. "I just—I need to, um—powder my nose." So now I sound like an idiot *and* a senior citizen!

Max is looking at me like I've lost my mind, but she follows me across the room into a far corner where I pull her up next to what is probably a real Warhol.

"How is *he* your brother?" I whisper forcefully.

She looks off to our right to where Brody is chatting with his parents.

"Who, Brody?" Max looks back at me with suspicion.

"No, the guy who jogs backwards down Sunset Boulevard," I hiss. "*Yes*, Brody! How is he your brother?"

Her eyes narrow.

"How do you know each other?"

"We just did an event at Twenty-Five," I answer quickly, and I suddenly remember his words from the night before . . . *If you were my little sister.*

Knowing he was talking about Max takes a little of the sting out of the memory.

"But that's not the point. Your last name is Jennings, how are you related?" I demand.

"We're not related, really. My parents divorced when I was little; my mom married his dad a couple years later."

"But that means your family owns, like, fourteen hotels and half the restaurants in this town! Your family founded Barker-Ash!"

"Yeah?" she says, like it's of no great consequence.

How is she so nonplussed? This is huge, crazy news! If my family was this cool, I'd probably have it tattooed on my face!

"How come you didn't tell me any of this?" I demand desperately.

"You never asked." Max shrugs.

———

I manage to spend the rest of the cocktail hour avoiding further awkwardness with Brody by throwing myself into a conversation between two serious-looking older men who are debating the Burden installation at LACMA. It takes at least ten minutes, but I finally gather what exhibit they are so worked up about. Serious guy number one thinks it was "sheer genius." Serious guy number two keeps throwing out words like "gauche" and "maladroit." I decide not to mention that the first several times I'd driven by the installation, I'd thought it was some sort of giant streetlamp delivery.

Dinner is called, and I follow everyone out to the back patio of the Ashtons' house and into the tented space beyond. Underneath the tent are six square tables, draped with luxurious paprika silk linens and autumnal centerpieces. Each place setting has a gold charger and stunning china, topped by a napkin and a chocolate-brown seating card with the guest's name calligraphed across the top . . . So not exactly the potluck that is happening at home back in Texas. I find my seat next to Max, and only after I glance around at the other seating cards do I realize I am sitting with her at the family table. I smile to myself . . . That is really sweet of them.

The rest of the guests take their seats and then our table is full. Her parents sit next to Max; Charlie's brother and his wife and their teenage son are next to them. When Brody sits down next to me I take a fortifying sip of my wine. I excel in this type of situation. Parents *love* me, always have. I will not act like an idiot in front of them! I will not let him intimidate me into silence, whatever his opinion of me.

I take another healthy sip of wine as the servers bring the first course of pumpkin soup that is contained inside actual little pumpkins. Vivian leans over to whisper to Max, but I can't help but overhear.

"Yours has fat-free milk instead of cream, Kenzie. They made it special."

I find it incredibly thoughtful that her mom would go so far to help Max stay on her diet, but the subject in question just looks annoyed by her mother drawing attention to it. Charlie must notice it too because he leaps into conversation, I'm guessing to break the tension between them.

"So, Landon, Mackenzie mentioned you work at SSE. How's that going?"

I look up from my soup nervously. Er, how to answer this? I haven't really spoken much this evening and starting off with a bitter diatribe doesn't seem like the polite thing to do. All around the table, pairs of eyes look in my direction as if they are genuinely interested in what I have to say. Normally I'd be honest about how tough it is, but surely etiquette prohibits insulting the host's business partner before the entrée has even been served.

"It's great. I've already learned so much," I answer brightly.

Max looks up, her soupspoon halfway to her mouth, and stares at me like I'm insane.

"What are you talking about? You work, like, seventy-five hours a week, and your boss is the Antichrist!" she barks.

Around me all eyes turn curious or pitying.

"Kenzie, I don't know that the Antichrist is appropriate holiday conversation," Vivian scolds her lightly.

"It'd only really be inappropriate on Christmas." Max waves a hand in her mother's direction like she is batting at a fly.

"Or Easter," Brody adds helpfully, and I don't know what surprises me more, the fact that it's the first time he's talked about anything besides work or the fact that he's trying to make a joke.

"That too." Max points at him with her spoon. "And besides, it's true in this case." She looks back at me.

"Yes," I answer her finally, "but it's not really anything I didn't sign up for." I look over at Charlie. "And my daddy always said that a dictionary is the only place where success comes before work. So I don't mind where I'm at now because it's a road to somewhere better."

I absolutely refuse to look at the person sitting next to me. How is he responding to the declaration that this silly little girl is interested in hard work?

Charlie smiles in recognition. "That's a Lombardi quote. Is your dad a big fan of the sport?"

"Sir, I'm from Texas," I say with mock severity. "It's not a sport, it's a religion."

"Oh, I bet Charlie and Paul could give your father a run for his money as superfans. Especially when Green Bay is playing," Vivian says, patting her brother-in-law's arm.

"I might have to challenge that. You'd be hard-pressed to find anyone as crazy as my dad when it comes to team obsession." On this point I am absolutely certain.

"Paul," Charlie calls across the cornucopia centerpiece, "as the only lawyer here, you'll agree that we're going to need some supporting evidence."

"Without question." Paul smiles at me from across the table. "Charlie and I have sat in more than one snowstorm to watch the Packers; we're pretty hardcore."

"Psh—" I wave my hand at him in dismissal. "Tom Brinkley has sat through dozens of snowstorms watching Dallas play, and in his case he drives twenty-six hours for the pleasure."

"That can't be the best you've got," Brody says from beside me.

I'm surprised to find him joining a conversation directly involving me, but even more surprised by the look on his face. The tiniest smile is playing around his lips, so I'm not sure if he's teasing or patronizing. But seeing the smile there makes me irrationally agitated, and I so badly want to get the last word, even if it is over something ridiculous.

I am going to have to bring out the big guns. I could tell them about the Cowboys flag my dad raises and lowers every day with military precision. Or the time he punched a tourist for badmouthing Troy Aikman. Honestly, though, none of the stories that come to mind really paint him in the greatest light, and I won't do anything to disparage the best man I know. I force myself to look away from Brody and back at the others.

"There are so many to choose from," I say, racking my brain. "Though truth be told, few of those stories would be appropriate if you found the Antichrist line offensive." I smile at Vivian. "OK, how about this . . . My middle name is Meredith."

"And?" Max looked at me.

"Lan-*Don* Meredith." I say it slowly. Surely they'd get it. "For Don Meredith." Still nothing from the group. "Dandy Don?" I try again. "Really?" I look around at the confused faces staring back at me. *What is wrong with these people?* "And you call yourself football fans!" I scold the two older men. "Don Meredith was one of the greatest quarterbacks Dallas ever had! He played all nine seasons of his professional career in Texas and led them to their first winning season." Everyone stares at me like I've just grown horns; clearly, little blonde girls rarely spout sports history for them at the dinner table. "Come on, guys, you're Green Bay fans, you have to remember the Ice Bowl?" Finally, comprehension lights up their faces. That game is so famous almost anyone their age has to remember it.

"I remember now," Charlie says, chuckling, "and I'll admit defeat on the grounds that I didn't recognize the name immediately. Your father, and his daughter for that matter, are far more knowledgeable on the topic than we are."

They all chuckle, and I smile happily at having proved my superiority on the topic. Vivian asks Max about her current course load, and Max launches into a tirade about one of her idiot professors. I glance up to smile at one of her particularly colorful descriptions and find Brody looking at me like I'm some unknown species.

After our last confrontation I know I should ignore that look, but I can't seem to stop from wondering what he's thinking. There are so many questions I could ask, but the one I whisper is:

"Why do you look so confused?"

He stares a second more, then leans in a little, like he's going to tell me some kind of secret.

"You're—" He pauses, struggling for the word. "Unexpected," he says, finally.

I'm momentarily surprised, but I recover quickly and grab for some sarcasm, wrapping it around me like a shield.

"Well, I suppose that's better than silly." I whisper it so as not to be overheard over the other conversation, but I refuse to drop eye contact with him.

He doesn't even have the grace to look embarrassed or guilty.

"Is it now?"

I can't tell if he's actually trying to piss me off, but he's succeeding marvelously.

"It is." I try and match his tone. "Unexpected could turn out to be a lot of things, but being described as silly, beyond the negative connotations, implies that you've somehow already figured me out."

"Can I offer you some advice?" he asks sardonically.

"No," I reply with equal sarcasm, "I don't think my ego can handle your advice twice in one week."

Brody's face brightens in surprise and then the stoic, pompous executive—whom I've never even seen crack a full smile—throws back his head and laughs. It's so incongruous with the person I've come to know that I'm actually startled by his response. A quick glance around the table tells me that this is just as shocking to the rest of the group because they've all stopped to wonder at the sound as if it's a new one for them too.

———

"That pie really was so good," I tell Max as I look out at the LA night slipping past the passenger-side window.

"I know; you've said that three times since we got in the car."

I don't turn towards her but I know she keeps looking at me every time we stop at a light.

"Did you use baker's chocolate for the filling or—"

Max's dramatic sigh cuts me off.

"Cut the crap, Landon, just ask."

Her words are a little harsh but her tone is resigned. I spin towards her, unleashing my excitement for as long as she'll allow it.

"You have to explain it to me, because honestly I can't even imagine! How can you be from *your* family but choose to bartend in order to afford our crappy apartment in Hollywood?"

Max doesn't look at me but she does answer.

"They paid for school, because that seemed fair to me. But I've done everything else on my own since I was eighteen."

When she stops speaking I prompt her. "Because . . ."

"My dad built the company from the ground up, and both Liam and Brody are partners now. It sucks a little for them because their last name *is* Ashton, so everyone assumes they just inherited their jobs, but that's not true. They both earned their places."

"And you want to do the same?"

She shakes her head slightly.

"I don't really know if I want work with them, but whatever I do I want to earn it on my own. It drives my mom crazy. She's positive my chances for gang rape increase by large increments every mile I live past La Brea."

"But they're so proud of you, anyone can see it."

This most definitely makes her uncomfortable; she sort of flinches. "I guess, whatever."

"Max." I grin at her even though she won't look my direction. "You're kind of awesome."

Her only response is a scowl, but at least I know she's heard me. After a few minutes she breaks the silence.

"Coconut," she says succinctly.

"Excuse me?"

"Coconut milk . . . in the pie. I use it to melt the chocolate down into the filling."

"Ah, that explains it."

Chapter TWELVE

"Shut. The. Front. Door!" Miko screeches dramatically and then throws herself down into Quade's old chair with the grace of a drunken toddler.

Selah's never mentioned getting a second assistant since the Volturi left, so the chair's only purpose now is to hold Miko when she comes calling. I'm guessing Selah's figured she's getting two assistants for the price of one, so she's not motivated to bring in anyone else. With so many things to manage, Miko was right about my salary; if I ever divided it by the amount of hours I spend working, I wouldn't be shocked to discover that I could make a better hourly wage at In-N-Out Burger.

"It's the God's honest truth. I wouldn't have believed it if I hadn't seen it myself." I smile down at the reports I am sorting and stapling at my desk. I knew she'd love this bit of news.

"This is—"

Selah's line buzzes and our conversation pauses so that I can answer, then take a message. The second I hang up Miko carries on.

"This actually explains a lot, if you think about it," Miko says contemplatively.

I look up from the papers in my hands. "How so?"

"Max, I mean. She acts all agro-nation but she's intelligent and even sweet when she wants to be. And she can wear all the sloppy, weird outfits she wants, but that kind of flawless complexion is achieved only through a lifetime of expensive facials. And her hair . . . You think someone at Fantastic Sams cut that?"

"I guess not." I really don't know. Mama's second cousin Terry works at Fantastic Sams, and she's pretty good at a spiral perm. I'm guessing she could cut a pixie if anyone in Texas would ever ask for such a thing.

"There's no question. Her highlights are so subtle, they look like they were painted on by fairies! I should have realized . . . I'm actually surprised I didn't think of this before."

"But even if you had guessed, would you ever in your wildest dreams imagine who her family is?"

"Definitely not." Miko has found a paper clip and is bending it into a new shape between her fingers. "But then, I don't really know much about Brody besides the few times I've seen him at SSE stuff, and then Selah's clinging to him like a bad suit because she—" Miko's eyes snap up from the now straight piece of wire in her hand. "She won't like this."

I frown at her.

"She won't like that you have any connection to him outside work."

"I just know his sister. It's not a big deal—"

"It will be for her. She doesn't play well with other kids, and she doesn't share anything, in any capacity. If she finds out you're friendly with what she thinks is hers—"

"We're not friends. I barely know him, and even if she finds out I was there—"

"You mean, if she finds out you spent a holiday with her would-be boyfriend and his family and she didn't," Miko challenges.

"Well, um, I guess she might not like that but—"

"No, Landon, seriously. She's irrational and as far as I can tell she's got sociopathic tendencies. One time an intern brought her the wrong salad during an off-site, and she berated her so harshly, the girl threw up in a trash can out behind the venue."

"That's not true." I giggle nervously.

"It is true. She asked for sautéed shrimp, but I accidentally brought her sautéed chicken. I've never been able to go back inside The Grill without getting a little nauseous," she says with a wink.

Even though she's teasing, my face falls a little. I don't doubt for a second that her story is real and that Selah's reaction was over seafood. Miko's right: Selah won't like me having been at the Ashtons for Thanksgiving.

"So make sure you have Selah sign off on that Swarovski order by tonight or we won't have them in time." Miko is suddenly all business.

I look up at her, confused. What is she talking about? Then Selah's voice rings out from the doorway.

"Brinkley, are we confirmed for that tasting for Kessler-Glen on Saturday?"

"Yes ma'am." I'm already whirling around to open up her calendar on my computer. "Confirmed for an eleven thirty with the caterer."

"You'll be there too; and then afterwards we're going for the final dress fitting."

I look up, and my confusion must show because she only looks more annoyed with me.

"Did I stutter?" she demands.

Why is she so annoyed? *Does she know?*

"No ma'am. I'm just surprised. But of course I'll be there."

Selah laughs, but there's no humor in the sound.

"No one is more surprised than me, but Kira wants you there. Whatever you assisted with this weekend must have made an impression on her. I don't need to remind you that you're there to be seen and not heard. You have to earn the right to interact with clients, Brinkley, and you're a long way from that."

The brazen part of me wants to point out that my interaction with her clients saved her at the Riverton party. Or that baking cakes with Kira while she chain-smoked and told me the entire saga of her relationship, complete with details that made my tender ears burn, would also be considered direct interaction. But as usual I just nod.

Selah's eyes slide to Miko.

"Jin, surely you've got something better to do . . ." She walks away before finishing her thought.

Once we hear the door to her office close behind her, Miko gets up.

"Someday, not now, but someday, I'm going to go all Jericho Barrons–inner beast on her, and it's not gonna be pretty." She glares at the wall that separates us from Selah's office like she can see through it.

I spin back around to my desk so she can't see my face. It's more than a little embarrassing for your friend to see you get put in your place. I try to sound lighthearted when I say, "I think you've finally found a literary reference I don't get."

"Yeah?" she asks, happy again. "I'll give you the series. It's, like, five books of buildup, but when they finally get together . . . *so good!* I'll see you later, 'k?" she asks from the door.

I don't reply, just wave at her with the papers in my hand. Selah seems annoyed but not hands-off-my-man annoyed, just general displeasure. Forget her bad attitude: it's really exciting to get to do something so personal with Kira. I've always wanted to work with brides on their wedding day, and this is the biggest bride and the biggest wedding ever! I can't wait!

———

The Monique Lhuillier store on Melrose Place is sort of magical. When I walk inside I have one of those breathless moments because the dress on the mannequin in the center of the room looks like something a princess might wear. It's the most beautiful combination of silk and lace, with a wide, full skirt that would probably swish a little when you walk down the aisle. I'd say it's the most gorgeous dress in the world, but then there are similar gowns in every direction that are just as pretty. Being surrounded by this many gorgeous gowns has got to be every woman's fantasy, and I have no idea how a bride might choose between them all.

"May I help you?" A well-tailored, older woman comes over to ask.

"Yes, I'm here for the Meeks fitting," I tell her.

This wedding is beyond high profile and almost every detail is in code, including the names attached to the appointments.

"And you are . . ." she asks kindly.

"Brinkley from SSE. I'm meeting Ms. Meeks." I smile back at her.

"Absolutely, they told me you were coming. Just wanted to check." She gestures for me to walk to the back.

I'm escorted to the back room where Selah and Kira's best friend, Meg, are already seated in fluffy white chairs, sipping on champagne. I take a seat next to them and decline the attendant's offer for a drink of my own. I'm fairly sure Selah wouldn't allow it, but I'm also too terrified to be responsible for any kind of beverage around this much expensive white silk. Selah and Meg chat a little about some restaurant they both like, but when Kira emerges from the back room with the help of two attendants, we all lose the ability to speak.

The dress has an empire waist with a low neckline and three-quarter-length sleeves. The entire bodice is like a second skin and made up of delicate lace. The skirt looks like a fluffy pile of whipped cream that's been pinned up into itself here and there, and its volume only makes the dainty bodice look all the more delicate and feminine. She looks perfect . . . And once again she doesn't even have makeup on.

"Oh, Kir—" Meg sighs.

"It's stunning, Kira, really," Selah tells her.

"Yeah?" Kira asks nervously. "It had a big bow here." She runs her finger along the waistline. "But I had them remove it. It was a little much."

"Here are the two veils you were looking at," a perfectly tailored attendant says, coming out of the back room.

She's got two veils in her hands. One is long and entirely lace. It's made to lay on the bride's forehead, completely covering her hair but not her face. The other is thin and sheer but short, and attaches to the top of the bride's head. It's sweet . . . sort of like something you'd see in the sixties. Kira tries on one and then the other. And then she tries them on again. She goes back and forth, and both Selah and Meg offer her polite opinions, but she's still undecided. Finally, after a twenty-minute debate, she settles on the shorter option.

"Oh, thank God!" Meg announces, rushing over to Kira. "I've been sitting here praying you wouldn't choose the lace because I didn't want to have to tell you you looked like Mary Magdalene!"

Kira laughs at her. "That doesn't even make sense."

"It does to me! That's all I could think of when you put it on. I expected *Ave Maria* to start blaring in the room at any moment." They hug and giggle, and I smile right along with them.

Once everything is decided and I have all the details from the attendants about delivery and so on, I say good-bye and make my way out of the store. I'm smiling as I go.

This job sucks some days, well, most days; but I've just spent the afternoon with a celebrity couple trying the most amazing food I'll likely ever eat and now I'm walking through a field of dresses so pretty they almost hurt my eyes.

Yes, some days this job sucks, but today is *not* one of those days.

Chapter THIRTEEN

If I thought a timeline for a mitzvah was intense, it was only because I'd never seen one for a wedding. The one in my hand is sixteen pages at last count, and I'm following along as Taylor and the production team tell the room at large the details for setup.

Kira and Jake are getting married at an old-cathedral-turned-event-venue downtown. I saw the space during the walk-through, and it's amazing, but I can't help but feel a little weird about throwing a party on consecrated ground. I'm hoping since Jesus's first miracle was turning water into wine, he won't mind the top-shelf bar or the six signature martinis we're serving during cocktail hour.

"Just want to confirm the strike time on this?" I ask Taylor because I know that's the next question Selah will ask.

"Midnight on this one as well," he says with that boyish smile that's so incongruous with the rest of him. Does he always smile like that, or is that look just for me?

"Can someone explain the cake thing to me again?" Miko asks out of nowhere. I'm glad she's said something because I don't really understand it myself.

"Jake's mother is making the wedding cake." Selah pinches the bridge of her nose like the very idea gives her a migraine.

"Is she a baker?" Miko asks the question everyone is wondering.

"No idea. She wanted to make the cake, and I advised against it, but they're letting her."

"Are we doing anything with that, or . . ." Taylor asks.

"Allegedly, we're dressing the cake table per the design and they, as in the MOG and some random aunt, are delivering it to the reception by four."

It's taken me weeks to decipher the wedding codes they all use. "MOG" is Mother of the Groom, "FOB" is Father of the Bride, and so on, and now that I understand it, I get a dorky sort of thrill when I use it too. It's like speaking in wedding acronyms makes me more official or something.

"How odd," Holt speaks up, confused. I'm pretty sure it's the first time I've heard her talk in one of these meetings.

"They're from Wisconsin or something. What am I supposed to do?" Selah says, throwing her hands up.

His family is actually from outside Chicago, but I don't correct her. I am pretty sure all the states in the center of the country are the same to Selah.

———

Saturday at 4:42 p.m. is when I start to panic.

Jake's mom was supposed to deliver the cake to the venue by four, and there's no sign of her. I have her cell phone number, but after meeting her yesterday at the wedding rehearsal I'm hesitant to call. Kira wasn't lying when she said Mrs. Kessler hated her, but I don't think she should take it personally. I'm pretty sure Mrs. Kessler hates everyone. It's hard to believe such an uptight woman gave birth to someone as dreamy and sweet as Jake.

I attach another seating card to a chain of Swarovski crystals and move on to the next. It's taking a while to put together this vignette since the chain and the custom clips that hold the cards in place are both delicate, but it'll be worth it. When guests enter the reception they'll come through hundreds of crystal chains of various lengths dangling from the ceiling. It feels like you're walking through a wall of rain, and the effect is only heightened by the blue lighting and the pin spots our team is using to highlight the crystals. It's stunning, even if the effort to achieve it is pretty tedious.

Thirty minutes later I finish the last of the 207 seating cards, and I've decided I'm going to have to call the grouchy MOG. Guests arrive at six, and the cake table is set up in the foyer, so they'll see it as they walk to the ceremony. I can't risk her being late and throwing off arrivals.

As I pull out my phone the far doors open and Jake's mom walks into the room. She's wearing a black dress with an ill-fitting matching jacket and black flats. It's like she actually tried to look as miserable as possible while still in formal wear. She holds the door open, and Taylor walks through it with a cake in his hands.

I am being generous when I call the thing Taylor's holding "a cake," because even from a distance it resembles a multi-tiered lump more than anything close to a wedding confection. Taylor heads my direction, and since the MOG beside him can't see his face, he looks at me and mouths a pretty distinct cussword.

For lack of any idea of what else to do I smile brightly and meet them at the cake table just as Taylor sets his burden down on it.

"Hi, Mrs. Kessler. This looks great!" I go for the bold-faced lie. *Crud!*

Surely lying isn't bad in a situation where telling the whole truth would hurt her feelings? Because the *whole truth* is that while there are four tiers, and they're roundish, the cake is falling and sagging and in some places about to collapse completely. I know enough about baking to realize she iced this thing when it was still warm, because the icing is full of red crumbs. And that's it . . . no piping, no flowers, no fancy scalloped edge. Just red-speckled icing on a troglodyte cake for the most well-publicized wedding of the year.

Crap!

Whether she was already coming over or she smelled fear and responded to it like a shark, Selah appears at the table next to me.

"Look, how gorgeous!" she croons to Jake's mom. "This is stunning!"

I'm beginning to realize that "stunning" is Selah's go-to word for everything.

That baby is stunning! Your dress is stun-NING! Did you see this rash on my arm? STUNNING!

Mrs. Kessler's thin-lipped mouth purses further, like she's just daring us to call her out on this monstrosity. Who would offer to bake their son's wedding cake if they didn't actually know how to bake?

"Thank you. I think they'll like it," she says finally. "Kira wanted red velvet, which I think is sort of tacky in a wedding cake, but I did it just the same."

I glance at Selah, who's still smiling like this is the prettiest thing she's ever seen. How the heck are we going to deal with this? Mrs. Kessler won't acknowledge that the cake is an obvious disaster, so we're supposed to just display it?

"Taylor, would you mind showing Jane where everyone else is? We're just about to start family pictures," Selah says smoothly.

As soon as they're out of earshot she spins around to me.

"You need to fix this right now!" Gone is the calm, collected wedding planner. Now she's all wide-eyed crazy-town, staring me down like I'm the one who made this lump on the table.

"Should I call someone or maybe order another—"

"No, you can't call someone! You can't offend her by replacing the cake. But you *will* find a way to make this look better!"

"But I—"

"I don't have time for this. I'm supposed to be with the bride, not here figuring things out for *you*." She looks down at her phone. "You have forty minutes." Then she turns around and walks away.

For a moment I just watch her go. What does she think *I* can do with this thing? Surely she'd be better equipped to deal with this sort of emergency.

"Left you with cleanup, right?" Taylor asks.

I hadn't even heard him walk up.

"Yes, but I don't know what she thinks I can do." I look between him and the cake anxiously.

"You don't get it yet, do you, Brinks?" He's called me that little nickname ever since the Riverton party, and it doesn't annoy me at all anymore. "Selah never gets her hands dirty with any of this. She doesn't dream it up or design it. She doesn't do setup or cleanup or anything else. And when something like this happens"—he points down at the cake—"she gives it to staff; then if it goes to hell, she always has someone to blame."

"But that doesn't make sense." I look back at the door where she just walked out. "If she doesn't do anything, how is this company so successful? How does she have these clients?"

"I didn't say she wasn't smart. She knows enough to hire good people. The rest was just family connections and a deep trust fund."

But if she doesn't know what to do in this sort of situation, how is she supposed to teach me? As if he's read the question on my face, Taylor steps closer and puts a reassuring hand on my arm.

"Maybe you can call Jin. Maybe she'd have an idea."

Miko left for San Francisco late last night after setup to make it home for her mom's birthday. I don't want to bug her, especially if I'm not even sure she can help. After all, it's not like this sort of thing happens all the time. No. We're tight on time, and I've got to figure this out myself.

Think, Landon, think!

"We just need some way to make it look *better*." I stare at the cake intently, hoping the answer will magically appear.

"We could cover it with a sheet," Taylor says sarcastically. "'Cause that's about the only way it's gonna look better."

A disguise!

"That's it!" I look around frantically.

Taylor looks with me, confused. "What's *it*?"

But before I can even answer him I see what we need. It's a crazy idea, but maybe people will think it's avant-garde.

"Taylor, how much of that Swarovski do we have left?" I say, staring at the vignette in the entryway.

Taylor looks with me, and understanding darkens his face.

"We have plenty. But damn, Brinks, that'll take forever."

"We've got," I look at my phone, "thirty-two minutes."

Taylor runs out to grab what I need and is back in less than two minutes, God bless him. I grab for the first strand, but he stops my trembling hand before I reach it. When I look at him, his face is serious.

"Brinkley, promise me . . . If we make it out of this night alive, you'll go out with me." I can't help but laugh at his acting skills and he winks at me, which calms me down enough that my hands stop shaking. I grab the first string and begin working frantically to wrap the long chain of crystals in neat rows on the cake. I'm careful to cover up every tiny inch of the icing that holds the gems in place like glue. SSE staff come up and murmur to each other behind me, but I don't even acknowledge them. My stomach is churning, and the crystals keep sliding through my fingers because my hands are sweaty. I finish the cake just before the first guests walk through the door.

I quickly shove my supplies under the champagne-colored linen of the cake table where no one can see them, and step back to look at the Frankensteined wedding cake. The lighting team has washed the table in amber and used pin spots to make the

entire cake shimmer. I hate to use Selah's word, but I will: it looks
stunning.

I'm sweaty and still fighting my nerves when I turn to go help
with the ceremony seating.

I have no idea at the time, but the image of this cake will get
a whole page in *People*'s coverage of the wedding. Because of the
massive press exposure, bejeweled cakes will become one of the
hottest wedding trends of the next season, and Selah of course will
take all the credit.

———

The ceremony is almost full, which according to the rest of the
team is sort of a miracle considering we're only fifteen minutes late
on our start time. I check in with the nondenominational min-
ister, who has charged more than my rent to be here today, and
then head back to Kira's dressing area. I want to see if Selah needs
anything else before we start, but when I walk in I sort of wish I'd
stayed out front.

Selah and Meg are looking on nervously, and Kira is pacing
the room mid-rant, looking like the most frantic but beautiful
bride I've ever seen. She's so pretty I'm momentarily stunned, but
then I see how hard she's fighting tears. I have to stop myself from
rushing over and giving her a hug.

"I don't, Meg. I really don't know. Maybe . . . maybe it was just
a silly thought. I fancy him and he fancies me, and so he thought
to ask me to marry him, because you know, that's what his people do. But I—that's not what *my* people do!" Kira keens before
turning to Meg, who automatically holds up the cigarette that's lit
in her hand, and Kira leans over, careful to keep her dress away
from the ash, and takes a long drag off of it. "My people," she says,
whirling away and continuing to pace, "drink too much and fight
constantly and tell their kids what cock-ups they are! *My people*

are the bloody poster children for divorce! What do I know about marriage or being a wife? I've only seen the very worst examples!"

"Calm down, Kir, you're lovely and Jake loves you—" Meg tries carefully. I wonder how long they've been back here trying to talk her down from the ledge.

"You have to say that!" Kira says desperately. "You're my best friend!"

Kira takes a deep, dramatic breath and seems to come to some sort of conclusion.

"No, no, I don't think I can do this to him. He convinced me to marry him, and I will *never forgive* him for that, but I cannot ruin his life. I won't do it to him!" She looks at Selah. "You have to tell him that I—" Her voice breaks and she starts to whimper. "That I can't do this."

I look at Selah, who is calculating her next words—carefully measuring, I'm sure, what a cancellation of this wedding would mean for her reputation—and I know what will happen next. I've seen this scene a thousand times in *The Wedding Planner*. It's the moment when Selah will deliver a rehearsed speech she's crafted to perfection. It'll have the perfect amount of sincerity and romantic words to calm the bride and get her down the aisle.

"Kira, take a breath, doll." Selah steps over to her, looking all calm and cool. "There are two hundred people out there waiting to see you in this gorgeous Lhuillier. Not to mention the press coverage of both this and the honeymoon will be ruined if you walk away now. It'll be disastrous for you. Let's get you some champagne." At this she snaps a finger at me, and I hurry over to fill a flute with champagne. "You can take a moment to calm down, maybe have another cigarette, and then just get through today. It's not like you can't get divorced later. Kim did it after what, three months, and now she and Kanye have the baby and her profile is bigger than ever. You just need to get through today." She says it emphatically as I hand over the champagne.

It's the least romantic speech I've ever heard in my life. It actually makes me a little sick to my stomach. Is that all this day is for them, just another opportunity for press?

Kira takes a big swallow of the champagne, and when she speaks again her voice is small and sad. "I really am sorry about all of this, but I can't do it. I won't do that to him. He'd end up hating me, and I can't—I couldn't ever handle that. At least this way, he could, I dunno, maybe move on or something." Tears slide down her cheeks, and without thinking I step forward and grab her hand. She and I both stare down at our joined hands for a moment, surprised.

"Kira, I don't know you and Jake well . . . But I know without question that you love each other very much."

"No, you know what you've seen on TV and in the magazines. I'm a very good actress." She sounds jaded and sad, but she's holding on to my fingers like a lifeline.

"No. I know what I've seen in you. How hard you worked on Thanksgiving to make it special for him even though you didn't know how to bake. And then at the tasting, I've never seen a man so excited to plan a wedding before. I don't think he let go of your hand once, and he gave you all of the tomatoes from his salad before he even took a bite."

"He knows I love tomatoes—" she says, sniffing.

"And he laughed at all of your jokes, which, please excuse me for saying so, really weren't that funny—"

"She's right, Kir, your jokes are terrible," Meg pipes up helpfully.

"Oh, sod off," Kira tells Meg weakly. But for the first time since I walked in, she smiles a little. She looks back at me. "I know he loves me. But I still can't marry him. I'll ruin everything. It's in my DNA."

I don't know what I'm talking about here, or if I'm saying the right thing. I only know that she's upset, and so I tell her what I'd tell my very best friend in the same situation.

"I don't believe that." I squeeze her hand emphatically. "It sounds like your parents didn't have a good marriage, but you know what? Mine do. They've been married for thirty-two years and you've never met two people who are still so in love and happy. It's possible to have a great marriage; it just requires some effort. But I've seen you two together, and I believe you both care enough to put the effort in."

"But he's so great, and I'm such a mess—"

"My mama always told me that grace is giving someone the opposite of what they deserve. I know I've never been married, but I think that means that sometimes he's going to have to let you get away with being a mess. And that sometimes you're going to have to let him get away with, well, whatever he does that bothers you—"

"That creepy collection of Dune figurines might be a good place to start," Meg says, handing Kira a Kleenex.

Kira twists up the tissue nervously in her fingers.

"You think—you think that I should do it then?" She looks me dead in the eye and a small part of my brain cannot believe this woman is asking me, a relative stranger, whether or not she should make such a huge decision. But I don't even hesitate.

"I think if you love him, and he loves you, that you shouldn't let what happened with your mama and daddy affect your decisions now. I think you say a prayer and take a leap of faith, and if you fall, well, now you'll have a husband there to help pick you back up." I smile at her, and I'm completely sincere.

After a few more tense seconds she smiles too. A full-out, gorgeous, bride-on-her-wedding-day-happy smile, and I know I've succeeded. Apparently, Selah does too because she snaps back to it.

"Brinkley, call hair and makeup back in so we can have a quick touch-up before we head to ceremony."

"Yes ma'am." I hurry to beckon the beauty team back inside and then watch as they quickly restore Kira's hair and cover up the lines the tears have made in her foundation. I feel a light pinch on my elbow, and look up at Meg.

"Well done, you," she whispers with a smile.

Saying thank you would feel a little odd since it was far too intimate a moment already and my interference could have just as easily backfired. So I don't respond. I just smile back and then slip out of the room to make sure the best man has the rings before lining up the men in their positions.

———

Later that night after a beautiful and extremely emotional ceremony, the first dance during which Kira and Jake giggled like grade-schoolers, and the near-inappropriate speech that Jake's little brother made after one too many of the specialty martinis, I am able to sneak back to the kitchen and swipe some food from the caterer. Dinner has long since passed, and all the kitchen has to offer is a hodgepodge of random appetizers and unclaimed vegetarian meals. Everything is cold and rubbery, but I haven't eaten all day so I dig in like it is my last meal. It is here where Selah finds me, crouched over a busser's tray, smearing butter onto my second sourdough roll.

"I'm leaving now." She holds out a white envelope like the object is personally offending her. "Kira asked me to give you this."

I lick a dab of butter off my finger. There are no napkins, so it's either that or wipe it on my dress, and I reach out to take it from her. She watches me intently while I open it, which makes me more than a little nervous. I don't know what I am expecting, but it's certainly not five crisp hundred-dollar bills.

"I don't understand." I look to Selah for an answer.

"It's a tip," she says, annoyed.

"But that's a ton of money! I didn't even really—"

"She likes you," Selah says imperiously. "Brides are emotional, and actress brides are the *absolute worst*. For whatever reason, you were able to calm her down. I suppose this is her way of thanking you. You should feel honored; assistants don't usually get tipped."

"Oh my Lord." I stare down at the money in my hand. Five hundred dollars cash is huge! Maybe not for someone like Selah, whose shoes probably cost twice that much, but for someone like me it's a cushion, a safety net. For me, this five hundred dollars is time, a little more time to keep living in LA, more time to keep reaching for my dream.

"Thank you so much for letting me work on this with you. I learned so much today," I tell her sincerely, because I really have learned more in one single day of working a wedding for SSE than I have in years of assisting random planners back home. Even though none of the knowledge has come from her, I am still grateful.

Selah turns to leave, not deigning to reply, but then she calls out as she walks out the door. "You did well today, Brinkley."

She says it sort of begrudgingly, but she said it! It is the first time—for all I know, the only time ever . . . But Selah Smith has just given me a compliment.

Chapter FOURTEEN

"Wait, is this one for this week's party or next week's? I can't keep them straight."

One of the designers on Miko's team waves a sketch dramatically in the air in our direction. We are all huddled around desks in the design team area long after quitting time, because we have to finalize the details of six separate holiday parties that have popped up on our radar out of the blue. Miko says it's typical for our corporate clients to hold out until the last minute before deciding whether or not to have their parties, but the end result means all of us scrambling to try and fit everything in before Christmas.

"That one is for next week," I say, pointing to the paper being waved at me like a flag. "Remember, they wanted the tropical theme?"

"Right. You're right." The designer studies the picture. "They're all starting to run together in my mind." She rubs at her eyes, desperate. "Jin, you've got to call it. It's almost nine and you know I'm incapable of dreaming up anything pretty after seven."

Miko and I both laugh.

"All right, fine, why don't you guys take off? We'll finish up in the morning," Miko tells her little crew. The small group packs up eagerly and hurries off towards the elevator, infinitely more animated now that they've been given a reprieve.

"You don't need to stay either," she tells me.

I look up from my laptop where I've been adjusting proposals and inputting numbers into bid sheets to go along with their design schematics all evening.

"Actually, I don't mind. I need to finish these proposals anyway." I look down and keep typing.

Miko looks at me suspiciously. "Writing proposals isn't even part of your job."

"It's not my job, but it's important that I know how." I've told her this at least three times today.

"I guess," she mutters, looking back down at her sketch.

We both work a few more minutes in silence and then she stands up.

"Come on, we're taking this on the road." She sandwiches her pencil in between the pages of her sketchpad and throws the whole thing into her shoulder bag.

"Where are we going?" I ask, but I'm already packing up my laptop to follow her.

"I need food . . . more specifically, orange chicken."

"Don't have to tell me twice." I follow her like a dutiful puppy as we jog across the street to grab a table at Chin Chin. We immediately set up our work on the corner table we are given, but it isn't quite as tedious now that we are both munching on fried wonton strips and sipping the first fruity cocktails we spotted on the menu.

"I think I'm tapped too," she says as she looks up from her sketch and takes a big sip of her drink. "Six designs in one day is a little much, even for me."

My phone buzzes with a text message and I grab it.

"Is Max gonna come meet us?" Miko guesses who my text is from.

"Doesn't look like it. She's still fighting that flu, and she says she's too exhausted to leave the couch." I read the text aloud.

Miko looks confused and I understand why. I don't think either of us has ever heard Max admit weakness.

"Did she work tonight?"

"Not sure, but she's been working a ton lately and writing her thesis nonstop. I'm sure she's just worn out." I drop the phone back into my bag.

The waitress comes over and sets down our "assorted pleasures" dim sum, and I reach for a piece of gift-wrapped chicken. Just like always, I burn my thumb on the hot foil wrapping when I try to open it up. "Which one are you working on now?"

"Donahue, Capell, and Michelson. You'd think a bunch of lawyers would be OK with access to an open bar and the musical stylings of whatever cheesy cover band they book every year, but they're pretty big on the design." She pinches a pot sticker with her chopsticks.

"What was the direction?"

Miko sorts through the piles of paperwork in front of her before finding the scrap she's looking for. She reads her notes to me.

"Elegant but unique. Whimsical without being gauche."

"Not very specific, are they?"

"Not this client, no. I'm just trying to think of something we haven't already done."

I stab the last morsel of chicken on my plate. "What about an Asian theme?" I point around the restaurant with my fork.

Miko looks at me like I've just suggested vomit as decor inspiration.

"Landon, that idea is long dead and the time of death was somewhere back in 2001. Also, nobody does *overt* anymore. It's all about subtlety in a theme or statement in an element."

"Um, can you translate that for the new kid?" I stare at her, confused, and take another sip of my cocktail.

"It's like this, you either have a sort of underlying theme that guides your hand with the decor . . . maybe the type of flowers or the colors you use. Or you have some big-impact statement piece at the party and everything else is just there to help show it off."

"OK, I get it. Let me try again." I look around for inspiration, but the decor in the restaurant is sort of nondescript. I give up and go back to my cocktail, hoping it will offer some insight. And as it turns out . . .

"What about this?" I hold up the little red drink umbrella.

"You're kidding, right? Drink umbrellas are beyond cheesy."

"Not a drink umbrella, dummy! What about regular umbrellas? I saw a wedding once in a magazine where they hung painted Japanese parasols upside down from the ceiling and it was really pretty." I hold the little umbrella upside down to illustrate the point.

"Hmmm." Miko considers it a moment. "I feel like someone did an art installation like that a few years ago. They were all the same color, I think."

I open my laptop and Google for a better example of what she's talking about. The page fills with various pictures of the example she's mentioned. Red umbrellas hang open, upside down, and create a canopy down the middle of the street. The effect is striking. I spin it around to show her.

"Could this be your statement element?"

Miko looks at the screen intently, and I start babbling to further support my theory.

"I mean, the ceilings in the ballroom are really high, so maybe you could, I don't know, create a trail of umbrellas that kind of float there. You could light them from above so they sort of glow? And the rest of the lighting and decor could be subtle so it's like the whole party sort of wraps around under this magical little canopy."

She smiles at me with a bemused expression on her face.

"What?" I ask nervously. "Is it terrible?"

"It's chic, it's different, it's impactful without being too expensive." Her expression turns into a full-blown grin.

"Hot damn, intern; you just designed your first party!"

I laugh loudly, thrilled that she likes my idea. We start brainstorming other ideas and different ways to set up the space to best highlight the design. Once we get the layout nailed down, we celebrate this milestone in my career by splitting the last vegetable spring roll.

Chapter FIFTEEN

"So this is Runyon." I look up at the steep dirt trail snaking up the mountain in front of me, then back over at Taylor. He's dressed for the excursion in black basketball shorts and a gray Henley that's pushed up on his arms, showing off his tattoos. I'm doing my very best not to mock his OU ball cap because, with the level of wear and tear on that thing, it's clearly cherished. I've never been hiking, so when he asked me to come with him, I had to make a guess about my own attire, which resulted in workout pants, a sweatshirt, and my running shoes.

"This is Runyon." He starts up the hill, and I hurry to follow him. It's Saturday afternoon, and the day is pretty chilly, but the trail is covered with people hurrying up and down the mountain like ants.

"So this is what you do . . . On your weekends or whatever?" Why do I sound like such a thirteen-year-old?

"Sometimes," he says and smiles over at me. "I actually brought you here because it's a popular *LA activity* and you're still looking for those, right?"

Several members of the SSE team know how excited I still am to be in a new town, and they're always quizzing me on what I've done so far. They've made it their mission to guide me through the experiences they say are thoroughly LA, and the ones that are just for tourists.

"I am." I grin at him. "So this is a cool thing to—" I stop short as a guy jogs past us with his dogs. "Was that Justin Timberlake?" I hiss at Taylor.

"Brinks." He grabs my shoulders and turns me to face the right direction again. "The only thing busier than the best Hollywood club on Saturday night is Runyon on a Saturday afternoon."

We walk for a few minutes in silence, and the incline increases with each step, reminding me of how long it's been since I hit the gym at my apartment.

"How did you end up at SSE?" I ask him between gulps of air.

"I came out here a few years ago after school to work in production . . . in movies, not parties. I had some different PA gigs, but the money was terrible and you're never guaranteed hours. I got a part-time gig working events for the guy who used to have my job. He left to do his own thing, and I got bumped up." He points out a hole in the path for me to avoid, and continues, "Working for Selah would never be my first choice, but the money's pretty good, and that's a priority for me right now."

"Aah . . . driven by the almighty dollar," I tease him.

"Nah, it's not that. I got a kid sister in her freshman year of OU and a single mom who'd have to work two jobs if I couldn't help her out." He shrugs nonchalantly.

My face falls. I feel like such a jerk, I had no idea he was helping support his family back home!

"Oh gosh, Taylor, I'm so sorry I opened my big mouth! I had no idea you were—"

He gives me a self-deprecating grin.

"Come on, Brinks, I'm not a martyr. I'm twenty-seven and there isn't really anything I want that I can't afford, and I'm able to help my family out too. The job sucks some days, but the checks always clear, so it's good enough for now. What about you?"

"What about me?"

"Why are you here?"

As if we had timed it perfectly, we come to a spot on the trail without trees or brush and the whole city is laid out below like a quilt. It's so grand and inspiring that I'm a little breathless when I finally look back over at Taylor, who's watching me.

"I'm here for this." I grin and open my arms to encompass the view. "I came for this!"

I start laughing, so overwhelmed by the spectacular sight before me. He chuckles and throws his tattooed forearm around my shoulders and pulls me back towards the trail.

"Come on, Brinks, you're too easily impressed. I haven't even tried that hard yet."

"Really?" I ask.

His arm falls off my shoulders, but he's still so close that our shoulders keep brushing each other as we hike.

"Really." He looks over and smiles at me, and even under the brim of his tattered cap he looks like a pirate or marauder on the cover of every romance novel I've ever read. "When I actually try, you'll know it."

Is he flirting with me?

Oh God, he's flirting with me!

Of course he's flirting with me! He probably thinks this is a date! Why am I so naive? I just thought—

"Hey, calm down." He bumps me with his elbow playfully. "I brought you hiking, not to an orgy. I'm a perfect gentleman."

"What are you talking about?" I'm terrible at schooling my features, and God only knows what he's just seen flash across my face.

Taylor makes an inarticulate sound and throws me a look that says he knows I'm full of it. I want to act cool, but now I'm just uncomfortable. I'm not sure how to feel about him or what the rules are for accidentally going on a date with your coworker. His voice breaks into my internal debate.

"See, this is why I saved the orgy for date number four; girls can rarely handle group activity this early in a relationship."

I look over at him in shock, and he's grinning at me. All the tension leaves my shoulders, and I stop right there on the dusty trail and laugh until my sides hurt. Pirate or not, Taylor is one of the most fun people I've met in this town.

———

One week later I'm standing under a canopy of at least a hundred red umbrellas lighting up the breathtaking room before me. We're fifteen minutes from the guests' arrival, but I allow myself this small moment to look up at my tiny idea come to life. For the first time since starting this job, I'm really, really proud of myself.

I'm still grinning as I turn to head across the ballroom to check on the wine delivery at the bars. That smile freezes on my face when I see Selah laugh her way into the ballroom, side by side with Brody Ashton. This hotel is one of Barker-Ash's biggest luxury properties, so I knew I might run into him, but I'd been really hoping to avoid it.

Seeing him walking with Selah, in her skintight red Prada dress, chatting in her "client" voice, only serves to remind me that I'm not supposed to know him at all. I'm a little sick with the idea that he might mention Thanksgiving and that she might use the opportunity to rip my head off and turn it into a purse.

Curl mouth at corners, raise up towards cheeks.

There. I hope whatever is on my face will pass for a smile.

I walk towards them to check in with her and see what she thinks of the space. I'd pitched the idea for the installation at an all-hands meeting, and it was met with a quick approval, which in Selah-world is apparently a huge coup. Regardless of how nervous I feel, the installation looks amazing; and ever since I'd gotten my one tiny Selah-compliment, I've been itching to see if I could impress her again.

"This looks incredible. I'm sure they'll be pleased," I hear Brody say as he peers up at the umbrella installation.

My umbrellas look incredible! And this from the guy who's incapable of a compliment.

"Well, you wouldn't expect anything else from me, would you?" Selah says in her gross, overly flirtatious voice, and my heart stops.

Did she just say—?

"How did you come up with the idea?" Brody looks back overhead. "I've never seen anything like it."

She considers the umbrellas for a second, which is as long as it takes her to come up with the lie.

"The painting by Cipolla. I've always admired his work, and it came to mind when I was dreaming up a theme."

Dear Lord! She's just lied her way through that entire sentence with the poise of a senator's wife! Worse still, I don't even know what painter she's talking about, so I'm not even smart enough to refute her claim! Here I am hoping she might give me some small scrap of a compliment, and she's not even going to acknowledge my participation at all.

I wonder, not for the first time, if she even realizes she's lying, or if she just does it so often that she believes it simply because it came out of her mouth. I've only just walked up to them, but I make up an excuse to leave.

"If you'll both excuse me." I try to keep my voice steady. "I just need to check in with the catering captain on a wine delivery."

I make to walk away but Selah stops me.

"While you're at it, check in with operations and bring the thermostat up a bit. It's freezing in here." She does a mock shudder and scoots closer to Brody in some weird pantomime of snuggling up close to get warm.

Any idiot could tell her: a large ballroom is always cool, but once it's filled with four hundred drunk lawyers it'll be too hot, and then it'll take ages to cool down again. But I'm not that idiot, so I just nod.

Brody steps away from Selah and directly into my path. *This is a really bad idea for all parties concerned.* I look up at him with questioning eyes.

"I'll walk with you, Landon. I need to check in with the captain myself."

It is a totally casual comment, but I know Selah won't like him leaving her side to go anywhere with me. That is what worries me, until I realize what he's just said. *Please, Jesus, Mary, and the Saints, did he just call me* Landon? I glance quickly at her. *Maybe she didn't catch him using my first name—nope, no, she definitely caught that.* I'm a goner.

"I, er—probably, yes. Mr. Ashton, if you'll . . ." I glance nervously at Selah, then back at him. "Excuse me, I have to—" I don't even finish the sentence because Brody looks utterly confused by my response.

When I look at Selah she's looking back and forth between us like she's trying to solve a particularly difficult riddle, and then I see it. It's the moment she decides something is up. Her eyes narrow and suddenly she's not looking at me like a worthless peon; she's looking at me like I'm an adversary, which is far more terrifying. I have a single crazy moment when I consider screaming, *Nothing is going on, I swear!* But I bite my tongue.

There's an intense, quiet moment in which Selah glares, I stare at my shoes, and Brody checks his phone like he's got ninety-seven better things to do than stand here in this tableau. I wait for the blowup, but to her credit she doesn't scream or fire me or say any-thing terrible. No, like only the very best villains, she attacks subtly.

"Brinkley, I need you to pick up my dry cleaning," she says abruptly.

I guess she's trying to embarrass me in front of him, which in the grand scheme of life isn't as bad as I expected.

"Of course, I'll add it to my list." I turn to go.

"No. I need you to go right now."

"Right now?" I look around me, confused; we're about to open the doors for a huge party.

"Yes, I have two events to attend this weekend, and I need more wardrobe options. I need you to go pick up the dry cleaning and drop it off at my house."

"But the event is—"

Selah smiles and it's pure evil. "Surely you don't think the absence of one little assistant can in some way negatively affect an event. Honestly, we've managed to get along just fine for the last five years without your help."

"Of course not, but I just thought—"

"But I don't pay you to think, do I?" Her eyes spark maliciously. "And right now, I'm *paying you* to go pick up my dry cleaning."

Brody turns back to her and inserts himself into the conversa-tion. "Honestly, Selah, you need her to go to the Westside during rush hour on a Friday?" All three of us can hear the annoyance in his voice, and I want to curl up and die right there on the plush ballroom carpet. Why is he picking this, of all moments, to be chivalrous? Doesn't he know this is only going to make it worse?

"B, are you trying tell me how to run my company now?" Selah says coquettishly.

Her body language is flirtatious but her eyes glitter with a challenge.

I lower my eyes. I can't look at her, and I definitely can't look at Brody. I don't have any choice, and she knows it. My job is whatever she says it is, and right now that's running errands. I nod and turn to go grab my bag, and she throws her last pass.

"Mia's leash is on the hook by the door. Be sure and run her around the block while you're there. You know she hates being cooped up while I'm out."

I don't acknowledge the statement. But then I don't really need to; she knows I'll do it.

I spend the next hour and a half sitting in terrible traffic, trying, yet again, not to cry. I was so excited about this event. It was the first one I'd worked on from start to finish, and I'd helped plan every single element, from the design down to the dessert choices. I'd wanted to hear what the clients thought about everything, wanted to see people's reaction to the umbrellas . . . umbrellas inspired by a cheesy cocktail garnish, *not* an old painting.

Ugh! I'm not gonna think about it. I'm gonna do what she's asked of me and head back over. With any luck I'll be back in time to hand out the gift bags we spent three hours stuffing.

I park my car in front of Selah's twenty-four-hour, eco-friendly dry cleaners and hustle inside. An older man is sitting in front of a portable TV. When he sees me he hops up.

"Hi, Mr. Agabalian. How are you doin'?" I slip up to the counter. "I just need to grab whatever she has in-house."

"She has more?" He looks confused. "Let me check." He scoots over to the ancient computer and clicks through for a bit, but his confusion only grows. "I'm sorry, I don't see anything in here. Are you sure?"

"Oh, I'm sure. She sent me all the way over to grab whatever it is."

"Do you think she dropped off something else? I was here when she picked up that red dress and a few blouses this afternoon, but I don't see anything else in the system. Maybe she brought them in when I was at lunch, and Eva hasn't put them in the system yet."

He looks up helplessly. I'm already pulling out my phone to text Selah to ask her which items I'm supposed to pick up. Her response is nearly on top of mine; it's like she has been just waiting for me to ask.

SELAH SMITH:
That's right, I picked it all up earlier.
Must have slipped my mind.

I'm still staring down at the text in disgust when the next one pops up.

SELAH SMITH:
Don't forget to walk Mia.

————

On the way back to the venue my feet hurt from walking the uneven pavement around Selah's house in heels. My hair has turned into a frizzy disaster from being in proximity to the ocean, so I have to pull it up into a messy knot on top of my head. And my once-pretty black dress is covered with white dog hair. God forbid Selah would have a little, yappy pocket dog like any normal socialite; no, Mia is a two-hundred-pound Saint Bernard who likes to pull my arms out of their sockets and ruin every outfit I wear in her presence. It takes another two hours to get back over to the hotel because of the wreck on I-10. I should have spent that whole time plotting Selah's ultimate demise. Instead, all I can do is worry about this pseudo-love triangle she's cooked up in her imagination.

When I finally trudge my way back into the hotel, I'm shocked to see that the only people left in the ballroom are the members of production tasked with striking the room and the catering staff cleaning up what must have been one heck of a party. The umbrellas are still there floating above the room, but with the house lights turned back up and the smell of spilled alcohol in the air, they don't look quite so pretty anymore.

Sort of like this job.

I ignore the little whisper in the back of my mind and pick my way through the room. I don't even know why I've come back. I should have just gone directly home to pajamas and a pint of Ben & Jerry's because, really, that's the only answer at this point.

I check in with our team and make sure they're good before going to grab the stuff I'd hidden under the candy table. First I pull on a black peacoat, then use the table for balance as I slip out of my heels and into my UGGs. I wiggle my toes down into the fluffy boots, and I already feel a million times better. Now all I need is a thousand calories' worth of chocolate-brownie ice cream, and maybe I can pretend this night never happened.

Chapter SIXTEEN

It's really late by the time I make my way back home. I'm exhausted emotionally, and I can't wait to crawl under my blankets. I slip my key into the lock, and when I open the front door I'm surprised to see all the lights on and hear music coming from the kitchen. Max must be pulling another late night working on her thesis.

"You are not going to believe the day I had," I call out to her as I round the corner to the kitchen. And then I stop cold.

Max is lying on the kitchen floor. She's unconscious in one of her ridiculous T-shirts, a huge puddle of blood collecting in a halo around her head.

Oh Jesus.

Air rushes out of my lungs, and I'm vaguely aware of the sound of someone hyperventilating. A moment later I realize I'm the one making those sounds. My friend is hurt and I still haven't moved. Time suddenly speeds back up, and I'm on the floor next to her. Some latent instinct takes over, and I'm already pulling my phone out.

"Max! Max!" I scream as I run my shaky hands over her body, trying to figure out what's wrong with her. Her coloring looks all wrong, pale even beyond her normally fair skin, and everywhere

I touch her she's clammy and cold. She's breathing but she doesn't respond to my voice or my touch. It looks like she's hit her head. *Was that before or after she passed out?* I don't know what's wrong with her. I don't know what I'm supposed to do.

"Ma'am, I need you to stop yelling. I need you to take a breath and tell me your address." The woman on the phone speaks in a stern but even tone.

I don't even realize I've called 9-1-1.

"I . . . um . . . my friend is hurt. I don't know . . . she's bleeding!"

I'm afraid to move her in case she's hurt her neck. *Am I supposed to try and stop the bleeding? Is she going to be OK?* I feel all at once numb and hyperaware. *Why won't she wake up?*

"Max!"

"What's your name, sweetheart?" the operator asks.

"Landon Brinkley. Max is my roommate—and my friend!" I stutter stupidly.

"Landon, I need you to stay calm for me, OK? Tell me what happened to Max."

I tell her what I know, which isn't much at all, and our address. When she asks for the door code for our apartment lobby, it takes me three tries before I can get it right because my thoughts are so frenzied. I can hear her typing feverishly in the background.

"Can I . . . Should I use a towel or something for her head?" I'm nearly sobbing but the operator is maddeningly calm.

"Yes, grab a clean towel and apply pressure to the area of her head that's bleeding. Be very careful not to move her neck at all, OK?"

I grab a kitchen towel off the handle of the dishwasher and very carefully hold it to the area on Max's head that's matted with blood.

"She's so pale and cold," I whisper.

"Does she have any illnesses that you're aware of?"

"I don't know—"

"Can you look her over? Can you tell me if she's wearing any kind of medical identification?"

"Medical what?" I'm confused.

"Look for a bracelet with a medical ID tag. It's important."

"OK—" I'm not sure what she means because surely I would have noticed something like that. I reach for Max's left hand and her wrist that's covered with all the different bracelets she never takes off. It doesn't take me more than a second: one is different from the others. It's got a red symbol on it.

"She does!" I almost yell when I pinch the tag with my fingers. "It says hypoglycemia. What does that mean?"

I'd never noticed it hidden amongst the other bracelets. *Is that why she wears them? Why didn't she tell me?*

"It means her blood sugar is dangerously low, especially with the blood loss. Do you think you can get her to drink some juice or to eat some candy?"

The side compartment of Max's purse pops into my mind. It's forever filled with mini–candy bars despite that she's on the most health-conscious diet of anyone I've ever known.

"I don't think so. She won't wake up. I can try, though—"

"No, that's OK," the operator says. "You don't want to force fluids if she's unable to swallow."

"Is someone coming to help? Are they close?" I whimper because now I'm really starting to freak out. *What happens if Max can't get her blood sugar up soon?*

"Any minute now. Just stay calm for me, OK?"

I hear the dispatcher speaking to someone else as I kneel on the floor. Blood is staining the knees of my tights. I keep checking her pulse with shaky hands, like they taught us in eighth-grade health. It's still strong but she won't open her eyes or respond when I call her name.

"Landon, the paramedics are in the hall. I need you to open the door for them, OK?"

Before she finishes her sentence there's a loud knock on my door, and I run to open it. A team of firefighters rushes through. I can't help but think that Max would be mortified if she knew all these men were seeing her in just a T-shirt and her underwear, but then I look at the group of them kneeling around her in the kitchen, and I want to curl into a ball and cry. A stretcher is wheeled in and they're lifting her onto it; suddenly, they're taking her back out the door. I stare after them for a moment, and then I grab my purse and chase them down the hall.

Outside the street is filled with fire trucks, and I run up just as they're loading her into the ambulance. One of the paramedics sees me standing there.

"Do you know if she's allergic to any medications?"

I panic a little at his words.

"Oh God, I don't know. Is that bad?"

"It's OK, it's just helpful if we know, but it'll be OK. Her vitals are good. We're taking her to Cedars. You can meet us there," he says.

I don't like this idea. I don't want to leave Max. What if something happens to her on the drive over and she's alone with strangers? I don't know where I find the strength to argue since it feels like a strong wind could knock me over, but I refuse to leave Max.

"I'll ride with her." I step towards the back of the ambulance.

"I'm sorry, miss, that's against policy. You can meet us at Cedars; I promise your friend will be fine."

I look him dead in the eye.

"You're either letting me ride with her or you're physically removing me from here."

He must see my resolve because he doesn't argue further; he just gestures for me to climb in. I find myself cramped into a corner of the ambulance, and I'm watching them shove needles into Max. No matter what they do to her, she doesn't respond. By the time we arrive at Cedars, I've stopped feeling numb. I'm sick with worry.

I hurry into the hospital behind the paramedics wheeling Max, but a nurse stops me.

"I'm sorry, you'll have to wait here," she tells me.

"I can't—my friend is back there." I point to the swinging doors beyond me. "I don't want to leave her alone."

"I understand, and I'm sorry, but no one is allowed back there. Can you answer a few questions for me? Do you know her date of birth?"

Another blank. I'm so angry with myself. Why didn't I ever think that I might need to know this information? It's so important, and I have no idea what the answers are.

"I—gosh, sometime in April I think."

Her eyes narrow slightly.

"Maybe there's someone you can call? Her family? We'll have a lot of questions about her medical history and—"

"Of course, yes, I'll do that." I fish my phone out of my bag, grateful for something to do.

"I'll just be over there at that desk. Come find me when you know more."

I nod and begin scrolling through my contacts. Only then do I realize I don't actually know how to contact Max's parents. I suppose I could drive over to their house, but then I . . . didn't bring my car.

Damn it! I chew my lip nervously, then I remember: I have all of Selah's contacts listed in my phone. For one idiotic moment I hesitate. *It's so incredibly rude to call someone at 1:00 a.m.* Then I shake myself and dial the number. It rings twice and then goes to voice mail, meaning that he doesn't recognize my out-of-state number and is ignoring the call. Well, at least that means he's awake. I don't even bother to leave a voice mail, I just hang up and hit redial as I pace back and forth in front of the nurses' station. On the fourth call he finally picks up.

"Who is this?" he demands.

"Brody, I'm sorry, this is Landon Brinkley—"

"Landon?" He sounds totally confused. "It's really late, and, um, not the best time."

In the background I can hear a crowd and music. A woman giggles and calls his name.

"I know and I'm sorry, but I—"

"Why don't we forget this happened, OK?"

It hits me. *He thinks I'm drunk-dialing, or worse.* I feel so embarrassed that in my shock at everything that's happened I almost apologize and get off the phone. I'm so overwhelmed by the entire night and feel like I'm looking down and watching myself from somewhere high on the ceiling. I don't know where it comes from but I'm crying before I even realize it.

"Brody, it's Max. I think she's OK but I came home and she was on the floor and I think she hit her head—" I hear him curse with feeling but I keep tripping over the words trying to get them out. For some reason I'm afraid that he's going to hang up on me. "The paramedics took her, and the nurse needs to know answers, and I don't know any. I'm sorry but I didn't know your parents' number—"

He interrupts me. "Landon, where are you?"

"Cedars, in the ER waiting room."

"I need you to find the nurse or the doctor who was asking you questions and let me speak to that person. Can you do that?"

"I can." I swipe the tears off my cheeks and walk towards the nurses' station. The nurse looks up when I walk over.

"I have Max's brother on the phone. He'd like to speak with you."

The nurse reaches out for my phone.

"Brody, I'm going to hand you over to her."

"Good girl." He sounds so calm. "I'll be there in fifteen minutes, OK? Do not move."

"OK," I mumble as I hand over the phone.

The nurse starts asking him questions, and now that someone else is involved I can take a deeper breath for the first time in an hour. I'm cold even though I haven't taken off my coat, and I curl my arms around myself protectively as I make my way over to a row of gray plastic chairs to wait. My thoughts are jumbled and confused, but I'm intensely grateful that someone else is involved now to help.

———

I huddle in the chair and watch people make their way in and out of the busy emergency room. Each person who passes is in some state of pain or illness. Some have broken bones or sick babies, and there's a palpable feeling of nervous energy while everyone waits for their name to be called. Nobody looks good but I find myself begrudging them their injuries; at least with a broken arm or a cut that needs stitches they *know* what's wrong with them. I still haven't heard anything about Max, and it's making me imagine the worst.

My brain is in such a fog I don't even realize Brody is standing right in front of me until he calls my name. He's wearing the nicest-looking tux I've ever seen but his hair is mussed in every direction, as if he's run his hand through it repeatedly. I stare up at him; I'm unable to form words because the weight of this night is starting to pull me under. He sinks down in a squat in front of me at eye level.

"Hey, are you OK?" he asks softly.

I still can't find words.

I shake my head. No, I'm not OK.

The look on his face is utterly soft as he reaches out to take my hand. I hear his quick intake of breath when his fingers touch mine, and I look down at them. My hands are covered and stained with blood. I hold them out in front of me and stare at them like they're not attached to my body. I notice the sleeves of my coat and then my tights. Her blood is all over me. I hadn't even noticed until that moment. I look back into his eyes in panic, but he's already pulling me to my feet.

"Come on."

He keeps ahold of my hand and leads me like a small child to the bathroom.

"Do you need me to come in there with you?" He looks at the door of the women's restroom, then back to me.

I find my voice. "No, I can do it."

"I'm going to check in with the nurse again." He looks off behind me. "I'll be right back."

I nod and walk through the door he holds open. The sight of myself in the mirror above the sink jolts me out of my trance. My hair is seconds from falling free of the elastic holding it in place. My eye makeup is smudged, and my nose is red from crying.

First things first. I turn on the water and wash my hands. It takes three rounds of soap until they come clean, and I'm so grateful for the reviving effects of cold water that I hold them under the faucet longer than necessary. There are dried patches of blood on the edges of my coat. I think I might be sick; the sight disgusts me more than anything else I've seen tonight.

I quickly take off the coat and without another thought shove the whole thing into the trash can. No amount of dry cleaning can ever make me want to wear that coat again, and even if I'm cold I don't want it touching me. Next I take off my tights and they land in a heap on top of the coat. I use the next several minutes to scrub the blood off my arms and legs. Now I'm just wearing a black cocktail dress and my boots, but at least I feel clean.

I wash up my face and pull my hair back into a bun. For some reason, looking a little better actually helps me feel a little better. I dig into my purse and find some Chapstick and some gum; I'm utterly grateful for both. Then I head back out feeling much more in control than I did on the way in.

When I come out Brody is leaning against the wall next to the door, and I wonder how long he's been waiting for me. He stands upright and then looks at me with confusion.

"Where's your coat?"

"Trash."

His lips thin a little, like the idea bothers him, but he's already pulling his jacket off and helping me into it. I start to protest but he silences me with a determined look. My arms shiver when they slide against the silk lining; it's about a million times too big but it's warm so I pull it tighter around me.

He holds onto my elbow, like I'm some elderly aunt prone to keeling over, and tows me back over to my seat near the nurses' station.

"Did you call your parents?" I ask as I sit down.

He nods absentmindedly. "They were up in Whistler skiing with Liam and Malin—they'll get the first flight out. Mom is freaking out though, and it won't surprise me if she makes him charter a jet."

I chuckle, but when he looks at me curiously I realize he is not actually kidding. I change the subject.

"Did the nurses tell you anything?"

"They don't have any info yet," he says, and runs his hand through his hair. "The doctor is supposed to come out and speak with us as soon as they have something to tell."

"What do they—" I start to ask, but he cuts me off abruptly.

"Did she not tell you she is hypoglycemic?" He looks at me accusingly. When he sees the answer on my face, he swears harshly.

"She promised, *promised*, she'd tell you! Having a roommate is the whole reason my parents agreed to stop harassing her about living so far away from them." His knee starts to bounce in agitation, his composure slipping with each sentence. "And I know she's been so stressed with her thesis, but she *knows* better. She knows she has to take care of herself!"

My mind is racing again. *I can't believe Max hid this from me.* My great-grandma was diabetic, which has something to do with blood sugar but I don't know how similar the two are. I look to Brody, about to ask him to explain it to me. His head is in his hands, and he looks utterly lost. It's shocking to see him so obviously upset. *When did he start falling apart?* Half an hour ago I thought he was going to be the grown-up here.

He runs a hand back and forth through his hair again in what I now realize is a nervous gesture. The helpless look on his face is so at odds with his usual confidence that it makes my heart hurt. All I can think about is that I want to make him feel better, and to do that he needs to think about something else besides his little sister being sick. So I start talking.

"I'm afraid of Bigfoot," I blurt out.

Brody sits up and blinks like he's not sure what I've just said . . . Honestly, neither am I, but I just keep going.

"It's true. He, or I suppose it could be a she." I wiggle my hands out of the sleeves and push them up on my arms. "*It* scares the bejesus out of me. When I was little my cousins used to threaten to tie me to a tree and leave me there overnight as a sacrifice. I was petrified."

"But . . . Bigfoot doesn't exist." Brody is baffled.

"That you *know of*," I tell him indignantly.

That earns me the smallest twitch of his lips. I keep going.

"I mean, someone breaks into your house, a robber or a mugger let's say—"

"I don't think muggers break in," he says conversationally.

"Well, whatever, my point is that some *human* comes at you
. . . You know what to do, what your options are. You can run or
fight back, you can find a knife or crawl out a window—"

"You've thought about this a lot."

"You have no idea," I tell him, deadpan. "But a creature, or an
alien, or a ghost . . . I mean, how are you supposed to know how to
deal with that? You have no *idea* what they're capable of. I'd probably pee my pants." I'm telling him the absolute truth. Supernatural
anything terrifies me.

I'm so wrapped up in the thought, it takes me a minute to
realize Brody is laughing at me. His eyes crinkle around the edges
with his smile, and my heart grows three times its size, just like the
Grinch, because I —I!—am helping *him* feel better.

"Thank you for that—" he starts to say, but the sight of a doctor walking towards us has us both springing to our feet.

"Mr. Ashton?" the doctor asks.

"Yes?"

"I'm Dr. Lacour. I attended to Mackenzie tonight. She's stable."

The little knot in my stomach unravels a bit.

"But she's still not awake. I believe she suffered a severe hypoglycemic reaction. It was advanced enough that she lost conscious-
ness and appears to have hit her head. We gave her some stitches
for the laceration, and it should heal up fine. I believe she'll wake
up in the next few hours, and then we'll have a better idea of how
she's doing."

I can see some of the tension leave Brody's shoulders. He clears
his throat once before he speaks.

"Thank you so much, doctor. I can't tell you how much I appreciate your help. What do you think caused this?"

"I'll have to speak with her to be sure, but typically it's a combination of not keeping her blood sugar up mixed with exhaustion,
or even stress. We usually see this type of thing after several days of
dehydration due to illness."

I remember then. How sick Max has been over the last week. I didn't even know to be worried about it.

"She's been fighting the flu," I croak.

The doctor looks over at me kindly.

"Well, that might do it. We'll know more when she wakes up. She's in a room if you'd like to go see her now."

"Thank you." Brody reaches out to shake his hand.

The doctor smiles at us and then directs us to Max's room. I walk back through the hallways crowded with medical equipment and feel more nervous with each step. I haven't visited many, but I'm fairly certain that I hate hospitals.

When we open the door to Max's room, we both stop short in the doorway. She looks pale and sickly and so tiny in the bed, connected to IVs and a heart monitor. I absolutely hate seeing her this way . . . She'd hate it too. I walk right over to her bed, grab her hand, and sit down in the chair next to her.

"Max," I call to her softly. "I need you to wake up so I can beat the crap out of you for this."

Brody walks up behind me and reaches out to touch her as if reassuring himself that she's actually there. He clears his throat after a moment.

"I need to call my parents. Are you OK if I step out into the hall?"

I nod, never taking my eyes off Max's face. I hear the door open and close behind me.

I feel bone tired, weary down to my toes. I look at the clock on the wall; it's almost four in the morning. The confirmation of time seems to release whatever tentative hold I have on my ability to keep my eyes open. I scoot closer to the bed, lay my head down on the mattress, and pull Max's hand closer until it's almost touching my head. I'm asleep before Brody comes back in the room.

It feels like seconds later that someone is shaking my arm. I open my eyes, confused, and look at the clock. It's nearly 8:00 a.m. Someone jostles my arm again.

"My hand's asleep, let go," Max rasps.

My eyes fly to her and then quickly scan the room. We're alone. I'm not sure where Brody is or when Max woke up. She wiggles her fingers, trying to get out of the death grip I've got on her hand.

I gasp. "You're awake!"

"It would appear so," she says, doing her best to sound sarcastic but the effect is lost in the whisper of her voice and the paleness of her skin.

"Don't. Don't even. I swear to God I will murder you myself if you try and act nasty to everyone this morning!" I scowl at her, and for a second she tries to scowl back but then her face crumbles. She looks away, blinking back tears. I don't give her time to feel self-conscious. I jump up and throw my arms around her.

"You scared the crap out of me! Don't ever do that again." I hug her fiercely, unconcerned about all the tubes and wires I'm disrupting. After a second she gives in and hugs me back.

"I'm sorry," she squeaks. "I didn't know it was going to—"

She's cut off by the sound of the door opening, and Vivian rushes into the room, looking like she's about to lose it completely. Charlie and Brody come in behind her.

"You're awake!" Vivian runs over to the bed.

I try to get out of her way but she gathers me into a sort of group hug along with Max, and then she's crying and hugging and kissing us both and I just let her hold onto me, unsure of what else to do. When Charlie walks over to tug her back I move to give him room next to Max.

"Let her catch her breath, Viv," he says as he rubs slow circles on her back. When he looks down at Max he gets choked up. "You gave us a scare, baby girl."

Max's face crumbles again. I'm not sure any girl can hear her daddy cry without getting upset, even one as tough as she is.

"I'm sorry, I don't know how this happened. I was fine and then I felt light-headed, so I went to the kitchen for a snack and then I just got so . . . confused. I woke up here," she says helplessly.

I inch closer to the door as Brody walks up to the bed. He gives Max a kiss on the forehead.

"Don't worry about it now, OK? Just get better. We'll figure it all out."

"There's nothing to figure out," Vivian says with sudden ferocity. "I knew it was a mistake to let you live by yourself." She shakes her head as if annoyed. "Maybe someday when you're not so stressed with school, but not now. You're moving home." She speaks with finality.

"Mom," Max groans, and at the same time Charlie says, "We can discuss this later."

"No. Absolutely not. I listened to you the first time and look where it got us, Kenzie!" She gestures around the room spastically, tears rushing down her face. "You could have . . . I can't even say the words. I can't even say the words!" She's nearly hysterical now, and Charlie's trying to calm her down. I'm sure I shouldn't be here for this conversation, but I'm unsure how to slip out without it being awkward.

"Mom, I know this scared you. It scared me too, OK? But I'm all right, it's not going to happen again." Max speaks to her carefully.

Vivian acts like she didn't even hear her.

"You have to come home."

"I won't discuss this anymore," Max says.

Her voice is stern, but her eyelids flutter with the effort to stay open. I can't imagine this sort of argument is good for her. Vivian must sense her exhaustion too, because her voice grows gentle.

"I don't want to upset you," she says as she smooths Max's hair out of her face. "We'll discuss it later, OK?"

"No, we won't—" Max says fiercely.

Her eyes slide to mine in the corner of the room. For one quick moment she looks at me beseechingly, and then her eyes dart back to Vivian. I follow her gaze and look at Vivian too. She has that intense mama-bear gleam in her eyes. This is an argument Max won't win, and Max knows it.

"You need someone to take care of you!" Vivian tells her.

"I don't—"

"You do—"

"I'll take care of her," I call over the top of them.

All their heads swing in my direction. Max looks like I'm her savior, and Vivian looks like she might tear me to pieces, but I hold my ground.

"I didn't know she had this—" As soon as the words leave my mouth, Max's parents turn and glare at her. She holds their look with one of her own, and I keep talking. "Condition. Which was wrong of her, and she can see that now." I point at my friend, who looks weak and repentant, and I don't doubt I'm telling the truth. "But I know now, and I'll do whatever you need me to do so you feel comfortable." Max smiles at me sadly, and Vivian turns back to her, ready to argue again, but I stop her.

"Mrs. Ashton?"

She looks at me warily.

"We all know Max isn't the best at expressing the way she's feeling. She's one of the toughest girls I've ever met, and she's fiercely independent. I think that's why she didn't tell me; she doesn't want anyone to see her as weak. I think she must get it from you, because you're pretty tough too." I smile at her. "But if you make her come home, she'll be miserable . . . And she'll resent you. I can't imagine how tough it is to worry about her when she's not with you, but she's an adult and you've got to let her try and do this on her own. I promise I'll help."

Vivian looks back and forth between Max and me. When she finally turns into Charlie's arms and starts to cry, I realize she knows Max won't ever move back home. Brody's voice breaks up the awkward sound of crying.

"Malin and Liam are waiting to come in, but two of us have to leave first."

"Of course." I hurry over to grab my bag off the floor, and as I stand up Max grabs for my hand. She doesn't say anything at all, just squeezes my hand so tight it hurts, and I squeeze back just as hard.

"I'll check in on you later, OK?" I whisper.

She nods and I turn and follow Brody out of the room. As we walk down the hallway together I realize I don't have a car. I try my best to lighten the mood.

"Would you mind giving me a ride home? I have to be at work in, like, an hour, because I'm pretty sure death or my own dismemberment is the only reason my boss would allow a sick day—"

Brody stops abruptly midstride. When I turn to see what's wrong he grabs me and pulls me in for a fierce hug. I'm so stunned, I don't move or raise my arms to hug him back; I just let him hold me while the last twelve hours of emotion pass back and forth between us. Finally he bends down and places the lightest kiss on my forehead, just like he did with Max.

"Thank you," he whispers.

I'm too overwhelmed to speak so I just nod and let him lead me out to the waiting room.

Chapter SEVENTEEN

We have four more holiday parties in the following two weeks. I learn to hate gift bags with the intensity of a thousand suns. Every event has both regular gift bags and VIP gift bags, and each takes an extraordinary amount of time to pack up and cart around. Regardless of the cool packaging or setup, the party guests rarely show much enthusiasm, even though each bag contains several hundred dollars' worth of loot. I wonder more than once why we bother at all.

Max comes home from the hospital halfway through that time. Her mom begs her to stay with them until after Christmas, but I think Max is afraid if she goes back at all, she'll never be allowed to leave.

She hates doing it, but I make her explain to me exactly how her diet works and when she needs to test her blood or eat something to get her sugar back up. I am totally ready to play nurse like I'd promised, but it turns out there really isn't much to do. Max has been dealing with this all her life, and she really does have it under control. She had ended up in the hospital after being sick for days and, as a result, dehydrated. As much as she'd known a coma was a possibility, I don't think she'd truly taken it seriously since it had never happened before. But now it has happened, and even though she'll never admit it, the experience scared her. She is more diligent than ever about taking care of herself, and because of that I go along with her demand: we will never discuss that night again.

I hover over her every minute I'm not working, but she finally gets fed up and says she'll rip out my hair if I don't leave the house for at least an hour. Which is how I find myself one weekend letting Taylor talk Miko and me into attending a coed dodgeball game. We're supposed to help defend his team, the aptly named Dodge Chargers. I think the whole thing is a joke until I get there and realize it is an actual league, with uniforms and everything. I explain to Taylor that this new athletic revelation only ups his nerd ante, but he just laughs and pulls out thick sweatbands for both his wrist and his forehead . . . He says that dressing in weird seventies paraphernalia is half the fun of the game. I guess he's right because everyone else is in some variation of the same.

Taylor and his friends are all really funny, if more than a little competitive. Miko refuses to get off the bench during the game, but I play and get pegged in the head by a member of the all-girl opponent team called the Ball-erinas. Afterwards we all go for drinks at a place called The Snake Pit, which isn't nearly as scary as it sounds, and the team has us laughing until our sides hurt with some of their colorful stories. It's a fun afternoon and one of those days that make me think I am actually putting down some little roots in LA.

The last month has been an emotional roller coaster. Max being sick and multiple holiday parties notwithstanding, Selah has been in a bad mood for weeks. I know that's a silly thing to say, because she is always in a bad mood, but ever since the umbrella party and the interaction with Brody, I can't seem to do anything right in her eyes. I spend the last remaining weeks before Christmas running myself into the ground. With my regular workload, her

Christmas shopping, sending out her holiday cards, picking up her
dry cleaning, couriering gift baskets, and all of the other whims
she can dream up in the course of a day, I am utterly exhausted by
the time I board the plane back home. Once I find my seat, I buckle
in and am asleep before we take off. I don't wake up again until we
are pulling up to the gate at the terminal.

The second I turn on my phone I find four texts and seven
e-mails from Selah, all labeled "urgent," though most are questions about where she's put something she can't find or a request
to arrange her oxygen facial. I sit in the seat dealing with each one,
and by the time I finish, I am the last one off the plane.

When I walk out of the small Midland terminal Mama is
already there, looking for me in the crowd. She looks exactly the
same with her sassy blonde bob and the colorful outfit she's recently
snagged from Chico's, no doubt. She's so pretty and has one of the
sweetest dispositions of anyone you're ever likely to meet. Before I
can stop myself I'm running towards her with my roller bag clunk-
ing awkwardly behind me. Then I'm in her arms, and we are both
laughing, and just like that everything feels normal again.

Mama reaches out and squeezes my hips through my coat.
"Baby, you're so *thin!*" she scolds. I don't want to get into a discussion about the downsides of my job, like rarely finding time to eat,
so I slip my arm through hers and change the subject.

"I'm fine. Is Daddy in the car?" I say as we head for the door.

"No, he had deliveries due this mornin', but we'll head over and
meet him for lunch."

She eyes my figure again, worried. I have lost weight, sure, but
in Texas we tend to run a bit on the curvy side so any loss is going
to get noticed.

We walk arm in arm all the way to the truck, and once I've
tossed my suitcase in the back I jump up in the cab to burrow
down next to the heating vent. Out on the highway I take in
the gray day around us. We pass by fields, big plots of land,

and taupe-colored landscape in every direction. It looks sort of depressing. Why does the land I've looked at all my life suddenly seem so dreary, I wonder. And then I realize everything is so spread out and one-dimensional. You don't think about it when you're in a big city, but because of the tall buildings and billboards and the palm trees lining the streets, your eyes tend to travel up and around to see all the color and landscaping. In LA things are pretty simply for the sake of being pretty, and it makes everything here in Texas seem a little flat by comparison.

"So the jobs goin' good?" Mama asks, pulling me out of my head. She's lowered the volume on her *Christmas with Sandi Patti* album and keeps looking at me every few seconds.

"Yes ma'am, just hectic. But it's great because I'm learnin' so much." My accent came back with a vengeance the second I stepped foot on Texas soil.

"Just don't work yourself too hard," she says, and looks at me pensively. "I know you think I'm bein' silly, but you are thin, and you've got dark circles under your eyes."

"Mama, I'm fine!" I singsong. "All I need is home cookin' and some sleep and I'll be perfect! Now tell me what's goin' on: did Rafe survive that knife attack?"

Mama fairly vibrates with excitement. She has to prioritize what to tell me first, because I've just thrown out a question guaranteed to get her talking about something besides me.

"Oh, Landon, you would *not* believe . . . Nobody knows who did it, and he's on all these machines, and he looks just terrible, and Kate, bless her heart, found him in that alley. I don't even know how she'll get through that, I really don't. And Nicole is having all of these fantasies about Eric even though she told him she only wanted to be friends, and, well, Sami and EJ are fightin' again, but you know how Sami is. She's been stirring things up since God was a boy."

There are three things in this world my mama loves passionately: God, her family, and *Days of Our Lives*, in that order. The happenings of Salem are a huge priority for LuJuana Brinkley, and she is absolutely unreachable between the hours of one and two, central time, while her "stories" are on. We spend the whole ride home recounting the intricate plot points from the current season, and I am saved from prying questions for the time being.

I spend the next few days proactively sharing stories from LA. I figure if I cut them off at the pass with info, they won't grill me to get more out. So I tell them about Miko and Max, my apartment, the trip to Sonic . . . really, anything I can think of to stay off the topic of my job. Both my parents believe in hard work, but I know they'd never understand the way SSE is run. I'm fairly certain that my status as an adult would be summarily dismissed if they ever found out the truth. They'll likely remove me bodily from Los Angeles County if they get a whiff of the things Selah does and says.

On Christmas day I get sweet little texts from both Miko and Taylor wishing me well. Max sends me a picture text she's snapped of a drunken Santa passed out in front of Pink Dot, which I guess is as close to a holiday greeting as I'm likely to get from her. I spend the whole of my weeklong holiday—an *excessive* vacation, as Selah has mentioned more than once—wearing sweats, eating my mom's cooking, and watching old movies with my parents. It's absolutely perfect, and by the time I land back in LA I feel energized and excited in a way I haven't since I'd first moved here months ago.

Chapter EIGHTEEN

"My friend Maya is having a party," Miko offers.

I look up from the living room floor where I am reading a back issue of *US Weekly*. Miko is stretched out on the sofa, snacking on Bugles and Fruit by the Foot because, she says, as everyone knows, calories don't count between Christmas and New Year's. Max is wearing her usual annoyed expression, sitting in the chair in the corner while she scrolls through her phone. We've been absolutely worthless all afternoon, spending most of the thirtieth in workout clothes (though I'm pretty sure no one actually worked out today) and trying to figure out what to do tomorrow for New Year's.

"She's pretty cool, but she lives in Venice so it's kind of a haul," Miko continues.

My phone chirps with an e-mail, and after reading it I get to work rearranging Selah's car service for the evening . . . Apparently, she doesn't want to leave her place until ten. It's the third time I've moved the reservation around today, and I am seriously nervous that she'll keep bugging me all night and ruin the holiday.

"What's she need now?" Miko asks me.

"Car service again." I smile up at them. "Selah's headed to some party in the hills; if you want I can see if she'll get us in." I'm teasing.

"I'd rather spend the night getting my yearly at the gynecologist than hang out with her on New Year's." Max tosses me a dirty look.

"How lovely." I toss the look back and drop my phone on the floor next to my magazine.

"What do you guys think of the Venice party?" Miko sings out.

"I'm down for whatever." I leave Miko and Max to figure it out and turn my attention back to the page with a picture of Bradley Cooper buying toilet paper, which proves that stars are *just like us*.

"Well I'm not down. No way am I trekking to Venice on the first New Year's I've had off in the past four!" Max gripes. She untucks her feet from beneath her on the chair and starts to peel her string cheese like a banana.

"Then it's on you, dearie, because you've vetoed every one of my ideas," Miko says, sitting on the sofa arm and then falling back to lay across it lengthwise.

"And you guys are the only people I know, and my only idea was having a Sandra Bullock marathon," I tell them.

"I would rather die first!" Max snaps.

"Dramatica!" Miko scolds in a tone that's pretty dramatic itself.

"Fine." I roll my eyes at Max's theatrics. "Then, I hate to point out the obvious, but you do sort of have some pretty sensational connections for a night like tomorrow."

Max's scowl only deepens, so I keep going. "Or we can stay in . . . *Hope Floats* is actually a lot better than people give it credit for, and I've got *Miss Congeniality 1* and *2* on DVD."

"What's the second one called again?" Miko asks, because she loves to harass Max almost as much as I do.

"*Armed and Fabulous!*" I smile brightly.

Max is already off the chair to grab her phone. "You should both be embarrassed," she calls over her shoulder.

When she comes back into the room a few minutes later she's texting on her phone. Without looking up she steps over me lying prone on the floor and then falls onto the couch.

"OK, Brody said he can take care of us at Twenty-Five if we want to go there. He promised he wouldn't do anything douche-y like give us bottle service."

"What's wrong with bottle service?" Miko whines.

"Bottle service is for tourists," Max informs us both seriously.

I am pretending to be highly engrossed in an article on what Barbara Walters likes to keep in her purse, but I feel a little uneasy with this plan. I haven't seen Brody since the hospital, and I'm not sure exactly how to act around him now. Surely we are more than work associates, because we've gone through something pretty intense together. But we definitely aren't friends. If I think about it, I don't actually know him that well at all.

"Does nine thirty sound OK? I need to tell him a time," Max is asking.

"Yeah sure," I say absentmindedly.

"I'll be here at eight thirty for my first cocktail," Miko says, tossing the now-empty Bugles bag on the coffee table. "Now, out of curiosity, what are you two wearing?"

———

I debate the topic for a while the next day, but the conclusion is foregone. I spend every day of my life in muted black, and I am going out on New Year's Eve in all the full glamorous glory I can muster up. There will be sparkle, there will be perfect curls, and *by God*, there will be lashes . . . a whole strip *and* individuals, because this is a holiday after all. When Miko starts drumming on the door around 8:45 p.m., I've just finished my makeup and feel like

I've done a pretty good job with the Brigitte Bardot thing I'd been going for. I'm only wearing my bra and my black opaque tights, so I throw on my fuzzy pink bathrobe and head to the door.

Miko is on the other side, holding a bottle of champagne and looking adorable in a sleeveless electric-blue romper. Very few people can pull off an outfit like that, but she of course looks fantastic. Her hair is perfectly disheveled, and her smoky eyes and berry-colored lip gloss look awesome. I wonder, and not for the first time, if I'll ever be as effortlessly cool.

"I stole this from my parents at Christmas," she says, waving the bottle at me as she walks past. "So you know it's good!"

"How exciting!" I check out the bottle like I have a clue about champagne. "I don't know if we have flutes, but I can find something—"

Just then Max walks into the kitchen, and we both stop dead in our tracks to stare. She's done her hair and makeup and is rocking a bright-red lipstick that almost no one other than Gwen Stefani can get away with. Her version of the LBD has long sleeves and a short hemline and hugs her perfect body like a second skin. Even though she still has her slippers on, she looks amazing!

"Miss Jennings, as I live and breathe," Miko coos, in a pretty terrible attempt at southern belle.

Max's eyes narrow at her, and she opens her mouth to retaliate, but I cut her off. "Miko was just about to open this very expensive bottle of champagne for us. Do you want some?" I ask sweetly, already pulling glasses from the cupboard.

Max considers it for a moment and apparently comes to the conclusion that good champagne is worth more than chewing out our guest, because she hops up on the counter and reaches for the bottle.

"Give it to me," she demands. "You'll blind yourself with that thing."

Miko hands over the champagne bottle, which is covered with pretty white flowers, and Max proceeds to remove the wire cage and pop the cork like she'd majored in it at school. Once our mismatched glasses are filled we hold them aloft, grinning at one another.

"What should we toast to?" Miko asks.

"To friends?" I volunteer.

"God, Landon." Max sighs. "This isn't a cheesy rom-com."

"To cheesy rom-coms?" Miko tries and succeeds in getting an aggravated look from my roommate.

"Ooh, ooh, I know!" I laugh. "To Sandra Bullock!"

"To Sandy B!" Miko is laughing now too.

And because we are both holding our drinks up towards her, and because it's two against one, and because she has to find us at least a little entertaining since she keeps hanging out with us, Max rolls her eyes and clinks her glass with ours.

"OK." I swallow a sip. "I need to scoot a boot." Miko is already blaring Tegan and Sara from her iPhone because, she says, *someone* needs to DJ, and she just waves me off while she dances around the kitchen with her juice glass of champagne. I head towards my room to get dressed, and Max dogs me down the hallway to her own room. Just before I turn into my doorway, I stop and grab her wrist lightly.

"I know this will annoy you, but I'm going to say it anyway," I say. "You look really pretty."

It takes her a second to respond, and I can see her fighting her natural instinct to say something rude, because I've made her uncomfortable. I'm sure it was only years of Vivian's training that makes her utter a quick thanks and hurry into her room before I do something crazy like try and hug her.

When I come out of my room twenty minutes later Miko and Max are in the dregs of the champagne and laughing about some video they are watching together on YouTube. When they look up I do a full 360 turn for them. My dress is a showstopper, and it deserves proper presentation. I want their opinions, though, in case the showstopping is more of a record scratch than the sort of silent moment of awe I'm going for. I am actually wearing a similar style to Max's dress, short and tight with long sleeves, only mine is gold sequins from head to toe. Back home twenty-three is practically an old maid, and most girls I know are already married so I'd worn this dress to three separate bachelorette parties. Even still I look at them for confirmation . . . hot or not?

"If you weren't my friend, I'd totally hate you. No one should look that good in sequins." Miko smiles.

"I accept that backwards compliment," I say, and walk over to grab my phone from the countertop.

"We tried to call a cab," Miko says sheepishly. "But they said it would be two hours, so we, um . . ." She looks at Max.

"So we both drank the rest of the champagne as fast as we could so you'd be forced to drive us," Max says with a little smirk. "But she and I will split a cab on the way home so we can all drink."

I consider the two Judases on our sofa and roll my eyes.

"You two are rude, and if I wasn't in such a happy mood because of how good these pumps make my legs look, I'd fire you both." I grab my keys. "Now let's get outta here before my hair falls."

———

Our happy mood carries us all the way to the club, which is good because Sunset Boulevard on New Year's Eve is the traffic equivalent of the seventh circle of hell. It takes us over an hour to get there, so by the time we shimmy up to the door with the small XXV sign next to it, it's almost ten thirty. The doorman had apparently been on the lookout for Max: as soon as we get within spitting distance he is on his walkie, and we are promptly ushered into VIP by the general manager, Marco.

We have a small lounge area in VIP, and apparently no one got the memo about bottle service because it is already waiting for us when we arrive. Max throws it a look of disgust and heads off towards the bar without a backwards glance. Miko has no such prejudice about free booze, and she happily starts to make herself some combination of vodka and juice.

A DJ is spinning old-school hip-hop that vibrates off the walls and makes it impossible not to sing along with the chorus. The entire space is packed with the energy of beautiful people yelling conversations over the bass line, and I can see at least four major celebrities in close vicinity. I wonder what it must be costing the bar in revenue to give up one of their premiere tables for us on a night like this.

Max comes snaking through the crowd with three clear shots and hands one to each of us. I take a sniff. Tequila.

This is usually the point in my night where I know: things are going to be really good or very bad. Being handed a shot of tequila, even if it's top shelf, always means you have a big decision to make. Are you gonna have *that* kind of night . . . the kind of night when alcohol isn't just something in the background but an active member of the party. And, just to be clear, in this mythical alcohol party, tequila is your older cousin Crystal whose bras are always a primary color and who is forever talking you into sneaking out to go to high school field parties. In other words, tequila is a bad influence.

"Ugh, I hate tequila!" Miko calls over the music.

Max is staring us both down, not unlike my older cousin Crystal actually. "Tequila is a natural upper, and it's only one tiny shot so stop being a baby."

The two of them go back and forth about the size of the shot and how Miko has an intense tequila gag reflex and is taking no responsibility for what might happen, and somewhere in there I start to laugh. I am with two girls who are quickly becoming the best friends I've ever had, in one of the hottest clubs, in one of the coolest cities in the world, sitting at a lounge next to Rihanna, and I am dressed head to toe in sparkly gold, and my hair and makeup are *working it* tonight. There are a lot of hard decisions to make in life, but what kind of night this would be isn't one of them. I hold up my shot glass, lime wedge at the ready.

"Ladies," I call, and they both stop to look at me. "To Sandra Bullock." I raise my glass and they immediately both clink with me. Probably because it is New Year's and shots are a foregone conclusion, but also because no one should disrespect Sandra, especially after Jesse did such a number on her.

We down them simultaneously, and some of us (Miko) grimace theatrically and some of us (Max) act like it doesn't affect her at all, but all of us are in a happy place approximately seven minutes later. It is, officially, the greatest New Year's ever!

A little while later we're all standing around our lounge area sipping some sort of muddled creation Max has talked the bartender into making for us, even though she is drinking water. I am engaged in a pretty fierce debate with a few members of Rihanna's twenty-person entourage about whether we should all start up some kind of dance battle (because, like I mentioned, tequila makes me dream up things like dance battles). My new friends and I are laughing hysterically, and I am just about to show them my own version of crunking when Brody walks up. He's with his brother Liam, whom I'd met quickly at the hospital but hadn't really had time to notice in the chaos of that morning. Liam is shorter and his hair a bit darker, but he is really handsome in his own right. He has an easy smile and a laid-back energy that stands in direct opposition to his older brother.

I'm still not sure how to act around Brody, but my mama raised me with manners, and at the very least I need to thank him for hosting us.

"And I think you know Landon," Max says as I walk up.

I stick out my hand. "It's Liam, right?"

"It's nice to see you again." He smiles at me sincerely. "I'm sorry I didn't get a chance to tell you before how much we appreciate everything you did for Mackenzie."

"Liam—" Max warns him.

Brody must sense her distress because he interrupts her with a swift change of subject.

"Looks like you were having quite a debate there." He nods towards my new friends.

I smile at him, grateful that he's helping Max and even more grateful for an easy conversation.

"They're backup dancers. I was challenging them to a duel of sorts," I say flippantly, because besides fueling great ideas, tequila also dissolves the filter between my brain and my mouth.

"A duel?" Liam laughs.

"A dance-off," I tell him with mock seriousness.

"Interpretive?" he teases.

"Hip-hop," I answer.

"You're a hip-hop dancer?" Max asks, incredulous.

"God no!" I giggle at her. "But even if I was terrible, I'd be able to say I went all *Step Up 2* with Rihanna's backup dancers, and that'd be awesome!"

Liam laughs and even Max manages to smile, but Brody isn't quite so joyful. I'm beginning to understand why everyone seemed so surprised on Thanksgiving; he clearly doesn't laugh easily. I take another sip of my drink and bop along while Timberlake brings sexy back over the loudspeakers.

A beautiful woman walks up dressed as a vintage cigarette girl, and I am so busy checking out her flawless makeup that I don't even notice her tray until Miko waltzes up to it.

"What are those?" she coos, and points at the girl's tray, covered with individual shots that are smoking. Dry ice maybe?

"Those are the Twenty-Five; they're our signature shot. You should try it." Brody takes shots from the tray and hands one to each of us.

I sniff it dubiously. It doesn't smell bad, but it does smell like gin, and mixing different types of liquor is probably a very bad idea. I look up at Miko, who is already half in the bag. But Max is actually sort of grinning happily for once, and she says, "To Sandra?"

And then Miko and I go along immediately, because that's the theme of the night.

"To Sandra!" we yell.

And then the bad idea is down my throat and it's too late to take it back. The Ashton brothers are staring at us with confused expressions, but I just ignore them.

Miko turns to me suddenly. "Should we dance?"

She asks the question the same way you might ask if you should get bangs or become a vegetarian.

"We *should* dance," I tell Miko, like it is the best idea I'd ever heard of . . . and right then it sort of is the best idea I'd ever heard.

"There's not enough liquor in the world," Max warns when we look to her. Then she plops down on the lounge with Brody following suit. Liam wishes us a fun night, and I wave to him as I bop and weave my way to the dance floor.

For the next three songs we jump and shimmy and sway, and at one point I do the sprinkler, and it's awesome because even lame dance moves are forgiven on New Year's. Finally the DJ puts on something a bit too techno for my taste, and we use the opportunity to bounce back to the table for water.

Miko gets there first and falls in a heap next to Max, which means I have nowhere to sit except next to Brody. He is lounging on a sofa in his perfectly tailored three-piece suit, sipping on a Perrier like he has nowhere better to be when, really, there must be a dozen cooler prospects for him on a night like this. Where is his latest hot date? Surely someone like him is a hot commodity as a New Year's date.

I grab for a bottle of water, and I look back at the crowd on the dance floor while I drink it.

"How was your Christmas?" he asks after a minute.

I turn around to frown at him . . . Are we making small talk now?

"Fine, thanks. How was yours?"

"It was good. Look, I meant to apologize for the, uh"—he seems to struggle for words—"dry cleaning thing. But then I forgot to—with everything else."

God, I can't believe he even remembers that interaction, especially after everything that happened afterwards. Why is he bringing it up now? Why is he still talking?

"I didn't anticipate her reaction. It was never my intention to get you into trouble."

I mean to dodge this subject altogether, but his first line mixed with the liquor in my bloodstream pulls me up short. How can so many people who work directly with Selah remain blind to the terrible things she does? I know he's a man, and she's gorgeous, but surely you'd be able to see through her crap after working with her a dozen times, right?

"You didn't think she'd react that way," I wonder aloud.

Can he really be that clueless?

"Of course not. I know events can be tense so she was likely stressed, but her reaction was completely irrational." He says it like that settles everything.

She was stressed out? Is he actually making excuses for the way she acts? As if it's a one-time occurrence. As if it can all be explained away in one moment of irrational-ness! *Is that even a word?*

"Irrational?" I screech.

I'm afraid the last bits of practical thought washed away with that smoky shot, and I'm officially a little drunk and a whole lot pissed off. Miko and Max snap to attention and are both staring at me, and it takes me a minute to realize it's because I'm laughing like a lunatic.

"*Irrational*," I say again. "She once made me work until midnight, changing all her hanging files from white to off-white because she said she wanted them to be 'white-*ish*' not 'white-*white*'! And you know what, I don't even know what that *means*, but I did it!" I slam the water bottle down on the table. "And the week before Thanksgiving, Mark at the Coffee Bean was having a really bad day—he must have put two pumps of sugar-free vanilla in her coffee instead of one—and when she tasted it she screamed at me for *nine minutes* about how even a monkey could do a better job than I do! *Nine. Freaking. Minutes!* I know because I actually timed it with my stopwatch app! And do you know how many times she called me on Christmas? Not the day before or the day after, but the actual holiday? Don't guess, I'll tell you: eleven! I left the table during Christmas dinner to answer a call about how to work her TiVo!" I'm absolutely indignant, and all three of them are looking at me nervously, but I just keep yelling and pointing an angry finger in random directions. "And once she made Miko throw up over dolphin-safe tuna!"

"Grilled shrimp," Miko corrects me helpfully.

"Same difference!" I glare at Brody because he officially represents every man who has ever made excuses for a woman's bad behavior because she has a nice rack. "And this is only the teeniest tiniest evidence of her being *irrational*! Which *you* should know because she's working at being your girlfriend like it's her part-time job! But maybe anorexic mean-girls are attractive to you, what do I know?" Brody opens his mouth to say something, but I hold up my hand to cut him off. "What I do know is that she doesn't even want me borrowing her stapler, so how are you *surprised* that she might have issues with me saying one word to you?"

"What are you talking about?" Brody asks at the same time Max barks.

"Ugh! No way. Brody might be a man-whore but he wouldn't touch her with a ten-foot pole!"

Now that my tirade is over I'm having a little trouble getting my heart rate to slow down.

"While 'man-whore' seems a little judgmental"—he rolls his eyes—"Max is right. I don't have any interest in Selah outside of work." Then, because he can't seem to help himself, he adds, "But just to clarify, the pole in question is nine feet at the absolute most."

Max and Miko laugh nervously, but when I don't join in the sound falls away. Even with Brody's attempt to diffuse the tension with a joke, there is no covering up the full-on trip I've just taken to Crazy Town.

I've screamed at him, a person who—in my mind, if I went back over every single interaction we'd had and, believe me, I'll spend the next week doing exactly that—had never been anything but professional at the very least and actually friendly in his own aloof way. I'm pretty sure that even if the tequila isn't going to make me puke, the embarrassment definitely is.

"Will y'all excuse me for just a moment?" I mean to sound breezy, but it comes out strangled.

Dang it! Stupid nervous accent!

Miko makes a move to come with me, but I wave her back down.

"I'll only be a sec." I grab my clutch and hurry to the women's restroom as fast as my five-inch heels can carry me.

Insider information . . . the line for the stalls don't take nearly that long in VIP. So I have to come up with a way to kill some more time. Once I wash my hands and spend five extra minutes adding lip gloss and fluffing my hair, I have no other choice but to go outside and apologize. I take a deep breath, suddenly feeling depressingly sober, and head back out into the hallway.

I walk a few feet and turn a corner only to find Brody blocking my way. He looks a lot like the first time I saw him, so serious, so grown-up . . . He makes me feel about five years old.

"I'm so sorry." I want so desperately to look anywhere but at him, but I don't want to be a coward. "I—it's been—a stressful month, and I have no idea why I took it out on you. You just—"

"Have this uncanny ability to say things that set you off. I swear it's not intentional." He says this with a little smile.

A loud rumble of sound starts to grow from the other room, and it distracts me long enough to lose my train of thought. Over Brody's shoulder I can see waitstaff handing out hats and noise-makers to the dancing crowd. I hadn't realized how close we are to midnight.

I open my mouth to continue the apology, but he cuts me off. "I'm thinking we should start again."

"I'm sorry?" I'm confused.

"We've gotten off to a rocky start. We should start again. No misconceptions, no muffin-induced near-death experiences, no advice—"

The muffin comment is below the belt, but also sort of the perfect thing to say because I'm smiling again, and five minutes ago I wouldn't have thought I'd ever feel comfortable in his presence again.

"Let's pretend we're meeting for the first time."

The idea is so sweet and so unlike anything I'd ever expect him to say. Maybe that's the point, though, maybe I don't actually know him at all.

He sticks out his hand.

Behind him the room of people start chanting.

Ten, nine, eight . . .

I look down at his hand and then back up into his face.

"I'm Brody." He smiles a little, only this smile isn't the sharp businessman smile; it isn't cocky or sexy or even a smirk. He looks a little shy, like maybe he feels sort of ridiculous for holding his hand in midair, waiting for me to make the next move.

Seven, six, five . . .

And I can't even help myself; I smile back. In fact, I think I fairly beam at this too-beautiful man who doesn't have any reason to try and make me feel better but is doing it anyway.

Four, three, two, one!

As the crowd starts blowing noisemakers and singing "Auld Lang Syne," I reach out and put my hand inside of his.

"I'm Landon."

This isn't the first time he's ever touched me, but it's the first time I've anticipated what it would feel like when he does. Tingles work their way up my arm and around the back of my neck.

Brody breaks out into a full-blown grin.

"It's nice to finally meet you," he says softly, and then, without letting go of my hand, he leans in and gives me a light kiss on my cheek.

I'm so startled, and he must see the question on my face because he shrugs and says, "It's New Year's."

———

After walking me back to the lounge Brody heads off to check in with his staff, and I'm relieved to see him go. For some reason I feel even more nervous around him than before.

Max hands me another shot of tequila as soon as I walk up to the lounge. I clink glasses with her, and we both mutter Sandra's name . . . Because now it just feels like bad luck not to.

"So . . . That was awkward," she says at last.

I sigh. "It really, really was. I'm sorry about screaming at your brother."

"I could have told you, had you just asked," she says earnestly. Then her face changes to one of annoyance. "Honestly, Landon, I can't believe you think anyone related to me would be interested in someone so vile."

"Well, she is really pretty . . ."

"And a terrible person."

She looks at me seriously. "Look, I don't like conversations like this but I've had a lot of tequila so you're going to have to deal, OK?"

"OK—"

"Landon, the stuff you said, the stuff she does and says to you . . . It's bullshit! No job is worth all of that! You need to stand up for yourself or leave altogether."

I smile sadly because I can tell how uncomfortable it makes her to have a serious conversation, and God bless her for being worked up on my behalf.

"I know what you're saying, I really do. But it's only been four months, and I know once I prove myself she'll see that I'm—"

"No, she won't!" Max spits at me. "You're being naive. It's not going to get better unless you—"

"I found snacks!" Miko singsongs her way into our midst bearing a platter piled high with sliders, little tomato soups with grilled cheese, and various kinds of cookies. It looks delicious, and it's a welcome distraction from the tense conversation. I grab a slider and take a bite.

"Where did you find these?" I ask between bites.

Max looks like she's debating whether or not to continue our conversation, but the late-night grub wins out. She plops down on the sofa in front of the tray.

"There are servers passing them around so I snuck into the kitchen looking official and did a swipe." She breaks off a piece of cookie and pops it into her mouth. "It was just like a Mentos commercial."

"Good work!" I grab a grilled cheese and ignore the soup it came with. "So should we have another drink before we wrap this night up?"

"We should!" Miko says happily.

"I'm on it!" Max gets up and heads to the bar.

Two hours later we've danced our way to last call. Well, Miko and I dance; Max mostly makes fun of us from the sofa while blatantly ignoring the overtures of every male in the room, but we're all laughing and out of breath by the time we decide we need to call a cab.

"I texted Brody to have someone call for us." Max looks up from her phone.

I've officially danced my hair into a sweaty rat's nest, so I pull it into a big messy bun on top of my head. I can't wait to get home and into my pajamas!

"Did Marco get us a cab?" Max asks someone behind me.

"Two a.m. on New Year's will take at least another hour and half a week's pay to get a cab home. I can drive you guys," Brody says, walking up.

He's removed his jacket, and his sleeves are rolled up on his arms. I must be drunker than I thought because all I can think about is how long he has to work out to have arms that look like that and how someone who works inside all day has skin so tan.

Bad thought, Landon. Bad thought! I blink twice to clear my head.

"You don't have to drive us. That would be such a pain."

I expect the other girls to back me up, but Miko looks like she's about to fall asleep and Max is already pulling on her jacket, ready to get out of here.

"It's no trouble. I don't mind." Brody reaches over to help Max with her coat.

Nobody else puts up a fight, so I don't either. I just follow them down to the main floor and out to valet.

"Where's your ticket?" Brody asks us.

Everyone looks at me, and I realize what he's asking. "You want to drive my car?" I ask incredulously.

"I have a parking spot here and you don't." He says it like it should be obvious. "Plus I'm sure you'll need it tomorrow."

"But what about you? How will you get home after you drive us there?" I try and argue.

"I'll manage, don't worry. Ticket?" he asks again.

All right, Mr. Moneybags wants to drive my crappy car? This should be interesting. I hand him the ticket, and the valet hustles out to get it. When he pulls up I get in the front seat with Brody, and Max sits behind me. Miko is asleep in the back before I even buckle my seatbelt.

I glance at Brody, and he's staring dubiously around my car's interior like something might give him tetanus if he's not careful. I can't help but smile at this millionaire sitting behind the wheel of my *twice*-previously owned clunker.

"What vintage is this, exactly?" he asks, with a little furrow in his brow.

"Ninety-seven. It was a good year for Ford." I smile brightly. "But I'm sure they'd bring your car around if this isn't up to your standards."

"I'm sure I have no idea what you're talking about." He makes an elaborate show of getting comfortable in the seat.

"Oh my gosh." I giggle. "You're a total snob."

Brody pulls the car out into traffic but he doesn't even try and defend himself.

"I am, a little. But it's a knee-jerk reaction that I blame entirely on my parents. A few minutes in and I'm totally fine." He taps the dashboard affectionately. "In fact, I really like this car. I think I'm going to get a fleet just like this one. Complete with the little vanil-la-scented trees." He nods at the air freshener hanging from my gearshift.

"Such a jerk." I shake my head and hit the button to turn on the radio.

The whole car shakes with the sound of ABBA's "Dancing Queen," which is where we'd left off in my New Year's playlist earlier.

Max groans in the backseat. "Not this again!"

I laugh. "I told you that if I had to drive, I also got to pick the music. Remember that the next time you want me to be your sober sister."

I reach for my iPod to change up the music.

"Oh no, you can't cover it up. Now we know all about your dark love of Swedish pop," Brody taunts playfully.

It's funny, tonight he seems so young and carefree and so very un-Brody-like. I lower the volume a bit but not all the way. ABBA is one of my favorites, and I'm not ashamed of it.

"This isn't the only thing I listen to, it's just what happened to be on when I shut the car off."

"Yes, I'm sure your musical taste is extensive." Brody doesn't sound convinced at all. Max snorts from the backseat.

"It *is* extensive. I listen to everything, and I know all the words," I challenge them both.

"All the words?" Max scoots over, rebuckles in the middle seat, and reaches for my pink iPod that's connected to a cord in the cigarette lighter.

Without missing a beat I start crooning about digging The Dancing Queen. I should probably be embarrassed because I've just unleashed my terrible voice on them both, but I've had tequila, so . . .

"Hmm . . ." she says, scrolling through the songs in my collection.

There are hundreds upon hundreds of every genre. I have no idea what she expects to find. She presses the button and Kenny Rogers is singing to us now.

So I sing right along with "The Gambler." I start with the train bound for nowhere, and end up well past the chorus before I start giggling.

"Kenny Rogers is how you thought you'd stump me? *Really*?" I laugh at her over my shoulder.

"Don't get too cocky yet, princess," Max says and presses the button again. Now the Black Crowes are singing.

I don't even miss the opening line; I jump right in there with them about being "Hard to Handle."

The song switches without warning but I don't even flinch.

I rap right along with LL Cool J to the old-school mix, including choreographed hand motions when the explosion sound effect hits the car's speakers.

I understand why she thought I might not know that one, but the joke's on her because all us girls learned the lyrics at Britney Thompson's slumber party in eighth grade.

"OK, hold on, this isn't challenging enough." Brody grabs the iPod from her and starts scrolling through the songs himself. It takes a minute since he's also trying to watch the traffic in front of us, and I wait in giddy anticipation. Finally he selects one.

The music comes out, a distinctly eighties sound.

"Ah—" I smile. "I see what you've done here," I call over the loud music.

Brody just smirks back at me.

"You've picked a Whitney Houston song, thinking I won't possibly embarrass myself further by trying to hit the high notes in front of you guys."

Brody turns the car down another street and looks over at me in challenge.

"But there's something you don't know about me," I say seriously.

"And what's that?" he asks.

"You don't know that—that—" I'm stalling, waiting for the right part in the song, and he must know it too because he starts chuckling silently. And then it's the perfect moment, and both Whitney and I are belting it out about wanting someone to dance with.

I'm bouncing along in my seat, well aware that I look and sound ridiculous, but far too thrilled to be winning this game than to care about it.

"You're such a nerd," Max says from the backseat.

I lower the music and nod in agreement. "Yes, but in my defense, I never claimed to be cool."

After that I turn the regular radio on because Max says her ears would start bleeding if she has to listen to anything else of mine. Thirty minutes later we pull inside our parking garage, and Miko springs up like a jack-in-the-box as soon as the car is in park.

"Ugh!" she moans. "I need some water and, like, half a bottle of Tylenol I think."

She gets herself out of the car with the grace of a baby rhino and drapes herself across Max for support, ignoring the annoyed sounds of protest she gets in response.

"Lead on, captain!" she says through half-closed eyes.

Max snorts, but starts helping her to the lobby anyway. Brody and I follow behind them, but by the time we get there they've already gone up in the elevator. I've removed my shoes; I'm suddenly hyperaware of how much taller he is than me.

"Let me wait with you until you get a cab." I turn and head for the doors to the street without waiting for a response.

He follows me out front and types something quickly into his phone. He drops it back in his pocket and looks down at me. I feel nervous again, and also very short as I look up at him. I need to fill the silence.

"Thank you so much for the ride and for everything tonight. We had such a good time." I swing my heels back and forth in my hand, anxious.

"I'm glad you had fun." He smiles sincerely.

I look down at my stocking feet.

"We need to go on a date."

My head snaps up in utter shock.

He's asking me on a date? He's asking me on a date. I open my mouth but no words come out. I'm fairly sure I look like a deer in the headlights.

I've never even been on a real date before, because I doubt this man would count football games and group outings to the Dairy Queen a "real" anything.

"We can't go on a date." My voice sounds strangled.

He actually laughs. "And why not?"

I clamber for some explanation that makes sense.

"Because we work together—well *sort of.* Because if my boss finds out, she'll freak!" I'm counting the reasons off on my fingers as I come up with them in exasperation. "Because I hardly know you. And you're, like, thirty—"

"Thirty-two actually," he adds helpfully.

"Thirty-two!" I point at him accusingly "See there, you're nine years older than I am! No. I'm sorry. We can't go on a date." I have the strongest urge to put my shoes back on like some kind of armor.

"OK, we won't go on a date," he agrees.

Well that was a little too easy . . .

Now I do start slipping my shoes back on because, even if it seems ridiculous, I need some height for this conversation.

He offers me a hand to steady myself but I bat it away. When I'm back on higher ground, I look at him in challenge. He runs a hand through his hair, but it flops right back over his forehead. I wonder if anyone has ever told him he looks like a Calvin Klein ad.

"We'll go on a *non*-date."

"What's a non-date?" I'm suspicious.

"Two people, hanging out together somewhere, with food involved, and maybe alcohol . . . but with the express understanding that it's *not* a date."

And dang it, I smile, because it's the most ridiculous and adorable thing anyone has ever said to me.

"But you just asked me out."

"And?"

"Then your non-date is just a date in disguise." I'm losing traction in this argument. I just know it.

"No, it won't be a date. It'll be terrible, I promise. I'll pick an uncomfortable location, I'll talk about myself the whole time, you won't enjoy it at all." He holds his hand over his heart like he's making a pledge.

This whole thing is a terrible idea, absolutely destined for failure. How does he not realize that?

"I can't date you!" I say desperately.

"Why not?"

"Because you're all," I flap one hand in his direction, "this. And I'm all," I make an inarticulate sound and flap the hand around myself, "*not* like you."

We're not in the same league; we're not even on the same planet!

"I like you," he says, like this solves everything.

I'm flustered and can't stop myself from asking.

"*Why*?" I'm staring right at him, which sort of makes me breathless, and the question comes out as a nervous little whisper.

He cocks his head to the side and studies me for a second. "Because you're sarcastic and funny, and you fought me over paying for your drinks tonight when you must know that I can afford it." As if on cue, a black town car pulls up to the curb. He gives it a quick wave of acknowledgment, then turns back to me. "You're smart, and you work so hard to do a good job even if you never get credit for it. And because I thought you were adorable the first time I saw you, which is saying a lot since you were choking." I glare at him and he chuckles. "I liked you then, and I didn't even know that someday you'd tell me embarrassing stories in a hospital waiting room, or sing Kenny Rogers, or do the absolute worst sprinkler I've ever seen."

He couldn't have shocked me more if he'd slapped me. I can't believe he's been paying attention this entire time . . . that he noticed me at all.

"But you said I was silly." It's a last-ditch effort to restore sanity.

"In the best possible way." He reaches for me slowly.

Oh Lord, Baby Jesus in the manger!

I've never been in this position before with someone who looks like him, so I panic. I throw my hands up between us and screech the first thing that pops into my head. "Don't try to kiss me!"

Dear Heavenly Father, if ever there was a moment for the rapture to come and spirit me away, it would be so great if it could happen right now.

I am mortified by what has just fallen out of my mouth. I have no idea how to do any of this, and I know that probably no one has ever said something so idiotic to someone so beautiful, but I'm incredibly nervous, and I don't even *hold hands* with guys I barely know. I definitely can't handle a kiss.

Brody takes a step back and puts his own hands up in mock surrender. I can tell he's trying hard not to laugh, and I would hate him for it if I didn't already hate myself so much.

"I wasn't going to kiss you, I swear." He smiles. "I was going to reach for your hand. But I'll just stay over here if that makes you more comfortable."

At this point I've lost all shred of dignity so I just go for broke.

"See, you don't want to go on a date with me. I'm absolutely clueless! I don't know how to flirt properly, I say the wrong things; I'm not at all like the women you usually date."

"I know," he says, taking a small step forward. "That's one of the things I like about you most."

One of the things I like about you most.

OneOfTheThingsILikeAboutYouMost.

Like. About. You. Most.

The words pinball around my brain.

He likes me?

His blue eyes look right into mine, and he has this little half smile on his face like he knows a thousand things I don't know. When I just continue to gape at him, he smirks . . . He knows he's won.

"So, next Saturday then?"

"Sure," I reply weakly.

He doesn't make any move towards me. Maybe he's worried I'll panic again . . . Smart man. He gives me a little salute and turns towards the black town car still idling at the curb.

"Who's that?" I call after him.

"That's my driver." He looks back. "I had him meet me."

I'm stupefied. "I thought you were taking a cab."

He shudders dramatically. "Come now, you must realize I'm far too snobby to take a cab. Now head back in the lobby so I know you got in safely."

I wave stupidly and let myself in the building without a backwards glance.

What kind of man has a car meet him at 3:00 a.m. on New Year's just so he can drive his sister and her drunk friends back to a crappy apartment in Hollywood? And what kind of money do you need in order to have a driver on call? Honestly, I'm not even sure I want to know the answer to that. *Oh man, I'm in so far over my head.*

———

When I get back upstairs to the apartment I find Miko passed out on our couch in a jumble of blankets with her clothes and makeup still on. At least Max has covered her up.

I pull off my heels and pad down the hallway but stop short when I see Max sitting on my bed, waiting for me. She's still wearing her dress and looks up as I come in the room.

"What's going on with you guys?" There's no preamble.

"What do you—"

"Don't patronize me. It's too early in the morning for that." When I don't respond she continues. "You blush every time you see him."

"I do not blush!" I say indignantly.

Do I?

"You do; and when he speaks to you you're either stuttering or having verbal diarrhea."

"I get it," I grumble.

"It's embarrassing to let a guy affect you like that. He clearly makes you nervous."

"Of course he makes me nervous!" I burst out. "Have you *seen* him?"

"Barf!! He's my brother." She scowls at me in the lamplight.

I blow all the air out of my lungs. She's right, he is her brother and this is totally inappropriate and likely only going to end awkwardly. As if I need another reason not to be interested in this person.

Wait, am I interested in this person?

Crap.

This breaks some sort of roommate code for sure.

"You're right, I'm sorry. But don't worry, nothing is going to happen."

Max taps her fingertips on her knees in thought, then starts speaking without looking my way.

"Don't be sorry; you didn't do anything. You're both adults, and you can do whatever you want." She takes a deep breath, and I can tell having two personal conversations with me in one night is her worst nightmare come true. "Brody is a good guy, and I love him. But honestly, he dates a lot of women. And you, I'm guessing, haven't really dated much and especially not someone like him—"

"Who said anything about dating?" I squeak.

How does she know?

Her look says she's not buying anything I'm selling. I become suddenly very interested in my manicure.

"I'm just—I want you to be careful. I don't want you getting hurt."

"That's really sweet of you—" I say quietly.

"Whatever!" She stands up abruptly. "It took me forever to find a roommate who only mildly annoyed me. I don't want to have to look for someone again if—no, *when* this whole *whatever*," she says the word distastefully, "goes up like Chernobyl."

"I understand." It's all I can think to say.

"All right then." She heads out of my room as quickly as possible.

I am totally baffled by the direction this night has taken. I want to replay everything in my mind and figure out the exact moment it started jumping off the rails, but my brain is too fuzzy. Finally I give up. I'm not going to figure out anything at this hour. I stare at the bed for a moment before slipping out of everything but my panties. Then in an act that goes against everything I believe in, I climb into bed and fall asleep without washing off my makeup.

Chapter NINETEEN

"I have some news," Selah announces as she walks into the all-hands meeting.

It's so out of character for her to walk into the room ready to actually start the meeting that everyone instantly falls silent. She sits down in her chair and looks around the table for dramatic effect.

"We're going to Sundance again this year."

I have to stop myself from gasping. This news is far too cool to even be believed! Clearly no one else agrees, though, because all around me groans and sighs fill the conference room. Everyone starts speaking at once.

"It's three weeks away. There's no way we can dress out a space on that notice."

"How will we lodge everyone? There's nowhere left to stay."

"What location is even still available?"

I can't believe anything would encourage this kind of mutiny. No one ever openly disagrees with Selah, but the entire staff is questioning her decision. Selah holds up a hand and signals for everyone to quiet down. I expect her to start screaming, but when she opens her mouth she's . . . *cajoling*. It's like she needs to convince them. I'm so confused.

"I know, it's an impossible task, but we have to do it. SSE is the best, and we do the impossible every day. Riverton decided that they absolutely have to go, and they've asked Barker-Ash to partner. They were decided before they even contacted me, so now it's either make this happen or allow them to bring in another firm. That's not an option," she adds sharply.

The room is still tense but resigned. Everyone here knows what it would mean for SSE if it allowed a client like Riverton and a partner like Barker-Ash to work with another event-planning firm. We'd run the risk of losing them both. I'm still unsure why there is even a debate. The Sundance Film Festival is one of the coolest events you could ever dream of working. It's a week where celebrities of every letter grade congregate to do press and ski down mountains in Utah. Some of the biggest restaurants and clubs set up satellite venues, and every kind of luxury brand jumps on board in the hopes that Ashton Kutcher will get snapped holding their product while running down a snow-lined street, trying to escape the paparazzi. It sounds like the greatest thing ever!

"Now, the good news is," Selah continues, "that I already called my contacts and found out there are still three spaces left. I decided to go with the same venue we had last year."

Taylor and the production team start to voice very strong opinions on the issues with the space from last year, but Selah cuts them off. "We're already familiar with the space, and yes there were issues, but we don't have time to start from scratch. Now, production, please work with Brinkley on who's handling what. Between pulling the permits, arranging the parking, calling in local vendors, booking travel, and finding housing, there are too many logistics and too little time. Jin, you and your team can follow me to my office and we'll talk about the design of the space. As soon as people hear that we have a venue everyone is going to want to book a party. I think it's best to go ahead and design ten to twelve layouts that we can easily pull off in the time allotted, and then when the parties are confirmed we'll talk them into choosing one of our existing concepts."

Everyone in the room looks miserable, but they don't say anything else. When Selah finally stands to leave the room, the design team follows, but I grab Miko's arm before she walks out. I look around quickly to make sure I won't be overheard.

"I know it's short notice, but isn't this good news? All of us up in the mountains for a week . . . it'll be just like camp, only with cool celebrity parties." I bump her with my elbow playfully.

She looks bleak. "That's what everyone thinks before they go the first time. As far as event planning goes, Sundance is the killing fields! It's ten days in this tiny town in the mountains, and you have to truck everything in from LA because God forbid Selah would use a local vendor. The space is open all day and then the parties go on all night, and Selah always overbooks us for events, so sometimes we'll have three parties in a single evening with, like, a twenty-minute changeover. Oh, and there's always a crazy publicist screaming at you about the two hundred people who should have been let in an hour ago or the fact that they want you to turn off the smoke alarms so Bai Ling can smoke indoors!"

"Is Bai Ling even still relevant?" I try to tease her out of her mood.

"It doesn't matter, she'll be there." She sighs. "I've gotta go. We have twelve different events to design, and she'll probably want options by tomorrow. Oh God, I thought we'd escaped it this year." She turns to go.

"I'll get you a coffee!" I call after her.

"And a cookie—two cookies!" Miko calls back.

I run to grab my wallet out of my bag so I can sneak out and get some sugar for Miko. I believe her, and I'm sure the festival won't be easy, but I can't help but be excited. It's such a cool thing to get to do, and I've seen pictures of it in magazines for years; I can't wait to see it in person.

I pull out my wallet and snag my phone while I'm in my purse. I see a text message from Brody, and my stomach flips. I haven't had any contact with him since New Year's.

BRODY ASHTON:
You never followed up, so I
assume you think I'll just forget.
I'm calling in the non-date. I'll pick
you up on Sat @ 6AM

What the heck? Six in the morning? Is he insane?

Are you insane?? I can't be functional
before noon!

His response is almost instantaneous.

BRODY ASHTON:
I promised you a terrible
experience. Sleep deprivation
will play into that nicely. 6AM.
I'll bring caffeine.

OK, I can't help it. I'm more than a little curious about what kind of outing might happen at six on a Saturday morning. I text:

Where exactly are we going?

BRODY ASHTON:
You'll see. Bring your swimsuit . . .

What?

My swimsuit??? It's January!

BRODY ASHTON:
See you Saturday.

He has a maddening habit of ignoring my protests, or maybe he doesn't even hear them because he's so used to girls just doing whatever he says. I'm trying to come up with some sort of cutting response, but Selah does the one-buzz summon. I drop both the phone and the wallet and hurry to jump into the Sundance frenzy. Soon the coffee trip and text messages are long forgotten.

Chapter TWENTY

When I open the door of my lobby on Saturday and step out into the still dark morning, the cold hits me in full force. I wrap my arms around my favorite Longhorns sweatshirt to hold in some warmth and don't even try and cover the miserable look on my face. I'll be honest, I don't look cute at all in my leggings and UGGs, and my hair is in a massive bun, but it's a miracle he got me out of bed at all. Looking good isn't possible at this time of day. There's a cherry-red vintage Bronco idling at the curb, and since it's the only car with the engine on I walk over to it. I'm more than a little surprised that this is what he's driving. Shouldn't he be in something flashier? I open the passenger door and the overhead light comes on, revealing Brody in a faded red hoodie. With the hood on he looks normal, young even, and far too awake and perky for this time of day.

"Good morning, sunshine!" He smiles and it lights up his whole face, and for a second I'm way less annoyed about the hour. That is, until I step up on the running board and my brain processes his outfit: board shorts? Then I notice the two surfboards hanging out the back of the jeep. I stare at the offending objects without moving to take a seat. I'd thought the request for a swim-suit might be for use at a spa or even in a possibly creepy scenario involving a hot tub. But going to the beach in the middle of winter? That has never even crossed my mind.

"Please tell me you're joking," I say miserably.

"I promised you a horrible experience," he says and gently pulls on my elbow until I'm forced into the seat. "And this has all the makings of one."

I snort inelegantly and buckle my seatbelt.

"First of all," he says as he reaches into a cup holder and hands me a to-go mug, "the promised caffeine. I'll have you know there isn't a single coffee place open this early. I had to make you that myself," he says with mock seriousness.

He's so cute with his hood pulled down over his ears. I cover up my smile by taking a sip of coffee.

"Thank you."

"So, like I was saying about the horrible experience," he says, throwing the car into first and driving down the street. "This will be one of the worst."

"You won't hear an argument from me," I grumble.

Brody ignores me. "First of all, it's winter and it's freezing and the water is so cold it feels a little like you're dying. Also, I'm taking you to do something that *I* like to do, with no concern or thought about what you'd prefer. Then we add in time of day." He looks over at me with a wink, and despite myself I'm feeling a lot more awake. "*And* the whole swimsuit thing. I mean, being half-naked on a first date—"

"Non-date," I correct him.

"Being half-naked on our first non-date, that's a lot of pressure for you."

I can't help the laugh that escapes my lips. "You're such a jerk."

"Totally. But you agreed to come, so now you're stuck with me for a while."

I'm a little disoriented by this laid-back version of Brody that's so at odds with the stoic, executive version. Regardless, I'm in this cool car with the prettiest guy I've ever met, headed out on the most creative date anyone's ever come up with. I decide not to overthink it. I tuck one of my boots up underneath me on the seat and watch the dark buildings zip by my window.

———

We drive to Santa Monica because, according to Brody, the easier waves there are good for a first-timer. I have to change in the public restroom, and I have to tell you, getting on a wetsuit by yourself in the freezing, smelly beach bathroom is pretty damn terrible. I finally squeeze into everything but it's a close call. I am starting to think that maybe he really is trying to make this day terrible and that it's not a joke.

But then I walk out onto the sand, and he is there on his knees, rubbing wax onto one of the boards, and I forget about whether or not the date is terrible or that I am cold or how my thighs look in this unflattering neoprene. At this point I might not be able to tell you my name. He is wearing a wetsuit but doesn't zip it up all the way, so it is hanging down from his waist, leaving his too-perfect back bare for public viewing . . . And, well, I guess this explains the whole question of why he's so tan.

His hair has turned wavy in the sea air and keeps falling into his face as he works. When he looks up at me he flashes a grin and sits back on his haunches, and it's the first time I get a full view of his abs. I may or may not have tripped in the sand. I try and cover it up by searching the sand for the imaginary impediment to my step.

Who has abs like that?

Who goes shirtless when it's fifty degrees out?

By the time I walk up next to him I've lost the power of speech.

"Are you ready for this?" he asks.

He stands and I look beyond him to the gray water already dotted with surfers. The terror of what he's asking me to do quickly takes over any giddiness I might have felt about the state of his six-pack. The waves aren't really big, but I can't even imagine forcing my cold feet into the surf, let alone throwing myself into the churning water. I watch as one of the surfers pops up on a wave and almost immediately gets dragged under.

"Absolutely not," I say, not taking my eyes from the cold water.

He zips himself into the rest of his wetsuit and hands me one of his boards. He props the other under his arm and turns towards the water.

"Don't be a baby—"

"I'm not a baby!" I say indignantly and follow behind him slowly.

My argument is quickly squashed, though, because as soon as my toes touch the surf I scream and run in the opposite direction. Cute boy or not, there is no freaking way I'm going in that icy water!

"I think I'll just wait for you here." I glare out at the ocean like it has just personally offended me.

"You didn't even get in." He chuckles. "Come on, once you're in it's not really cold anymore."

"That's because your body goes numb!" I whine nervously.

"Landon," he says earnestly. It's almost a whisper; so soft and sweet-sounding that my toes curl into the sand. "It'll be fun, I promise."

I look down at his long elegant fingers reaching out to me and back at the hair whipping around his blue eyes, and I don't even care what he is asking for at this point. I will say yes to anything. I stick my cold hand inside his warm one and walk with him into the water.

I stay in the ocean with him for almost an hour, and he is right, after a few minutes I don't even feel cold anymore. I fail miserably at any attempt to get up on a wave, but I'm content to straddle the board and bob along the surface of the water. Brody finally gives up on pushing me to try and surf when it is clear to both of us I don't have whatever innate surfing gene makes it look so easy when he does it.

While we wait for waves we talk about anything and everything: his family, my own, where we went to school, what he did at work all day (which was impressive), and what I did at work all day (which was not nearly as cool).

"So how do y'all decide who works where?" I ask, watching my feet swing back and forth on either side of my board.

"What do you mean?" Brody looks back behind me to judge the coming waves.

What is it about being in proximity to a guy that makes you suddenly fascinated with inane things: the way his jaw looks when he hasn't shaved or that one stubborn piece of hair that keeps curling around his ear?

Wait, did he just ask me a question?

Oh, right . . .

"I mean, do you cover some and Liam does the others? Do you have managers who aren't family members? How does it work?" I'm not sure if it is impertinent to ask, but business fascinates me, and I'm so curious about how theirs is structured.

"We have several general managers, and Liam and I oversee them. It's geography more than anything else . . . He's on the Westside so he takes everything west of the 405. I look out for everything else when I'm not managing Twenty-Five."

"You manage that space by yourself?"

"I *own* that space by myself."

I look up from the water swirling around my board.

"Really?"

"Really. It's the first time I've ever gone out on my own." He looks a little sheepish.

I'm totally impressed.

"That's fantastic! How's everything going? Is it doing as well as it seems?"

He smiles again. "It's doing pretty well. It was a significant investment but it's close to being one of our most popular venues."

"Honestly, that's so incredible. I can't even imagine." I shake my head in wonder. "What does Twenty-Five stand for?"

He chuckles a little. "It's sort of childish."

"Oh man, do I want to know? Is it something gross?" I laugh with him.

"Don't be absurd, of course it's not something gross! It was Mark McGwire's number, and I was a huge Bash Brothers fan when I was little."

"Didn't he get busted for steroids?"

He puts a hand over his heart like my words physically hurt him. "Don't bring that up. I'm still not over it!"

We both laugh, and then I bring up something I've wondered for a while.

"What's with the Roman numerals?"

He shrugs. "Just seemed cool."

I nod at that. He's right; it is cool.

He's cool, and smart and incredibly successful, and I have no idea how we got here. It's hard to reconcile the godlike man from the elevator with the surfer sitting in front of me. I smile to myself. I guess he's just as unexpected as I am.

I'm having so much fun that I'd happily sit out in the water with him until sundown, but he says my lips are blue and so we both finally paddle for the shore.

Before I am even all the way out of the water, Brody runs up to our stuff and comes back with a big fluffy beach towel. He wraps it around my shoulders and tucks it in on itself, and then uses his hands to rub up and down my arms to warm me up. I look down at the towel bound tightly around me.

"I feel like a burrito." I look up at him, and the giggle dies on my lips.

He is staring down into my face, and his hands are paused on my upper arms, holding me still. Water is dripping from the ends of his hair down onto the front of my towel, but I don't move, I don't even breathe. He reaches up and runs his index finger lightly over the bridge of my nose.

"You have freckles here," he whispers. "I never noticed."

He cups my face in his hands and tilts my head back to further meet his eyes. My heart stops.

"Just so you're prepared." He smiles. "This time, I *am* going to kiss you."

And then his lips are on mine, and they're so warm against my cold ones that it almost burns.

He tastes like salt water, or I do. I'm not sure. I only know that I'm kissing him back, and it's so perfect I think I might die. It's soft and sweet, and the whole time he holds my face like I'll blow away if he doesn't keep me in place. I push up on my toes to get closer to him and the pressure changes, becomes more intense. Brody's kiss is utterly him: confident, sexy, and thoroughly grown-up. After a minute, or an hour, his lips slow down into a few sweet pecks on my lower lip, my nose, my cheek.

Finally he pulls back and looks at me with a slow smile. My heart starts beating again, and I say the first stupid thing that comes to my mind.

"That wasn't very non-date-like." I try and sound stern, but I'm grinning like an idiot.

He grins back and kisses my nose again, and then his smirk is back.

"Your lips really are blue, I was only trying to warm them up."

He reaches down and scoops up all of our stuff, and then looks up at me. "Other parts of you might be blue too. If you want I can check, kiss those too."

I roll my eyes dramatically and walk past him to change into dry clothes. I never look back, but the whole way to the bathroom I keep my head ducked underneath the edge of the towel so he won't see my smile.

I walk back to the Bronco, feeling warm for the first time in hours. Brody is already back in his hoodie, with the heater going full blast. I jump in and put my fingers against the vent, shivering gratefully when they warm up a little.

"Do you like pancakes?" he asks abruptly.

"I love pancakes." It's the truth . . . And right about now I think I could eat a dozen.

He nods approvingly. "I know a place."

He pulls the jeep back onto PCH, and I study him while he drives.

"What?" he asks when he catches me staring.

"You surprise me."

"And why is that?"

"You—this." I gesture around the car. "This isn't what I expected from a date with you."

"And what did you expect?"

"I don't know. Something involving reservations maybe?"

He frowns. *What did I say wrong?*

"Is that what you would have preferred?" There's an edge in his voice and that aloof, haughty mask is back on his face.

"Don't do that!" I scold.

"Do what?"

"Don't pull that face, or that voice." I turn in my seat to look right at him. "I don't know what I said, but I sure didn't mean to startle you back into Brody Ashton."

Confusion clouds his features, but at least it's not the look he just wore.

"I *am* Brody Ashton."

"Not today." I smile at him. "Today you're just a guy who took me surfing."

He looks startled and then a little sheepish.

"And surfing was . . ."

"Surfing was perfect." I smile at him, "Best non-date ever."

His own little smile starts to play around the edge of his mouth.

"I am curious, though. Why did you choose something so different from your usual dates?"

He looks over at me quickly and then back at the road in front of him. I can actually see the wheels turning in his mind as he debates his answer. We come to a stoplight before he looks over at me again.

"Because you're not like other dates, and so the usual wouldn't work with you."

Meaning I'm not composed or cultured enough to warrant a sophisticated evening from him. My spirit plummets.

I try to keep the disappointment off my face, but he must see something there.

"It couldn't be the usual date, because you're different," he says softly.

His tone only makes me more confused. I search desperately for something to keep myself from embarrassing myself further, and settle on rubbing my hands together in front of the heating vent. I'm watching my hands rub back and forth nervously when Brody grabs one, brings my fingers to his lips, and kisses them sweetly.

"Landon." He says my name like a caress. "It had to be something different, because everything feels different with you."

I'm stunned by what he says, and when I smile stupidly over at him in shock, he leans over quickly and kisses the grin off my face.

The car behind us honks, angry that our speed has dropped, and he leans back over and winks at me.

"They were looking a little blue again," he says with a grin.

———

The next day I'm sorting and folding laundry in my room while I catch Mama up on my week. I don't know how she knew, but she must have sensed something in my tone because she asks point-blank if I've met any nice boys lately, and I find myself telling her about the non-date.

"Well, he sounds like somethin' real special, Landon." She practically croons into the phone.

"He's very nice, but I'm not sure yet if he's special." I ignore the flutter in my belly that says I'm lying; I'm not going to admit it to my mother when I haven't even admitted it to myself.

"Oh, pish," she says dismissively. "I knew the first time I saw your daddy that he was the man for me. He'd come to my cousin Margie's Fourth of July barbecue, and she introduced us, and he reached out to shake my hand, and I swear, that was it."

I keep folding the T-shirts in front of me but can't help but smile along as she talks, even though I've heard this story a million times before.

"Mama, he just took me surfing and then to breakfast. It's a little harder than you think to find *the one*."

"See, that's where you're wrong, baby. When you find your man, it's almost *too* easy. Gettin' married and havin' a mortgage. Kids and a business to run and findin' a way to stay in love day in, day out, that's the tougher part. But the beginnin' . . . that part's easy as pie. That's why they call it fallin', because it happens before you have time to stop yourself."

"OK." I roll my eyes. "I'll remember that, Mama. I'm gonna let you go, though. I gotta put all this laundry up before it starts to wrinkle."

She probably knows I'm avoiding the conversation but doesn't call me out on it.

"OK, girl. Love ya. Call me later."

I hang up with her and drop the phone onto the bed. I'm still smiling at the conversation as I grab a pile of towels and turn around to put them in the linen closet in the hall.

Max is standing in my doorway, holding her bag, with an odd look on her face. I hadn't heard her come home.

"He took you surfing?" she asks me incredulously.

I hadn't anticipated her wanting to talk about this, but I'm confused by the look on her face.

"He did," I say carefully. "Is that . . . bad?" I ask for lack of a better word.

She shakes her head slowly back and forth.

"No—he doesn't really—not since," she says as she catches herself midsentence and closes her mouth completely.

I stand there waiting for her to finish her thought. Finally she speaks.

"I'm just surprised."

With that, she shrugs and heads off to her room. I'm left standing there, holding a stack of towels, wondering what the heck that was all about.

Chapter TWENTY-ONE

The next Wednesday we host the Riverton group and a small team from Barker-Ash in our conference room to finalize details for Sundance. The lead from each SSE team is sitting around the table, along with Selah, Diego, Brody, and me, of course, since I'm the official catchall for just about everything. Diego is going over design layouts, and I absolutely refuse to look at Brody for fear that Selah will see how bad I'm crushing on him. We've exchanged texts a few times, but it is the first time I've seen him since our non-date.

I take diligent notes and offer Selah answers when she needs them, trying not to gag when she flirts with every man in the room.

"And it's possible to have this many parties in one space?" Diego asks finally.

"Possible and necessary." Selah beams at him. "The more cast parties you host, the more your brand gets featured. The association with Barker-Ash, and Twenty-Five more specifically, is a huge draw, so everyone came calling when they found out we'd be in town."

"Is everything sorted out with the liquor delivery?" the man sitting next to Diego asks.

"It's always a bit of a pain working in Utah because they won't allow alcohol to be shipped cross state lines. We deal with that by having a local restaurant there order an excess amount of product in exchange for a small markup, and we buy it off of them," Taylor explains.

"And everything is handled with the permits, the licenses, et cetera?" Brody asks.

"We're all set. Walker flew out on Monday and met with the City. So we're good," Taylor answers.

"And what's the weather supposed to be? I heard there was a blizzard last year," Diego asks.

When no one answers I look up at him.

"Upper twenties is what they're estimating now, though I'm tracking it regularly. I'll let you know if there's a drastic change in either direction."

"And lodging?"

I look down at my notes and then back up.

"I sent details to your assistant this morning; both your teams are booked at the Waldorf."

"And featured drinks?" he fires back.

"Will change daily depending on the party. Each is themed in some way to the movie and the cast you're hosting."

"And you got the margarita mix?" His eyes narrow, but I don't even change expression.

"At the Patron party maybe, but not at any of ours. You asked us to come up with several inventive variations, and we've done that, but none of them are margaritas."

Ever since the first party, and Brody's warning that people will treat me with as much or as little respect as I allow them, I've done my best to be only professional with the Riverton team. Diego is still a flirt, but when I don't encourage it he tends to mellow out in the course of a meeting.

"Very good, *querida*." Diego smiles beatifically. "I think we're good here unless you have any questions." He looks at Brody and then the rest of the team, and when they all shake their heads he stands to leave.

Everyone files out on either end of the room, and I'm one of the last to leave after packing up all of my paperwork and my computer. I head in the direction of the door and only then do I notice that Brody is dogging my steps. I'm still not going to acknowledge him in this setting, and I think he gets it because he hasn't tried to engage me in conversation or make eye contact once. He now knows as well as I do how Selah might react to that. Still, it's more than a little odd to not speak to him at all.

Just before I reach the door I feel a playful tug on the back of my ponytail, and I giggle quietly and throw him an amused expression over my shoulder. As soon as I do Brody's face goes completely blank. At first I think I've done something wrong but then I turn around to follow his line of sight.

Selah is standing in the doorway, watching us.

Yea, though I walk through the valley of the shadow of death . . .

She's seen the exchange, and there's no covering up what has just happened because no way is hair pulling professional behavior. Her face is frozen in a grimace, but her eyes dart back and forth between the two of us like she's trying to solve a particularly difficult riddle. I feel myself blush, and just like that, I've answered the question for her.

You know that scene in *Willy Wonka* where Veruca Salt loses her mind over the golden goose? Well, Brody is the golden goose, and Selah has just realized he's unavailable to her . . . and she's pissed. Her eyes nearly glow with rage, but then just as quickly she schools her expression.

I have no idea what I should do, so I just keep walking past Selah standing in the doorway and straight down the hall to my office. I don't look back at Brody, I don't acknowledge any of my coworkers; I just jump on my computer and start following up on e-mails. I'm running through a million possible scenarios in my mind . . . Will she fire me? Surely that's illegal or something. I didn't really do anything wrong, did I? Maybe she'll just scream. It'll be unpleasant, but I've been there before, and if I just stay quiet and let her get it out—

The door to my office clicks shut, and Selah is standing in front of it wearing a beautiful Gucci dress and an ugly expression.

"Is this how you thought you'd work your way to the top then? On your back?"

Her words are a physical blow, a sucker punch to my stomach that pushes all the air from my lungs. I look up expecting her glare only to find a totally controlled expression on her face, as if getting worked up over me is beneath her. She stands there without speaking. *Is she waiting for some kind of response?* I shake my head slowly, and finally I find my voice, "I didn't—"

"Do I *look* like an idiot? This isn't anything new. The scenario has played out a million times before, but usually the girls doing it are a bit more obvious. I'm actually a little impressed . . . You pretend to be sweet and innocent, when really you're just scheming like all the rest."

I don't want to listen to her. I want to get up and run away but I'm frozen to my seat.

I will not cry. I will not cry. I will not cry.

"Ma'am, I—"

"Give up the act, Brinkley. No one's buying it! You saw a meal ticket, and he saw another cheap lay," she snarls viciously, and it's the first break in her composure since she walked in the room.

"Another?" I squeak.

Selah's face softens the slightest bit while she considers me and then morphs completely into concerned.

"Oh, sweetie, don't tell me . . . You thought you were *special*?" It's the most-popular-girl-in-school voice, the one she uses on the

SSE team when she wants to make them feel like her best friend. "Let me guess, you're different from all the others, right? He made you feel pretty and interesting, and you thought maybe the two of you had a future?"

Her voice sounds kind but the words are intentionally sharp. My eyes blur with tears so I stare down at my hands. I can't have her watch me cry. It was only one date, but he did make me feel special. Now I just feel stupid. I don't answer, but then I don't really need to.

"You really are naive, aren't you, sweetie?"

Finally I find my voice enough to squeak.

"We're just friends."

She takes two steps forward until she's looming over me, eating up all the air in the little office.

"Ah, but perception is everything, Brinkley. I'm sure people already assume the worst."

"I don't want—"

She interrupts me. "Do you want to keep your job?"

My head snaps up. "Of course I do!"

"Then you have a choice to make. I won't allow the reputation of my firm to be tarnished by your indiscretion—"

"But I—"

"You will have no further contact with anyone from Barker-Ash professionally or otherwise! If I find out about any kind of relationship, even a purely platonic one, I'll be forced to let you go. Do you understand?"

I can't believe any of this is happening, and I can't believe I've made such a fool of myself that even Selah, who doesn't seem to care about anyone, is concerned for me. I nod slowly.

She seems mollified by my response and turns to go, but at the last second she looks back. She starts to speak and with every word her tone changes; it becomes hateful.

"And Brinkley, I'm rarely this explicit with employees, but since you seem to be slow on the uptake, let me make myself perfectly clear. This is your only warning. If you disregard it, I won't just fire you, I will *ruin* you."

I stare at her in wide-eyed shock. No one has ever spoken to me like this in my life, and I'm paralyzed. I have no idea how to react.

"I know what you all say about me behind my back; I'm a crazy bitch, right?" She bends down, nearly in my face. "But I promise you, you don't want to see how far I can take that title."

Then she straightens herself up, smooths out her dress, and leaves my office with the door clicking quietly shut behind her like she was never there at all.

For a minute I just stare at the closed door, too shocked to move. I knew she'd be upset, but I never thought she'd imagine I was sleeping with Brody, or that I'd do something like that to get ahead. *Is that what girls in LA do? Is that what girls in LA do with him? Is that all I am, just the latest conquest?* I cover my face with my hands and let go of the tears I've been holding in. I don't understand this game, and I'm not sure how to play when I don't even know the rules.

I will ruin you. Selah's words repeat on a loop in my head. Even if I don't understand anything else, I know she means it. She's done it to McKenna. She's absolutely ruthless. But I don't know what I'm supposed to do; how am I supposed to keep working for her when she clearly hates me? But I can't leave; she'll probably see that as a personal attack.

My phone starts ringing, and I know who it is before I grab it. Just the same, seeing Brody's name on the screen makes my stomach plummet. I hit "Decline" and silence it and shove the phone to the bottom of my bag. I don't know what I'm going to say to him, but I know I don't have the courage to say it right now. And I can't have the conversation with Selah nearby.

I can only focus on one thing at a time; right now that *thing* is my ability to stop crying. I swipe a tissue under my eyes and take a few deep breaths. I turn on the Frankie Valli station on Pandora, because *no one* can be sad listening to Frankie Valli, and I remind myself for the hundredth time that I've come too far to fail now.

Once my hands stop shaking and my heart rate slows down I open up my e-mail and get back to work.

———

I spend the next several days sick to my stomach, waiting for more fallout from Selah. But maybe she feels confident in the level of fear she's inflicted, because she's gone back to being her regular disdainful self. We never mention Barker-Ash again. Brody sends me several text messages and leaves a handful of voice mails, all of which I delete without opening.

The more I think about it, the stupider I feel. Of course he was interested, he'd told me himself that I was different. For someone who'd probably grown tired of the same easy women, my inexperience would seem like a fun new distraction. Or maybe he did think I was trying to sleep my way to the top like the others, and that this is all some kind of game we were playing together.

The whole idea really upsets me. If I am being honest with myself, I really liked Brody, and even though it was naive I'd thought he really liked me too. So whenever I start thinking about it, I open up a timeline or reconfirm a delivery or answer another e-mail in far more detail than is necessary. At night I have trouble sleeping, and when I lie in bed too long I keep crying. So I mostly try not to go to bed. I work nearly around the clock and thank God for Sundance more than once because there is plenty of work to keep me busy.

On Wednesday morning I finish packing my suitcase for my afternoon flight to Salt Lake City, and I head into the bathroom to finish my hair and makeup. I give myself one brief, sad moment to acknowledge how thin my face looks and how dark the circles are under my eyes.

Don't be dramatic, Landon. You should be ecstatic. You're working a film festival!

I give myself a mental pep talk and pull out the under-eye concealer to cover up the worst of it.

"What's going on with you?" Max demands from the doorway.

She is in her disheveled morning glory and is glaring at me through the smudge of last night's makeup.

"I'm just getting ready for the airport; my flight is this afternoon."

"Bullshit!" she barks so loudly that I jump. "You've been avoiding me all week and Miko too . . . and Brody for that matter."

"I don't want to talk about him." I keep applying my makeup and refuse to make eye contact. Maybe if I act like I'm nonchalant, she'll leave me alone.

"You think I want to talk about him with you?" She sighs, annoyed. "He keeps bugging me about how you are, and he says you won't return his calls—"

"Max, I swear on all that is holy if you don't stop talking—" My voice starts to vibrate with anger. Anger is good. Anger I can handle, because at least if I'm angry I'm not crying.

"Then tell me what's going on!" she yells.

And because I am angry now, I yell louder.

"Oh yeah, because you're so forthcoming about all your stuff!" I glare at her.

"It's not the same thing—"

"No, you're right. Your secret was much worse because it was dangerous! You never tell me *anything*, and the only reason I did find out was because I found you in a fucking coma on the kitchen floor!"

I never curse, *never*, and I can't believe I just screamed that at her. My hands are shaking, and I look down at them, afraid to see hurt in her eyes. I just want her to leave me alone.

Neither of us speaks for a minute, and when she finally does her voice is soft in a way I'd never heard.

"And look what happened to me . . . when I didn't let anyone help. You're my friend, and I should have trusted you with what was going on, just like you should trust me now. Brody says he thinks he got you in trouble at work again. You've spent the last week avoiding everyone, you barely sleep, and you don't look like you've had a meal in days. If she said something—or did something—you don't have to work there, you can find another—"

With each word my composure slips a little more until I feel like I might drop to the floor in a blubbering heap. I interrupt her with the line I've been telling myself over and over for the last couple of days.

"I've been busy this week. Just need to get through Sundance and everything will be fine. Maybe when I get back, we can have drinks or—"

"Landon." Concern fills the single word all the way to the brim. "I'm worried about you. We all are."

I can handle her scowls, her bad moods, even her anger. But Max being so sweet, talking to me softly like I am a skittish animal—it's going to make me start bawling for sure and I'd just finished my eye makeup. I give her my best beauty pageant smile and hope she can't tell how fake it is.

"Don't be silly, I'm doin' great." I throw the blush brush into my makeup bag and then gather the whole thing up along with my toiletry case and scoot past her to my room. Both bags go into my suitcase, and I zip up in my big winter coat and head to the front door in under two minutes. It is the first time in my life I am traveling with my makeup only half-finished and my hair in a bun. But I get out the door before Max can ask any more questions.

When I wheel my carry-on up to the gate at the airport, Miko is waiting there. She's wearing a black parka bigger than she is, her gold headphones, and dark sunglasses even though she's inside a building.

As I walk over she pulls off her headphones and hands me one of the two coffees in her hands.

"What kind of coffee is this?" I let my shoulder bag sink to the floor next to my suitcase.

"It's the cheer-up-because-you're-starting-to-freak-me-out kind," she teases.

My smile crumbles. I can't handle another altercation this morning.

"Don't get upset." She touches my sleeve lightly. "Max said you wouldn't talk to her—"

"So you're going to start in on me?"

So now I'm back to being mean to my friends, who are really only trying to be nice to me.

"Hey, just talk to me. What's going on?" she asks quietly.

I look around the gate that is slowly filling up with passengers and more than a few members of the SSE team. I don't want to have this conversation ever, but especially not in the Jet Blue terminal with my coworkers around.

"Please," I squeak, "please, I just want to get through this week. I promise it'll get better after. I promise I'm going to cheer up and get sleep and stop living off coffee. I promise we'll have fun and I'll be the absolute life of the party." I smile weakly. "Just please don't make me talk about it now, OK?"

Miko looks me over pensively. Maybe she can see how close I am to the edge of tears, because she finally nods.

"OK, I won't ask anymore. But you better find that sunny disposition I know and love because this week is going to suck enough already. If we don't have your eternal optimism to keep us warm, I don't know what we'll do."

She smiles at me, and this time I am able to return it without much effort. I'd never get through the next ten days like I'd gotten through the last several. If I am going to keep it together, I have to find the positive in this situation. Producing an exclusive lounge at Sundance is a dream come true, and I am going to find a way to enjoy the opportunity I've been given.

Landing in Utah the first time you go to Sundance is sort of anticlimactic. In the weeks leading up to the festival you spend so much time stressing and worrying and planning for every possible event-disaster scenario that you expect to walk into utter chaos. So when you arrive in Salt Lake City, and it's just a moderately sized city in the middle of snowy mountains, you get lulled into a false sense of security. By the time you leave the very same airport on the way back out of town, you fully understand just how badly you've been duped.

Walking through the airport that first day, you believe the whole trip will be as easy and wholesome as the southwestern-themed souvenirs in the gift shop. Departing through that same terminal, you know the truth about the soul-sucking nightmare it is to produce film festival parties, but by that point, it's too late.

We drive from Salt Lake City up to Park City in a rented minivan that calls for more than one joke about soccer moms and the sweet sorts of perks of being SSE lackeys. Chadwick drives us through the canyon since he'd grown up in Colorado and says we are all babies for being afraid of a little snow. The "little snow" covers every bit of ground and falls in a steady flurry all through the hour-long drive, and when we finally arrive in town I am shocked by how tiny it is. The festival doesn't officially start until Saturday, and we've arrived a couple days early to finish setup, but it is already a crush of delivery trucks and people hustling in and out of the little storefronts that line the main street.

"It's so packed," I say, looking at the activity.

"Wait 'til Saturday," Miko tells me. "This is nothing."

We drive through the quaint little streets and finally pull up in front of the rented house the staff is sharing on a hill above town. The SSE staff, consisting of eight people—with the exception of Selah, who is staying at the Waldorf along with the clients—is sharing this modern-looking log cabin for the next ten days. Our house is a quick walk into town and boasts a hot tub and a game room . . . all a huge upgrade from last year's property, according to the rest of the team. They'd also told me it had been an act of God and an incredibly big budget to find any place to rent with so little lead time. Evidently most places book out six months in advance, and whatever hotel rooms are left cost four times what they would during any other time of year.

As soon as I step out of the van into the driveway I am grateful for my new snow boots; the snow comes up above my ankle. Holt had worked out more than one deal so that we all got a new pair of Sorel boots. All she had to do was mention which space we were producing and she'd been able to snag cold-weather gear for everyone on the team. I chose a pair that is cherry red with a white toe and tan furry trim across the top because I still want a little color to balance out our eternally dreary wardrobe requirements.

In the house little signs of habitation are everywhere. Taylor and two other production guys had arrived a couple of days ago to oversee the unloading of the trucks from LA. The big kitchen is clean, and someone has already made a grocery run because one part of the center island is a tidy little collection of various snack foods. On the other counter next to a coffee pot are enough kinds of beer, wine, and liquor to throw a block party. I point it out to Miko. "Looks like someone is planning for a good time."

She laughs at me. "Believe me, you will never need a happy hour as badly as you do here. Plus Utah is really weird about liquor. You have to go to this special store to buy it, and they look at you all judgey and weird and make everyone show their IDs even if they're not the ones buying. It's a total pain. We usually stock up at the beginning of the week so we don't have to deal again."

"Ah, makes sense."

We wander around checking out everything from the beautiful view out the floor-to-ceiling windows in the living room to the coveted game room. Finally we search upstairs until we find an unoccupied room with two double beds. The house has five bedrooms, which means that most of us are going to share, but I don't mind bunking with Miko; it just makes it feel even more like summer camp.

I've just thrown my bag down on the bed closest to the window when Revere pokes his head in.

"First crisis," he sings to us.

"What happened?" I grab my shoulder bag with all my perfectly organized binders and permits in triplicate.

"Oh, let's see . . ." He leans against the doorjamb. "Davies's floral delivery showed up, and it's all wrong. Tay says he's already gotten a parking ticket because one of the drivers forgot to keep his load-in permit on hand, and while they have the down inserts, they can't find the custom pillow covers for the lounge setups."

"Which pillow covers?" I'd had to rush-order seven custom pillow-cover orders for multiple parties; it had been a nightmare.

"All of them." Revere winks at me.

"Oh man." I sigh.

"May as well head over there." Miko grabs her own bag and walks to the door; I follow her and Revere out. We tramp out into the snow one after another, and I walk towards the van.

"Brinkley, parking is a total pain. It'll be a million times easier to just walk," Chadwick explains.

"Oh, right."

I pull the hood of my parka over my head and move towards the road. One by one we trudge through the snow and the slippery sidewalks into the chaos of our event space. Out of the frying pan and into the fire.

Our venue is a two-story real-estate building owned by Realtors who have packed up and left town for the three weeks around the festival. Most of the spaces on Main Street do the same thing; the rent they earn for their little storefronts during Sundance is the best profit they'll make all year long.

The production team, along with a crew of hired local guys, have cleared the space and rebuilt it to Miko's specifications. Now it doesn't resemble an office at all. Instead, it looks like a sleek, comfortable daytime lounge that can change into a sleek, comfortable nighttime lounge with the proper lighting and some well-placed pop-up bars.

———

Unfortunately, the mysteriously missing pillow covers never surface, which is why I find myself on Friday afternoon in the small upstairs conference room of our space, creating an alternative with Wal-Mart shams and some iron-on printer paper. It is tedious work, but Selah is bringing the clients in for a walk-through in the evening before we open tomorrow, so I have no choice but to finish. Fueled by a lunch of Skittles and Diet Coke, and pop music pumping from my phone into the room, I have a false sense of energy. The door behind me opens and closes, but I don't look up. This little room is our staff's satellite office, and people have been in and out all day.

"You didn't text me back."

I nearly drop the iron but manage to set it down gently before turning around. Brody is wearing jeans and snow boots with a cream-colored fisherman's sweater. His style is perfect and effortless, but his smile is unsure.

I'd known I'd have to see him at some point on this trip, but I'd just refused to let myself think about it. Well, he's here now. I need to be *adult* and *professional* and deal with him. I take a deep breath.

"Mr. Ashton—"

"Brody." His smile is gone, replaced by the frustration in his voice. "You know my name. Why are you calling me that?"

"I think it's better if you go, and you shouldn't contact me anymore. I'm sorry if I gave you the impression that I—" My voice cracks, and I look up at the ceiling.

"Landon, what the hell are you talking about?"

He takes three steps eating up the space between us, and then he is right in front of me. He smells so good . . . earthy and fresh. *Just like the snowy mountains outside.* I know that doesn't really make sense, but it's all I can focus on, and my head is foggy with it. I need to get him out of the room with as little emotion as possible. I need to explain to him the professional ramifications of us being friends because that is the only part I *can* talk about. The other part, the one in which I am either a slut sleeping her way to the top or a new conquest for a player, is the thing that's had me crying myself to sleep through most of the past week. I definitely can't talk about that with him.

"It was inappropriate to have seen you outside the office, and I apologize for whatever impression I might have given. Going forward, Selah will be the direct contact for our Barker-Ash events." I look away from him.

"This is crazy." He grabs for my hand, but I back away, bumping into the conference table behind me.

"She can't tell you who you're allowed to see outside of work. You understand that, don't you? I'm not a client of SSE. In fact I've already told Selah: this is the last event she'll do with us. I don't agree with the way she does business, and truthfully, I just don't like her as a person. Not even our buyout minimums are worth risking association with some of her shadier practices."

What is he talking about? I am surprised to hear this because she hasn't mentioned it at all, but I try not to let it show.

"So there's nothing wrong with us hanging out. Honestly, the only inappropriate part of this whole situation was her reaction to it. Come on." He grabs my hand before I can pull it away, and it feels so good it's almost painful. "You look so sad; it's not like you at all. Let's sneak out of here for a quick lunch. I'm starving and you can't survive on candy alone." He eyes the empty Skittles bag on the floor next to my finished pillows. "I'll even make you pay so it's not date-like at all."

He smiles at me, and that grin is gold and glitter and everything magic, and for one single moment I consider letting him hold my hand all the way down the stairs. I let myself have that single breath to dream about what it would be like go to lunch at some cozy little bistro as the snow falls on Main Street outside the window. And then I remember Selah telling me how naive I am to believe I am special, and how many other girls Brody has taken on similar lunches. And, lastly, what she would do to me if she ever found out. I remove my hand from his and watch his face fall.

"Please leave," I whisper, miserable. "This is all I've ever wanted to do, and if she finds you here I'll never get an opportunity like this again."

He nods slowly and gives me a tight smile as he moves towards the door. Just as he reaches it, he spins back around and the look on his face is one I've seen before, that night at Twenty-Five. Like he is fighting with himself about whether or not to say something.

"You're smart and ambitious, and I absolutely respect working hard to get somewhere. But Landon, you are too sweet to work for someone like this. She's harsh and fake, and if you let her, she'll rub out all the best parts about you. If you want to work in events, there are a ton of different opportunities at one of our properties. I can make some calls."

He's so earnest in the offer, but it's exactly the kind of thing Selah alluded to when she said I'd use him to get ahead, and maybe that's why he's doing it . . . because it suits his plans too.

I spin back around to the pillow I had been working on.

"I appreciate your offer, but if you'll excuse me, I have a ton of work to do before the walk-through."

He doesn't say another word and I never see his face, so I don't know how or if my words affect him. I stare down at the logo in front of me as the door opens and then closes again behind me.

Chapter TWENTY-TWO

"How you doin', Brinks?" Taylor calls to me over the music.

It is the third day of the festival, our fifth in Park City, and the fourth party we've thrown in the last two days. The night before we'd left the venue at 3:00 a.m., and the alarm on my phone went off at seven this morning so we could open up the venue as a daytime lounge. It is now nearly midnight, and I am fairly sure that a constant stream of caffeine and Emergen-C packets are the only things keeping me upright.

"I'm hanging in there." I smile at him as he removes his big jacket and runs a hand through his hair to get the snowflakes out.

"What's tonight's drama?" He leans against the hallway wall next to me in the near dark. Once a party is off and running, the latter part of the evening just turns into lurking somewhere in the shadows and babysitting the room in case there is trouble.

"Let's see . . . The landlord came by and tried to sneak his teenage daughter in again to get pictures with celebrities. Security stopped him at the door, and he was really annoyed. I had to kindly explain that it was a private event and even if he owned the building he couldn't just waltz inside. It didn't go well. I ended up giving him three of the VIP gift bags, which finally calmed him enough to leave. Hmm, what else? There was an issue with capacity, and we had to turn away a bunch of people. The personal publicists were freaking out, but I think it was mostly their friends who were trying to get in, so whatever. At some point I commandeered a plate of appetizers from Revere, but I put it down for a second and a busser cleared it and I'm starving." I smile over at him. "How about yourself?"

"Well first of all," he says, reaching into the pocket of his jacket and tossing to me a bag of pretzels. "It's not gourmet but—"

"Thank you!" I beam at him. "You're always feeding me!" I am already opening the bag to pop one in my mouth.

"You're welcome. Now as for me, I've just spent the last hour huddled outside the back exit helping Rodriguez fix the security camera."

"I didn't know that came under your purview." I smile through a mouthful of pretzel. "Purview" is another one of Selah's favorite words.

"It doesn't. I mostly just held the flashlight for him. It had to be done because we're contractually obligated to have one for security purposes; it was just our good luck that it decided to crap out after sundown and during a snowstorm."

"I've had a ton of that sort of luck this week myself."

"And have you started counting down the days yet until you get to fly out of here?" He reaches and snags a pretzel for himself.

"Five more to go," I say, miserable, and he laughs. "But tomorrow night we're off, and I plan on sleeping for at least twelve hours straight."

"You haven't gone out with us once yet. Tomorrow night is perfect." He gives me a sidelong glance. "There's a really good Thai place down the street, and then there's a couple of parties we could go to."

"Yes to the Thai, but as takeout only. As for the parties, thanks for the offer, but I won't even pretend to be interested. I don't think I've ever been this tired in my life." I look down at my watch and grumble, and then hand him the bag in my hand. "Here, you finish these. I have to go make sure the hipster DJ got his cocktail; part of his rider was a fresh gimlet every forty-five minutes."

"At least he gets points for an original drink choice."

"The best part is that I serve it to him in a to-go coffee cup so no one knows he's drinking alcohol. Apparently, he's, like, five minutes out of rehab."

"Ah, Brinks . . . You sound jaded already." He laughs at my pained expression and bumps me sweetly with his shoulder.

"I can't help it. I watched one of America's sweethearts scream at a barista this morning because we ran out of soymilk. And I'm pretty sure that one of MTV's *Teen Moms* was dancing on the bar earlier . . . and if she's here, Taylor, *who's* watching her baby?" I say warily. "And the worst of it is, I'm too tired to care. I promise I'll go back to being appalled by it all once we're back at sea level."

I turn to walk down the hallway, and he calls after me. "Now you know why we all hate Sundance!" I can hear his laughter, and I consider turning around to stick my tongue out at him, but I'm too exhausted and can't work up the necessary energy.

———

The next night I let everyone talk me into going with them to Thai on Main for dinner. I've long since passed the tired phase and am floating somewhere in a sort of numb, giggly state, but so are the rest of them. We make for quite a group when we finally snag a table by the bar. Everyone else orders drinks, but I'm positive I'll fall asleep in my curry if I have a drop of alcohol. I opt for hot tea, which is perfect for my scratchy throat, and I share *gang keow wan* with Miko. It's so spicy it makes my nose run, but that's a nice change from the stuffiness so I don't care. Apparently another side effect of Sundance: everyone working there spends the entirety of the trip fighting off various forms of illness.

After dinner we trudge back up the hill to the house so people can change into their "going out" clothes, and Miko and I can change into our "staying in" clothes. I'm snuggled up with a box of double-stuffed Oreos on the sofa in the game room while Miko tries to figure out how to work the DVD player in front of me.

"What are we watching?" Taylor walks by me and steals a handful of cookies, stretching himself out on the loveseat catty-corner.

He's wearing sweatpants and an old concert tee . . . clearly not his "going out" clothes.

"I thought you were all headed to a party." I break apart a cookie so I can eat the icing out of the middle.

He shrugs. "Movie night sounded better. What's the choice this evening?"

Miko beams at him as she plops down next to me. "*Twilight.* And just so you know, it's not even the fourth one when they had a big budget. This is the very first one where their makeup doesn't even go down onto their necks, and Kristen Stewart does that whole exorcism thing before Edward sucks the venom out. Sure you wanna stay?" she taunts.

"The acting is pretty terrible," I warn him solemnly.

"If it's so bad, then why are you guys watching it?"

"Because it's a classic and neither of us has the brain capacity to watch anything deeper . . . and because Rob Pattinson is pretty and will make us feel better," Miko tells him.

"Sounds good to me." Taylor snags a blanket hanging over the back of the sofa and wraps it around himself.

The movie starts up, complete with the random piano music and the wide shots of the forest. He teases us for the first twenty minutes about what kind of adults watch something this terrible.

But then he quiets down, and by the time Edward saves Bella from the street thugs he's incensed.

"Wait, why is he being so weird to her in the car?" he demands suddenly.

"Because the smell of her blood bothers him. He's a *vampire!*" Miko says, annoyed.

"I'm not sure why she thinks he's such a catch. He's basically rude to her all the time." He grabs a bowl of popcorn from the coffee table and shoves some in his mouth.

"He's not rude to her. He's afraid he'll accidentally kill her! He has to keep himself in check constantly . . . Can you even imagine?" Miko screeches in exasperation. "This is one of the great literary love stories and—you know what, stop talking! If you want to watch, you have to quiet down!" She scolds him like he's a little boy, and I'm laughing so hard by the end of her tirade I'm in tears.

The two of them continue to bicker about plot points and soundtrack music, and this is the happiest I've felt in weeks. I lay my head on the arm of the sofa, content that I'll make it through the rest of this festival in one piece. I'm asleep before Bella even gets to watch them play vampire baseball.

———

The next four days fly by in a blur of party production, frigid temperatures, and sleep deprivation. On the plus side, I now totally understand why people who fight wars together remain close even after they return home. There's something about spending intense, stressful time with other people that bonds you forever, and I can safely say that the members of the SSE team working this week will be lifelong friends. Taylor wasn't kidding when he said that Selah was smart enough to hire good people; I've seen evidence of it over and over. Every single person on our team is the epitome of grace under pressure. I've watched Davies create thirty-nine centerpieces, by herself, with only half her expected flower order. I've watched the production team change our space over three times in one day, once during a snowstorm. I've seen Revere remember the food likes, dislikes, and allergies of at least one hundred VIPs and never once break a sweat when they complained or asked for something different. Probably most impressive is that everyone has managed to keep a good attitude despite how tired we all are. Between Revere's bawdy jokes and Miko coming up with endless games of Would You Rather, we've managed to laugh our way through most of the long days on site. The only tense moments happen when Selah comes in, but since she spends most of her time wining and dining the clients or skiing with her friends, those moments are few and far between.

We are nearing the end of a cast dinner on the second-to-last night in town when Miko and Revere find me in the back room sorting gift bags.

"Tonight we're drinking!" Miko declares.

"Hold on. Thirty-eight, thirty-nine, forty, forty-one, forty-two," I say, counting the bags. I look over at Chadwick, who's been helping me get them ready. "Can you take them down to the lobby area and put them on that table we set up?"

"Sure thing."

I turn back to Miko and Revere, both grinning like naughty children.

"We. Are. Drinking. Tonight." Miko enunciates each word.

"I don't know." I grab some lip gloss from my pocket and swipe it on. "Tomorrow's one of our biggest events—"

"Yes, but it's our *final* event, and tomorrow night we go too late to celebrate. This is our last night here that we'll be off early enough to do anything."

I smirk at them both and head back out to the party area; they follow closely behind, extolling the virtues of one last hurrah.

"You haven't had a single drink the entire week," Miko whines. "That's not even human!"

"I've been too tired and I've been fighting a cold and I've had to get up early every morning—"

"You don't have to get up early tomorrow!" Revere sings. "We don't have to be on site until noon."

"And we've already invited people," Miko adds.

"What people exactly? You know we have a security deposit on the rental and if anything happens—"

"*Mom!* Stop freaking out, it's like eight extra people, not the makings of a rave," Miko barks. "Now then, *we're* done here so we're going to do a run for snacky-poos and more wine."

"Did you already have a drink?" I look closer into her eyes, but it's too dim to see anything clearly.

"Neither here nor there, miss!" Revere says haughtily. "You guys finish up quickly, and we'll see you back at the house, OK?"

"Fine." As soon as I turn around I feel a swift smack on my bum. I whirl around but they're both running like mad back down the hallway to escape any retribution. *Those two are trouble.*

I smile and walk back out to the lower floor of the space. We've transformed it into an elegant dining room for tonight's forty-person party. I straighten the custom napkins on the bar and return a few abandoned wine glasses to scullery. The cast's movie is premiering tonight at nine, and it's already 8:40 p.m., so they are starting to make their way out in groups to make it to the theater on time. I chat with the DJ one last time about lowering the music and playing something really mellow . . . the event-planner equivalent of flashing the lights on and off. When I turn around again Selah has entered the space with the Riverton group. Behind them are the Ashton brothers. She is guiding Diego around the party, using the opportunity to introduce him to some of the celebrities, I'm sure in a bid to remind him how well-connected she is. I don't want to watch her work the room any more than I want Brody to spot me, so I sneak out before they notice me. I swipe my jacket from the partition I'd hidden it behind, and slip out front to check in with security.

When I open the door hundreds of flashes fill the air in the split second between me stepping out and the paparazzi realizing I'm not anyone famous. I step over to two men who have been our door guys all week as the flashes come to an abrupt halt.

"Joey," I call to the bigger of the two. "Revere says he left plates of food for your team back in the kitchen. They'll keep them warm for you, just head back when we're done here and grab them."

"Thanks, Brinkley. We really appreciate it."

I turn back to go inside. "You're lucky too," I call. "I think they had extra filet so you're livin' large tonight, gentlemen!" I laugh at their happy expressions.

Every single event we work has security, and the easiest way to their hearts is through free dinners. Just as I turn to grab the door, it opens inward. The flashes go off again but die off when the Riverton team steps out. Selah follows behind them, ahead of Brody and Liam. I cringe at the vision of Selah in her stiletto boots, tights, cashmere sweater, and fur vest paired against me in my dirty snow boots, ponytail, and practically no makeup since I'd sweated it all off long since. I turn back to the guys. "Joey, can you escort them to their cars, please?"

"Absolutely. Right this way, Ms. Smith." Joey offers Selah an arm, which she clutches rather than fall off her six-inch heels. *Honestly, what idiot wears those boots in the snow?*

I turn back for the door. Brody gives me a hopeful grin, and Liam's face brightens in recognition. "Hey! How are you—?"

"Excuse me," I mumble quickly and duck back inside the space. *Great, now I'm being openly rude to everyone. Ugh!*

I walk slowly back to toss my jacket in its hiding place and start overseeing strike of the party. I decide right then that Miko is right: we *are* drinking tonight.

"There she is!" Miko squeals from her perch in the middle of the kitchen island. The main room is full of people, but true to her word, there can't be more than twenty total. There is music and lots of loud, happy conversation, but nobody appears to be doing anything that might get them (or us) into trouble.

"Here I am," I say in agreement with Miko. "Let me just drop my stuff off in the room, and I'll be right back."

I jog up the stairs to our shared bedroom and change into clothes that don't smell like the food we'd served at dinner. I redo my pony, pull on a pair of UGGs, and apply gloss. Back down in the kitchen, Miko, Chadwick, and Revere are lining up shots of Jameson and cackling like hyenas . . . Clearly they've been drinking since they left me at the venue.

"Come on, comeoncomeon! It's your turn," Miko croons.

"All right." I grab a shot and throw it back without hesitation.

"You drink like a guy," Revere slurs.

"Or a pirate," Chadwick agrees.

I laugh. "Either way, I just want a buzz as fast as physically possible." I grab another shot.

"Hey, careful there, slugger." Taylor comes up next to me and stops the forward motion of the shot by grabbing my wrist. "The altitude will mess with you if you've never been up here before. You get drunk a lot easier, so you might give it a minute before your next one."

He must have just taken a shower because his hair is wet, and he's changed into an old Rolling Stones shirt.

"You can have this one then." I hand him my shot and he drinks it for me. "And I'll just get the next." I grab the next in line and swallow it before he can stop me. The group assembled around the kitchen gives me a round of applause, during which I stop to curtsy.

"You're going to feel that tomorrow."

"Yes, but at least I won't think about anything tonight." I smile at him as the whiskey starts sizzling its way through my veins.

"Who wants to play I've Never?" Revere asks, sloshing around the dregs of the Jameson bottle.

"I do!" I laugh. Because right about now I want to drink and be silly and not think about my crappy boss or the way Brody's face looked when I ignored him tonight. So we play games, and we drink a ton, and I end up teaching Revere and Chadwick the first eight counts of my favorite routine from junior high cheer squad.

The last thing I *sort of* remember is a group of us creating suits out of trash bags so that we can make snow angels without getting wet.

Chapter TWENTY-THREE

As soon as my eyes catch the smallest bit of daylight, I wince and slam them shut again. I reach a hand up to rub the clumpy mascara out of my right eye but keep them shut until I can assess my wounds. My head is pounding, probably because I didn't drink any water last night. I remember that I did eat my weight in Costco pizza that someone showed up with last night; it must have absorbed the worst of the liquor because I don't feel as terrible as I should.

I slowly open my eyes to test out the level of my hangover . . . and see Taylor's head asleep on the pillow next to mine.

"Oh my God!" I spring upright in bed with a yelp.

Taylor jumps up too. "What's going on—?"

He's wearing a rumpled white T-shirt and pajama bottoms.

I look down at myself, wearing only his "Back in Black" T-shirt.

"Oh my God!" I cry louder this time.

What did I do?

What did we do?

I don't remember anything after the trash-bag snow angels, and I'm . . .

"Calm down, Brinks, it's not as big of a deal as you're making it out to be." He flops back down on the bed with a yawn.

"*Not that big of a deal*?" I clutch the blanket and pull it up above my chest. How have I gotten myself here? And with a guy who doesn't even seem that worked up over what happened?

"How can you say that? I don't do things like this, Taylor!" I'm either going to cry or be sick . . . maybe both.

Taylor sits up, suddenly very awake.

"Brinks, you didn't do anything, I swear. Well, you did a few things that I'll tease you about until the day I die; but *we* didn't do anything."

"But why am I in your bed?" I ask weakly.

"Everyone was down in the game room playing pool, and you must have ferreted in here when no one was looking. I came in and found you passed out across the covers, apparently having helped yourself to some pajamas." He gestures at the shirt I'm wearing. "You wouldn't wake up, and I was too tired to care, so I just left you here."

"I can't believe Miko didn't stop me from doing something so stupid," I gripe.

"Don't be too mad at her. She was the first one who went up to bed. And even if she was awake, I doubt she was sober enough to have kept you in line."

"OK, yeah, you're probably right." I look around me, a thought occurring suddenly. "But why didn't you sleep somewhere else?"

"*You* snuck into *my* bed!" He laughs. "I'm gentleman enough not to touch you but not gentleman enough to sleep on the couch just because you want to pull a Goldilocks!"

The tension in my shoulders eases.

"You're right. I'm sorry. I'm such an idiot." I run my hand through the rat's nest on my head.

Taylor's smile is slow and sleepy. "No, you're not an idiot." He reaches out to push a piece of hair behind my ear. "You're actually kind of adorable."

My breath hitches a little at the gesture because I know what it means. How many girls would kill to be in this position with Taylor right now? He's sweet and funny and completely gorgeous, and I just . . . I just don't feel excited or nervous or get goose bumps on my skin when he touches me.

I look down at my hands nervously. "Taylor, I—"

He starts to chuckle a little and leans back against the head-board. "No, Brinks, don't even say it. I know that tone of voice, not that I hear it a lot, mind you, but I know what it means."

I look up at his kind expression. He really is the best.

"I'm sorry. I really do care about you so much as a friend, I just don't—"

"Want to make out with me?" he finishes for me.

"No, I don't." I give him a helpless shrug. "And I don't know why either, because you're totally gorgeous. But I don't think make-out sessions are in our future."

"It really is your loss," he says playfully.

"Oh, I'm sure it is." I look around for my phone or my clothes or something, but I don't see anything helpful. "What time is it?"

Taylor looks at his watch on the nightstand. "Just after ten o'clock."

I scoot to the edge of the bed and do another cursory search for my clothes.

"I don't know where they are either. I tried to find them last night," he says as I hunt. I pull an afghan off the end of the bed. It's an ugly, crocheted mustard color, but it's big enough to wrap around myself like a cloak so I can get upstairs.

"Lord, I'm the worst!" I laugh at the idiocy of the situation and wonder if he'll ever let me live this moment down. "If you wanna meet me in the kitchen, I'll throw actual clothes on and make you some coffee; it's the least I can do."

Taylor peels himself out of the bed. I shouldn't notice how nice his body is, but I do. Someday he's going to make some lucky girl very happy.

I keep the afghan draped over my shoulders like a cape and use one hand to hold it in place. The other hand slowly turns the knob on his door, and I listen for a moment to see if anyone else is awake. The house is still, so I'm assuming everyone else is sleeping off last night.

Taylor's room is in the basement next to the game room, so we have to trudge up steep steps to the kitchen. Just as I get to the last step up, Taylor accidentally snags the edge of the afghan, which makes me trip, and then he trips, and both of us sort of half-tumble into the kitchen, laughing.

I straighten back up and pull the blanket tighter around my shoulders, still snickering. "I'm honestly the least graceful person you're likely to meet, I just—"

A throat clears.

I look up at Revere, who's standing in the archway of the kitchen . . . next to Brody.

I look at Taylor and then back at them and . . . and . . . I'm wearing his T-shirt and my hair's a mess and I don't have pants on and I . . .

Oh God this looks so bad!

Revere clears his throat again. "I'm sorry, uh, Mr. Ashton asked to speak with you, Brinkley, and I, uh, thought you were in your room."

Brody's face has drained of all its color. I start to say something, but then his features shift and for one fleeting moment I see a look of disgust that makes my heart hurt.

"Excuse me, this was my mistake." Brody turns around and heads back out the way he came.

Damn it!

I leave Taylor and Revere standing in the kitchen still gaping at the spot Brody just exited, and I chase after him. I'm wearing an old T-shirt and a mustard-colored blanket; I pick out a random pair of snow boots from next to the front door that end up being two sizes too big, and I run out into the snow.

"Brody! Brody!"

He's almost to his car but he spins back around.

"Oh *now* it's Brody?"

I'm stumbling through the snow. I nearly crash into him when he comes striding back to me.

"I'm sorry. I know how it looks but I—"

"How it looks? It *looks* like you were in bed with Bennett . . . who's your coworker, by the way!" he shouts. "Which is really confusing because you said we couldn't even be *friends* because it was unprofessional!"

"I know you have no reason to believe me, but I promise—"

"You *promise?*" he sneers, and I shrink back and hug the blanket tighter around myself. "Are we back to pretending then? You're going to play good girl again, and I'm supposed to buy it?"

I know it's an utterly ridiculous thing to say, but it falls out of my mouth like a plea.

"I *am* a good girl."

Brody leans closer and points an accusing finger at me. "Hard to believe that when the only thing you've got on is *his shirt.*"

His face blurs in my vision, and tears start rolling down my cheeks. I am so damn sick of crying all the time! *When did I become this girl?* I scrub them away with the edge of the blanket. My brain races to figure out the right thing to say, to make him understand. He's looking at me like he's finally figured out who I really am and it's disgusting to him. I don't know what to say. He's practically vibrating with anger, and I have to fight the urge to reach out to him.

"Why are you so upset?" I ask in a small voice.

"That's the question of day!" he says contemptuously. "I came over here because I was *worried* about you. Every time I've seen you this week you looked upset, and I thought you were having a hard time. I wanted to make sure you were OK. But the joke's on me, right?" He's almost yelling by the last sentence.

"Please don't be angry. Just let me—"

"Brinks, are you OK?"

I turn to see Taylor standing in the doorway of the house, looking pretty angry. He's clenching his right fist at his side, and I wonder if the bad boy image isn't actually an act after all.

"I'm fine. Can you give us a minute?" I call over.

He doesn't look happy about it, but he closes the door. When I turn back Brody is smirking.

"You've just got all kinds of men checking up on you, huh? The damsel in distress is a good game. I certainly fell for it." He looks out into the snow for a minute, and when he speaks again his voice is quiet. "The worst of it is, I don't know why I'm so upset. I've been in this scenario plenty of times, I just thought this time—no, I thought *you* were going to be different."

"Brody, please listen to me. I'm in this situation, and I know how it looks, but it's not my fault. I had too much to drink, but I didn't do anything!" I'm pleading; I need him to understand.

"And that's your thing too, right? You don't *do* anything. You let Selah control your life and make you miserable and you just take it. You're depressed for weeks and your friends try to help and you're rude to them. But that's not your fault, right? They should have left you alone? You end up drunk in bed with some guy, but you don't take responsibility for that either!"

"Please." I'm really crying now. "I'm not like that."

My tears only seem to make him angrier.

"You're *exactly* like that! But you know what? I don't get to tell you how to act; you can be whoever you want. But at least take responsibility for it. Stop pretending that your life is just *happening* to you and that you have no control over it!"

I can only imagine how pathetic I look sobbing here in the snow, but I can't stop. He's so angry and each word cuts like a knife. I am so tired of people being mad at me but the worst of it is . . . he's right. I have let Selah boss me around. I was rude to my friends, and I did get drunk and end up in bed with Taylor. What would have happened if it had been someone else's bed? For the first time I realize how dangerous my actions were last night. I've been so wrong, so much lately. I'm sorry about all of it, and I don't know what I can fix, but I have to make him understand. I can't let him leave here without knowing what really happened. I swallow back more tears, and start at the beginning.

"I'm s-sorry. I shouldn't have let Selah tell me that we couldn't be friends—"

Brody holds up a hand to stop me.

"You know what? Don't even worry about it, really . . . I don't want you as a friend."

He walks away through the snow back to his car, and drives all the way down the hill before I can stop crying long enough to go back inside the house.

Chapter TWENTY-FOUR

"OK, so the day started off truly sucky. That's a given." Miko and I are changing out the pillows in the lounge for the last Sundance event. "But we're an hour and a half removed from the start of the very last party, and we get to go home tomorrow. These are bright sides, and I think we should focus on them."

I'd told her the whole sordid story while crying and shivering under the blankets from both my bed and hers. I'd finally let her coax me into the shower and downed two cups of coffee and three of the dozen donuts Revere ran out to grab; apparently, he's on Miko's emergency diet of sugar. I'd spent almost an hour doing my hair and my makeup, because everyone knows about the restorative effects of good hair. But I am still floating in that weird sensitive place where a slight breeze might make me start crying. *But I'm going to hold it together long enough to get through this party!*

"I'm good." I smile at her weakly. "I'm just going to get through tonight, and then I'll deal with everything else when I get back."

She studies me for a second, and then drops the pillow she'd just stuffed into a new cover.

"You need more sugar," she says decisively. "Wait here. I think I have some SweeTarts in my bag!"

———

It stands to reason that the party that night would be our biggest and would present the most issues. Within the first forty-five minutes of opening the door, we've reached our two-hundred-person capacity; we still have a line of at least seventy-five people out front who are screaming about being on the guest list and demanding to be let in.

I have to ask at least three people to stop smoking inside; celebrity or not, if they set off the fire sprinklers, I'll have to beat them to death.

A former boy-band member swipes an entire bottle of Riverton and is halfway through it when I have to ask Joey to escort him out for belligerence.

It's been a hellish night, and I haven't stopped running from one fire to another, but the party is packed with A-list celebrities, and there are at least fifty paparazzi out front. Everyone involved is going to get amazing press out of this. As tough as it is, it is nice to end the week on a success.

"Did you see this e-mail from Selah?" Revere asks as I stare dubiously at a group of unruly guys who keep causing trouble at the bar.

"About Brian Paul coming in?" I smile at him. "Yeah, I had a lounge area cleared for them. She said they were fifteen minutes out . . . and coming in through the back."

"And aren't you excited? I thought you loved pop music, and it doesn't get any bigger than him." He winks at me.

"I liked his music better in the beginning . . . now he's turned sort of . . ."

"Douche-y?"

I laugh at the pristine Revere using such a common word.

"Exactly. I guess it doesn't matter, though, since I can't imagine anyone who would garner more press. I'm sure Selah is salivating at securing his presence. Ooh, do you think he'll have Katie with him?"

Katie is a former child star turned wild child, and she and Brian are forever having blowouts in public. The tabloids go crazy for them.

"I don't know. Are they on or off right now?"

"Who knows?" I throw my hands up. "Can you have the chef wait to fire the apps for their table until we know how many are in the party? I can only imagine how big the entourage is for someone like him."

"Already on it, girl. I'm just going to check in with the kitchen. Will you text me when they come in?"

"Will do." I'm distracted. The rowdy guys are trying to create some sort of tequila bomb with a Riverton shot and Red Bull . . . *This won't end well.* I call for security on my mouthpiece. They are going to have to come deal with this group before it gets out of hand.

I've just finished the unpleasant job of getting the group out of the party when I get word that Brian and Katie are coming in through the back entrance. Odd that Selah would bring them in through there since I'd assume she'd want all the press shots she could get.

I hustle to meet them and find Selah leading the group through the long hallway with Joey's help. Brian and Katie are both so much shorter than I thought they would be. He is wearing an oversize sweatshirt and a huge beanie with dark Ray-Bans, even though it has to be hard for him to see in the dim party. Katie can't weigh more than one hundred pounds. She has on snow boots with fuchsia tights and a matching fur jacket. Honestly, I have sports bras that cover more skin than her leather miniskirt does, and I have the strongest urge to find her a blanket or something.

They all come sauntering down the hall with Selah cooing praise about Brian's last album and Katie's stunning fashion sense. I'm actually sort of embarrassed for her . . . Pandering to teenagers is just gross. Brian, Katie, and their entourage don't seem to mind at all, though. They soak in the attention like it's UV rays, and they fairly glow in the aftereffects.

As we snake our way through the crowd the other guests pretend to be oblivious while surreptitiously checking out Brian's and Katie's every movement. When they arrive at their lounge they plant themselves in the middle of a sofa while their crew covers every other available surface and starts working on the bottle service.

"Can I get you anything else?" Selah asks flirtatiously.

Brian gives her a grin that I'm sure is his very best version of sexy, and crooks a finger. Selah bends down to let him whisper in her ear and then stands up with a nod.

"Of course," she purrs.

She turns around and signals me to step away with her; I follow quickly.

"Brian wants a rum and coke and Katie would like champagne. Go grab them from the bar and have the servers put them in coffee cups," she calls over the music.

I look back at the already-rowdy circle around the young couple, then back at Selah, confused. "They're—I don't think either of them is even twenty yet. We can't serve them."

"Don't be a moron," she hisses. "This is a private event. We can do whatever we want!"

My parents have owned a restaurant for longer than I've been alive. I know that private parties don't change the stipulations of a liquor license or the legal drinking age. I shake my head slowly.

"Selah, this is really dangerous. If anyone finds out it could be so damaging for the clients—"

"There you go again, trying to think for yourself when that's not what I pay you for." She glares at me. "Those two get served all the time, and they show up to parties like mine because they know they'll be accommodated. Now go get them a drink."

She has that look in her eye . . . the one that makes me think she might eat her young if she ever finds a man willing to give her any. I know she wants to bully me into doing something I know is wrong, but I just can't.

"I'm sorry, ma'am. I really don't feel comfortable—"

"You know what? You're a child!" she spits. "I'll do it myself."

Then she huffs off to the bar while I stay glued in place. Five minutes later she comes back over with two to-go coffee cups and hands a drink to each of them. They laugh and Katie gives her a big over-the-top hug, then Selah sits down on the arm of the sofa to chat them up.

I'm still watching half an hour later when she gets them a second round. When they finally get up to go around midnight, I relax a little. I don't know what I thought was going to happen, but the whole scene made me nervous . . . Maybe I really am immature? I shrug it off and go to grab vendor checks to distribute.

———

Very few things have ever felt as joyful as waking up the next morning and realizing that Sundance is over. I have to stop by the venue this morning to grab a couple of things, but other than that I am free! I plan to spend the whole weekend in my pajamas, and I cannot wait!

I take my shower, do my hair and makeup, and put on some skinny blue jeans, my red snow boots, and a kelly-green sweater . . . I'm technically not working today, and I can't handle another second wearing anything black. I grab my phone only to realize it's dead; I'd been too tired last night to remember to plug it in. Miko is still passed out so I tiptoe down the stairs, grab my jacket, and start the short snow-covered walk to the space for the last time.

Once I get on site I end up helping wrap up some of the more delicate decor. Taylor and his team would spend at least two days breaking everything down. My flight isn't until four, so I figure the least I can do is help them until I have to leave for the airport.

I am just taping some bubble wrap around a lamp base when Selah comes hurrying into the room. She looks impeccable as always in her dark wool Fendi coat and dark Jackie O–style sunglasses, but she's radiating nervous energy.

"There you are!" She practically runs over to me.

I jump up off the floor; I'm more than a little surprised to see her here today . . . Selah doesn't stick around for cleanup, not ever.

"I've called your cell phone at least twenty times." She whips off her sunglasses, annoyed.

"Oh, I'm so sorry. I left it charging back at the house." I wipe my dirty hands on my jeans. "Can I help you with something? Was there an issue with your flight?"

"You haven't heard then?" She looks around nervously.

I look the room over with her, confused. The production crew is busy breaking down furniture; no one is paying attention to us.

"Heard what? I'm sorry, I should have had my phone on me. I can find a laptop and make whatever changes you need."

"No, come with me." She grabs my elbow and pulls me upstairs to the tiny conference room that has served as our office all week. I am so stunned—she is actually touching me—and I just hurry along with her.

Once we get inside she closes the door behind her and looks me up and down.

"There was an issue—last night at the party."

I had been here cleaning up with the crew until almost 3:00 a.m. and no one had told me about any significant drama. I have no idea what's going on, only that she's on edge, and it's in my best interest to back her off of there.

"There was? No one told me. But if you let me know what happened, I can see what I can do to make everything right."

"It's all over the news! I can't believe you don't know this already; who doesn't follow the news?" She is as exasperated as ever but keeps biting her bottom lip, a nervous gesture I've never seen on her before. What could have happened at our event that was newsworthy? I have no earthly idea.

"Was there an issue . . . with capacity permits?" It's the only thing I can think of. The Park City PD has hounded us about it all week long.

"No, you idiot!" she snaps. "It was Brian fucking Paul! He and Katie ran out of here and jumped into a neon-yellow Hummer and then drove that fucking cliché right through the 'Welcome to Park City' sign!"

I gasp in shock but she ignores me.

"They're fine, not a scratch on them, but the Mormons are going crazy. His blood alcohol was way over the limit, and he's only nineteen! Christ! There were paparazzi everywhere! It's a fucking shit-storm!"

"Oh God." I stare at her in horror. What would this mean for SSE, or Riverton, or Barker-Ash? "What can I—"

She looks at me, calculating, and then her face turns sweet. "See, that's just like you, Brinkley. You're always looking for ways you can help. That's what makes you such a great addition to our team." Her tone is cloyingly sweet and concerned. She sounds just like she did on the day she talked to me about Brody. The memory makes me anxious.

"I think you've more than proven yourself to me this week. When we get back we need to talk about moving you up to event coordinator."

Wait, what? A promotion?

I'm so taken aback by her abrupt change in topic, and the offer she's making, that I momentarily forget about what we are discussing.

"Really?" I am in shock. I've heard it usually takes a couple of years for her to consider promoting anyone.

"Of course. You've earned it!" she says enthusiastically. "Let's get your stuff, and then you can ride to the airport with me and we'll discuss it." She shoos me towards the door.

"OK. So you're not worried about the Brian Paul thing?" I ask nervously, sure she's going to fly off the handle again. But she loops her arm through mine like we're the very best of girlfriends and walks with me down the stairs.

"Nothing to worry about. I've explained the situation to Diego, and once he calmed down, he understood that no responsibility would fall on his brand and he was fine. In fact, I dare say, sales of Riverton tequila will triple after this . . . There's no such thing as bad press after all."

I grab my shoulder bag and my coat. *She's going to take responsibility for the situation?* I'm surprised, given how serious it is. Maybe her persona is just that. Maybe she's not as terrible a person as I thought, because admitting that she's in the wrong regardless of how it might affect her business just shows how deeply principled she is.

"I'm surprised you'd be willing to do that," I tell her as I shrug into my parka.

"I'm willing to do whatever is necessary for my company, and I appreciate that you are too." She smiles. "Now, Brinkley, I don't want to worry you, but there's a fair amount of paparazzi and press outside. Security is keeping them in check but, well, with a profile as high as mine is, they're bound to ask questions. So for now, and over the coming weeks, if anyone asks you questions, just go along with my story and we'll be fine. Understand?"

I'm more than a little intimidated by the look in her eye and by the idea that anyone in the press might try and ask me anything, so I just nod.

"Good girl." She pops her sunglasses back on her face, loops her arm through mine once more, and pulls the door open.

All at once we're rushed by dozens of paparazzi and a couple of them have handheld video cameras. A thousand flashes blind me momentarily. But unlike the other times this week they don't stop when they see that it's us; they keep on taking pictures. Everyone is yelling her name and trying to get closer to us as we make our way to the car.

"Selah! Selah—"

"Selah, can you comment on Brian and Katie's accident?"

"There are rumors they were given the alcohol here—"

"Selah, did you know?"

They all scream over each other at once, and I clutch Selah's arm tighter. She seems totally unaffected, though, like this is exactly what she'd been expecting. Finally she stops trying to move forward and looks up at them with an indulgent smile.

"Fine, guys, I'll give you a statement. Just back up a little. You're stepping on my Louboutins!" she says in her flirty voice and most of the men laugh with her and inch back a step.

I look up at her in a little bit of awe. She's so composed; I can't imagine ever fessing up to something with so little fear.

"Last night Brian and Katie did attend one of the parties we produced here. As it was a private event, they were allowed in to celebrate the premiere of the film along with the other guests. While I didn't see exactly what happened, I've heard from more than a few of my staff that the team at Twenty-Five was perhaps a little indulgent with them."

My head snaps up in shock. The noise of the crowd rises, and Selah raises her hands like Moses parting the Red Sea.

"Now, who knows? Perhaps the bartenders were a little starstruck or just don't think much of serving minors, but whatever the reasons, it resulted in an unfortunate situation, and we can only be grateful that no one was hurt."

The camera flashes explode again and everyone starts screaming at once.

"Selah, are you saying that someone from Twenty-Five knowingly served minors?"

Someone shoves a microphone in front of her, and I recognize the reporter from TMZ. Oh God! This is so bad.

Selah smiles at him indulgently. "I'm only telling you what I heard secondhand, but more than one of my staff saw this all happen. Right, Brinkley?" She looks at me calmly. The microphone is shoved in front of my face, and I stare at it in shock. Selah jostles my arm a little. "Isn't that right, Brinkley?" she asks again with a bite in her tone.

I look at her and then back at the press in front of me, and I know what she wants me to do. It's something I've done a million times for her already. All I have to do is nod my head.

I don't even have to say any words, just a simple nod like I've been trained to do, and this will all be over and we'll be in the car chatting about my promotion.

It would be so simple, and with the weight of her stare and the press inching closer, I almost do it. I almost agree with the whole thing because that's so much easier than the alternative.

And then I think about what this will mean for Brody. Because my parents own a restaurant, I know that he'd lose his liquor license and what that would mean for his business. He'd lose everything. It's not just him either, but Barker-Ash as a whole. Max, Liam, Vivian, and Charlie, an entire family who has worked so hard to build up their company and whose only mistake in all of this is that they trusted the wrong woman with their reputation.

When I was a little girl, Daddy took me to get an ice cream. As we were driving away he looked down in his hand and realized that the kid at the counter had given him too much change. He turned the truck around in the middle of the highway and drove back to give her the difference. I always remember the amount specifically because when he got back in the truck I asked him why he bothered to drive all the way back for four extra dollars. He looked at me very seriously and said, "Kid, your integrity is the only thing they can't take away from you, and it's worth a helluvalot more than four bucks."

As I stand here staring at a sea of photographers, seriously considering taking the easy way out, I wonder at what point in the last four months I stopped being my father's daughter.

I pull my hand loose from Selah, but I don't dare look at her when I open my mouth to speak.

"Actually no, that—" I clear my throat. "That's incorrect."

I hear Selah gasp, and the flashes come faster now and for some reason it gives me courage.

"Barker-Ash and Riverton Tequila are completely without fault. I watched Ms. Smith get drinks from the bartender herself and serve them to Brian and Katie—"

"You're a liar!" Selah screams. "She's sleeping with Brody Ashton and trying to cover for him now!"

I wince internally at what my parents are going to think when they see all of this, but I keep speaking and for some reason feel calm. The worst has happened, my career is over, but I can at least protect my friends on the way out.

"No, that isn't true." I shake my head. "I have e-mails from Selah asking me to get a lounge ready for Brian and his friends. There's a security camera in the back entrance that will have video of her bringing them in and escorting them back out. I'm sure if you speak with the bartender or some of the other staff, they'll confirm what I'm saying."

The last of my sentence is lost in the sounds of the press screaming at Selah for comment, but she must know there isn't anything she can say because she hurries to the back of the town car and slams herself inside. In less than a heartbeat the car has peeled away from the curb and everyone's attention is back on me.

For a moment I'm frozen in place as they scream questions at me. Only when Joey comes up and physically pulls my elbow towards the building do I break out of my trance. I hurry after him and back inside the safety of the venue to hide. Joey shuts the door behind me and then comes to stand next to me while I try and catch my breath. When I look up at him, he's smiling.

"Good for you, girl," he says with a wink.

And the whole thing is so ridiculous and unreal that I can't think of anything else to do, so I just start laughing.

————

By the time I land in LA the laughter has worn off, along with the shock of everything that's happened.

When I get back to the apartment Max is sitting in the living room waiting for me. I am so exhausted and overwhelmed that when I see her get up to walk towards me, I start bawling. Not quiet, ladylike tears, but a full-on breakdown of everything I've been holding in the whole way back to LA. When she throws her arms around me, I am so shocked I cry even harder.

"You're going to be OK," she says in a soothing voice I didn't even know she possessed. "I know it doesn't feel like it right now, but you're going to be great."

"I lost my job," I sob.

"Landon, seriously. What you did . . . was just . . ." She pushes me out to arm's length so she can look into my eyes. "Everyone in my family is so grateful . . . especially Brody. He's called me four times already because your phone is off."

"I don't want to talk about him." I wipe my cheeks with my sleeve.

Max looks a little sad. "He told me what he said to you—"

"I didn't do anything with Taylor! I tried to tell him, but he wouldn't listen to me—"

"I know . . . He knows. I told him he was an idiot. He's really sorry, Landon, I swear."

"I can't talk about this right now." I sniff. "I've spent the cab ride home trying to explain this whole situation to my parents, but they're both so upset. I can't handle anything else. I just need to go to bed."

Max nods, but when I walk down the hall she follows after me. As I walk into my room she grabs my hand, stopping me in place, and looks at me seriously.

"Thank you," she says sincerely.

I don't have any more words, so I give her a jerky nod, then walk into the room and shut the door behind me.

Chapter TWENTY-FIVE

I spend the next week in bed. I rarely leave my room; if I do, it is only when I'm sure Max is at work. I call my parents once a day so they won't worry, but beyond that I don't turn on my phone. I don't answer when Max knocks on my door. I keep the curtains drawn and mostly cry and sleep.

I don't know how my life has taken such a drastic and ugly turn, but I don't even recognize myself anymore. Being an event planner is all I've ever wanted to do, and there is no way that's possible anymore. Selah promised to ruin me for a lot less than publicly damning her company, and I am terrified of her retribution.

When I'm not worrying about Selah, I torture myself remembering all the things that Brody said to me that day in the snow and the look on his face when he saw me in the kitchen laughing with Taylor. I eventually cry myself back to sleep.

I wake up one day to the sound of my doorknob jiggling. I've barely registered the sound when the door bursts open. Miko is on her knees, holding a bobby pin, and Max is standing next to her. A flicker of pity washes across Max's face before being erased with her token scowl.

"All right," she says, striding over to my drapes and throwing them open. "We've let you wallow, and now it's time to get out of bed!"

I squeeze my eyes shut as bright sunlight fills the room, then roll over to face the opposite wall.

"Leave me alone. I'm not in the mood," I whisper.

"Come on, Landon. I'm all for a good dramatic shut-in, but it's been over a week. You can't stay here forever." I feel Miko sit down on my bed. "Come on, I brought you a latte. I even went all the way to Intelligentsia to get you the good stuff." She shakes a bag. "And a blueberry scone!"

I stay right where I am, and I hear her sigh. When she speaks again her voice is quieter.

"We're really worried about you. Please get up."

It reminds me of the things Brody said.

You're depressed for weeks and your friends try to help and you're rude to them. But that's not your fault, right? They should have left you alone?

I slowly roll over and sit up in bed.

"Atta girl," Miko says, handing me the coffee and the scone.

My eyes are swollen, my mouth is dry, and I haven't showered in days. I can only imagine what I look like right now. I take a sip of the latte. It's chai and it's perfect. I nibble the edge of the scone and for a minute nobody speaks. Finally, Max comes and sits down on the bed next to Miko in a huff.

"This is the part where you talk to us about what's going on," she says, annoyed.

I nod but keep my eyes down, watching my fingers tear the scone into little pieces.

"I'm going to go home, back to Texas," I say quietly.

"Are you kidding?" Miko demands, at the same time Max yells, "Like hell you are!"

I look up at them in shock.

"Don't you get it?" I demand. "I can't handle it here! I'm not strong enough for LA; I can't keep up. I thought I could come and that I'd be brave enough or smart enough, to—I don't know, do something big with my life. But I'm not!" I didn't think I had any tears left in me, but they are running down my cheeks, mocking me. "All I did was screw everything up and embarrass myself, and I just want to go home!"

"You're one of the smartest girls I've ever met," Miko says seriously. "You went from intern to assistant with hardly any training, and you never missed a beat. You covered the holiday parties and you absolutely ran the event space at Sundance. You're twenty-three, and you managed a staff of forty people and multiple events for ten days straight. That's epic, Landon; how do you not see that?"

Max speaks up. "You stood in front of the press with Selah breathing down your neck, and you did the right thing even though you knew you'd lose your job. That's not just brave, that's valiant."

I give them a small, sad smile. "It doesn't matter, though. She promised I'd never find a job working at another event company, and I believe her. Even if she doesn't try and ruin my reputation, every other firm will know I was a snitch. No one will hire me."

"Then start your own company, Landon. Don't be stupid." It is Max's version of a motivational speech, and it is so ridiculous an idea that I laugh outright.

"Oh sure, because that's so easy," I say sarcastically.

"You have a laptop and a cell phone and the necessary connections. What else do you need?" Max asks.

"I couldn't do that—I need years of experience, I need—" I stutter.

"You managed to figure out everything this far. It can't be that hard, can it?"

"But I'd never find any clients, nobody knows who I am," I try to argue.

"Are you crazy? You just outed one of the biggest celebrity event planners on national TV. *Everybody* knows who you are!" Max says, exasperated.

"And besides," Miko says as she smiles at me, "if you don't start your own firm, where else am I gonna find a job?"

"You didn't . . ." I stare at her in utter disbelief.

"I did," she squeals, "and it was spectacular! I told her at least four different places she could shove her bad attitude and then I stormed out in a huff!"

"No!" I am laughing now with her. Lord, I would have loved to see that.

"Yes! And I will tell you all about it, but first you have to take a shower because you look like a Garbage Pail Kid."

Miko stands up and tugs on my hand. For the first time in days I feel the smallest flutter of hope, but just as quickly it's squashed. That naivete is what got me here in the first place.

"You guys, this is impossible. Do you remember what you told me? This town was gonna chew me up and spit me out, and it did! I don't have it in me to keep trying!"

I fall back down on the edge of the bed, defeated, but Max is already pulling me back up.

"And you remember what you told us?" she says, getting in my face. "That you were going to love proving us wrong! So stop whining, go brush your goddamn teeth, and let's come up with some kind of plan!"

I look between the two of them: at Miko, who's beaming at me like the sun, and at Max, who looks like she's close to punching me for my own good. The three of us could not be more different, and yet for some reason God saw fit to bring these weird, lovely girls into my life.

Right now it doesn't feel like I've got much going for me at all, but I've got these girls. Strange and odd and incongruous as they are, they're still here, willing me to believe in myself . . . And so I do.

Chapter TWENTY-SIX

"Thanks, Nick." I smile at the server as he refills my coffee cup for the umpteenth time today. My laptop is sitting in the midst of various piles of paperwork on the table I've commandeered. For the last three weeks I've come to the coffee shop down the street from my apartment every day to work. Most days Miko meets me here, but today she's having lunch with one of her friends, who's a web guy, to try and talk him into designing a website on our measly tech budget (which is basically like seventeen dollars). The whole prospect of having our own events company is terrifying, but we're both focusing on what we do best. With her designs and my ability to keep an event organized and in-line, I think we have the potential to create something really great.

When I finally turned my phone back on after my week in bed, I found a voice mail from Diego telling me to call him immediately. When I worked up the courage to do so, he raved about my work on Sundance and told me he'd heard I'd branched out on my own. I'm sure someone at Barker-Ash encouraged him to reach out, but when he offered to let me produce a small taste-maker event for them next month, I'm not stupid enough to turn down the offer.

I'd put together a proposal based on exactly the same kind of numbers Selah would charge because, I figure, if they'd pay for her at that price, I might as well try for the same. Once we booked the event with him, Miko convinced me that since we've basically declared war by poaching an SSE client, we might as well go for broke. I'm not interested in stealing business, but I do reach out to a few of the clients to whom I'd been closest.

When Paige Blakely gave birth to her beautiful baby girl, Kherington, I had Daddy ship her enough brisket to feed a small army. She was so touched that I remembered, she asked me to help her with the christening after-party. I didn't even know those existed but I am thrilled to book my first celebrity client. The party is only a few weeks away so I need to spend most of the afternoon working on it, but first I have to get everything squared away with Diego's paperwork.

The current budget breakdown I am working on is taking forever, but Diego has an uncanny ability to remember every line item so I want it to be perfect before I send it over.

I sense the server walk up to the table again, and I reach a hand out to cover my coffee cup.

"I'm good, thanks. If I have any more, I won't sleep for a week." I look up to smile at him.

Brody is standing there in jeans and that faded red hoodie. He smiles sheepishly.

"You never texted back."

"You need a new line," I say, and slide my hands down on the table to brace myself.

"Can I sit?"

"Sure." I wave at the chair across from mine and lower my laptop screen to see him better. I don't feel nervous, or sad, or upset. I just feel sort of resigned.

"I forced your location from Max."

"It's OK."

"I wanted to apologize to you—"

"It's OK."

"No. It's not OK." He speaks emphatically. "It's inexcusable. I shouldn't have assumed the worst, and Max has reminded me more than once what an asshole I am because of it."

I look right at him, because I want him to understand what I'm about to say. I take a deep breath. "In a lot of ways you were right, though. I did end up in bed with him."

Brody winces but I keep going. "And even though nothing happened, it's not something I'm proud of. If you were upset by what you saw, it's because I allowed myself to be put in that position. You wouldn't have been there at all that day if you weren't checking on me. I'm sorry about everything—"

"You don't have to apologize—"

"No, let me finish. I've thought about this a lot and what I wish I would have said to you that day—what I need you to know." I look up and he nods for me to continue.

"I wasn't playing any kind of game with you. I wasn't pretending to be something I'm not. I know it's hard to believe that anyone could be this gullible or naive, but I really am most of the time." I smile sadly. "And I hope it doesn't sound ridiculous, but it would make me feel a lot better if you understand that I'm really not, like—like other girls who've done stuff like that to you before."

My voice cracks on the last few words, but I'm pretty proud of myself for keeping the tears in check.

"God, Landon, of course!" He sounds almost desperate. "I said so many stupid things that day, and I'm so sorry. In business, you're supposed to leave emotion out of it, and I tend to be good at that. But with you, I just—" He sighs, seemingly at a loss for words, but then he continues. "The way I acted was inexcusable, and in light of that, what you did for me, for my family . . ." He searches for the words. "That was one of the most mature things I've ever seen. Thank you. You are such a bigger person than I am."

I nod to let him know I heard him and run an index finger through the water ring on the table.

"We never even got a chance to—but then we've been through all of these really intense situations together—and I . . . I just wish we could start again."

"We've already done that once."

"I know," he says and runs a hand back and forth through his hair. "You're right. We have already done that once. So maybe we just keep going from here to—wherever—somewhere, I don't know." He looks right at me. "Look, I know I don't really deserve it, but I was wondering if you'd let me take you out. A real date this time." His voice is earnest.

The air around us both feels heavy and tense, and it makes me sad because I remember a time when we were relaxed and play-ful; I remember how he kissed my fingertips to keep them warm. But those kisses are blurred by harsher memories of crying in the snow, and I know this is one game I can't join in again. He is so far beyond my scope of understanding, and I don't think I'd survive another round.

"Brody, I like you a lot, maybe too much—"

"I didn't know that was a bad thing," he teases, and for a moment he looks like that boy who tried to teach me how to surf.

"I'm just—I'm trying to figure out myself right now. I don't think I can do that and figure us out at the same time."

He blows all the air out of his lungs like he's been holding his breath. Finally he stands up with a sad smile.

"Can we still be friends?" he asks quietly.

I start to shake my head no because I'm unsure how I'm sup-posed to be friends with someone I want to kiss this badly. But my head is nodding on its own.

"I'd like that," I tell him.

He smiles back down at me and then turns his head sideways to read some of the scribbles in my notebook. He points down at my list of ideas for company names.

"I like this one," he says with a grin.

I see what he's pointing at and smile too.

"The definition is 'a fashionable lifestyle, ideology, or pursuit.'" Feels like that's all I've done since I moved here. You don't think it sounds too girly?"

"Chic Events," he says, testing it out. "No, I think it sounds just like you."

Chapter TWENTY-SEVEN

"Have y'all seen my wings?" Paige calls into the living room where Miko and I are huddled on ladders, hanging individual white garden roses on fishing line so they appear to be floating.

"No ma'am, I thought your hairstylist had them," I call down to her.

"Landon, don't call me 'ma'am'; it makes me feel old!" She laughs, then hurries off in a flurry of white gauze in search of her wings.

When she told us she wanted an angel theme for her baby's christening party I didn't so much as bat an eye. It might not have been my first choice (and it most definitely wasn't Miko's), but our job is to make our client's vision come to life as beautifully as possible, not to tell them what that vision should be. And so we'd spent the last couple days turning Paige's sprawling home into, well, heaven . . . or at least heaven as interpreted by us.

Each table is covered by white silk and topped with dozens of white candles at varying heights. The white roses hanging from the ceiling are gorgeous and make the whole house smell amazing. A huge golden harp is being set up in the entryway so the music can spill into the rest of the house, and all the guests have been asked to wear white to match the theme. Paige and her two-month-old are wearing matching white gowns and matching wings . . . if she ever figures out where she's left them.

We are just finishing up our work with the decor when we hear Paige scream from the other room. I've learned long ago with her that she's loud and a little crazy, so the scream could be because she saw a spider, won the lottery, or just found a cute sweater online; you never could be sure. I climb down the ladder and roll my eyes at Miko.

"I'll just make sure everything is OK."

"Good idea." She smiles back.

As I'm walking through the room, the sounds of Paige's squeals are growing more pronounced. So I'm surprised when I come into the entryway and find her there with her boyfriend.

Privately, Miko and I refer to Damon Kress as Paige's baby daddy, but to the rest of the world he is the lead singer of Liquid Six, a hugely popular rock band that continues to blow away both critics and existing record sales with each new album. He looks like he should be in a biker gang and is tattooed to the hilt, but he turns into an absolute gummy bear every time Paige is around. And I'd rarely, if ever, seen a grown man so in love with his own baby.

Paige is still giggling and squealing when I walk in, and they are locked in an embrace so tight I feel like I'm intruding.

"I'm so sorry. Please excuse me." I turn to go.

"No, Landon, come look! Come look at what DK got me!" she yells after me.

I turn back around obligingly and am nearly trampled by Paige as she hurries towards me with Damon in tow. She waves her left hand wildly towards my face. The diamond on her finger is so big I embarrass myself by gasping.

"It's my Push Present!" She beams. "He meant to get it before Kher-Bear was born but she came so early and there wasn't time. He surprised me today! We're gettin' married, Landon, can you believe it?" She doesn't wait for my response but jumps back into his arms and hops up and down a few more times like a little girl.

"Oh, congratulations, guys! I'm so happy for you." I can't mean it more.

"Thanks," Damon manages right before Paige grabs his face for a kiss.

"Come on, DK, let's go tell Kherington! She'll be so excited!"

Paige starts to pull him towards the stairs as I turn to head back into the living room to finish up before the guests arrive. They are almost to the top when Paige turns and yells down to me.

"Girl, in case I forget to tell you later, everything looks real, *real* pretty. I can't wait to see what y'all come up with for the wedding!"

She doesn't wait to see the surprised look on my face, but it's still there when I walk back into the room with Miko.

"What was all that about?" she asks as she hangs the last of the roses.

"I think . . ." I try to hold back my grin and fail. "I think we just booked our first wedding."

———

Later that night I wander down the street with Taylor, doing a pretty good job of walking in high heels on the rough terrain of a Hollywood sidewalk.

Over the last several weeks he's let us take him out for coffee or dinner or drinks at least a dozen times in exchange for answers to our endless questions about production and timelines. He's been absolutely invaluable as we learn to navigate the waters of independent event planning, and he's quickly become one of my closest friends. He's agreed to come with me to Max's birthday party tonight because he knows I'm nervous about the prospect of seeing Brody again after almost a month.

I teeter along next to him in my high, high shoes that are necessary when I'm wearing my short shorts. I've paired them with a vintage T-shirt and black blazer, and my hair is big and wavy. The whole outfit says, "I'm too cool and confident to wear a dress to this ritzy bar." So you know it took me hours to pull it together. The question of why I'm working so hard to look good for someone I've turned down isn't something I want to explore too deeply.

"So is Sara the one that you like or—" I ask, interrupting Taylor's recounting of his latest date.

"Sort of . . . I mean, yes. I like her. I wouldn't have asked her out if I didn't. But Julianne keeps popping back up and—"

"Wait, I thought Julianne was the crazy one." I look over at him, confused, just as we arrive at the front of the club.

"She *is* the crazy one." He looks equally confused by my confusion.

"But why would you want to date a crazy girl?" I ask, pulling my ID out of my clutch to show the doorman.

"Because crazy girls are kind of hot," he says, handing his ID over too.

At my shocked expression he looks to the bouncer for confirmation.

"True or not true?" he challenges him.

The doorman looks back and forth between us, and laughs. "True."

I roll my eyes in disgust at them both and head in the door. "You men deserve whatever rabbit-boiling scenario dating crazy women gets you. I wash my hands of this."

Taylor follows me into the dark lounge, still laughing at my reaction as we snake our way through the crowd to the back bar where Max's party is gathering.

We wade through another huge cluster of people, and I see Max is already at the bar with Miko and a pretty big collection of school and work friends. Brody and Liam are at the bar talking to each other, and I'm so grateful that he's not there with a date I exhale a breath I didn't even know I was holding.

"You ready for this, Brinks?" Taylor whispers in my ear, startling me.

I didn't realize I'd stopped walking. I turn to stare at him in wide-eyed panic.

"How's my hair?" I demand.

"Large and in charge. Now come on." He spins me back around, and we keep walking. I head right to Max who is, shockingly, wearing a skirt for the occasion. It's a leather mini and she's paired it with an old Queen T-shirt, but it's a skirt just the same, and it makes her legs look about a hundred miles long.

"Happy birthday!" I reach out to hug her.

She's gotten better about me hugging her and bears it with the same stoicism she reserves for all my other "necessary signs of emotion."

"Can I buy you a drink or—"

Her eyes narrow at Taylor, and she abruptly cuts me off.

"Who are you?" she demands.

I start to intercede before she offends him, but Taylor doesn't even bat an eye.

"Who are you?" he challenges her back.

"Are you serious?" She scowls at him.

"In general? Or right this moment?" he says, and then God help him, he actually smirks at her.

Her eyes narrow dangerously, and I look at Miko for help, but she's watching the whole thing like a spectator sport.

"Do you actually sit around and dream up clever responses so you have them at the ready?"

"So you think I'm clever?" Taylor takes a step closer to her, and I watch her eyes grow bigger at the audacity. Usually by this point guys have run off in the other direction.

"Maybe . . ." She dangles an empty shot glass between her fingers. "But just like all the other girls you know, it's taken me three shots of tequila to arrive at that destination."

I look back and forth between them nervously and whisper to Miko. "Should we do something?"

"Are you kidding me?" Miko looks at me with an evil gleam in her eyes. "I've been waiting for this little intro for months!"

"Can I get either one of you a drink?" I ask Taylor and Max in an attempt to distract them. Neither acknowledges me from the depths of their staring contest.

"OK," I say to no one in particular and turn around to head to the bar. I catch Brody's eye before I remember that I was going to try and ease into this moment, not run for it headlong.

Nothing for it now . . .

I head over to where he and Liam are sitting at the bar.

"Hi guys!" I paste on my best smile.

Liam stands up to give me a hug and a perfunctory LA kiss on the cheek, and my stomach drops out because that sort of awkwardly sets the standard for greeting. I brace myself for the feel of Brody's lips on my cheek, so when all he does is raise his glass in salute I feel oddly bereft.

"Since you're here now to keep this guy company, I'll excuse myself. I'm half an hour late for a date already." Liam gestures for me to take his stool.

"You always did know how to impress the ladies," Brody calls after him.

"Not a complaint yet, big brother." Liam laughs over his shoulder without looking back. "Not a complaint yet."

I scramble to think of something to say as I take my seat but I'm saved for a moment by the bartender's arrival.

"What would you like?" Brody asks before the server can.

"Jack rocks, please."

The bartender nods and turns to make the drink, and even though I'm not looking at him I can feel Brody's stare. I pretend to be enthralled with the creation of a cocktail that has exactly one ingredient.

"Unexpected," Brody says as the glass is set down in front of me.

I take a sip while turning to look at him, hoping the liquor will help with this whole staring into the sun thing. He really is just stupid good-looking.

"I like unexpected." I try for cheeky and repeat the line I told him months ago. "Unexpected could turn into a lot of things."

"God, I hope so." He says it with far more gravity than the situation warrants.

I've told myself a million times that it probably took Brody Ashton all of five minutes to move on to his next date after the last time I'd seen him. I've come here tonight expecting to see a goddess on his arm or, at the very least, a Russian model. I'd never anticipated him coming alone or our conversation turning intense so quickly. I don't know how I'm supposed to respond, so I grasp for something to talk about.

"We produced our first event today."

He can always be counted on to navigate away from awkward conversation and today is no exception.

"How did it turn out?" He takes a sip of his beer.

"It turned out great." I can't help but smile at the memory of Paige and Kherington dressed as angels. "I think the client was really happy."

"That's fantastic, Landon. I'm so happy for you."

"Thank you. I'm pretty happy for me too." I grin at him and he smiles back. Before I can even guess at what that smile means he stands up and waves at the bartender.

"Scotty, just keep my tab open. Whatever they want tonight, OK?"

When I realize he's leaving, my heart starts to shrivel up and die like one of those time-lapsed flowers in ninth-grade science. The words are out of my mouth before I can stop them.

"You half an hour late for a date too?"

Kill. Me.

Brody stops moving and looks down at me in surprise. I want to beat my head against the top of the bar repeatedly until I pass out and can forget the last two minutes, but some masochistic side of me needs to hear his answer just the same.

"No," he says with his almost-smile. "I'm covering for Marco tonight at the club."

"Of course. I'm sorry I said anything. It was rude of me to ask." I shrug awkwardly.

His smile gets a little bigger as he considers me.

"Don't be sorry . . . That worried look on your face just now gave me more hope than I've had in a while."

The look on my face now must be one of utter shock because it makes him chuckle. He leans down and kisses me lightly on the cheek, and it feels so good I have to fight the urge to rub my face against his like a cat.

He pulls back and looks into my eyes. I open and close my mouth like a goldfish struggling to find the right words or the courage to say them. Neither comes.

"Tomorrow, or next week, or the middle of the night a year from now . . . I hope you'll call me when you figure out whatever it is you want to say."

He kisses me once more, on the forehead this time, and then he's gone. And I know I'm young, and fairly inexperienced where men are concerned, but I'm positive that even when I'm ninety years old I'll still remember exactly what it feels like to have his lips on my skin.

It's such a depressing realization that I immediately head off in search of my friends so I don't have to be alone with my thoughts any longer.

Chapter TWENTY-EIGHT

A month later I'm in the midst of utter chaos.

We have more people trying to get in than space to put them. The cigar roller gets into a car accident and Miko has to go pick him up and they barely get set up before the doors opened. Two of the bartenders don't show, and I make Max, who has promised to strangle me some night in my sleep, come work on her day off to fill in for them. It ends up being amazing, though, because Max is one of the best mixologists in town, and the Riverton team is thrilled with her creations.

The DJ is sort of a pain and uses the wrong mix for cocktail hour, and the light that is supposed to shine the gobo onto the brick wall of the loft burns out. It's only through the help of really good deodorant and a constant stream of prayer that I'm not chewing through my wrist right now.

But in the end everything looks gorgeous, and I can't wait to add the pictures to our growing portfolio. The party design isn't subdued or modern or muted in tone. It's vibrant and loud, the antithesis of a Selah Smith Event. The atmosphere is energetic, and admittedly a little wild, but it's a hell of a lot of fun. It is the hardest thing I've ever pulled off in my life . . . It's also a massive success. Diego and his team come over to us at the end of the night for kisses on both cheeks and words of praise and the promise to speak about their summer events. Miko and I make sure strike is taken care of and then hug the crap out of each other in the excitement of having survived. While Paige's event was our first, it was small and intimate. This one is corporate, with a potentially huge client. By all accounts we are over our skis a bit, but we've done it!

My feet hurt, and I am starving and exhausted, but I fairly float to my car.

As I pull onto the road I dial my parents because they'd made me promise on a fictional stack of bibles that I would call them no matter what time I got finished.

Mama answers on the second ring, sounding a little tired but so excited.

"Hold on, Daddy's goin' into the kitchen to jump on the other phone—*Hurry up, Tom, she's waitin' on ya!*" She giggles at whatever his response is, and then I hear him pick up.

"Hey, kid, how'd it go?"

"It went great! They're already talking about what we can work on for them next."

"Baby, that's wonderful! I can't wait to see pictures!" Mama says.

"See now, I knew it. I told ya you'd do great," Daddy agrees.

"You did." I laugh into the phone. "I might not have believed you, but you were right."

"Kid, what most people don't know is that the hardest part is just having the courage to try. You never learn how to swim if you don't jump into the water first. Mama and I are real proud of you."

"Thanks, guys. Now go to bed. It's so late. I'll call you tomorrow and tell you all about it, I promise."

I wish them both a good night and hang up. As I drive home I get more and more excited.

I'd done it.

I'd produced a successful event for my very own client, at my very own company. Tonight we'd achieved something I'd dreamed about since I was a teenager, and I am filled with such intense emotion it takes me a minute to identify the feeling: pride.

I'd allowed someone to tell me I was worthless and inept for so long, I'd almost started to believe her. I'd almost forgotten what it felt like to be proud of myself. The thought is sobering.

I keep running Daddy's words around in my head. It had taken a heck of a lot of courage to get through the last couple of months, to start this company, to try and manage an event for a client of this caliber. There's integrity in the work we've done; it's something to be proud of.

I smile at my own inner monologue. I am proud of the woman I'm becoming, someone who's strong and smart and courageous, just like the mantra I've whispered to myself continuously over the last year.

Only, I'm not really courageous, am I? If I'm being honest with myself, I know I keep avoiding the thing that scares me most. Brody stays on my mind whether I want him there or not. And whenever he's on my mind, I think about his words: "Tomorrow, or next week, or the middle of the night a year from now . . . I hope you'll call me when you figure out whatever it is you want to say."

I chew on my lip nervously, running the thought over and over in my mind . . . Do I have the guts to do what he asked?

Maybe Daddy is right. Maybe the hardest part of life is just having the courage to try. At least then I can say that if it doesn't work out, it's not because I was just too afraid to admit that I'm scared.

An idea pops into my mind.

It's stupid and reckless and thoroughly embarrassing, but I am so damn sick of being afraid to speak up. I'm gonna do it anyway.

I'm stopped at a red light and before I can stop myself or think better of it, I jump into the deep end. I pull out my phone and send Brody a text.

I figured out what I want to say.

I hold my breath while I wait. One second. Two. Three.

His response pops up on my phone before the light changes from red to green.

BRODY ASHTON:
1422 Mission St. off Sunset.

I refuse to be flustered by the fact I'm driving to his house at midnight, or that it probably sounds like a thinly veiled booty call . . . He's made that mistake before. I refuse to think about anything at all except what I'll do and say when I get there. I drive the whole way there rehearsing my speech over and over in my head, willing myself not to back out.

———

The gate in front is already open, so I pull my car in the driveway and jump out before I can think better of it. The only way I am getting through this is just to do it. I'm not going to be intimidated by the mini-mansion in front of me, or his brand-new Range Rover in the driveway. Or even the way he's framed in his doorway, looking rumpled and sleepy but so very handsome.

I just keep walking towards him and try not to chew on my lip like a nervous moron.

"You wore pink." He smiles at my dress, and for a moment I lose my train of thought.

"Oh yeah. It's a requirement at Chic Events. Color is a must!" I smile stupidly.

"Would you like to come in?" He moves to the side so I can step by, but I don't move from my spot on the porch.

"No, no, thank you." I square my shoulders. "I'm making an overture."

"An overture?"

"Yes, the big over-the-top gesture that happens at the end of the movie? It's the overture, that's what I'm doing . . . It's all very John Hughes. Just bear with me."

"Oh, OK," he says, looking bemused. "Go ahead."

I hold up my iPhone and press play. Whitney in all her eighties pop glory starts serenading us both. Brody laughs and I grin nervously.

"OK, here it goes . . ." I take a breath. "You scare the crap out of me."

"What?" He laughs again.

"No. This is my overture. You have to be quiet."

He nods solemnly, but he's fighting his grin.

"You terrify me. You're all," I wave my phone in the direction of his house, "grown-up, and it makes me feel so immature. I constantly say the wrong thing, and I never seem to be wearing the right outfit. My hair is usually big, and I'm almost always going to want to wear lashes if we go somewhere special."

Brody's grin is full-blown now, and he must have given up on waiting for me to finish, because he's stepping out of the house. For a moment I just watch him walk towards me. I can't wrap my brain around the idea that I know someone this beautiful, let alone am engaging in this conversation with him. He stops in front of me, and I clear my throat nervously.

"And you should know that I've never even been on an actual date before. So I'm going to be nervous, and say ridiculous things, and you're going to have to be patient with me," I tell him hurriedly.

He cups my face in his hands like he did that day on the beach, and it makes my heart flutter and I lose my breath for a second.

"But—I mean, in spite of all of that—if you're still interested, I was wondering if you'd like to go on a date with me. A real one this time."

I stare at him, waiting for some kind of response, and finally he speaks.

"Am I allowed to speak yet?" He's playful.

I roll my eyes. "Yes."

"Good. Then you should know that I love everything you wear, old sweatshirts, pink dresses." He touches my sleeve. "Wet suits and bright-red snow boots. And the things you say are usually these madcap, left-field ideas that I'm positive no one else has ever even thought of before."

I open my mouth to protest, but he rubs his thumb across my bottom lip to shush me.

"I love the things you say. And I love that you've never been on a real date before. I love that this is all new for you. I love that you are so very different from so many other people. But I never want you to be nervous around me. I swear, the shine will rub off really quickly and you'll wonder how someone who annoys you so much could have ever made you apprehensive." I giggle like an idiot, and his eyes crinkle around the edges when he smiles.

"So, I promise if you'll be patient with me when I'm pretentious or overbearing or showing one of the million other character flaws you haven't yet encountered, then I'll be as patient as you need. I'll be Job. I'll be—"

And it's so sweet, and perfect, and exactly what I need for him to say to me in that moment, I throw my arms around his neck and lean up on tiptoes to kiss him.

And just like the last time, my belly flips and tingles run down my arms all the way to my fingers. When he pulls away from our kiss, he runs his fingertip over the bridge of my nose where he knows my freckles are hiding.

"Do you want to come inside?"

I bite my lip nervously.

"Not ready to come in yet?"

"For what purpose exactly?" I ask dubiously.

He looks away into the yard searching for a good option, and then his eyes light up.

"You like pancakes?"

"I love pancakes," I answer, just like I did on our first non-date.

"I know a place." He gestures behind him to his open front door, and I can't help but grin.

The smile is all the encouragement he needs, because he grabs my hand and pulls me into the house, and I laugh the whole way there because I'm so grateful that this grand scheme didn't explode in my face.

Daddy was right. Half the battle is just having the courage to try.

Sometimes you aim for the sun and fall short. But if you keep fighting for your dream, it becomes something so much better than you even knew to hope for.

That little girl who wanted something bigger, that country mouse who never quite found her place, found it here. In her favorite pink dress, eating pancakes and telling the cutest boy she's ever seen all about where her dream will take her next.

About the Author

Rachel Hollis is the founder of the popular lifestyle site www.thechicsite.com and the Los Angeles–based event planning firm Chic Events. At twenty-seven, she was named by *Inc. Magazine* as one of its "Top 30 Entrepreneurs under 30." She has designed and produced parties for many Hollywood stars, including Bradley Cooper, Al Gore, Jennifer Love Hewitt, Ivanka Trump, Rashida Jones, Marcia Cross, Jamie King, and Cuba Gooding, Jr., among others. Rachel is a lifestyle expert for *The Talk*, *EXTRA*, *The Nate Berkus Show*, and *The Steve Harvey Show* and has been featured in *People*, *InStyle*, *Cosmopolitan*, *OK!*, *Entertainment Weekly*, *Better Homes and Gardens*, and *Traditional Home*. Rachel lives in Los Angeles with her husband and three children. Connect with Rachel via:

Facebook/MsRachelHollis
Twitter @MsRachelHollis
Instagram @MsRachelHollis

To Brandee James, my work soul mate, sounding board, therapist, and dear friend. Thank you for always helping me figure out how to build the rocket ship.

To my mom, Sheree Edwards, who flew to town over and over to hang out with my boys so I could write away the weekend . . . And for always knowing exactly when I needed a surprise snack.

Lastly, to Dave Hollis, my best friend and the cutest boy I've ever met. So much of Landon and Brody's relationship is sourced directly from the story of us, so thank you for 1,001 sweet memories. Thanks too for being the most supportive husband any girl has ever known and for going along with all my harebrained schemes. I thank God for you every day.

Acknowledgments

If you've made it this far then that means you read my book! *Holy crud, I can't even explain what a big deal that is to me! Thank you* so *much for giving Landon (and me) a chance. I hope, hope, hope you loved her as much as I did! ~Rachel*

To Simone Blancato (and her parents) who helped me with the Spanish . . . Any mistakes are mine alone.

To Cynthia Lavers for all your help with the medical info: from insulin to hypoglycemia to diabetes and 911 operators. Max is a richer character for all your insight . . . Any mistakes are mine alone.

To Jacqueline Pilar who didn't so much as hesitate when I asked her if she'd help me shoot a book cover. Your work is incredible, JP, and I'm so grateful for more than twenty years of collaboration.

To Amanda Pittman, my beautiful friend and favorite Texan. Thank you for answering a million questions about football, your home state, and the intricacies of sorority life.